THE GOLDEN TROLLOP

THE GOLDEN TROLLOP

NATALIE ANDERSON SCOTT

CUTTING EDGE

ISBN-13: 978-1-970848-07-6

Published by
Cutting Edge Books
PO Box 8212
Calabasas, CA 91372
www.cuttingedgebooks.com

PART ONE

I N AN OLD London museum there are three portraits.

Two, life-size—a tall gross man in white satin breeches, diamond buttons on the plum-colored coat, diamond buckles on his shoes, the abundant folds of the exaggerated neckcloth propping a fat florid face with its haughty eyes and thick sensuous mouth, and wearing a wig of glossy brown locks. The other man also tall but slender, very elegant, his fawn-colored breeches of plain material, plain bone buttons on the impeccably fitted tan coat, the neat neckcloth of fine linen, his lean face handsome, manly; if he had a wig on it was unnoticeable, or perhaps he was wearing his own hair. Everything about him was unobtrusive— he aimed at simplicity, naturalness, in other words, perfection, the epitome of genuine good taste.

In the catalogue it says of the first man—Prince Regent, later George IV. And of the other man, quite matter-of-factly— Mr. Brummell.

Napoleon had his Josephine, Lord Nelson his Lady Hamilton, the Prince Regent had Beau Brummell. The artist had painted them at the height of their friendship. And so they went down in history …

There they are, side by side, life-size, life-like, no hint there of the eventual, never to be conceived, violent quarrel; Brummell's flight for his life to France, into exile, poverty, sickness, ignoble end from starvation; the petulant Prince adamant in his vicious, cruel unforgiveness. The reason of the sudden breakup to remain a complete mystery, the historians to this day searching in all the available papers and documents, official archives, and memoirs, printed, handwritten—searching, searching, to unravel the tragic secret …

But it is in front of the third portrait, comparatively small, and tucked away in a corner, as if unimportant, that the visitors to the museum always stop, and, forming a little crowd, they stare at the woman's lovely face, her neck, at the breasts half-bared by the low cut of the crimson silk bodice. Her smiling luscious lips match it in color, laughter sparkles in her dark eyes, her warmly tinted skin has the velvety softness of a magnolia petal, while the lustrous auburn hair is gathered in fashionably bunched curls on either side of her lively head.

The same artist who had painted the two famous men had painted her also, and evidently at about the same time, according to the catalogue. And though there's no information whatsoever about her, except for a crisp statement—portrait of a woman, unknown—and notwithstanding the fact that there's only the top of the bodice to give an idea of the rest of her figure, down, the visitors feel that they *know* just how tall she was, and how supple was her body, and how becoming the long crimson gown. There's so much vitality and mirth and daring about her, it seems to them tantalizingly that any moment she might move and, suddenly, with a swish of silk, step out of the old ugly frame and come over to tell them something, laughing. And so they stare, silent, strangely hushed, as if held there by that eternal secret which no historian would ever attempt to probe—the mysterious power of a beautiful, desirable woman.

CHAPTER ONE

T HE NIGHT BEFORE Carbuncle Joe was to be hanged at Tyburn, a girl was dancing on a table in the Waterfront Tavern. Her short skirt was very shabby, the brief blouse torn at the armpits, and even the green satin shoes of which she seemed very proud, with high heels and of surprisingly fine workmanship, showed signs of wear. Her dark hair tumbled in a wild mass over her shoulders as she whirled around, pirouetted, or swayed her body about, to the gay music of a screechy old violin. Or sometimes she would suddenly, throwing her head back, start kicking her legs up very high. She had no underwear on and there would be a roar of coarse laughter from the men and they would bend low where they sat at the tables to catch a glimpse of her long gleaming legs. She laughed back at them.

Perspiration stood out in drops on her forehead, trickled down her neck, and when it gathered on her upper lip she would lick it off swiftly with the tip of her sharp pink tongue. Her cheeks and mouth were lavishly rouged, the eyelids smudged with charcoal, and the strange heady scent she always used wafted towards the men through the many unsavory smells around, of gin and rum, tobacco, stale food fats, of unwashed clothing, human sweat, women's cheap cosmetics, and the everlasting acrid stench of the fog hanging thick over the Thames, whose sluggish dirty waters passed under the tavern's outer wall. The men's uplifted noses followed the whiff of that scent eagerly, voluptuously.

Little Mr. Davey, who had made the treasured shoes, without payment, as one artist to another—made them to her specific measurements, quite as if she were a duchess or something—had also given her the scent, in its strangely shaped flacon fashioned out of a yellowed bone. It was called the Green Perfume, and as he had explained very impressively, it was supposed to have come from some faraway outlandish spot, beyond Palestine, and to contain a rare ingredient, worth a fortune, and endowed with some wonderful potent powers …

"Higher, Clarissa. Higher!" "What a wench!" "There's no other like her!" They stamped their feet, struck the tables with their fists, with their liquor mugs, cutlery, raising a deafening clamor. Or they would egg her on, "Come, my pretty, you can do better than *that!*" And Clarissa, in her own enthusiasm, carried away by the joy of dancing, and happily aware of all these men looking at her, eating her up with their eyes, would suddenly give a little scream of triumph, and throw her lovely arms towards them all, and stamp, wildly, gaily, with the heels of her green satin shoes.

There was hardly a man present who didn't have a woman sitting beside him, and so far it had been the women trying to cuddle up to the men, who, busy with their liquor, dice, or food, would push them roughly away. But now, excited by Clarissa's dancing, they started to hug and kiss them, and pull them on their knees, to slip a hand inside the invitingly low bodices. Everybody who was anybody was there: One-Eyed Tom, Slimy Jackson, Honest Gregory—so called because he would disguise himself as a parson, or a lawyer, or even as an out-of-town magistrate, to ply his dishonest trade—and Ugly Frank, Knock-Kneed Malachen, Take-the-Road Timothy, Crooked Mike … There was also Black Moll, the procuress, a plump, motherly, cheerful woman, always dressed in dignified black, with long black veils of unconsolable widowhood. And Maggoty Jane, the "fence," who looked like a respectful housewife, with her mobcap, apron, and shawl, and who was always knitting a stocking, as she was now. And, of course, there was Slippery Jack, young, handsome, indolent, dandified; the awareness of his boundless attractiveness to women reflected in the shrewd glow of his eyes and in the catlike walk.

There was one other person, sitting all by himself at a table in the corner, and scribbling away. From time to time he would suddenly stop and, the quill pen poised in mid-air, stare into space unseeingly. Curly black hair, which he wore very long, as became a poet, framed a thin pale face with its aquiline features and passionate black eyes. After dipping the pen into the inkpot he would again, bent almost double, scribble on.

The white ruffled shirt, the short coat and narrow breeches, showed how little attention was paid to such prosaic details. He was very young. Nobody could remember exactly just when he had first wandered in. Since he was obviously starving, they fed him. They treated him as if he were some sort of a pet, a peculiar one certainly, but quite harmless, and they called him the Poet.

They were all there because of a very important occasion; Carbuncle Joe was to be secretly let out and brought to the tavern in order that he might spend the few hours remaining to him, between midnight and the sunrise meeting with the hangman, carousing with his friends, drinking, gambling, eating heartily, enjoying a woman. The jailers were corrupt and it had cost the underworld such an enormous sum of money as to leave them virtually broke for many weeks to come, but they owed it to him, to his fame. In the course of almost three decades Carbuncle Joe's exploits, while being a constant challenge to the constables and a source of despair to the magistrates and of nervousness and even terror to the nobility and the wealthy, had made his name a household word. The fact that he was so famous had naturally pre-cluded any efforts to buy his escape, since the chief jailer would lose not only his lucrative job, but probably also his head, on failing to produce his renowned prisoner at the hour appointed.

"That's enough," Clarissa announced, after kicking a leg especially high, "until Carbuncle Joe comes."

As the coins thrown by the appreciative audience began to fall about her feet, Slippery Jack, though he had been sitting at some distance, was suddenly right there, scooping up the money, slipping it into his pocket. It happened every time, no matter how prepared she was to forestall him. He was just too quick for her, was Slippery Jack, as he was for everybody else.

"You pig!" Clarissa screamed.

She jumped down and slapped his face. He slapped her bottom, so painfully that tears sprang to her eyes. But he pulled her to him and began to fondle her, and, though she hated Slippery Jack, she was so afraid of him that, as usual, she let him do it. Then he released her, and she saw the Poet, who, having jumped to his feet, and holding in an upraised hand a tankard which he had unceremoniously borrowed from a neighbor's table, was trying to proclaim a toast.

Striking a dramatic attitude, the Poet shouted;

"To Clarissa!"

"To Clarissa!"

As if she were a renowned actress, or one of those famous women kept by men of title or wealth.

He drank. Then, returning the tankard to its rightful user, he as suddenly sat down and went on scribbling.

Clarissa followed Slippery Jack over to the table where several men were examining pieces of jewelry, evaluating them, then bargaining with Maggoty Jane, who seemed interested only in her stocking-knitting. She was a hard one. But she always paid them something in advance and she never failed to sell the stuff. How she did it, what were her contacts, nobody knew. Most of it probably had to be smuggled across the Channel, abroad, to avoid recognition of the jewels, which were generally heirlooms.

"You'd never guess from whom I took this little trinket!" One-Eyed Tom was saying, holding up a fat gold watch studded with big diamonds to form initials and crest. It was really a fabulous piece, priceless.

"The Prince Regent?" Clarissa said, her face flushed and eyes shining with greed at the sight of the precious stones. How they glowed and sparkled, as if with a mysterious hidden fire. Whenever she saw diamonds a little shiver would run over her body, like a shiver of desire.

"Well, not quite," One-Eyed Tom had to admit. "Duke of Cumberland, his brother. The neatest job I ever pulled off! And with only Ugly Frank here to help me. There we were, the two of us, waiting in a dark narrow street, and along comes a hired coach, no guards, no outriders, just the coachman and a footman. Going incognito like that is supposed to conceal the frequency of the Prince's visits to gaming houses and brothels.... Anyway, Ugly Frank stops the horses, shows his pistol to the men on the box, and I open the coach door, and you should have seen the rage the Prince Regent got himself into when I poked my pistol at him. Sitting beside him, of course, was Mr. Brummell, and they had with them the Duke and a lady. 'Sorry, Mr. Brummell,' I said, 'but I'll have to relieve your friends of a few of their possessions.' I wouldn't take anything from him," One-Eyed Tom explained, "he's all right; besides, being all out for simplicity the way he is, he wouldn't have anything on him, not even big money, since he doesn't gamble. Well, the lady, naturally, screams and clasps a lily-white hand to her throat, but I take the diamond necklace from her and the matching earrings and the bracelets, and the Duke gives up this watch, while His Royal Highness, still raging, has to shell out all the money he'd won at the gaming place. Then I bang the door shut, Ugly Frank prods the horses' rumps with his pistol, and away the coach gallops. It was as simple as that."

When everybody had laughed their approval, Black Moll, who was in the same group, spoke up:

"Well, don't I always give you the right information?"

The girls she prepared for the titled or the wealthy men were trained to keep their ears open for bits of gossip, news, plans, and Black Moll then would pass on the obtained information to her friends.

"But what about the necklace, the bracelets?" Clarissa said excitedly.

"The set was of recent make, not an heirloom," Maggoty Jane explained professionally, while calmly knitting her stocking. "So I was able to get it off our hands right away, and the money will go to make up the rest of the payment to Carbuncle Joe's jailer. Compared to the gems' actual value it was a mere pittance I got," Maggoty Jane complained, as usual, "but people like us are always taken advantage of. Anyhow, that lady, whoever she was, can certainly love wisely. Such gorgeous jewels."

"And she didn't have half your good looks, Clarissa," One-Eyed Tom remarked, passing the Duke's watch over to Maggoty Jane and watching it being dropped carelessly into the seemingly innocent reticule in which she carried her knitting.

The gray-haired, distinguished-looking man who had been playing the fiddle had meanwhile put his instrument carefully away in its shabby case and was having a drink in company with Dumb Clara, the ragpicker, and Clarissa hurried over to join them.

"How was I, Lafonte?" she asked anxiously. "Was I good? Tell me, please."

Once he had been a fine musician, a well-known dancing master; young ladies of gentle birth and daughters of the wealthy merchants had been his adoring pupils, and he had coached professional actors, actresses—all this before the gambling passion, taking possession of him, had dragged him gradually down. Now he was old and frail, his eyes red-rimmed, the thin face heavily lined, his neck like parchment, the sensitive hands tremulous.

"Of course you were good," he said quietly. "Hadn't I myself taught you everything you know? I, Lafonte. The great Lafonte."

As far back as Clarissa could remember, and patiently, untiringly, he had been giving her lessons in dancing, music, acting. He had even taught her some French, and a little Italian, and how a performer should come onto the stage, and how to make a bow.

"A pupil of Lafonte should go far," he went on proudly. "That's why it pains me to see you perform here, being treated like a cheap little dancer."

"And your poor father wouldn't have liked it a bit, either," Dumb Clara said, dropping a tear into her gin, and then taking a great gulp of it from the tin mug. Since she couldn't afford to indulge except rarely, on great occasions, the liquor would hit her hard, almost at the first sip, and she was already tipsy.

All the money Dumb Clara made with her ragpicking went to pay Lafonte's gambling debts. She also took care of his clothes, washed and ironed his linen, kept him immaculate. She was very proud of his distinguished appearance. When sometimes Lafonte, assailed by a sudden fit of frustration, would suddenly disappear, she would go to search for him. And eventually she'd find him in front of one or another of the great mansions or famous theaters whose doors were now closed to him forever, and behaving in the strangest manner, almost raving. Terrified

lest he attract the attention of the authorities and be taken away
to Bedlam, Dumb Clara would knowingly calm him, cajole him
somehow into going with her, and so bring him back.

"Ah, it would have broken your poor father's heart, hic.... It
sure would."

"You old bitch," Clarissa said, and she laughed. "You told me
a hundred times you don't even know who *was* my father."

"Is that a nice way to talk to your poor old mother?" Dumb
Clara whimpered. "Besides, how could I know which one it was,
in particular? There's been so many ..."

Though almost toothless, she wore a coquettish velvet bonnet, probably found somewhere while ragpicking, and rouge
stood out in clownlike patches on her cavernous face. Her shawl
and skirt were shabby and soiled. The implements of her trade, a
large sack, empty as yet, and a long stick with a metal hook at one
end, lay on the floor beside her chair.

Lafonte moved closer to Clarissa and, after glancing around,
said, lowering his voice:

"I've been trying to explain the situation to you all of this
last month, ever since they got Carbuncle Joe, a most fortunate
situation as far as you're concerned. You may never get a chance
like this again to leave, run away.... Because of his notoriety, high
pressure is being put on the authorities to clean up this section
of the waterfront, rewards have been posted for almost every one
of the men here, with the result that the constables are keeping
a close watch from the outside. Of course, they'd no more dare
venture in now than they would have before, well knowing what
would happen to them, but they're there, waiting, just beyond
the section's limits. And this means that very few of the men
here would venture out, take the risk of being caught. You know
yourself, Clarissa, how inactive they've been lately, just sitting
around, waiting for it all to blow over. The very brave ones like

Honest Gregory, Ugly Frank, or One-Eyed Tom, well, they naturally don't care, they'd dare anything. But not the rest, certainly not Slippery Jack. He's too indolent, nothing could make him take chances. Spurred by anger he might start after you, but it wouldn't be far. And you could get away ..."

"What about that sharp little knife Slippery Jack carries concealed somewhere on his person?" Dumb Clara grumbled. She passed a hand across her own throat, demonstrating. "That's what will happen to her if he catches her!"

"She'll have to risk even that," Lafonte said. "There's no future for her here. Slippery Jack behaves as if he owns her. He's her enemy, and Clarissa knows it. And eventually he will destroy her.... She *must* leave this place. Anywhere else, and away from Slippery Jack, she could make something of herself, become somebody. With her beauty, her talent, she's entitled to everything money can buy. Beautiful clothes, jewels ..."

"So now we're not good enough for her." Dumb Clara complained with biting irony. "Leaving her poor old mother." She shed tipsy tears.

Clarissa, who with her chin cupped in a hand seemed to be listening attentively to Lafonte's urging, suddenly said:

"Who is that man in a black cloak, sitting on a bench near the back door? I've never seen him here before. Who can he be?"

There was a striking calm and dignity about the stranger as he sat there, the cloak wrapped about him, arms crossed on his chest, the shadow cast by the broad-brimmed hat over his long strong face failing to conceal the piercing gaze of his eyes.

"I noticed him a while back," Lafonte said. "He couldn't be a spy, since all the entrances tonight are guarded on the outside. He's either known to someone, or may even have a friend here."

The stranger so far had evinced no particular interest in anyone or anything, but now, for a fraction of a second, Clarissa saw his gaze directed upon her, as if studying her, evaluating.

Dumb Clara's voice broke upon her:

"Isn't it almost twelve by that clock? Carbuncle Joe should be here ..."

As a matter of fact, the clock over the mantel showed more than five minutes past twelve. Rising anxiety began to be reflected in all the faces. Another five minutes passed....

Never had the interior of the old tavern looked so nice and cozy. The floor freshly swept, the rough tabletops cleaned of the usual messy stains; on the generous hearth huge logs blazed, crackling, sending sparks all around; the proprietor, a rotund person with a red-cheeked jolly face, had put aside his dirty apron to wear instead his best fancy vest; while from the kitchen came the appetite-teasing odors of roasted meats, boiled fish, pigeon pies, mutton patties, and juicy fruit tarts. Every one of the crude lamps suspended from the thick beams had been lit, producing such a bright illumination that the two coarsely made comical cartoons, pinned crookedly on the wall near the clock, were clearly visible. Both cartoons were aimed at the Prince Regent, the favorite target of the poor people's humor.

In one, and depicted naturally much fatter than he actually was, he was showing the door to his weeping young wife, Princess Caroline. And the caption said: "Trumped-up charges or not, the court had to obey me, and it has deposed you, and sent you into exile, and gave your child to me. So there!" In the other cartoon the Prince, surrounded by obsequious tailors, was trying on a new coat, while just outside the door Lord Nelson, with a group of anxious statesmen, stood waiting to be received. And the caption said: "Tell him his naval engagements can wait, but this coat must be finished in time for the supper party I ordered Mr. Brummell to give in my honor."

Another five minutes passed. Now they were really worried. Just then a secret door in the side wall suddenly opened inward; until a spring was touched nobody could have suspected its existence, it merged so perfectly with the rest of the wall. First to come in was one of their own men who had been standing guard at the end of the long passage, one of the many passages connecting the various parts of the rambling tavern. Next came the two assistant jailers in their green coats, trimmed with bits of red cloth, their matted hair cut in a circle all around, so that in front it reached to their eyebrows, and in the back exposed their grimy necks.

And, at last, Carbuncle Joe appeared. He had been allowed to exchange his prison garb of coarse brown wool for his own clothes and, big, muscular, grinning broadly, he looked resplendent in tight-fitting white breeches, dark blue coat of good material and trimmed with silver braid, tall boots of yellow leather, and, dangling at the hip, an ornamental sword, an integral part of a gentleman's formal costume. His hat was fashioned like an admiral's tricorn and under the hat the curly wig he wore was lavishly powdered.

It was the period when men were just starting to give up wearing powder. The titled and the wealthy because Beau Brummell disapproved of this artificiality, while with the poor people, who liked to adhere to old customs, it was a question of expense. Since the beginning of the war against Napoleon the tax on flour had been raised so high they just couldn't afford to have it, except on great occasions, holidays, weddings, when going to a fair, or some sort of special celebration. And so Carbuncle Joe came to them in powder.

He was anything but handsome, the skin of his face and hands rough, weather-beaten, and there was the disfiguring feature, the carbuncle—a big, horribly purple, slimy thing, growing out of his right cheek, as if a living leech had fastened itself there permanently, mercilessly.

But they were all used to his rather terrifying appearance. He was at once surrounded, and joyful greetings, exclamations of relief, questions were showered upon him. What had delayed him?

"I had to shave twice, the beard was grown so thick and stubborn." Carbuncle Joe passed a great hand over his cleanly shaved chin and jowls.

How like him that was, wasting precious minutes to look his best!

After the little bag containing the gold coins, the second half of the payment to the jailer, was thrust into the hands of one of his assistants, the honored guest was led to a table in the center which was the only one covered with a clean cloth. The proprietor, bowing and scraping, kept repeating:

"Plenty of pigeon pies ... Everything the way you like it ... Most tempting ..."

"Rascal host," Carbuncle Joe said, taking the rotund person by the scruff of the neck, lifting him bodily, and shaking him till the man's teeth rattled; all this by way of showing his appreciation. "After the fare I've been getting since they clapped me in irons, anything, even *your* vile food, should taste mighty good."

And leaving the proprietor to scramble to his feet as best he could from the spot where he had been flung, Carbuncle Joe addressed the gathered company:

"First let's eat and drink and be merry. Afterwards, I'll choose me a woman."

He glanced around and, his bloodshot eyes catching sight of Clarissa, he leered to himself in anticipation.

CHAPTER TWO

C LARISSA WENT TO CHANGE into one of her "costumes," as she liked to call them, for her next number. There was no such thing as a dressing room, of course, but she had improvised one for herself in one of the pantries adjoining the noisy kitchen. Sacks of potatoes, dried peas, beans, onions, and shelves crowded with earthenware jars, containing condiments and preserves, made the little room very cramped and it was stuffy and smelly with pickled cabbage, garlic, and rancid cooking oil. The treasured piece of a broken mirror (brought back by Dumb Clara from one of her ragpicking trips) was propped against a jar on a lower shelf, and there also were ranged neatly the pot of rouge, homemade from the juice of beets and of cranberries mixed with lard and a little starch for a base; the box of powder, which was merely flour strengthened with starch; and bits of charcoal, used for the primitive eye make-up. Seated on an empty barrel, turned bottom-up, and by the light of a candle end stuck in a discarded bottle, Clarissa began to clean her face with lard, taking it out by the handful from a wooden pail nearby.

Prickly Gil had followed her in, soundlessly, secretively; a manner characteristically and unpleasantly hers. She was one of the younger girls, still virgins, who hung about the tavern waiting to be appropriated either by Black Moll or by one of the men. She was very small, and everything about her was sharply pointed— the little upturned nose, the tiny breasts, the scaly elbows—so that she reminded one of a prickly pear; hence the nickname.

Sallow skin and shrewd little eyes, the color of unripened goose-berries, completed the image of something unsavory, unclean, indecent. To the men she had the unexplicable attractiveness based on natural revulsion, and several had had their eye on her.

She generally went barefoot, and the shape of her feet and the way they moved was somehow startlingly reminiscent of a goat. Over her shift, which rumor said was never taken off or washed, she wore a rather long full skirt, and it concealed her legs to below the ankles.

Stationing herself just behind Clarissa so she could see her in the bit of mirror, Prickly Gil said, at once, without any preamble:

"Are you going to take Carbuncle Joe? Everybody knows you're the one he'll choose. And tonight, especially, Slippery Jack couldn't refuse him. Even if he had a mind to, which he probably wouldn't, anyhow," she added, giving a little giggle of derision.

The men shared everything among themselves, including their women on occasion. It was an old custom.

"And what business is it of yours whether I'll take Carbuncle Joe, I'd like to know," Clarissa said, wiping the lard off of her face with a piece of rag.

"I could give you something for him. Something far more valuable than money, more precious than jewels, something that nobody could give you. I have the powers," Prickly Gil said.

And she glanced towards the darkest corner, as if what-ever or whoever was there was clearly visible to herself, while it remained invisible to anyone else.

She always behaved in that queer way. She would sit alone for hours at a time, staring into a corner and mumbling to herself strange-sounding words. There was, in fact, much bad gossip about Prickly Gil. Her habit of absenting herself regu-larly at certain days of the month which coincided with the moon's periodically strange influence on the elements, such as the sudden rise or fall of the river Thames, was certainly suspicious. There were even witnesses who were absolutely certain of having seen Prickly Gil coming out of the Kenerevy woods, which had a very evil reputation—no one dared go there, ever—and that at the most ungodly hour, just before the first cock's crow.

"Carbuncle Joe has murdered so many people," Prickly Gil went on, "any girl would jump at the chance of having him make love to her, just for the sake of the unusual experience, to see how different he'd be at it compared to any other man. That's why I'm willing to give you something, something very special, if you would arrange it for *me* to have him instead."

"I have no say in the matter, you know that," Clarissa said, intent on rouging her cheeks, her mouth. "It would be very difficult. Impossible, really." Secretly she was intrigued by the thought of the promised payment; what could it be?

"Ah, but you are clever," Prickly Gil argued shrewdly, "you'd be able to arrange it. You're the most popular girl here, so you could get away with something nobody else could. Unless, of course, you *want* Carbuncle Joe."

"I wouldn't say I'm *dying* to have him," Clarissa said. "That horrible carbuncle of his ... Do you know, it actually *leaks?*"

She could see in the bit of mirror that Prickly Gil behind her was licking her colorless lips as if something deliciously tasty had been mentioned.

"Do you have a familiar?" Clarissa asked.

"Not yet. But I will be given one if I please the Master, by getting Carbuncle Joe. I'm an underling and it will be my virginity that Carbuncle Joe will be violating. The Master will be very pleased indeed."

"The Master. Do you mean the ..."

Prickly Gil cut in with an anxious "Sh!"

"His name must never be mentioned." The horrible little creature looked actually scared.

"Pshaw!" Clarissa said.

Nonetheless, she was impressed.

"Seems to me," she said casually, "you should be able to get him by using these powers you're talking about, instead of asking my help."

"It would be too long to explain," Prickly Gil said, "why some things must be achieved without the interference of our powers. All I can say is that Carbuncle Joe must come to me of his own will—only it'll be of your doing."

"And what is this something important you'd give me in exchange?" Clarissa wanted to know.

"I'd give you the upper hand over your secret enemy."

"But I have no enemies," Clarissa laughed, "secret or otherwise."

"I don't mean the kind *you* mean, the ordinary kind. It's like this," Prickly Gil explained. "Suppose there's smallpox raging in the city, now there'll be those who get it and those who don't. It may be you or someone else, someone you've never even dreamt of. Or suppose something frightens the coach horses and they gallop along the street. Somebody is liable to get hurt. Again, it may be you or someone else. Or it may be something simple, like a girl trying to make a man notice her, or trying to get hold of a ribbon of some particular color. Every day, a hundred times a day, there are two people trying to get the same thing or to avoid some harm. There's you and the other person, and that other person is your secret enemy."

"Goodness," Clarissa said. She was so astounded, she stopped sewing up a tear in the harem trousers she had put on for her next dance. "I never thought of that."

"Well, do I get Carbuncle Joe? Just promise me to do your best."

Clarissa, who ever since his leering glance in her direction had been wondering how to try to wriggle out of having the man, because of his horrible carbuncle, said:

"Oh, all right."

"Now I'll do my part," Prickly Gil said. And stretching out a hand, she touched with her fingertips first the shelf, then a nearby sack of potatoes, then Clarissa's shoulder. "We call it the power of the Unbroken Line."

And to demonstrate, she drew with a hand an imaginary line between the three points she had previously touched: the shelf, the sack, Clarissa's shoulder.

"Now you're protected against your secret enemy."

And as quietly as she had come, Prickly Gil was suddenly gone.

What silly gibberish the queer creature always made one listen to, Clarissa told herself. But her mind was on the makeshift apparel which went by the glamorous name of "costumes."

The really suitable materials, such as satins, taffetas, brocades, gauzes, were terribly expensive. Even among the wealthy a good gown was considered on a par with the family furniture and silver, even with the smaller heirloom jewels, and like these valuable items would be carefully enumerated in the wills and so pass on from one generation to the next. Famous actresses to appear at their best—and that meant costumes, *real* costumes—had to depend completely on the size of their pocketbooks and the generosity of the men who kept them. And they too hung on to the treasured gowns, restyling them as fashion dictated, changing the lace, ornament, flounce, from one to another. Nothing was ever put aside, discarded, thrown away. Consequently, it was very seldom that Dumb Cora managed to find and bring home even so much as a button, or a bit of satin or velvet ribbon.

Clarissa had to use all her inventiveness to create whatever she needed out of anything she could get. The harem trousers, for instance, had been fashioned out of several pieces of crude muslin which the tavern cooks used to wrap their puddings in and which had become so threadbare in the process that they were about to be thrown out. The material, at least, was absolutely transparent. The trousers, gathered at the ankles, left her flat stomach bare. A narrow band made from bits of ribbon was tied across her breasts, just covering her nipples.

She had two other "costumes," also makeshift affairs, and these she now spread out over the sacks, in readiness for a quick change. Then she hurried to rejoin the gathered company.

All the faces flushed with too much food and too much liquor, they were singing lustily and at the tops of their voices an old song, something about:

Cherries, I have cherries!
Who'll buy my cherries?

As she jumped on the table, the men on seeing the harem costume, roared with delight. But Lafonte started on his fiddle. And she began to dance, moving her hips knowingly.

The stranger in the black cloak, she noticed, was gone; and the Poet, also, had already left, the latter's comings and goings always quite unpredictable. After she finished the harem dance, she hurried back and almost at once, or so it seemed, instead of the harem girl, there was one of the so-called blackamoor boys whom great ladies like to keep about as a sort of ornament: narrow breeches, a short coat trimmed with brass buttons, an oriental turban on his saucy head, and the grinning face absolutely black. The surprise of the sudden metamorphosis was as always a rousing success.

It had taken Lafonte many patient months to teach her the tricks, the art of a quick change, so important to a dancer, an actress. Now the struggle with the hooks and eyes, the lacing of stays, of removing one make-up and putting on another, or fixing her hair in quite a different way, meant nothing to her. The process had become mechanical.

After strutting about coyly as a blackamoor boy to the roaring laughter and indecent remarks of the men, she next reappeared as a cute drummer girl, the kind who entertains the crowds at a fair. Everything about her was white and pink, the short striped skirt, the pretty face under the pink bonnet, and the white blouse so tight it pushed her breasts up and almost out. She beat her little drum loudly as she marched towards them, marched backward, then came forward again ...

But it was getting late. Carbuncle Joe had beckoned Slippery Jack over and was saying something to him, and through the suddenly subsiding clamor Clarissa caught Slippery Jack's polite answer:

"Tonight, Carbuncle Joe, anything I have is yours for the asking."

And, raising his voice, Slippery Jack called to her:

"Clarissa, it's you he wants."

She blew kisses to Carbuncle Joe, who, having risen to his towering height, swayed slightly, ready to lunge in her direction. In a few flattering words she thanked him for the honor. But this was such a very special occasion, as far as Carbuncle Joe was concerned, a girl shouldn't allow herself to be selfish.... She knew how to talk to men, instinct guiding her in the choice of words, tone of voice, that would bolster up their vanity, increase their self-esteem. Never again would Carbuncle Joe enjoy a woman.

He was entitled to the best. And what could be better than a virgin? Clarissa suddenly stretched an arm out, to point straight at Prickly Gil.

"The youngest of them all," Clarissa cried enthusiastically. "That's what we have for you, Carbuncle Joe, the best!"

"That's just like Clarissa to think of the man first, instead of herself," somebody declared approvingly. "She's right," several voices cried. "He's entitled to the best, and that's what we're giving him."

Carbuncle Joe made a gesture which might have been one of protest, but he had so gorged himself with food and liquor it was obviously beyond the power of his faculties to start an argument. With everybody pointing towards Prickly Gil, he lunged awkwardly in that direction, grabbed her, swung her over his shoulder, and so carried her out to one of the private rooms with which the tavern abounded.

Clarissa, laughing to herself—it had been so easy, after all—slipped away to exchange the drummer girl's outfit for the shabby skirt and blouse she always wore. She was hanging up the "costumes" on the back of the door of her improvised dressing room, when the rotund proprietor put his head in.

"Clarissa, would you mind coming with me?" He sounded not a little excited. "The lady is here," he added, somewhat mysteriously.

"So the Princess Caroline has arrived safely," Clarissa said. "I'm so glad."

"Sh ... The idea mentioning her name, after all the trouble we've had, too. Walls have ears...."

"Was there trouble?"

"You don't imagine it's as easy to smuggle people in as it is goods, do you? Besides, the awful risk we run, doing it for a person of such an exalted rank ... I took her into my own living room," the proprietor went on, wiping the perspiration off his brow on his shirt sleeve. "The crossing was rough, and the poor lady has had nothing to eat since leaving Calais, and seeing the kind of sheltered upbringing she's had, the rough manners of our men must have unnerved her quite a bit, I guess. So I thought it would give her comfort to have a sensible girl like you keep her company while she's waiting for the Countess of Argull's coach, and maybe the Countess herself, to come to her."

The old Countess was the only remaining friend the Prince Regent's deposed wife still had at the English court.

Clarissa followed the proprietor to his own apartment, which to ensure privacy was separated from the tavern's public rooms by several intricate passages.

The frail but stately woman who sat on the bench alongside the wall had loosened her dark outer wraps and the pale brocade gown she wore underneath shimmered in the sputtering light of the crude bracket lamp. She had untied the velvet streamers of her bonnet, and holding a tiny lace handkerchief in a slim white hand, she was dabbing at her eyes.

Only a few years back, Clarissa, from the ranks of the noisily curious crowd, had seen this very same woman, then a happy, smiling girl-bride, bowing graciously from the gilded coach, while surrounded with all the pomp and pageantry of the royal procession returning from the historic Westminster Abbey. The change these few years had wrought was truly pathetic. The grief of being parted from her only child had etched premature lines into the small porcelain-like face and the once-blue eyes were faded with much weeping.

"I brought you a girl in case you need help, ma'am," the proprietor said, bowing respectfully. "Clarissa is her name. And here's the hot broth," he added, as a kitchen helper hurried in with a deep pewter dish.

"You have all been so very kind," Princess Caroline said, in her low melodious voice. And again she dabbed at her eyes with her handkerchief.

The proprietor moved closer the little table on which had been placed his best silver spoon and a clean linen towel, and with his own hands he set down the dish with the steaming broth. Then, gesturing the staring kitchen helper out, he also withdrew.

Clarissa sat down on a stool near the door.

This woman, she thought, might look unhappy, but what a beautiful gown she had on—brocade, such a rich material, and what a lovely pale color! The bonnet was of the latest fashion, straight from Paris, and how stylishly it was perched on top of the little ash-blond ringlets, the very latest way of doing one's hair. And the exquisite skin of the face and hands, *that* was no work of nature, Clarissa told herself, but the result of costly special creams and lotions …

Princess Caroline had picked up the spoon, rather uncertainly, then she glanced down at her brocade gown, put the spoon back, and looked towards Clarissa helplessly.

"Let me help you, ma'am," Clarissa said.

A person of such a high rank naturally was accustomed to being waited on, and here she was, the poor soul, feeling quite lost without her women, maids.…

And hurrying over, she swiftly shook out the folded towel, spread it over the woman's knees, moved the dish of broth a little closer.

"Thank you."

Clarissa went back to her stool.

Princess Caroline while daintily drinking the broth didn't seem to take any notice of her, but when she finished, she suddenly said:

"Come here, child."

Clarissa came over and stood before her.

"You're very beautiful," the older woman said, observing her. And for the first time she smiled.

Clarissa curtsied.

The Princess' interest seemed to deepen.

"You curtsy beautifully, too. There are very few ladies at either the English or French court who can curtsy as gracefully, just right."

"Lafonte taught me."

"Lafonte ... The name sounds familiar. Wait. Of course, wasn't he the dancing master of the Duke of Cumberland's sisters, when they were little girls?"

"The very same one," Clarissa said proudly. "The great Lafonte."

"Something very sad happened to him later, I remember ... Well, you're very fortunate to have such a wonderful teacher. And then the perfume you have on, Clarissa," Princess Caroline went on, frankly intrigued. "It's very rare, did you know that? I recognized the fragrance as soon as you came in. Empress Josephine's favorite scent, and everybody knows how fabulously extravagant *she* is!"

"Little Mr. Davey, the shoemaker, gave it to me."

"Oh ..." The Princess politely tried to mask her amazement. "Well, it's very strong, but it becomes you, your coloring, your vitality. My type of a woman has to stick to lavender or mignonette," a note of bitterness crept into the melodious voice. "But you should always use it," she advised, again observing Clarissa with kindly interest. "With your beauty, your talents, and I can see you're very talented, you're certainly entitled to quite a different setting."

"I'm Slippery Jack's girl," Clarissa said simply.

"But you do not love him, I can sense that. As for myself," Princess Caroline then confided, "though I have loved, it was most unwisely.... You know, I had been warned, my family, everybody warned me, about the Prince's character, but I truly loved him." The Princess dabbed at her eyes with her tiny lace handkerchief. "And now he has my child. That's why I'm here. I heard she was ailing. If I could see her, even for only a few minutes ... Mr. Brummell, the only person who has a restraining influence on the Prince Regent, promised to arrange it somehow. But in his letter he told me it might take several weeks, months perhaps, before he finds an opportune moment to persuade the Prince to give permission.... And, meanwhile, I will stay with Countess Argull."

The proprietor came in to say that the Countess Argull's coach, with the old Countess herself, had arrived and was waiting in the alleyway at the side entrance. Princess Caroline stood up, closed her wraps, tied her bonnet streamers. With the proprietor leading the way and Clarissa bringing up the rear, they took her through the labyrinth of passages. They had to pass through the main room where the merrymaking seemed at its height. On recognizing the Princess, however, everybody quieted down. The people's sympathy had been always on the side of the deposed wife.

Carbuncle Joe, having rejoined his friends, had Prickly Gil on his knee, and the queer creature kept cuddling up to him nauseously. Because they were all so proud of Carbuncle Joe's fame, they felt duty bound to introduce him to the Princess as she was hurrying past. Putting Prickly Gil aside, he stood up and, buttoning up his silver-trimmed blue coat hastily, he made the frail stately woman a low bow, the admiral's tricorn, clutched in his hand, almost sweeping the floor.

"Carbuncle Joe," Princess Caroline murmured nervously. "Of course, I have heard the name ..."

But as the men nearby explained the cause of the celebration, the look of fear in her eyes gave away to one of admiration, and then of pity.

"You're a brave man," she said. And she added, "I'm sorry."

"Don't be sorry for me, ma'am," Carbuncle Joe exclaimed, grinning broadly. "I'll be merely paying for the kind of life I chose to have, an exciting, rich, happy life."

"And with me it's been nothing but misery...." the Princess murmured.

And she walked on swiftly to the side door, held open for her by the proprietor, who then hurried out after her, followed by the two heavily armed men who were to accompany the coach to the old Countess' estate on the outskirts of London.

In something less than half an hour it was time for Carbuncle Joe to leave. After being bid many an affectionate good-by by his friends, he went, accompanied by the two assistant jailers, and the gathering began to disperse.

CHAPTER THREE

CLARISSA, ON COMING OUT, had merely to cross a narrow fog-filled yard to reach the shack which was her home. All of that section of the waterfront was crowded with such shacks, barely visible at the moment because of the darkness and the dense fog. From a window in the tavern, the only two-storied building, a solitary light shone dimly through the murk, and even that went out as she fumbled with the latch of the shack's door.

Slippery Jack was sitting on the one available rush-bottomed chair, paring his nails with his little knife. From behind the thin wall came the sound of Lafonte's regular snoring, and she could hear Dumb Clara muttering tipsily in her sleep.

"What kept you so long?" Slippery Jack grumbled.

"I was putting the costumes away."

Which, in a way, was true.

Without taking off her skirt and blouse, Clarissa jumped into bed. And since tonight it was more important than ever before to please Slippery Jack, to conceal from him the fact of how odious he was to her, she called out to him, invitingly:

"Come and have the joy of me!"

He began to undress. The little knife was no longer in sight, and who could tell where he secreted it? No matter how closely she watched him, she had never succeeded in finding out. She naturally had never dared to search his clothes.

Oh, well, she now told herself recklessly. If not the knife, it'd be his fingers at my throat....

He was very particular about his clothes and, as usual, proceeded to drape each garment very solicitously over the chair back. At last, with nary a stitch on him—nightshirts were unknown to the shack dwellers—he joined her, and at once grabbed at her thighs.

After a good romp, he was suddenly asleep.

She waited a moment, then pulled the tattered blanket over him and slipped out of bed. He had snuffed out the candle, but she needed no light to find the money. A man made no secret of where he kept it, for the simple reason that his woman knew it'd be the end of her, an ugly end, if she so much as touched it. The four deep pockets of Slippery Jack's vest bulged proudly with the coins. Her hand, groping in the dark, came in contact with his clothing, and it didn't take long to remove each separate garment, letting it slip softly to the floor, and so reach the vest. This she lifted off the chair back with both hands, very carefully, lest the coins should ring one against another—*that,* surely, would awaken him—and, so carrying the vest, she moved to the door. She had purposely left the latch raised and, the door opening at her touch, she slipped through and out. After swiftly folding up the vest, with the dampness of the fog silencing her footsteps, she ran back across the yard to the tavern. At a certain spot there, just around the corner of the nearest wall, concealed in a clump of weeds, she had left the small bundle containing all her possessions: her "costumes" and make-up, the piece of a broken mirror, and what was left of the Green Perfume in its tiny flacon. The whole was tied up in an apron she had found in the tavern kitchen.

All out of breath now, and tense with fear, she pulled the bundle out and thrust the folded vest in. The two knots she had made in tying up the bundle formed a sort of flexible handle, and, slipping it over her arm, she was about to move on when a powerful slap across her face sent her suddenly reeling back-ward. Just in time, she ducked, tore sideways; one instant, she was pinned against the wall—the little knife's sharp gleam ter-ribly close—the next, with the sound of her skirt ripping, she was suddenly free, and running, as fast as her legs could carry her.

She hadn't dropped her bundle, she realized, and the thought that Slippery Jack had been left behind, with a good part of her skirt clutched in his hand, made her giggle hysterically. But he was after her, at once.

Her original plan had been to make straight for the nearest thoroughfare, a busy city street which marked the limits of their section. By ducking in and out between the shacks, she could have made it easily. But his swift pace was pressing her in the opposite direction, towards the river. The fog was so dense that only the gentle splash of the water against the unprotected bank warned her, in the nick of time, to swerve suddenly left, and run on, guided by that occasional almost inaudible sound of lazy splashing. The shacks stood away from the river, nothing behind which she could duck, to hide, gain a momentary respite. Her only hope now lay in the swiftness of her feet. Further on, much further, there would be the beginning of the enbankment, and then the bridge.

Meanwhile, the weight of the bundle was becoming a handi-cap; several times she almost stumbled. Her strength was defi-nitely ebbing when quite unexpectedly, in sheer desperation, she remembered a certain secret spot where as a child she used to hide so successfully from her playmates. And as the ground under her feet started to slope upward, which meant the begin-ning of the embankment, she stopped and, knowing herself to be concealed by the darkness and the fog, moved close to the water and thrust a foot in, feeling with it for the remembered narrow ledge that ran along the embankment's stone wall. Holding on to the wall, she put the other foot in, swung round so as to face the wall, and, hugging it with her body, she began to move along the submerged ledge slowly, carefully. Only some fifteen yards away was the protective shadow cast by the bridge span.

The hours Lafonte had made her practice at her dancing had made her very agile. But the slimy stones sometimes eluded her grasp; once, twice, she almost lost her balance. The cold water, slipping into her green satin shoes, reached up to her knees. She had grazed an arm and it was bleeding. Then something cold and horribly sleek ran up her thigh and across her back, with the lightning speed peculiar to rats. The revolting contact would have sent her toppling backward, but for the sheer instinct of self-preservation which forced her to cling to the wall. Besides, she was already in the shadows gathered under the bridge and, resting there, she could have laughed—for Slippery Jack was within a few feet of her, and didn't know it.

He had continued up the embankment, just as she thought he would, and now he was standing, hesitant, on the bridge; she could see his reflection in the dim rippling water. Of course, he had had to get into his breeches and shirt before giving chase. Such a waste of precious time, the poor fellow! she thought humorously.

There was comparatively little navigation thereabouts, but one of the hulks, where lived the prisoners condemned to transportation to the colonies, stood a little way off, a sinister black shape barely discernible through the fog. There was a splash of oars and then Clarissa heard the thud of the boat being moored nearby, and after a while the clang of irons against the stone pavement: a batch of prisoners, under heavy guard, brought for the day's labor of building or repairing roads in the city. Slippery Jack must have heard them, too. The guards naturally worked hand in hand with the constables. He had disappeared from the bridge, and then Clarissa saw him moving swiftly along the embankment, beating it back to the safety of the section from which they had both come.

Making use of the submerged narrow ledge as before, she made her way back, then walked up the embankment and stopped to wring the water out of her hair. She thought gratefully of Princess Caroline, for strangely enough, in spite of Lafonte's recently insistent urgings, it was the Princess' kindly interest in Clarissa, the flattering remarks she made about Clarissa's beauty, Clarissa's talents, and, yes, the lovely brocade gown the older woman wore, which had decided Clarissa to delay no longer the decision, long contemplated, to run away.

Thank you, dear Princess Caroline, Clarissa said to her in her own mind. And someday, maybe, I'll have a gown exactly like yours....

She was soaking wet. She took off her shoes, let the water run out of them, then put them on again. They were probably ruined. Disheveled, and with a part of her skirt torn out, she must look a sight. She had the money, she could buy something decent to wear, but who would believe her that it wasn't stolen money? Besides, she wanted to be out of the city before the shops opened. Yet, clothes she must get, somehow.

Across from the embankment stretched a row of houses and there she hurried. The several doorways she peered into were empty, perhaps it was too close to morning for the prostitutes to be still out seeking customers. Then the unmistakable smell of gin led her to another doorway. There was someone sitting there, probably a woman.

"Hey, there," Clarissa called.

"What do *you* want?" It was a woman's voice. But because of the gin having made the voice hoarse it was hard to judge of the woman's age. If she was young she wouldn't part with her finery.

"Look," Clarissa said, "if you give me your dress, and ..." she peered closer, trying to make out what the woman had on her, "and yes, your shawl, and your bonnet, I'll give you money for them."

"Money?" the woman's hoarse voice said. She gave a laugh, which sounded even more horrible than her voice. "And how could the likes of you have money?" In her turn, she too had evidently been peering at Clarissa, and she had formed her judgment.

"I'm in a hurry," Clarissa cried angrily. "Give me the clothes and I'll give you a guinea."

She felt in her bundle for the vest, found the pockets, and drew out a handful of coins. Even in the dark the gold of a guinea stood out. She showed it to the woman.

"I know where you come from," the woman suddenly said. "You come from the Thieves' Village."

"Never mind where I come from," Clarissa said. "You give me the clothes. You're smart enough to keep the money for yourself. You can tell your madam your last customer was a pervert, and that he had insisted taking your clothes away with him; perverts get the strangest ideas."

The woman suddenly began to whimper.

"I don't have a madam. Not that I haven't worked for the best of them once. Why, Black Moll herself, how she used to fuss with me ... But I'm old now. I'm on my own."

"Then you can spend it all on gin. Come on, get that dress off your stupid carcass." Clarissa tugged at the dress impatiently.

"Since you want it that bad, it'll be two guineas."

"You gin-sotted swine!" Clarissa cried, and so furious she was, she stamped her foot. "You know those rags you have on aren't worth even a shilling."

"Two guineas."

And, willy-nilly, Clarissa had to get out another gold coin.

"Now get them off, whore. And quick," and darting into the doorway, she dragged the shawl off, and the bonnet. Then, pulling the woman to her feet, she swiftly unhooked the dress, and dragged that off too, over her head.

"My, but you're certainly in a hurry, and no mistake," the old prostitute muttered, amazed, as she stood there, in just her shift and petticoat, clutching the money Clarissa had thrust into her hand.

But Clarissa was already half a block away. After turning several corners, she reached a certain house, the inhabitants of which were all known to her. On the first floor lived Flaxy, a young blond boy, with his numerous trained dogs which performed at the fairs. On the second, little Mr. Davey with his family. On the third, the old wigmaker, who because he bought up the hair taken from the heads of men and women who had been hanged, went by the name of the Spider. As a spider waits for his prey, so he, too, had to wait for someone to be hanged, so he could have their hair. A very aged woman, known simply as Granny, who sold secondhand clothes to the prostitutes, lived on the fourth floor. The fifth was actually the attic, the single small room in it a mere garret, and there lived the Poet.

Clarissa ran up the dark stairs all the way to the top, pushed the door open, went in, then, pulling it shut, leaned against it.

By the light of a tallow candle, the Poet, sitting at a little table, was busy, scribbling away. Besides the chair he sat on, there was only a narrow bed, pushed under the sloping rafters, and another rickety chair. On turning round and seeing who it was, the Poet, after springing to his feet, stepped back dramatically and, in a voice shaking with emotion, exclaimed:

"Clarissa! You, in my garret!"

"Well, since Slippery Jack sooner or later will start searching for me, I didn't want to get any of my friends involved, for one thing," Clarissa said. "And those who maybe are not my friends, why, they'd be sure to run and tell him, and that'd help him trace my movements eventually. So instead of going to Granny to buy something decent to wear, I had to get *this*." Clarissa, in disgust, flung the old prostitute's clothes over the bundle which she had dropped to the floor. "But you're such a befuddled-looking fellow," she added, "nobody would think of asking *you* any questions."

"Clarissa," the poet again exclaimed, "there's blood on your arm, and, yes, some on your cheek, too."

"A few scratches." She waved a hand airily.

She glanced towards the small empty fireplace.

"Come on," she said, "I'm chilled all the way down to my beautiful bones." She was, indeed, shivering. "I'll catch my death of a cold if I don't have a fire. Where's your firewood?"

The Poet explained apologetically, while passing a hand ruefully through his black locks, that Mr. Davey had told him he could have some of his, but that he had forgotten all about it.

Clarissa, after a glance around, said decisively:

"Then we'll have to use that chair. It looks broken to me, anyhow."

The Poet obediently brought over the spare chair. Taking up a small hatchet from the grate, he tried to break up the chair, but he wasn't strong enough. Clarissa pushed him aside.

"I'll do it. And if there's such a thing as an old newspaper lying around somewhere, get it."

With a few dexterous blows of the hatchet, she swiftly chopped up the chair. Then, kneeling by the grate, using an old newspaper which the Poet handed her for kindling, she built up the fire.

"Now a match."

One had to tell him everything.

He brought it to her. She struck it against the chimney wall, lit the paper, and instantly the old wood of the dismembered chair burst into flames. Then, the Poet bringing over some water in a basin, which he had poured from a bucket at the door, and a rag of a towel, she first of all washed the traces of blood off her face and arm. The scratch on her cheek wasn't very deep, and after a few applications of cold water, it stopped bleeding. But the arm, which she thought she had merely grazed, showed a small gash. The Poet, following her instructions, tore up the towel and succeeded in making quite a decent bandage over the hurt spot. Then, quickly shedding her dripping skirt and blouse, she basked her suddenly naked body in the warmth of the bright fire.

Driven into the brick of the chimney were several big nails, probably used by some previous tenant for holding kitchen utensils, and on these she hung up her wet clothes to dry. Only then she became aware that the Poet had walked away to the little window, so as to stand with his back turned modestly towards her. She burst out laughing.

"Come on, look your fill," she cried invitingly. "I like it."

But he wouldn't turn around.

"Oh, all right," Clarissa laughed, "I'll get that blanket from your bed."

She went to fetch it. Then, wrapping herself in the blanket, she sat down on the floor in front of the fire, and shook out her hair so it would dry quicker. The Poet came over and stood gazing down at her with his passionate eyes, adoringly.

"I'm going to do everything according to Lafonte's plan," Clarissa said. "He's been planning it for months. He gave me a letter to an old friend of his who's gone down in the world, like Lafonte himself has, except maybe for a different reason. Anyway, this friend now is the manager of a cheap little theater in the provinces. Colchester is the name of the town." Clarissa prided herself on remembering previously unheard names, words, on being able to pronounce them.

"Lafonte hasn't heard from this friend for some time," she went on. "So I was thinking maybe he isn't there any more, lost the manager's job, and there'll be nobody to give *me* a job, as an actress. Lafonte thinks I'm more than ready for it. But Lafonte was quite angry with me. He said, unless one remained an op … optimist, one would never get anywhere. 'Always be an optimist, Clarissa,' he told me. So," Clarissa added, "I have to catch the first stagecoach that'll be going to Colchester. And I want you to put me on it. I don't know anything about traveling."

"I will consider myself honored, Clarissa," the Poet said.

But he looked sadly disappointed; perhaps he had imagined that she had come to stay with him, share his struggles.

Vaguely aware of his emotions, Clarissa said:

"Let's go to bed and you can have the joy of me."

"Your heart, Clarissa, would not be involved."

"You mean I don't get a tickle between my legs every time I see you?" Clarissa said, smiling up at him roguishly.

The Poet, without answering, went back to his little table, sat down, took up the quill pen.

Clarissa dozed off.

CHAPTER FOUR

S HE WOULD PROBABLY have slept on for hours, but for the urgent tugging at the blanket she sat wrapped in. The candle was still burning, but the rose and gold of dawn was reaching into the garret through the little window. The Poet, who had been shaking her awake, seemed terribly excited. In an out-flung hand he held a sheet of paper covered with his scribbling. And now, stepping back dramatically, he exclaimed:

"Clarissa! Your coming here has been an inspiration to me. I have it, at last, a truly great poem. Fame! Listen …"

And he began to read aloud from the scribbled sheet:

Like to Diana in her summer weed,
Girt with a crimson robe of brightest dye,
   Goes fair Clarissa.

"But I don't have a crimson robe," Clarissa cried.

"Well, you should," the Poet told her. "Crimson is for royalty, and beauty is royal; you should be wearing a crimson robe. Please don't interrupt."

And he continued reading:

Her tresses dark, her eyes like glassy streams,
Her teeth are pearl, the breasts are ivory;
   Thus fair Clarissa
Passes fair Venus in her bravest hue

And Juno in the show of majesty,
    For she's Clarissa!

There was a lot more of the same stuff, not a word of which could she understand.

"Goodness," Clarissa said, when he at last finished.

The Poet, however, was jubilant.

"When Mr. Brummell sees this, he will ask me to one of the exquisite little supper parties he's so famous for, to read my poem. So far, all the poems I sent him kept coming back. But this! Beau Brummell will be my patron. Fame. Fame!"

Clarissa, suddenly interested, got up swiftly and, clutching the blanket about her, came very close.

"Does that mean you'll be given a title, and an estate, and have money, lots of money?"

"Well, not exactly … I may get a meal now and then at the patron's table. He may give me a small stipend. That's customary. Fame, Clarissa, means that my name and your image will be known to posterity, to people many years hence, that is; long after the two of us are mere dust!"

"Pshaw!" Clarissa said, moving away. "What good will anything do me *then*?"

She put on her torn skirt and the blouse, both of which were dry by now. They'd serve her in place of a shift and petticoat, which one was supposed to wear under a dress. She was about to take up the dress, but ran to the window instead.

"I almost forgot about Carbuncle Joe. They always pass along here on the way to Tyburn."

The Poet joined her. The street below was already jammed with a crowd, everybody wearing his holiday attire, and all moving in the same direction. From every window in the row of houses opposite, people were leaning out, the better to see. Some, the more daring ones, had found places of vantage on the roof tops, over which the shreds of fog still lingered, obscuring the yellow sun.

The tolling of the bell from St. Sepulchre's, which meant that the condemned man had left the jail, could be heard all over the city, the sound came so clear and loud. And now a clamor was starting to rise from the crowd below. Shouts rang out, some of derision, others of encouragement. Then Clarissa saw the traditional cart. Beside the driver sat the hangman's assistant, Herb the Younger. No matter what the man's real name or age might be, he was always called Herb the Younger. The hangman himself never appeared in the procession, but waited for it at Tyburn. *His* was a hereditary post, and since the family name was Herb, it seemed natural to the people to call his assistant Herb the Younger.

But all eyes were on Carbuncle Joe, and there he sat between two guards, in the center of the cart, bareheaded, wearing a clean white shirt, dark breeches, big irons clapped on his legs, a long chain around his waist, and in his hands a nosegay, as was the custom. And, running alongside the cart, holding on with a hand to its edge, was Prickly Gil. To the constables and the guards, who were present in the milling crowd in a far greater number than usual, keeping a sharp lookout for the condemned man's associates and friends, Prickly Gil was the only person who had dared leave the Thieves' Village, and being a mere girl, and a queer one at that, of no account. But Clarissa caught a glimpse of and recognized another familiar face, that of Honest Gregory, who, wearing the dignified garb of a parson, moved along solemnly and at a prudent distance.

The cart and the crowd gradually passed out of view.

"I'll miss that stagecoach if I don't hurry," Clarissa cried.

And hastening away from the window, she put on the old prostitute's dress. Though Clarissa had never owned a real dress in her life, by sheer instinct, which is inherent in every woman, she knew exactly what was good and what wasn't, and whether a gown, a bonnet, was fashionable or lagging far behind the reigning style, and what kind of rosette, bow, or lace was in good taste or not. Consequently, she was very critical of the dress she had to wear.

The ugly purple color of the cheap material was faded, soiled; the satin edging of the wide flounces, shabby … It was, besides, much too large for her. The old whore evidently was as big as a horse. Ripping off one of the flounces, Clarissa tied it around the waist, making a big bow in the back. The bodice, at least, was cut very low, as she could see in the piece of mirror which she had taken out of her bundle and propped against the Poet's inkpot. And now, appropriating his chair, she put on rouge, face powder, colored her mouth lavishly. The bonnet was no better than the dress, one of the nodding ostrich plumes broken, the streamers worn into strings. But once she had it on, the mirror reflecting the young radiant face, framed in the mass of natural ringlets, it didn't look so bad.

Of course, she knew that too much of her hair showed. She had no pins to fasten it up with. She had pushed as much of it as she could under the bonnet, in the back, but that didn't help much. There was just nothing she could do with her hair, it was so abundant.

"Anyway," Clarissa said, getting up, picking up the shawl, arranging it about her shoulders, "I look the part. A poor dancing girl, or a cheap little actress. Except that neither would be traveling with a *bundle*."

Since her first quick look around the garret on coming in, she had been aware of a real traveling bag, a small valise, lying on one of the otherwise empty shelves near the bed. Now, hurrying over, she wrenched the metal clasps open, raised the lid.

"Clarissa," the Poet cried out, with a kind of frenzy. "That's where I keep my manuscripts, my poems!"

"Nothing will happen to them," Clarissa said calmly, dumping the contents onto the shelf.

She then quickly packed all her things into the valise, having transferred the coins from Slippery Jack's vest into the deep pocket of her skirt. Her green satin shoes, which were still not quite dry enough for comfort, just peeped out from under the flounced dress as she walked.

"I don't want anybody to see me when we go down the stairs," Clarissa said, giving the Poet the valise to carry. "You go ahead of me, and if someone comes out on any of the landings I'll keep out of sight, until whoever it is goes back in."

The Poet opened the door, and they began to descend, moving cautiously.

The first door they passed, on the landing immediately below, was Granny's. The aged woman was in the habit of talking aloud when alone, and they could hear her grumbling, using indecent language, and the rustle of the tarnished finery she was arranging for display to her sluttish customers. The landing of the next, the third floor, also seemed empty. Clarissa, after pausing, just in case, behind the turn of the stairs, started to follow the Poet, when a door opened and the old wigmaker, the Spider, came out, barely giving her time to slip back, out of sight.

"It's you," he said to the Poet. "I was expecting someone who was to bring me something," the wigmaker explained, and he chuckled in the most horrible manner. The traffic in human hair procured from the heads of the hangman's victims could incur very unpleasant punishment and the Spider, consequently, always talked in riddles.

An untidy, dirty-looking old man, wearing a disheveled dirty wig, he bore a striking resemblance to his namesake.

Especially the way he had come out of his door, unexpectedly, swiftly and soundlessly; a spider, darting out of its secret corner at the approach of the potential prey.

"I suppose you saw Carbuncle Joe go by," he said. "Now there's a fine head of hair! Every time I saw him, I'd admire it. What a head of hair, I'd say to myself. Well, now he's gone, should be, Herb's a fast worker. But the trouble is, because of Carbuncle Joe's notoriety, they'll have guards stationed for the twenty-four hours that he's to remain dangling there, at Tyburn. And then they'll bury him secretly, in some unknown spot, where nobody will be able to find him. Maybe outside the city somewhere, so long as it's unconsecrated ground. Who is that with you?" the wigmaker added suddenly. "I know it's a girl, I heard her. No mistaking the sound of a woman's skirt. You probably had her with you all night. Anybody I know?" And the Spider chuckled again, in that horrible manner peculiarly his.

It was no use hiding any longer. The senile idiot wouldn't go back in till his curiosity was satisfied. Clarissa, holding up her shawl in front of her face, walked swiftly past.

"Whoever she may be," the wigmaker called after her, chuckling, "it's a fine head of hair she has on her. What a head of hair!"

Clarissa felt a shiver of strange dread pass along her spine, starting from the spot in the back of her head where the gruesome stare of the Spider's eyes seemed to bore into her skull. But the sensation of this sudden terror lasted only a moment, and she forgot all about it almost immediately.

The Poet had followed her, and from behind little Mr. Davey's door in the next landing came the peaceful sound of the kettle hissing in the grate, and the clink of dishes being set on the table. Mr. Davey's wife was a very orderly woman. Then, even before they reached the ground floor, the air was suddenly rent by the barking and howling of Flaxy's numerous dogs, impatient for their breakfast. At last they were past Flaxy's door, and out in the street.

The Poet led her quickly by way of back alleys and narrow side streets, and so into a small cobbled square, where the stage-coach was to stop at the Rose and Crown to pick up passengers. The sun was shining brightly, the sky was a pure blue, and the surrounding buildings, after the night's dense fog, sparkled as if they had been freshly washed. There was a great deal of move-ment and noise. Now that the hanging was over, people hurried along intent on their everyday business. The farmers' carts and wagons stood drawn up in front of the hostelry, which appeared to be crowded, the men inside discussing over their morning meal the fine show Carbuncle Joe had provided them with. The food venders passed by, crying out, "Small beer. Small beer ..." Or, "Penny loaves. Who'll buy a penny loaf?"

A prim old maid, the daughter of a wealthy merchant, judg-ing by her rich clothes, was crossing the square on the way to the church whose spire rose just beyond the Rose and Crown. Wearing a gown of yellow satin trimmed with green ribbon, and a mobcap of starched dimity with streamers of the same ribbon, she carried in one hand a prayer book and in the other a fan. Just then, a couple of dandies, each embracing and mauling a young slut, came out of the inn, shouting at the top of their drunken voices. The old maid tapped her chin with her fan in hypocritical disapproval, but the glance of envy she cast at the revelers made Clarissa laugh. The old maid's eyes were like the eyes of a fish, a dead fish.

Then Clarissa caught sight of Black Moll, clad in her respect-ful widow's weeds. The procuress was talking with two shy young girls who had just arrived from the country in search of honest work in the big city. Well, Black Moll would promise to place them as housemaids with a nice family, and then ... A thin little

old man, very richly dressed, Lord Charters, the famous profligate, was not far away. He had his pimp, who went by the name of
Skiff, with him, and the two of them were watching Black Moll's
expert endeavors with great interest and very closely.

At the other end of the square, the milkmaids had arranged
their earthenware jugs and tin pails in a neat row, and were per-
forming a crude country dance while waiting for customers.
They were big strapping young women, wearing linen aprons
over their homespun skirts, and large flat straw hats, tied with a
string under the chin. Regular giantesses they were, and the way
they moved their big feet, now to the right, then to the left, was
really grotesque. People watching them laughed so hard, tears
streamed down their cheeks. But the milkmaids didn't care. They
went on hopping and jumping, perfectly satisfied with their ludi-
crous performance.

The Poet, who had gone into the Rose and Crown to inquire
about the stagecoach's scheduled arrival, just then returned to
say it was due any minute. But Clarissa sent him right back on
the pretense of bringing her something to eat; she was famished.
Oh, anything, some bread, cut from a regular loaf—she was sick
and tired of penny loaves—and, yes, some cheese. Hastily, she
gave him a few coins. Traveling by the stage was quite expensive,
she'd hardly have any money left by the time she reached her
destination. And if Lafonte's friend was no longer there …?

"The sharpest cheese they have," she ordered. "Go on. Do
hurry!"

For she had already caught sight of the man whom she had
noticed in the tavern the previous night, the stranger in the black
cloak. The broad-brimmed hat casting a shadow over his long
strong face, and arms crossed on his chest, he stood leaning
against a house wall nearby. She could see at once that the sole
reason for his presence there was herself, and that he was waiting

for an opportune moment to approach her, speak to her. And as soon as the Poet again hurried off, the mysterious stranger strode over. His strikingly commanding appearance was especially evident when he walked. People turned to look at him with respect.

"What I have to say to you, Clarissa," he said at once, "won't take long."

"But … how did you know I'd be here? And my name …" Clarissa stammered, surprised, not a little afraid, and excitingly intrigued, all at one and the same time.

In her present outfit of flounced dress, shawl, and bonnet, she had felt perfectly secure against possible recognition, even on the part of the sharp-eyed Black Moll.

"So long as she doesn't see your face, Black Moll won't know it's you," the stranger said quietly, rightly guessing her anxiety. "I noticed how, on seeing her, you placed yourself so's to have your back to her, and you're right to be so cautious. A procuress always sides with a man, and Black Moll would lose no time in carrying the information to Slippery Jack. But she's so used to seeing you always wearing that short shabby skirt and the torn blouse …"

The strong features of the long face, and even the eyes with their piercing gaze, when seen close, somehow inspired confidence. She spoke up boldly:

"You seem to know a great deal!"

"I am a Rosicrucian," the stranger said. As if that explained everything.

"I'll never be able to pronounce *that!*"

"Rosicrucian," he repeated it slowly, syllable by syllable, for her benefit.

"Ros … Rosicru … cian," Clarissa said. "A Rosicrucian."

"There, you have it right now. I knew you'd be clever, besides being very beautiful," he studied her face and the partly bared breasts with judicious approval. "And that is why you have been chosen to perform a certain service for us, when the time comes."

And, unmindful of the fact that she stared at him with her mouth open in astonishment, he went on calmly:

"The Rosicrucians are a secret society. Our existence was first discovered in the fifteenth century through the learned writings of Rosenkreuz, but of course we had been active long before then. Our organization already existed when the first of the great pyramids on the Nile was being built. The Fama, which is our Book, contains much of the hidden wisdom of the East. We bring Light into the world, and now that the Beast, which is described in the Apocalypse, has again appeared in the person of Napoleon, who hopes to possess all of the globe, we had to become very active again to protect it. We must keep peace among the great nations."

"And do you … do you believe in the Line?" Clarissa asked, remembering Prickly Gil's weird talk. "The power of the Unbroken Line?"

"We believe that the Line can be broken," the Rosicrucian said, "without disastrous consequences to the person involved. But, of course, there must be exonerating circumstances."

"Oh," Clarissa said. "You mentioned something about doing you a service," she went on, rearranging the shawl about her shoulders in a manner which she thought to be very ladylike, and even haughty. "And what will little *me* get out of *that?*"

"Rest assured, you'll be justly rewarded." And seeing the Poet hurrying towards them, the Rosicrucian added quickly, "So be prepared. I myself will contact you, or perhaps another one of our members. The most unlikely people are actually Rosicrucians. That's how I came to be admitted into the Waterfront Tavern last night. Let nothing surprise you henceforth," and he strode swiftly away, disappearing around a house corner, just as the Poet came up.

"Here's the bread and the cheese," the Poet said, handing them, wrapped in a scrap of greasy paper, to Clarissa. "The sharpest cheese they had. I'm afraid it actually smells."

The cheese, indeed, smelled to high heaven. But that's how Clarissa liked it.

The rumble of wheels over the cobbles, and the shouts of the postilion warning everybody to get out of the way, announced the arrival of the stagecoach. The two sweating horses moved at a swift pace, and drove up in front of the Rose and Crown. The heavy old-fashioned coach was crowded beyond its capacity, both with the passengers and their luggage. Two male passengers sat on the roof, among the heap of valises, bundles, and traveling bags. A little railing ran around the coach's roof to prevent the luggage and the passengers from sliding off it. The two men sitting there were the first to scramble down with the help of the postilion, a young surly fellow who had at once jumped down from his place on the box beside the burly driver.

Then the passengers from inside the coach began to come out. Two women, one richly attired, the other evidently her servant. A portly merchant. Two young, blue-coated naval officers, their hair tied in the back with a black ribbon, just as Lord Nelson wore his hair, and their tricorn hats like his, except that they lacked an admiral's gold fringe. There was also a red-coated officer from the Army, which was already under the command of Wellington; but since the struggle with Napoleon was at the moment wholly concentrated on the seas, the people paid marked attention only to the men who were lucky to be serving under Nelson. The last to come out was a shabby little clerk, followed by an old woman with a bundle.

Most of the passengers looked completely worn out; their insides all shaken up by the continuous jolting of the coach, their bodies cramped from sitting for hours in the same position. Clarissa smiled roguishly at the naval officers, and they grinned back, their handsome faces flushed, excited looking all of a sudden. With the Poet carrying the valise, she had hurried over to stand at the coach door, waiting to get in.

"Let's have your fare," the surly postilion demanded.

Without bothering to add "miss," or "ma'am," or simply "lady," polite words which she was quick to notice he had used in addressing other female passengers.

"I'll thank you to mind your manners!" she flared up, busy trying to get the money out of her pocket.

But the fool, instead of apologizing immediately, only grinned and stared at her breasts, so invitingly exposed by the low-cut bodice.

"The valise goes on the roof," he said to the Poet.

The Poet handed it to him.

"It's going with me!" Clarissa declared.

She snatched the valise from the postilion, who seemed quite unprepared for such behavior. To make short work of his protests, she at once flung the valise inside the coach, and since she was at the same time holding the fare money ready and clutching at the greasy package containing the bread and the cheese, the coins were suddenly scattered all over the cobbles. The postilion, cursing, and with the Poet helping him, both crawling about on their knees, began to pick the money up.

When, at last, the surly fellow had her fare in his possession, he reciprocated by giving her such a push, under the pretense of helping her get in, that she fell, landing in somebody's lap. The door banged shut. The coach began to move at a brisk pace. Clarissa thrust her head out the window.

"Good-by. Good-by!" she cried, waving with one hand, and with the other throwing kisses to the Poet, who stood, looking very sad, as he too waved in his turn.

"Never good-by, Clarissa. Farewell!"

CHAPTER FIVE

WHEN CLARISSA, at last, and in her own good time, drew her head from out of the window—it was so amusing to watch the houses flash past and the people scamper in all directions out of the stage's way—she suddenly became aware of the excitement her landing in somebody's lap had created among her fellow passengers. Indignant exclamations, ferocious glances of resentment, the stout matron to whom the lap belonged having hysterics, voices raised in an attempt to soothe her, and someone trying to reach with a smelling salts flacon the nostrils of the panting victim.

"Get off my lap, you painted hussy," the matron hissed right into Clarissa's ear. "You wicked, wicked woman. Shameless Jezebel!"

"Pray compose yourself, Mrs. Purdy. Do compose yourself." And the gaunt woman, dressed in an old-fashioned brown traveling costume, with a matching cape and turban, again offered the smelling salts.

Clarissa let them all fume. She could have, of course, at once slid off the lap and so put an end to the turmoil, but the lap's indignant owner sat in the corner next to the window, and that was where Clarissa wanted to sit. So sliding gradually towards that side of the coach, while working with her bottom and an elbow on the matron under her, she wedged herself in, between the window and the matron. A final powerful shove, which sent the gasping Mrs. Purdy sliding along the leather-covered seat to its center, and Clarissa was comfortably installed in the corner.

Mrs. Purdy, her fat face red as a beet, her mouth compressed tightly, shook out the folds of her taffeta skirts and of the paisley shawl very pointedly, as if contact with Clarissa might give one some horrible disease, something much worse than smallpox.

"Ugh ..." she gasped, venomously.

The valise? Clarissa had a moment of panic. But there it was, on the floor, where it had landed. There were racks under the coach's roof for the passengers' luggage, but Clarissa pulled the valise over close, and placed both her feet very firmly on it, in order that no one could steal it from her. Then she opened the package containing the bread and cheese and, breaking off a good chunk of each by turn, from the greasy paper on her knees, she began to eat her belated breakfast with relish. On chancing to glance up, she saw that everybody now had a hand to the nose, the fingers pressing the nostrils tight, because of the smelly cheese. Clarissa laughed.

She had been aware that someone was watching her with interest. Clarissa could feel the lively interest, but when she looked up, the serene young lady, who sat in the corner opposite hers, dropped her eyes demurely.

The dark dress the young lady had on was very simply made. A white cambric kerchief, worn around the neck and crossed over the bosom, was pinned at the throat with a small cameo brooch. Under the plain bonnet, her hair, parted exactly in the center, was all very smoothly drawn back, except for two long, sausage-like curls on either side of the clean sweet face. She was obviously not rich. The dress was badly worn, but it was immaculate. And everything about her, especially the quiet way she sat, proclaimed her to be of gentle birth.

That's why, naturally, she had been given the best seat, facing the direction in which the coach was going. And sharing this privilege with her were a man who, judging by his good black coat and the sour look on his big face, was probably a magistrate, and a red-coated, florid-faced soldier, with big mustaches. While Clarissa, Mrs. Purdy, and the gaunt woman in brown sat with their backs to the horses.

Clarissa, who had not often seen a gentlewoman at such close quarters, stared at her with frank curiosity. The young lady raised her eyes and smiled. It was a sweet, kind smile. Nobody had ever smiled like that at Clarissa before.

"Have some of my cheese," Clarissa said impulsively.

Instantly, she was ready to bite her tongue off, for being so forward.

But the young lady surprisingly was not at all offended.

"You're very kind," she murmured. "Yes, I would like to, just a little piece."

"Dear Miss Gray," Mrs. Purdy was heard to say with saccharine obsequiousness. "One naturally expects you to be extremely polite and kind to almost *anybody,* because of your gentle birth. But surely there's no rule in the etiquette book to act so familiarly with an *actress!*"

Miss Gray, after removing one of the black lace mitts she wore, took the piece of cheese out of Clarissa's hand, put it in her mouth.

"Very delicious."

And though she at once, taking a snow-white handkerchief from a small satchel on her knees, hastened to wipe her mouth and fingers with it very daintily, there was quite a wicked gleam of enjoyment in her eyes, considering her sheltered upbringing. She had really liked the cheese—even its awful smell, maybe!

The magistrate and the soldier, of course, once they got over being indignant with Clarissa, had been ogling her, though doing it in such a way as not to be caught at it by the other women, the respectable ones. And Clarissa had winked back every time, which seemed to make the men quite excited. They moved their feet nervously, frowned, coughed. But the swaying of the coach gradually sent them all to sleep. Mrs. Purdy was heard to snore. Miss Gray, leaning forward slightly, and speaking in a lowered voice so as not to disturb the others, said:

"So you're an actress!"

"If I get the job that's supposed to be waiting for me in Colchester. Up to now I was just a dancing girl in a tavern."

"A dancer! But how thrilling! And the young man who was seeing you off is probably your fiancé. I could see he's very much in love with you. I was watching you all the time," Miss Gray confided, smiling gently, a little sadly. "You're so full of life, so gay, so free ... And your name is Clarissa. I overheard the young man call you that."

"What's that word you used?" Clarissa said, anxious as usual to broaden her vocabulary. "Fiancé?"

Miss Gray explained what the word meant.

"Pshaw," Clarissa laughed. "He is just a friend."

"I suppose you have many friends like that—men friends, I mean," Miss Gray smiled wistfully.

She gazed out at the countryside that was now flashing past the swiftly moving coach. From the sky's infinite blue the sun was pouring its light in brilliant shafts upon the summer landscape. Sheep grazed peacefully on the green pastures. A lonely farm laborer was ploughing a field. Barefoot children ran out of the thatched cottages to wave at the passing stage.

"It's beautiful, isn't it?" Miss Gray said. "You see, Clarissa," she explained with her gentle smile, "I was brought up to love scenery, nature, poetry...."

But she didn't look very happy about it.

Maybe her health isn't so good, Clarissa told herself, wondering. She's just a young girl, like I am. If she looks older it's only because of her dignified manners ...

Aloud, Clarissa said:

"I guess you've been away to some fashionable boarding school and now you're going back home, to the big estate your family has."

From Lafonte she knew all about the ways of the gentlefolks.

"The estate, the land, everything, was lost to us many years ago," Miss Gray explained quietly. "Then my parents died ... It's true I'm just out of a boarding school; there was a little money left to pay for that. My headmistress had arranged a position as a governess for me. She corresponded with my employers; they've never seen me. Her recommendation, of course, sufficed, since she's famous for supplying governesses to our nobility. So now I'm on my way to Ravisham, the family seat of the Marquis of Trall, to take up my post as governess to the two youngest daughters.

"You said, Clarissa, you'd be getting off at Colchester," Miss Gray went on. "Well, about five miles before this coach reaches *your* destination, it will stop briefly at a small village, Wickhem St. Paul's it's called, and there a trap will be waiting for me at the inn to take me to Ravisham. My headmistress explained it all to me, very explicitly. And, of course, she gave me a letter which will formally introduce me to my employers. It's in my satchel," Miss Gray gave a little pat to the satchel reposing on her primly clad knees. "I should feel very grateful, really. And, of course, I *do*. Ravisham is a beautiful place, always crowded with guests, titled, important personages. The Marquis Tralls is one of our oldest families, enormously rich, and very influential at court. As a matter of fact, the Prince Regent frequently comes there to hunt."

"The Prince Regent," Clarissa gasped. "Why, you'll be meeting Beau Brummell himself then."

"You don't understand," Miss Gray said sadly, though smiling a little at Clarissa's enthusiasm. "None of those glamorous people will take the slightest notice of me. A governess is a nothing. A gentlewoman forced to earn her livelihood is universally despised. Even the servants treat her with contempt."

"But you're young, pretty," Clarissa argued. "Surely you could somehow make a man look at you. And once a girl gets a man to look at her," Clarissa snapped her fingers triumphantly, "why, the rest is easy."

Miss Gray laughed. Surprisingly, she had quite a merry laugh.

"You don't understand, Clarissa," she said, again trying to explain it all. "My behavior must be always beyond reproach. Modest, reserved, quiet. When it comes to men I'm not supposed even to see them, let alone look. I must keep my eyes down. Otherwise it would be considered highly improper. In fact, my reputation would be ruined, I'd lose my post, disgrace my family. I have some distant relatives left, a great-aunt somewhere in Scotland.... No, there's really nothing for me to look forward to. But I'm in a rather frail state of health, so it doesn't really matter....

"In the boarding school," Miss Gray went on, after remaining silent for a little while, "we were never allowed to see anything of the outside world. A high stone wall surrounds the place and within that wall we had to take our walks. So many wonderful things beyond it, we'd tell one another. Girls of my class are not allowed to go to the theater until they're married—think of it!

I've never even seen a fair ... That's why I so enjoyed watching you, the way you snatched your valise from the postilion and the way the man stared at you, admiring your good looks. *You* are free. And I envy you."

Clarissa laughed, convinced as she was that Miss Gray was joking.

"Well, I certainly envy *you,*" she said. "If I had your chance of having all those titled, wealthy men near me, I'd for sure get something out of it! You see," Clarissa explained in her turn, "a cheap little dancer or actress never comes in contact with the men who are of any account. *They* wouldn't go to a tavern or a little provincial theater where she happens to perform."

"Then all we have to do," Miss Gray said, laughing merrily, "is to change places."

"Oh, let's do that," Clarissa cried, also laughing. "We're about the same height. And our hair is almost the same color."

"But quite differently arranged," Miss Gray pointed out, scrutinizing Clarissa with lively interest.

"And, of course, our clothes are quite different," Clarissa laughed, in her turn studying Miss Gray.

"But all that could be changed, you see," Miss Gray reminded her, continuing her pretense of being very serious about it all. "And since you're an actress or about to become one, which means you must have had a great deal of training in the art, I'm certain you could play the role of a governess to perfection! There's so little a governess has to do or say ..."

At that moment, an especially severe jolting of the coach, as it took a sharp turn in the road without diminishing speed, almost sent them all flying out of their seats, pell-mell. Miss Gray tried to clutch at a strap, missed it, and would have had quite a bad fall but for Clarissa, who, sustaining her own balance by pressing her feet against her valise, had quickly leaned forward to grasp Miss Gray by both arms and so push her back against the leather upholstery. Their fellow passengers had somehow either retained or reassumed their sitting position—Clarissa, busy with Miss Gray, didn't notice what was happening to *them*. Anyway, they were all wide awake now.

"Quite a jolt, that," the red-coated soldier said, his florid cheeks puffed out and the big mustaches undulating, as he tried to regain his breath. "I hope the driver knows his business."

"Probably drunk," his neighbor, the magistrate, said sternly.

"A wicked man, that's what he is," Mrs. Purdy shrilled. "Why, he might have killed *me!*"

"A stagecoach driver," the gaunt woman in brown announced with authority, "always tears along as if the devil were after him. And maybe that's exactly what the stupid lout deserves. Anyhow, all we can do is hope that no bones are broken till we reach our various destinations."

Not until *that* excitement had subsided, did they notice that Miss Gray looked a little tired.

"Are you feeling all right, Miss Gray?" the magistrate, who sat next to her, inquired. Even his stern voice softened somewhat when addressing Miss Gray.

"Let me wrap this rug about your knees, Miss Gray," the red-coated soldier offered with surprising solicitude.

"Pray have this little cushion, Miss Gray," the woman in brown said. "Put it behind your back and you'd be ever so much more comfortable."

A mere few hours in Miss Gray's company was enough to inspire everyone with respect and affection for the gentle governess. Even Mrs. Purdy, in her own disagreeable way, expressed her concern.

"The actress woman was probably annoying Miss Gray, that's what it is," she was heard to say, while glancing daggers at Clarissa.

Miss Gray, however, politely declined all proffered ministrations.

"Pray do not be concerned. I think I struck my shoulder slightly against the window. But it's of no consequence. It might have been so much worse but for Clarissa here. Thank you, Clarissa."

"The painted hussy would have some such name," Mrs. Purdy could be heard grumbling. "Clarissa! Downright smacks of grease paint."

Miss Gray, leaning back, took a little nap. And at noontime the coach stopped at a big hostelry and everybody got out and went in to have something to eat. The little nourishment the governess partook of very daintily seemed to revive her strength, for as soon as they were back in the coach and on their way once more, she again fell to talking with Clarissa, while the others dozed, their heads nodding ludicrously.

"You mentioned Mr. Brummell," Miss Gray said, lowering her voice. "Eventually, of course, I'm bound to meet him, since wherever the Prince Regent goes, he has Mr. Brummell go along with him. Governesses, because of their gentle birth, are always introduced to the guests. And there I'll be, curtsying to Beau Brummell. Perhaps it will happen in the rose garden. But, of course, he won't even notice me....

"At the boarding school, all the girls, naturally, raved about him," Miss Gray went on. "They can't wait to meet him. The Prince's favorite ... But I think of Mr. Brummell quite differently. I've never told this to anyone before," she confided, her sweet face growing a little pink, a hand at her heart. "But Mr. Brummell is my ideal of a man. What a wonderful person he must be! Courteous, kind, everything about him in the best of taste, a perfectionist. Patron of the arts, and a poet at heart himself. Lonely, probably. For who could truly understand him? Friendless ... You must have seen him, Clarissa. Free as you were to go about London."

"Everybody knows Mr. Brummell's elegant little carriage. It's painted in stripes of bright yellow and blue," Clarissa said. "So a crowd would gather, and I'd catch a glimpse. The horses are very fine, dapple-gray. Mr. Brummell himself would be holding the reins. And beside him on the box, a groom in yellow and blue livery."

"And is he very handsome? Elegant?"

"That he certainly is," Clarissa said.

"But he doesn't look happy?" Miss Gray persisted.

"Well," Clarissa thought it over. "Now that you mention it, I guess he doesn't. But then the Prince is terribly jealous, and he sets spies on Mr. Brummell. Anything Mr. Brummell does, if it's merely going into a shop to buy himself a new neckcloth, right away the Prince Regent gets an account of it, in every detail."

"He is lonely, friendless," Miss Gray said, not listening to Clarissa, but speaking her own secret thoughts aloud. "I have a little book of poetry, in my satchel here," she went on, "and every time I open it and begin to read, the beautiful words, I don't know why, make me think of Mr. Brummell. Since the headmistress told me it was Ravisham I'd be going to, I've been reading the little volume every single day. But, of course," Miss Gray added sadly, "he won't even notice me. He'll be very polite, naturally. And then ... Well, he won't even know I exist!"

The coach had stopped at a town's outskirts to let the red-coated soldier get off. The sun was starting to set, Clarissa noticed.

"When you get back from your furlough," the magistrate was saying sternly, "try to get a shot at that monster Napoleon."

The soldier, already standing in the road, laughed.

"Seeing as we're the land forces, he hasn't given us a chance, so far. Napoleon is in Egypt now. He had one of their sacred obelisks moved to Paris. Robbing that country now of all its treasures. But Lord Nelson is right there, on the Nile, waiting to give battle to the French fleet."

And banging the coach door shut, the soldier hurried away.

"Lord Nelson, Lord Nelson, that's all one hears nowadays," Mrs. Purdy complained, as the stage continued on its way.

Not even the man who was fast becoming the nation's hero could escape the woman's vicious petulance.

"All the treasures *I* have in the world," Miss Gray said to Clarissa, "are in this satchel." She gave it a little pat. "There's a lovely miniature of my brother, for instance, painted when he was a little lad."

"You … you have lost your brother?" Clarissa said, trying to word her question gently, since her idea of miniatures was associated with persons already deceased.

It made her almost jump to hear Miss Gray's answer:

"I hope not. Not lost, no." And then she explained. "When I was placed in that boarding school, my brother, who was several years my senior, left the country to seek his fortune in foreign lands. India, Australia, Africa … I was too young then to understand, but I remember his enthusiastic talk about diamond mines, gold mines. Anyway, the idea was that he would return only when he makes a lot of money, to buy back our home, the family estate, provide a proper dowry for me … But there's been no news from him for all of ten years."

"Ten years!" Clarissa exclaimed. But she at once tried to bolster up the governess' pathetic hopes of her lost brother's return. "Of course," she said, "for a young man trying to make his fortune away from home, it would take longer than *that*."

"That's exactly what I think," Miss Gray smiled at her grate-fully. "Of course, it is quite possible," she went on sensibly, quietly, and with a great show of courage, "that he might have perished, at one time or another, and in some awful manner, through ship-wreck, or illness perhaps, cholera, the plague, or by losing his way in the African jungle. But I like to think that none of these things happened to darling Richard, and that, instead, rumors of Napoleon's ambition to conquer the world must have reached my brother, somehow, and that he was able to make his way back to civilization, in order to offer his services for the defense of his country. In which case he would, sooner or later, suddenly appear at Ravisham, a man grown, wearing a uniform, to claim his adoring sister! I would have liked to show you the miniature, Clarissa," Miss Gray added, smiling, "but it's already getting dark."

No illumination was provided inside the coach, while out-side it was, indeed, quite dark. Soon night closed in all around. Clarissa caught a glimpse of the moon, which, just starting to show itself from behind a distant hill, shed no light as yet. It was, in fact, pitch dark. The coach, however, seemed to be going at as fast a speed as before, if not faster. They could hear the driver lashing the horses.

"The wicked man," Mrs. Purdy whimpered, "is trying to make up for the time he lost drinking his ale at the Rose and Crown and then at that hostelry where we stopped for lunch. I *saw* him. Thank heavens, it's only five more miles and I'll be home. I know all the landmarks...." She prattled on.

Judging by the grand airs the stout matron gave herself, her husband had a very profitable business in a butcher shop, in Sudbury, a small town halfway between Wickhem St. Paul's and Colchester.

"Then it's less than two miles to Wickhem St. Paul's," Miss Gray exclaimed.

And she began to collect her luggage. Besides the satchel, there was also a valise. The coach had made two stops previously, first to let the magistrate off, then the woman in brown. There were now just the three of them: Mrs. Purdy, Miss Gray, and Clarissa. The magistrate, before getting out, had very gallantly removed Miss Gray's valise from the rack, placing it beside her on the seat.

"Oh, dear," Miss Gray said, hurriedly retying the neat streamers of her plain bonnet, putting on her short traveling cape, patting the skirt of her dark dress into smoothness.

The vague fragrance of lavender, which hung faintly about the governess' prim clothes, was momentarily intensified as, opening her satchel, she drew out a small flacon of cologne, sprinkled a little of the contents on a clean handkerchief, and passed the handkerchief over her face to refresh it after the long journey.

"I suppose I'm a little nervous," Miss Gray confided to Clarissa, closing the satchel, and laughing merrily at her nervousness. "Ravisham is such a magnificent place...."

The coach suddenly swayed. First to one side, then to the other. It all happened so quickly, Clarissa was to remember later ... There was a terrible jolt, a loud thud. The door on her side flung open. And she felt herself being propelled out bodily, as if by some tremendous force. Then something hit her, senseless....

CHAPTER SIX

W HEN SHE CAME TO, it was to find herself sitting in a field, her back against a haystack. It was the haystack that had broken her fall and so saved her. The moon was shining brightly now and she could see everything as clearly as if it were daylight. Some twenty yards away, the road, and the overturned coach, half of it sunk in the ditch, half sticking out. One of the wheels had come off and there it lay, a little distance away, gleaming in the moonlight. The harness had been torn and the horses, set loose, had walked over to the hedge and were peacefully nipping at the leaves.

The only sound was Mrs. Purdy's hysterical screams coming from within the coach. She was all right then. Nothing would ever happen to *her,* Clarissa thought.

"Get help!" Mrs. Purdy screamed. "You stupid lout. Fool! Go fetch help, I tell you. Run!"

The postilion was bending over the driver, who had been flung into the ditch. Clarissa could see the fallen man trying to rise, with the postilion's help, then he fell back.

Mrs. Purdy's screams continued:

"Get help, stupid. Go. Run! You lout!"

The postilion, thus encouraged, set off at a run down the road, and soon disappeared from view.

Clarissa had already caught sight of Miss Gray's prostrate form. The governess lay close to the hedge, which, while it screened her from the road, cast a shadow over the motionless figure, thus preventing Clarissa from perceiving her immediately. But even before Clarissa, getting up and hurrying over and kneeling beside her, took up one of the lifeless hands, she could tell that Miss Gray was beyond help. The hand, in its black lace mitt, already felt so strangely cold to the touch that Clarissa hastened to lay it down gently. There was a little blood on the left temple. Miss Gray's head had struck a stone. And there it was, jutting out of the soil. She had been killed instantly.

"Dear, dear Miss Gray."

Why, it might have been me, instead of you, flashed through Clarissa's mind. And vividly, she recalled Prickly Gil's weird talk. The power of the Unbroken Line … Had she Prickly Gil to thank, then, for being alive, while Miss Gray was dead? For a moment there, in the stillness, in the moonlight, Clarissa knew the horror of supernatural fear. But—*her secret enemy?* Miss Gray had been her friend. And it seemed to Clarissa that the gentle governess was looking at her, as if expecting her to do something. Sheer imagination, of course …

Then, suddenly, this something clicked in Clarissa's mind. She swiftly took stock of the situation. Mrs. Purdy, obviously, intended to remain inside the coach until help arrived. The driver had evidently been knocked senseless; anyway, at the moment he was unable to move. And the hedge provided a perfect screen to what Clarissa would be doing.

Any opportunity that comes your way, Lafonte used to tell her, you must at once take advantage of. Or, if an opportunity is lacking, you should create one. Clarissa would do both.

It was a bold scheme; but to miss the kind of chance that comes once in a lifetime? She set to work. First of all she removed Miss Gray's short traveling cape, her bonnet, the cambric kerchief, and the cameo brooch. Then, unhooking Miss Gray's dress, she slipped it gently off the lifeless form. She took out all the hairpins with which the governess' hair was pinned back so smoothly, and using her own fingers for a comb she fluffed it all out, including the sausage-like curls. Then removing her own bonnet with its nodding ostrich plumes, she put it on Miss Gray's head, tied the stringlike streamers. To remove the old prostitute's flounced dress which Clarissa had on, and slip it on the prostrate figure, was a matter of a few minutes. A quick-change artist, Lafonte had called her proudly. The only difference was that, since it was a corpse that had to be dressed, the weight of it slowing her down somewhat, it took a little longer, that was all.

Then, with the aid of the hairpins, she quickly arranged her own hair as Miss Gray's had been arranged, parted exactly in the center, drawn back very smoothly, except for two long curls on either side of the face. She made the curls as sausage-like as possible, by wetting a finger with her tongue and then passing the finger over each curl. She put on Miss Gray's plain bonnet, tied the neat streamers. As she began to get into Miss Gray's dress, she heard Mrs. Purdy's voice shrilling out angrily:

"Where's everybody? Somebody help me get out of this darned coach! Help. Help!"

The horrible woman had gotten tired sitting there all by herself, and she'd be getting out.

Clarissa pushed her arms into the sleeves, closed the dress as best she could, and started in the direction of the coach. The mitts! One never saw Miss Gray without them. Besides, Clarissa's hands were not nearly as white and smooth as Miss Gray's, and they might attract attention. She turned back, to peel the mitts off, then swiftly slip them over her own hands.

Now—the first test of how good an actress she would prove to be. Mentally, she prepared herself. How to use her voice to make it sound like Miss Gray's. How to hold her body, erect yet modestly. How to move, walk, gently and lightly, yet with a certain dignity … She still had her green satin shoes on, she suddenly remembered. But that wouldn't be noticed in the dark. She hurried along.

A little delay was caused by looking for a break in the hedge which would allow her to come out onto the road. At last, she was crossing it. She approached the coach window. A hand in the black lace mitt placed ever so gently on the sash, she said:

"Pray compose yourself, Mrs. Purdy. Do compose yourself, I beg you." Her back was to the moonlight; all Mrs. Purdy could make out was Miss Gray's plain bonnet, above Miss Gray's smooth hairdo, and the hand in Miss Gray's black lace mitt placed lightly on the window sash.

"Oh, it's you, Miss Gray. For a moment I thought …"

"For once, Mrs. Purdy, I beg you not to think of others, think of yourself. Under no circumstances should you bestir yourself, try to leave the coach. Any physician would tell you that for a person involved in an accident, to merely *move* is certain to bring on an apoplexy."

"Apoplexy! Oh, Miss Gray …"

"You must remain exactly as you are. For your own sake, dear Mrs. Purdy."

The coach's upset had sent Mrs. Purdy in a sprawled position into the furthest corner, and there, because of her stoutness and cowardice, she had remained, looking very uncomfortable.

"But I'm afraid that girl Clarissa," Clarissa went on, speaking in Miss Gray's soft voice, and gently, kindly, "well, she's … she's beyond help. In falling, she evidently struck her head against a stone. She must have died instantly."

"Well, I'm glad it was her and not you, Miss Gray. That painted hussy, an immoral woman, what kind of a life would she have led? A *wicked* life. But, Miss Gray," Mrs. Purdy suddenly said, "where's the white kerchief you wear around your neck? And didn't you have your traveling cape on?"

"I was thrown out of the coach, remember," Clarissa explained gently. "I found the cape, but then you called ... As to the kerchief, my cameo brooch must have come undone. That's why I want to hurry back and look for it."

Yes, and wash the paint off my face, Clarissa thought.

"Then I'll be back to keep you company, Mrs. Purdy, until help arrives."

And Clarissa hurried back into the field.

There was a little brook flowing somewhere nearby; the sound of it was the first thing she had been aware of on coming to. It was easy to find it in the brilliant moonlight. Crouching by the brook, dipping her hands into the cool water, after having removed Miss Gray's mitts, she washed the paint off her face. She had ripped a piece off her old torn skirt, which she was wearing under Miss Gray's dress, and used it for a washcloth. As to the underwear which clothed Miss Gray's lifeless form—petticoat, drawers, camisole—Clarissa knew she needn't worry about such under the old prostitute's flounced dress. Anybody might have that kind of plain underwear, even a poor actress.

Meanwhile, with movements swift, precise, soundless, she was already arranging the white cambric kerchief about her neck, crossing its ends over her bosom neatly. She pinned on the cameo brooch high at the throat. Then she put on the short traveling cape. Now, she felt, she was really Miss Gray, except for the shoes. She was just removing the governess' plain black shoes and replacing them with her own green satin ones when she suddenly saw a pair of eyes watching her over the top of the hedge. Such panic seized her that she almost screamed. She had, however, instantly realized who it was—the driver—and her self-control returned. The man had a hand to his head and looked dazed.

"In being thrown from the coach, I lost one of my shoes," Clarissa said, assuming Miss Gray's most sweetly conciliatory manner. She put on the second shoe. "But the important thing is, how do *you* feel?"

"I couldn't make out what you were doing," the man muttered. He stood there, swaying, holding on to the hedge for support. "That awful knock I got on my head is making me see things, I guess, miss."

He had called her "miss," which he certainly wouldn't have done addressing Clarissa. Besides, from his side of the hedge he could see the lifeless form, clothed from head to foot in Clarissa's apparel.

"The actress Clarissa," Clarissa told him gently, "is beyond help, I'm afraid. In falling she evidently struck her head against a stone. She must have died instantly."

Now, besides Mrs. Purdy, there would be also the driver avid to tell the story, and in exactly the same words, when help arrived.

Her hands clad in Miss Gray's black lace mitts and daintily patting the skirt of Miss Gray's dark dress, Clarissa sailed forth into the road, the driver staggering after her. While he sat down by the ditch to nurse his aching head, she got into the coach, settling herself gently into the seat the governess had occupied. The moonlight didn't reach inside the coach, and the resulting darkness and shadows, Clarissa knew, disguised her facial features by making them a mere blur under Miss Gray's prim bonnet. Mrs. Purdy, obedient to instructions, had remained in the same half-sprawled position in her corner, her state by now having been reduced to mere groans and moans. The luggage had all slipped to the floor and lay piled up against the door on that side.

Clarissa retrieved Miss Gray's valise, placed it on the seat beside her. She picked up the small satchel, and opening it, drew out the flacon of cologne and a handkerchief. After sprinkling the handkerchief with the lavender-scented liquid, she dabbed at her face—in case any traces of rouge still remained.

"So refreshing, isn't it, Mrs. Purdy?" she said.

What a horribly dowdy smell, she thought. How different from the Green Perfume! But it was a good thing that only a few treasured drops of it had remained, so that she had had to use it meagerly, or now a mere whiff of that heady, lusty scent would have aroused suspicion. As for this stuff, a woman might as well scent herself with spinach....

"Pray let me offer you some, Mrs. Purdy."

"Oh, Miss Gray ... You're so kind."

The rumble of approaching wheels announced the arrival of help from the village. A cart drew up alongside the upset coach. A constable got out and came close, followed by the three men he had brought with him, two of them carrying lanterns.

The constable put his head in, his sharp eyes scrutinizing Clarissa. The way she was dressed, the way she held herself, made him take off his cap.

"Miss Gray?"

"Yes," Clarissa said. "I'm Miss Gray."

"The trap sent over from Ravisham is waiting for you at the inn, miss."

"Thank you."

She did not have to say anything more, for Mrs. Purdy and the driver, who had come up, were already gushingly recounting the whole story of the mishap, and how a woman passenger, an actress, Clarissa, must have been killed instantly ...

"Struck her head against a stone," the driver declared excitedly. "Over in that field there," he pointed towards the field.

"An actress," the constable said. "Thank heavens it wasn't anybody important! But I better take a look at the body, anyhow."

And he and the men with him went off with the driver, who volunteered to lead them to the spot. On coming back the constable said that he had left one of the men to stand guard over the body, and then he asked if anything was known about the deceased. The family, if any, could be notified perhaps.

"She was absolutely alone in the world, the poor woman," Clarissa said gently. "I know, because the poor soul had made quite a confidante of me."

"That actress woman was annoying Miss Gray with her stupid prattle all the way since we left London," Mrs. Purdy broke in.

"Did she have any luggage?"

Mrs. Purdy pointed out Clarissa's valise for him.

My costumes! Clarissa thought, watching one of the men pick it up, throw it into the cart. She'd never see them again!

"But where is the postilion?" she asked quietly. "I hope the poor man wasn't hurt? But perhaps he's a local man...." Hoping that he wasn't. Somehow, she didn't trust the postilion.

"Just a bit dazed he was, that's all. He thought only the driver maybe was hurt. They are both Colchester men, miss. They'll be put up at the inn for the night. And in the morning they'll have the coach repaired and off they'll go."

With Mrs. Purdy bound for her home in another town, there'd be nobody then in the immediate vicinity of Ravisham who had actually seen the real Miss Gray.

"There's one other little thing," Clarissa said. She glanced around the little group of men, gathered about the side of the coach where she sat, to make sure they were all listening. "I was so sorry for the poor woman ... I found a little brook and I ... I washed the paint off her face." The lack of paint on the supposed actress' face had to be explained. "I thought she'd like to meet her Maker looking decent, at least in that respect. But I suppose you'll think me very foolish, doing such a thing."

Clarissa dropped her eyes demurely.

"That was a good charitable thing you did, Miss Gray," the constable said, impressed, even moved. "But don't you be worrying about her any more. I'll have a wagon sent for the body, and the workhouse will provide a coffin and they'll dig a grave just outside the churchyard. Seeing as she was an actress, the parson won't let her be buried in consecrated ground. But we know her name—Clarissa, the driver said it was. And that's how the grave will be marked."

So that's how they'd bury me, the stupid fools! Clarissa thought. Inwardly she was highly incensed. But she merely smiled sweetly.

The constable helped her out of the coach. Mrs. Purdy, moaning, was helped out by the other men. Then, in the same order, they were helped into the cart, which took them to the village. On the way they met with a group of men, some carrying glowing lanterns, and all talking excitedly. The news of the coach's upset had spread quickly and they were hurrying to the scene of the mishap, curious to see it all for themselves.

"Wait till they hear that a woman has been killed," the constable laughed. "They'll be coming in droves!"

Clarissa alighted at a cozy-looking inn on a corner. The men who had come with the constable also got out, and while he drove on with Mrs. Purdy to take the badly shaken-up matron to her Sudbury home, they hurried into the inn. The lit windows gave Clarissa a vivid glimpse of the villagers gathered inside around the postilion. Then, as the new arrivals entered, voluble with more exciting news, she saw everybody's attention swing over to them. The postilion picked up his ale mug, and it seemed to her that a look of cunning caution passed over his coarse face.

But a young, crude-looking fellow, dressed as a groom, came out just then and hurried over to her.

"Miss Gray?"

And right away, picking up the valise, he led her to the trap, helped her in, got in beside her, took up the reins, and at once they were off, at a brisk trot. Through the village, and then along a road winding between fields flooded with moonlight.

"You were lucky," the groom said. "Just heard, at the inn, a woman got killed, an actress. Clarissa her name was, they said."

"Yes," Clarissa said. "Are there any guests at Ravisham?" she asked quietly.

"Left last night, swarms of them, stayed a whole month. Others will be coming soon, I guess. But right now there's only Lord Cavor, very wealthy, too, besides having a title."

"Oh," Clarissa said.

"And Mr. FitzMaurice," the groom went on. "*He* has more money than any of them. Mines, gold mines. In Africa."

"Oh," Clarissa said.

After about ten minutes' ride, the trap suddenly turned into a veritable forest of ancient trees, or so it seemed to Clarissa. She turned round just in time to see the enormous iron gates, which had stood open to let the trap pass through, closing behind them.

"Ravisham Park," the groom said, indicating the huge trees with his whip. "Goes on for miles."

The fellow had a nice homely face.

A ghastly, human-like shriek suddenly rent the air around. Another shriek, equally horrible, followed.

"Oh!" Clarissa gasped. She was nervous enough without these ghastly shrieks, that made one's flesh crawl, coming on top of everything else. And quite forgetting who she was supposed to be, she threw her arms around the groom for protection.

"It's only the peacocks," the fellow laughed. "Ravisham is famous for its peacocks. You'll see them in the morning, strutting about on the green terraces. But for the night, the male and the female birds are put in separate enclosures, and they start calling to one another."

Horrible birds, how I'd like to wring your necks! Clarissa thought, reseating herself primly, making sure Miss Gray's satchel hadn't slipped off her knees.

The home of the Marquis of Trall all at once came into view; a huge pile of gray stone, as big as the Prince Regent's palace back in London, but older in architecture, more imposing. Several of the windows on the ground floor, in the right wing of the house, were ablaze with lights.

So this was Ravisham.

Clarissa gazed towards it.

"Pshaw," she thought, "I'm not afraid of you, and your peacocks! I'm not a cheap dancing girl or a little actress from the Thieves' Village, whom you could string up at Tyburn for stealing a sack of coal or a loaf of bread. I'm Miss Gray, the governess …"

She must keep imagining that Lafonte was watching her, and she just *had* to make him proud of her acting talent. And Miss Gray, too; how Miss Gray would have laughed, her merry little laugh, to see her succeed with the role.

The trap, circling the lawns which seemed to go on for miles, stopped in front of the big door. As she got out, she suddenly remembered that she didn't know Miss Gray's first name. They'd ask her, of course. Panic seized her. But it was too late, anyway. A flunky, with powder in his wig, was holding the door open, and she went up the stone steps, and then in, very quietly, her eyes downcast demurely, as befitted a perfect governess.

PART TWO

CHAPTER SEVEN

N THE HALL, as big as a barn, the flunky pointed at a hard chair and, his footsteps ringing over the stone floor slabs, left her alone there. Several doors stood partly open, offering a tantalizing glimpse of illuminated, luxurious rooms beyond. But Clarissa, intent on playing her role to perfection, had to curtail her curiosity. She obediently sat down and, after patting her skirt into smoothness—for all she knew someone might be watching her—she sat there very quietly, her hands in the black lace mitts clasped primly at her waist, as she had seen Miss Gray sit, even in the jolting stagecoach.

The shimmering suit of armor in a corner scared her for a moment. In the metal headpiece there were slits for the eyes and it seemed to her as if a pair of living eyes was watching her. But, of course, there was nobody inside it. The silly thing stood there just to show how far back stretched the lineage of the Tralls. Large swords, as old as the suit of armor, were on that wall, some in their heavy scabbards, some bare and showing the brown spots on the sharp blades—tarnish, probably, though it might have been human blood which had been shed so ruthlessly by the Tralls.

There was also a huge stone fireplace, guarded on either side by a stone lion holding a stone shield embossed with the complicated crest. The hall was full of drafts, but only a couple of logs sputtered angrily, and in front of this stingy fire some half a dozen enormous dogs lay sprawled. Hunting dogs, Clarissa knew them to be, remembering the stories Lafonte used to tell her. The more illustrious a family the more they hunted, chasing a scared fox or a little rabbit over some poor farmer's fields, ruining his crops.

Suddenly three of the hunting dogs rose and came over, first to sniff at Clarissa's skirt, then to thrust their noses underneath. Maybe her old torn skirt, which she wore in place of a petticoat under Miss Gray's prim dark dress, aroused their suspicion? Their exploring tongues licked her thighs, tickling her skin, making her want to giggle. Then, snarling, they withdrew their heads and, sitting back on their haunches, their red tongues dripping, they stared at her accusingly. They must have heard the sound of loud footsteps.

The footsteps sounded exactly like a man's, but it was her ladyship herself who came in. She walked like a grenadier, had a face like a horse, but was magnificently gowned in green velvet, with a regal train several yards long. Right there and then, Clarissa, with the quick aptness of a Thieves' Village dweller, named her the Ogre. That's what the woman obviously was, an ogre, in every sense of the word. Around the Ogre's ugly, veined neck was wound a rope of enormous emeralds, which hung down almost to her knees. And right away she began to bellow at the dogs.

"Caesar! Brutus! Nero!"

And picking up one of the whips with which a stone bench nearby was cluttered, the Marquise of Trall lashed the air with it.

"Wooze!" the whip went. "Wooze ... Woozzzee!"

The dogs, their tails between their legs, leaped back to the fireplace and again lay sprawled there, absolutely still with terror.

"Discipline must be maintained," the Ogre announced. "Or they'll be poking their noses under *my* skirts next!"

Which, of course, was unthinkable.

Flinging the whip aside, her ladyship seated herself in a satin-covered chair.

"Miss Gray."

Clarissa, who was already standing, her eyes modestly downcast, curtsied very low.

"Sit down."

Clarissa sat down.

The Marquise had bulging eyes which, besides, were shortsighted. And to look Clarissa over, up and down, up and down, she had to have the help of her ridiculous lorgnette. That's what the rope of emeralds, worth a fortune, was for—to have a lorgnette dangling at its end.

"And your first name, Miss Gray?"

Clarissa pretended that she was about to answer the Ogre's question, then she suddenly looked pathetically helpless. With a fluttering little gesture she put a hand to her forehead.

"I'm afraid I feel a little faint," she murmured. "The coach's upset … My sensibilities were quite … I beg Your Ladyship to forgive me.…" Meanwhile opening Miss Gray's satchel, putting a hand in to feel for the letter Miss Gray had spoken of. Thank goodness! There it was. Clarissa drew it out, handed it to the Ogre.

"The news of the coach's upset had reached me through the servants' grapevine before your arrival," the Ogre said. "And now Henderson, my butler, informs me that a woman passenger was killed, some actress—Clarissa, her name was, he said. Which was very fortunate, considering it might have been *you* instead, Miss Gray. And Ravisham has been without a governess for almost a month! *Most* annoying."

She opened the letter and scanned it through her silly lorgnette.

"Your first name, Miss Gray, is given here, of course. Not that it matters, since you will be called Miss Gray by everybody, including the servants." And the horrible woman slipped the letter into the pocket of her regal skirt, thus keeping the secret of Miss Gray's first name with her. "As to your duties," her ladyship went on, "I need not waste my time in enumerating them. You've been well instructed, according to the previous correspondence I have had with your headmistress, and this formal letter of introduction from her confirms the fact. You will therefore assume your duties as of this moment, Miss Gray."

"May I be permitted to ask Your Ladyship," Clarissa said quietly, "if there are any guests?"

"You're quite right to ask," the Ogre said, nodding her horse-like head approvingly. "Since if there were, you'd be eating alone in your little upstairs room, naturally. But there are only Lord Cavor and Mr. FitzMaurice"—Clarissa pricked up her ears, remembering the groom's description of their wealth—"and they're just like members of the family."

The gleam of triumph in the bulging eyes made it quite clear that the two gentlemen mentioned were intended as future husbands for the two brats, as Clarissa mentally called her prospective charges.

"When there's just the family, Lady Flo dines with us, and since she's much too young to do so without being attended by the governess, you, Miss Gray, will be allowed to dine downstairs tonight."

Lady Flo couldn't be more than twelve. Wasn't it ridiculous to call her by a title! Clarissa wondered about the other brat, when, suddenly, screams were heard, the patter of small feet, the sound of anxious adult footsteps in hot pursuit ... Followed by a capped, aproned housemaid, and three flunkies, exact replicas of the one who had opened the front door for Clarissa, a homely little girl of about four, already undressed for bed except for a small petticoat and camisole, rushed in, screaming:

"I won't go to bed. I won't. I won't! Not until I *pinch* the new governess."

"Now, Lady Sue," the housemaid pleaded. "You're supposed to be asleep. Her ladyship's, your mamma's orders ..."

At the sight of the Ogre, the housemaid and the flunkies stopped in their tracks and looked scared, while the four-year-old Lady Sue ran on.

"Mamma, I want to pinch the new governess!"

"Well ..." Her mamma indulgently smiled. Besides having a face like a horse, the Ogre also had buck teeth.

Lady Sue pounced on Clarissa and pinched her in the right arm so hard that Clarissa had to use all her will power not to let out a little scream of pain. In fact, she needed all her self-control not to kick the horrible brat in the shins.

"What's going on?" a petulant voice inquired, and a girl of about eleven or so, but dressed in the height of fashion, in a long, pinksashed, white satin gown, came in languidly. On her frizzed hair she wore a wreath of artificial strawberry leaves, made of velvet and sprinkled with seed pearls. But neither the strawberry leaves—symbol of her rank—nor the fashionable dress helped. She was as homely as Lady Sue, had the same sallow skin, and both had their mamma's buck teeth and bulging eyes. The female Tralls were, as a matter of fact, hideously homely.

"Flo, I pinched the new governess. I pinched her hard," the four-year-old bragged.

Lady Flo giggled. Then, as her bulging eyes ran over Clarissa, her upper lip curled, in utter contempt of any such person as a mere governess.

"You may remove your traveling cape and your bonnet, Miss Gray," the Ogre commanded. "Leave them on the chair. They will be taken up to your room. Dinner will be announced any moment now."

Lady Sue was then duly hustled out, screaming and kicking, by the housemaid and the three flunkies. Clarissa, meanwhile, took off Miss Gray's short cape, Miss Gray's plain bonnet, laid them on the chair. With a few pats of her mitted hands she made sure that her hair lay very smooth, including the long, sausage-like curls which dangled over her ears.

And then two men came in, both over fifty, portly, dissipated-looking, but splendidly attired. Probably equally bald under their curled wigs, Clarissa told herself. They wore no powder, doubtless just to show that they followed the fashion dictated at the Prince Regent's court by Beau Brummell. One had a monocle stuck in his eye, the other twirled a lorgnette suspended on a black ribbon from the rich white neckcloth.

When the Ogre performed the introductions, saying "Miss Gray," in that tone of voice which immediately explained that this person was a nothing, and then mentioned the gentlemen's names, Clarissa discovered that the one with the monocle was Lord Cavor, and the other was Mr. FitzMaurice. Both bowed politely as she curtsied, but Clarissa understood what Miss Gray had meant about not being noticed. They simply didn't see her. She might as well not have been there at all!

You just wait, Clarissa told them mentally. I'll make you take notice of me, I'll make you *look* at me!

Then she realized that this very lack of notice proved how well she played her role. The qualities of modesty, reserve, sweetness, were so perfectly portrayed as to be mistaken for the genuine article. Lafonte would have been very proud of her performance.

But now the butler, a distinguished-looking elderly man, dressed in black silk from head to foot and wearing an enormous powdered wig, announced dinner and flung the doors open. The

Ogre sailed in first, on Mr. FitzMaurice's arm. Lady Flo literally hung on Lord Cavor's arm and, trying to enchant him, made the most horrible grimaces imaginable. Clarissa was the last to go in, alone. The brilliance of the chandeliers almost blinded her. Sheer instinct guided her to the seat next to her eleven-year-old charge, Lady Flo. A flunky stood behind every chair, except, of course, the governess' chair. (That honor was not for the likes of her.) More flunkies were lined against the walls, while more of them moved about carrying the covered silver dishes. The Ogre sat at one end of the long table; at the other end, in a crest-embossed chair, sat a little old man, and he was eating porridge. Whenever the porridge trickled down his tremulous chin, the flunky standing behind him would wipe it off quickly with a napkin. That, Clarissa understood, was the Marquis of Trall himself. And then she suddenly asked herself—a feeble old man like him capable of having sired the four-year-old Lady Sue? Or even the elder brat? Clarissa wondered....

But on either side of her plate there was laid out such a confusing array of spoons, forks, and knives, each of a different size and shape. A cup of creamed soup had been placed before her. Everyone was having creamed soup. Clarissa waited to see which of the spoons was supposed to be used for the soup. Lady Flo beside her picked up a spoon. But Clarissa didn't trust her. Then out of the corner of her eye she saw Lord Cavor, who sat directly across, pick up a spoon of quite a different size and shape. Clarissa followed his example. And she heard the Ogre bellow:

"Flo, stop playing with your dessert spoon."

Lady Flo giggled, then threw a glance full of venom at Clarissa. The trick hadn't worked.

But Clarissa was afraid to take any more risks as far as the correct selection of spoons, forks, and knives was concerned. So after the soup course she gently declined all dishes offered, though each looked so tasty it made her mouth water. She was very hungry, having had nothing to eat since the quick snack the coach had stopped for at that hostelry at midday. She could feel the pangs of hunger gnawing at her stomach.

But the Ogre looked her approval of such a meager appetite. The woman, in addition to everything else, was also stingy, probably starved her servants ...

And aware that nothing escaped the Ogre's eyes or ears, Clarissa was quick to remind herself that a governess had certain duties to perform and that she, Clarissa, had better make it clear, right there and then, that she knew what these duties consisted of. Noticing how straight and stiff everyone sat, as if each had just swallowed a poker, except the eleven-year-old Flo, who slouched most disgracefully, Clarissa said gently, but firmly:

"Lady Flo, please don't slouch."

And though the vain brat snickered, she had to sit up straight.

Well, wasn't a governess supposed to reprimand her young charges constantly? Aloud, Clarissa said, very modestly:

"Correct posture is so very important."

The Ogre overheard and, her rope of emeralds rattling, she bellowed from her end of the table:

"Every governess we had made the poor child walk up and down the schoolroom floor while balancing a couple of books on her head, for a whole hour, every single day. Not that it did any good, as I can see!"

"In *my* boarding school," Clarissa said quietly, "we had to do that for two hours, every single day."

"*Two hours!*" Lady Flo wailed, horrified. "Oh, Mamma!"

But her doting mamma, though her eyes bulged more than ever, with sheer envy, as through her raised lorgnette she observed Clarissa's naturally graceful posture, nodded a shrewd approval.

Which meant that, with one brat balancing books on her head in the privacy of the schoolroom and the younger brat maybe forced to take a nap, Clarissa would have those two hours to herself, to do with as she liked.

But, meanwhile, how pompous they all were! The occasion, instead of a family meal, might have been a coronation—or a funeral. Clarissa, however, very sensibly, took it all in, noticing every detail, putting it in the back of her mind for future use. The two unsuspecting gentlemen, Lord Cavor and Mr. FitzMaurice, naturally claimed most of her surreptitious but lively attention. The monocled aristocrat was just the type to set up a mistress in a luxurious establishment, shower her with jewels, then display her ... The other fop, being a plain mister, probably preferred something more showy, more public—an actress. He'd pay a fortune for the most promising play, provide the most extravagant *costumes*.... And both the mistress of one, and the kept actress of the other—since both, of course, already existed, back in London—could easily be supplanted. All a woman had to do ...

But they were all getting up, leaving the dining room, moving on through the drafty hall, and towards the luxurious rooms beyond; except, of course, Clarissa. A housemaid appeared, not the one who had come after Lady Sue, but another, gruff, unfriendly, and took Clarissa up a side stairway all the way up to the fourth floor. A door opened and a woman, all in black, with a black apron and black mobcap, and a bunch of keys hanging from her stout waist, came out. The housekeeper.

After looking Clarissa up and down, she said:

"The governess!"

And back in she went, banging the door shut.

An enemy, Clarissa told herself. She was surrounded by enemies....

The housemaid pushed a door open and, going in first, struck a match and lit the candle. It was indeed a little room. A narrow bed, a washstand, a small bureau, and along one bare wall a row of clothes hooks. The short traveling cape and the bonnet, which Clarissa had shed downstairs, had been hung up there, and Miss Gray's valise had been placed on one of the two cane chairs.

"And don't expect me to be emptying your chamber pot," the housemaid suddenly cried out in the most insulting manner.

And out she went, banging the door after her.

Clarissa, first of all, locked the door, turning the key carefully, not to make any noise. Then she hastened to open Miss Gray's valise. On top lay a hairbrush, comb, and a small sewing kit with its dainty pair of scissors. Next came two changes of plain underwear: petticoats, drawers, camisoles, long-sleeved nightgowns, all neatly folded. A wrapper, of cotton, with an edging of crocheted lace. And under that three dresses. One of dark material, and the other two more summery, of white muslin, but Oh! ever so prim-looking, with their matching neckerchiefs and narrow, pale-blue sashes. The vague fragrance of lavender hung about the garments.

Shaking the dresses out impatiently, Clarissa hung them up on the hooks. She had a fleeting regret for her own valise and the colorful costumes—and the stolen money. Then, hurriedly getting out of the dress she had on, she quickly shed the old torn short skirt and the blouse which she wore underneath, the presence of which had worried her all along. So utterly inappropriate they were for the role she was enacting! Suppose she tripped, fell, the disreputable rags glimpsed—everything would have been ruined. What a weight off her mind to put on instead the camisole, the long, modestly ruffled drawers, the petticoat. She got into the dress again, pinned the cameo brooch into place on the cambric neckerchief. But how to get rid of the old skirt and blouse? There was no lock to the valise. The servants, the housekeeper would be poking their noses into her things. For the night, anyway, Clarissa decided, the safest hiding place would be under the pillow.

Hurrying over to the bed, she pulled back the covers, raised the pillow. A small snake lay curled there. How the unexpected sight of it made Clarissa jump! Then it dawned upon her that the four-year-old Lady Sue would naturally have various ideas of how to plague a governess besides pinching her very painfully. Boldly and swiftly taking hold of the disgustingly small snake by its middle, Clarissa hurried to the window, pushed it open, and flung the now-writhing viper out. Then hasting back to the bed, she stripped it bare and found, near the footbed, another little snake, this one already starting to writhe, the tip of the tiny tongue showing threateningly. Getting rid of it as she had the first, she made a thorough search of the room. And on the bottom of the water pitcher, on the washstand, she found two large, lively frogs. She had to fish them out one by one, then throw them out the window.

Now she could remake the bed, hide her old clothing under the pillow. She put the hairbrush, comb, and the little sewing kit on the bureau top, and the rest of the underwear into a drawer, and pushed the emptied valise under the bed. Then she opened Miss Gray's satchel.

Clarissa was rather curious to see the "treasures," as Miss Gray had called the satchel contents. Half a dozen freshly laundered handkerchiefs. The small flacon of lavender cologne, which Clarissa had already seen and used. A thin little volume of poetry. Well, at least it had a pretty cover. And then something, oval in shape, lovingly wrapped in tissue paper and tied with a narrow blue ribbon. Maybe a piece of jewelry. No matter how modest, it'd be something ... Clarissa tore the wrapping off. The miniature of Miss Gray's long-lost brother Richard, painted when he was just a lad. Sixteen, maybe seventeen? But what a handsome face it was! And now, if he was still alive, he'd be a man grown. Clarissa, in spite of herself—she had more important things on her mind—carried the miniature close to the sputtering candle, the better to admire the attractive features, the healthy coloring, the way a lock of the dark, glossy hair fell over the strongly molded, open brow. The eyes, already even then full of a daredevil sparkle, seemed to be smiling at her.

Suddenly becoming aware of a sound coming from somewhere beyond the door, she hastened to shove everything back into the satchel, and the satchel itself into a drawer. The sound was unmistakably that of a girl's muffled sobbing. Clarissa unlocked the door, slipped out into the passage. A stone arch, just a few yards away, separated the passage from the servants' dark back stairs. And there, huddled in the corner, was a little kitchenmaid. Somebody had given her a beating. The cook probably, or maybe the housekeeper.

Clarissa touched her on the shoulder.

"Don't be frightened. I'm Miss Gray, the new governess."

At the sound of her voice, which Clarissa had infused with all of Miss Gray's gentle, kindly tones, the girl raised her tear-stained face.

"Oh, miss ..." she said.

The little slavey might be of some use, was Clarissa's instant decision.

"Come with me."

Once the two of them were in Clarissa's room and the door locked, Clarissa sat down on the cane chair, while the girl stood before her, shivering, giving out a sob now and again.

"Now tell me all about it," Clarissa said.

CHAPTER EIGHT

"IT'S THE HOUSEKEEPER, miss. She beats me something cruel. No matter how hard I work, paring potatoes, or washing vegetables, or cleaning the knives, there's no pleasing her. Always she finds fault...."

"She's been slapping your face, I can see that," Clarissa said. "But that's over now. So don't cry any more."

But the little kitchenmaid, all of a sudden, covered her face with her skinny hands and began to weep all over again.

"It's not only the beatings I get," she tried to explain between sobs. "It's ... it's Pete."

"And who is Pete?" Clarissa asked.

"You saw him, miss. He ... he's the groom who drove you from the village. Pete, well, he takes no notice of me. He kisses all the housemaids, even Bertha—that's the unfriendly one—But ... he never once tried to kiss me."

Without saying a word, Clarissa got up, went over to the bureau, pulled a drawer out to take out of the satchel the narrow blue ribbon from the miniature wrapping. Then she picked up the hairbrush, comb, the little sewing kit with the scissors. She brought all these things over, put them on the chair. The kitchenmaid just stood there, her eyes wide with expectancy.

The girl wasn't pretty, but then neither was she homely. There were, definitely, possibilities. But her hair was like a mat. Clarissa began to brush it energetically.

"Don't you have any lice?" she said.

She had expected to see half a dozen of them, at least, hopping on the brush after the first few strokes.

"I use an ointment."

"What kind of an ointment?" Clarissa thought of the one she used to buy from Prickly Gil.

"A little old woman, Nellie Harris, makes it," the kitchenmaid explained readily. "She lives all by herself, in a tumbledown shack, far away from everybody. But when she's gathering fagots she goes everywhere, she's not afraid. Though the villagers tried to stone her several times, only the constable interfered…. There are all kinds of rumors about Nellie Harris."

"What kind of rumors?"

"Well, for one thing, once a month she goes to Kenerevy woods. Maybe you've heard about the place, Miss Gray?"

"I've heard about it, yes," Clarissa said, again reminded of Prickly Gil.

"Well, that's on the other side of London, so it takes two days from here, on foot, and Nellie Harris is too poor to pay for a ride in a wagon or cart. But the funny part of it is, she doesn't leave till late at night and if someone sees her the next morning she tells them she's been to Kenerevy woods. So the people say Nellie Harris has other means of getting there, fast, not human means."

Clarissa, having brushed the girl's hair till it shone, tied it in the back with the narrow blue ribbon. Then, turning the kitchenmaid around by the shoulder, observing her critically, Clarissa said:

"Your blouse is too loose, and too high in the neck. Take it off."

The girl obediently took it off. She was too poor to wear anything underneath, and her young breasts were exposed, firm and rounded.

Clarissa swiftly threaded a needle.

"We'll make the blouse tighter."

A few stitches accomplished that.

"And we'll cut it very low in front."

A few snips of the scissors.

"When a woman sets out to get a man, she's supposed to show what she has, not hide it," Clarissa said.

Then she helped the girl put the blouse on, tightened the sash of the homespun skirt.

"Now go and look at yourself in the mirror," pushing her towards the bureau.

"Oh, Miss Gray ... oh ... oh!" was all the girl could say at first, admiring herself in the little glass over the bureau, astonished at the sudden metamorphosis. "Is it really me? What a difference! I can't wait for Pete to see me. He's bound to notice me *now*.... Oh, Miss Gray, how can I ever thank you?"

And tearing herself away from the mirror, she hurried back to Clarissa.

"The housemaids will never do anything for you," she explained eagerly. "They never do, for a governess. Maybe just sweep the floor here. But I'll tidy up your room properly, and make your bed, bring hot water for your bath first thing in the morning, and empty your chamber pot. Do let me, please. And if there's anything you want me to get for you, why, I'll do my best ..."

Clarissa laughed. She'd have her own personal little maid.

"I don't even know your name, you silly child," she said.

"It's Sally."

"Well, Sally, what about food then?" Clarissa at once said. "I'm terribly hungry."

Sally's face fell.

"Oh, not food, no, never. Everything is kept under lock and key. The housekeeper has her own bunch of keys, and so has the butler."

"I see," Clarissa said, a plan how to procure something to eat already forming in her mind. "But there's something else you could do for me, Sally."

Going over to the bed, taking her old skirt and blouse from under the pillow, Clarissa brought them over, threw them on the chair.

Sally, her honest eyes wide with amazement, gave a little gasp.

"To think that anything so disreputable-looking should be in your possession, of all people, Miss Gray!"

"Shh …" Clarissa said, lowering her own voice. "Walls have ears."

"Don't I know it," Sally nodded her head sagely. "Here at Ravisham especially."

"Someday, maybe, I'll tell you all about it," Clarissa said. "The important thing now is to get rid of them."

"I should think so!" Sally was very emphatic about it. "Why, they make one think of a trollop!" She fingered Clarissa's old skirt and blouse curiously. "There aren't any trollops around here, naturally. But when the cook goes to market in Sudbury, she sometimes takes me along, and I saw them hanging about the hostelry there. And that's the kind of an outfit they'd have on, the skirt is as brief as this one. Somebody must have put these clothes in among your things, on purpose, to make you lose your job here! That's the only explanation I can think of. Soon as you're out of the room in the morning, the housekeeper, and that Bertha, and a few other housemaids that I could name, will be slipping in to look through your things. They always do. But don't you worry, Miss Gray. I'll get rid of them for you tonight."

"But how, Sally?" Clarissa asked. "That's the problem."

"Why, bury them in the ground somewhere. Simple enough."

"But the dogs! The dogs would dig them out."

"Not only dig them out, but bring them right into the house, and to her ladyship. That's how they've been trained. But I forgot about the dogs.... Suppose I throw the clothes down into the privy, then?"

"And the person who happens to go there next might see what you dropped in. Whoever heard of discarding clothing, no matter how worn? Every scrap of material so valuable, because of the war. There'd be no end of talk. It would look very suspicious. Oh, Sally," Clarissa laughed merrily, just as Miss Gray might have laughed on finding herself in a situation which was really amusing, though rather tiresome. "I wish the disreputable rags were miles and miles away...."

"I have it," Sally suddenly announced. "Your saying 'miles and miles away' reminded me." And then she explained. "Just outside the village, in a meadow, the gypsies are camping. They've been staying there for a week, but tomorrow, with the sunrise, they'll be on the move again. The housemaids were talking about it, and they'd know, because they keep running over to the gypsies to have their fortunes told. So," Sally went on excitedly, "soon as I get back to the kitchen, I'll slip out, and make straight for their camp, and I'll leave the trollop's clothing there, throw it on a hedge nearby. Now you may not know this, Miss Gray, but the gypsies, if they find anything, they never talk about it. They simply put it away in their wagon, and nobody ever hears about it again. And since they'll be leaving early in the morning, by nightfall tomorrow they, and what you want to be rid of, will be miles and miles away."

"You're a very smart girl, Sally," Clarissa said.

She let Sally out, waited a few minutes, then went out into the passage, found the side stairs, and so descended to the third floor. The landing here was much wider and several flunkies stood about. To explain her presence, in case she had no business to be roaming thus freely through the great house, Clarissa approached one of them and said:

"I'm Miss Gray, the new governess. Please show me which is Lady Flo's room, and which is Lady Sue's."

The two brats would have their own personal maids to attend them on going to bed, but a governess doubtless was expected to look in on her charges last thing at night. The flunky's attitude proved that Clarissa's supposition, a mere shot in the dark, was correct. He led the way. Then, halting, he said, pointing first at one door, "Lady Flo's," and then at the door directly across, "Lady Sue's."

"Thank you."

The flunky, however, didn't go away, but went to station himself alongside a nearby wall. So Clarissa had no choice but to turn the knob of the first door and go in. An enormous room, magnificently furnished, and in the big, canopied bed, all satin, laces, ribbon bows, the homely eleven-year-old Lady Flo, her hair in curlers, was half-sitting up and, taking advantage of a night candle, was polishing her nails with a large buffer. Clarissa didn't give a darn how her supposed charge amused herself when in bed, but she had to make a right impression.

"You should be asleep," Clarissa said primly.

And, crossing over, she stretched a hand out for the buffer.

This too evidently was expected of her, for Lady Flo, though making nasty grimaces, handed it to her.

"Good night," Clarissa said, replacing the ridiculously large nail buffer on the gilded dressing table.

And though the spoiled brat smirked her disdain, she had to say, politely enough:

"Good night, Miss Gray."

Clarissa sailed out. The flunky was still there. So, crossing over to the other door, she turned the knob, looked in. The room was just as enormous and as magnificently furnished. The four-year-old Lady Sue, however, Clarissa could see, was truly asleep.

"About large frogs and little snakes, I'll talk with you tomorrow, young lady," Clarissa mentally told her.

And closing the door and, with the flunky still there, watching her—let the fool think what he chose!—she boldly sailed on, down to the second floor, and then to the first. In the wide corridor there she came face to face with yet another flunky, but he took no notice of her, probably assuming that she was on some legitimate errand, to fetch a glass of milk maybe for one of her young charges. It was very quiet and she had no idea whether the adult members of the family and the two guests, Lord Cavor and Mr. FitzMaurice, had already retired or were still in one of the drawing rooms, perhaps playing cards or just yawning politely at one another. The place, however, was so huge that there was no danger of her movements being overheard from any other part of the house.

The pantry would be somewhere behind the dining room. Since she already knew where the dining room was, it was easy to find the corridor running parallel to it, sail along it swiftly, and then she pushed the first door open and walked in. The room, though spacious, was obviously a pantry, and there stood Henderson, the butler, taking a bottle of wine out of a cupboard.

Clarissa, exhibiting every sign of sudden confusion, embarrassment, and even awe, said:

"Oh! Oh, Your Lordship ..."

And she curtsied very, very low.

"I crave Your Lordship's pardon," she murmured, her eyes modestly downcast. "I'm Miss Gray, the new governess. I missed my cameo brooch and I hurried downstairs to look for it and I ... I found it, as you can see," a fingertip touching the brooch pinned to the cambric neckerchief. "And then I lost my way...."

"But, hmm ..." the butler said. "I'm not ... hmm ... his lordship...."

However, he looked terribly flattered.

"Your Lordship is kind enough to joke," Clarissa protested. And again she curtsied. "A man so dignified, so ... so aristocratic ... why, who else could such a man be?"

"Hmm." The butler again coughed.

With every word Clarissa uttered, his severe mask of a face, under the big powdered wig, looked more and more human, until he was almost grinning. So gratified he was to be mistaken for a titled personage.

"It's very kind of you to say so, miss," he said. "But, hmm ... I'm merely the butler here."

Clarissa looked astonished.

"His lordship," the butler went on, "was at dinner, in his chair with the crest...."

"That feeble little old man eating porridge! Why, I thought he was some distant relative.... Well," Clarissa at once went on, "it being my first day here ... I couldn't even eat, I was so nervous. Would you believe it, Mr. Henderson, all I had was a little soup ... But I musn't intrude myself upon you. A man burdened with so many important responsibilities ..."

"It's been a pleasure talking to you, Miss Gray."

"You're most kind, Mr. Henderson. And I'm sure," Clarissa went on with a little sigh, "once I'm asleep, I'll forget this gnawing feeling of hunger ..."

And with these words Clarissa quickly went out.

She hurried back upstairs and to her room. Out of Miss Gray's satchel she took, first, the miniature, to prop it against the bureau mirror. Then, taking out the little volume of poetry, she sat down with it close to the candle, which stood on a little table, and waited. The miniature, the pretty book open on her knees, both well in view, added a vivid touch of authenticity to a governess' genteel background. She didn't have long to wait. Soon there was a discreet knock on the door.

"Come in, pray," Clarissa said.

The butler came in, carrying a tray. Half of a cold chicken, some pastry, a small pot of coffee, and a bottle of wine.

"Oh, Mr. Henderson!" Clarissa exclaimed, obviously quite overcome with surprise.

The butler, after closing the door, set the tray on the little table.

"And pray don't go away," Clarissa went on. "Do have a glass of wine with me." Hungry as she was, the food would have to wait; she dared not expose her eating manners in front of a butler, the most severe of critics. "I see you've brought only one glass, for *me*. Oh, how kind you are! But I can use this coffee cup.... Pray sit down, Mr. Henderson."

"Hmm," the butler coughed appreciatively.

"And *pray* do not stand on ceremony, Mr. Henderson," Clarissa implored. "That big wig they make you wear must be quite a weight. Do take it off, put it on the bed, and if some of the powder gets on the spread, it's of no consequence."

The butler gratefully removed his wig, placed it on the bed, then, moving the other cane chair closer, he sat down. Without the wig, and with his own graying hair covered sleekly with a string net, his head looked like a vulture's bereft of its feathers. He poured the wine.

"Tell me about his lordship," Clarissa said, sipping hers daintily. "How does he amuse himself?"

"Bugs."

"Bugs!"

"In his lordship's study there are shelves from floor to ceiling and those shelves are crowded with jars full of bugs, in some kind of liquid. Horrible-looking things, *I* think, alive some of them, too. But his lordship dotes on them. Spends all his time with them, in fact."

"Then what about all those stuffed animal heads in the hall?" Clarissa went on.

"Her ladyship is responsible for *that*. Wonderful shot she is. Famous for it."

He poured himself more wine.

"And what about the housekeeper?" Clarissa said.

"Don't you worry about *her*. If she tries to pin anything on you, the way she did on the other governesses, and that's why they got discharged, she'll have me to count with this time. And a butler, Miss Gray," Mr. Henderson explained very impressively, "has more influence than a mere housekeeper."

"Oh, Mr. Henderson!" Clarissa clasped her hands in a gesture of gratitude. "You're so *kind!*"

Just because I pretended to mistake you for the Marquis of Trall you're ready to fight my battles for me, you stupid oaf! Aloud, Clarissa said:

"Everything you say is *so* interesting. Do, pray, tell me some more."

"Well," the butler said, pouring himself another glass of wine, "there's the ghost."

"A ghost!"

"A place as illustrious as Ravisham naturally has a ghost," the butler explained proudly.

"Is it white?"

"Why, of course, it's white."

"And when does it appear? At night?"

"Naturally, at night."

"When all the lights are out?"

"Well, at that hour, as a rule, all the lights would be out, yes. But you needn't be afraid of it, Miss Gray," the butler assured Clarissa patronizingly. "The Ravisham ghost has never harmed anybody, that I heard of. All we have to do if any one of us happens to see it is hurry back to our rooms and close the door."

"Have *you* seen it?" Clarissa was very curious.

"Several times. Since I'm the last one to turn in, after locking up for the night. And during the last fifteen years it's been appearing pretty regularly."

"And before that?"

"Before that there's been a period of almost a hundred years when nobody had seen it. It became a mere legend, the Ravisham ghost. Some people even thought that it didn't exist. But, as I said before, fifteen years ago it started to walk again."

"And where does it walk?"

"It appears on the second-floor landing, near the main staircase. It is a fast-moving ghost, and that's the stairway it uses to reach the third floor, and then the fourth, and then it moves along this passage right past your door, Miss Gray. And then as it reaches the servants' stairs it suddenly disappears. That's what I've seen with my own eyes," the butler said. "And I can take my oath on it."

"And its course never varies?"

"Never. A ghost always walks along the same route. But the reason I mentioned it, Miss Gray," the butler added, "is because I have a feeling that it may appear quite soon."

"You mean the ghost gives a warning of some kind *beforehand?*"

"Nothing like that, no. It's just that a new groom was hired for her ladyship yesterday. Young and handsome her ladyship's grooms always are," the butler put in, parenthetically. "And the last time that I saw the ghost it happened two days after a new groom had been hired."

"But what possible connection could there be between her ladyship's new groom and a *ghost?*" Clarissa said.

"None whatsoever, of course. Perhaps I didn't make myself quite clear. I said I have a *feeling* about it appearing again. And the last time when I had exactly the same feeling there'd just been a new groom hired, and that's what made me think of the groom who was hired yesterday. That's what I meant."

And now that he had finished the bottle, the butler glanced around the room. He was well aware, Clarissa could see, of the pretty volume lying open on her knees, and of the miniature on the bureau.

"My brother Richard," Clarissa explained sadly. "Left the country to seek his fortune ... But for ten years now there's been no news ..."

Both of Miss Gray's "treasures," besides supplying Clarissa with the needed background, so showed up by contrast the bareness and the shabbiness of the room that the butler couldn't but be struck by the pathetic fact.

"A cushioned chair, some nice drapes, and hmm ... a soft rug," he said. "And a coal fire in that grate, since it gets quite chilly here at night ... would make quite a difference, wouldn't it? I'll give the necessary orders in the morning."

"Oh, Mr. Henderson!"

The butler put on his big wig. Traces of the flour with which it was thickly powdered were all over the bedspread, Clarissa noticed as she saw him to the door.

Then she softly turned the key, and hurried back to the laden tray. She had snatched up the towel from the washstand rack and now, tying it about her neck, as one would a large napkin, and then peeling off the black lace mitts, she attacked the cold chicken with a fine appetite, using her bare hands, and with gusto licking the grease off her fingers. She sucked at the delicate bones. The coffee had gotten cold, but she drank it anyway, and then the cream, which tasted delicious. The pastry, as compared to the kind they served at the Waterfront Tavern, was something out of this world.

In a few minutes she was undressed and in bed and laughing to herself. Everything was going so smoothly! The brilliant moonlight, now that the candle had been snuffed out, streamed in through the open window. And what a strange shadow it cast on the opposite wall! Then, her heart in her mouth, she was suddenly sitting bolt upright, and staring hard. The shadow was that of a man climbing in through the window. The fact that the window was on the fourth floor presented little difficulty since he'd had one of those huge trees, standing close on this side of the house, to make use of for the purpose, besides a drainpipe and the old ivy creeping up the wall with stalks as thick and sturdy as any bough.

And there was the man himself, already in the room and moving towards her, while grinning from ear to ear. The postilion!

"What is the meaning of this?" Clarissa demanded, swiftly assuming Miss Gray's voice and an air of righteous indignation. "One more step and I'll call for help, rouse the whole house...."

"And I'll tell them who you really are," the postilion said, moving closer and grinning as before. "You can't fool me, my pretty. I was in that field when you were still senseless, propped against the haystack, and I touched you and I knew you'd be all right. And then I hurried over to where Miss Gray lay under the hedge and *she* was dead. I guess by the time you came to I was back in the road, trying to help the driver, who had been flung into the ditch. And right away you took it for granted that that's where I'd been all along."

So that's how it was. The stupid fool would have to be got rid of, somehow, eventually if not now, that was certain.... Aloud, Clarissa said:

"What do you want? I have no money to give you."

"All I want is yourself, my pretty!" The surly fellow had removed his jacket and was taking off his breeches. "The minute I laid my eyes on you, as you waited to get into that stagecoach, I'd set my mind to have you, by hook or by crook."

And he got into the bed beside her.

"You lout," Clarissa said.

But it was a relief, in a way, to cease being Miss Gray and return to being herself, being Clarissa, again, temporarily at least. Crude though the fellow was, he was also young and strong.

"You'll make the bed creak," she warned him, between smothered fits of laughter, while he giggled.

After a good romp, both of them of course being very careful not to make the bed creak, which somehow added to the fun, the postilion announced:

"I'll be coming to you pretty often. Every time, that is, that the stagecoach, on its run from Colchester to London and back again, stops at the village inn here. So ..."

Sounds, as of some kind of commotion, suddenly reached their ears. Bell ropes were being pulled throughout the house, and the flunkies could be heard running back and forth, answering the summons.

"Out," Clarissa hissed. "Maybe you were seen.... Out. Quick!"

Since illegal entry, no matter for what purpose, was punishable by hanging, the postilion was already getting into his breeches. Grabbing his jacket, he leaped for the window, swung himself over the sill, and disappeared from view. Not a minute too soon, for there was a knock on the door and the butler's voice said:

"Miss Gray."

"Just a minute, Mr. Henderson. Let me get my wrapper."

Clarissa, out of bed by now, snatched it from the clothes hooks, put it on, hastily smoothed her hair, then opened the door. The butler had dressed himself in a hurry, the big powdered wig set askew on his head.

"I thought you'd like to know ..." he said. "In case all this commotion made you anxious ..."

"Well, it certainly awakened me, Mr. Henderson." Clarissa pretended to stifle a yawn.

"A messenger has just arrived from London, from His Royal Highness, the Prince Regent. The Regent will be here tomorrow, for an indefinite stay. And, of course, Mr. Brummell. At such a short notice, can you imagine, Miss Gray?" the butler complained. He wanted sympathy, so he had come to gossip. The old oaf might become quite a nuisance.... "But then it's always like that with the Prince Regent," he confided. "Evidently the usual thing happened."

"And what *is* the usual thing?" Clarissa was instantly intrigued.

A bell rope, obviously pulled by the Ogre herself—it made such a terrible clatter—sent the butler hurrying away, however.

Clarissa closed the door, removed her wrapper, and got back into bed and was soon asleep, the only person calmly asleep in the huge house where everybody now was up and about, everything abustle and scurry and haste, with the anxious preparation for the royal visit.

CHAPTER NINE

THE "USUAL THING." as Clarissa was to learn surprisingly soon and from the lips of one of the participants, started to happen at precisely the moment when the stagecoach in which Clarissa was traveling away from London and with Colchester for her destination, as she then thought, had stopped at the big hostelry for a quick midday snack.

The scene had taken place, as it generally did, in the Prince Regent's palace in London. In a spacious, luxuriously appointed and sun-flooded anteroom, a little group of statesmen, with old Mr. Pitt in the lead, stood waiting in front of a closed door which, as everybody knew, led into the Prince's private apartments. A special courier early that very morning had come in haste from Lord Nelson with Nelson's urgent demand for supplies—ammunition, clothes, food for his brave sailors. And the document which the old Mr. Pitt held in his hands, glancing at it from time to time with ever-growing anxiety, contained the detailed lists of the urgently needed supplies, set down in Nelson's bold, clear handwriting.

Mr. Pitt was dressed in simple black. His wig was unpowdered. Notwithstanding his advanced age he held himself very erect. His hands, though thin and veined, were perfectly steady. Only the deep lines of his grave face reflected the continuous worries which, since the Regency, had beset this most venerable of statesmen.

Standing beside him, the Minister of War, a heavy-set, rough-looking man, wearing but a single star on the red coat of his plain uniform, whispered discreetly:

"Does Mr. Brummell know we are here for an audience with His Royal Highness?"

He glanced towards the closed doors with badly concealed resentment. They had been waiting in front of that door for almost three hours....

"I was fortunate enough to speak to Mr. Brummell personally," the old Mr. Pitt said quietly. "Before the tailors arrived."

"Ah, yes, the tailors." The Minister of War's robust face turned a brick red. But he dared not express his thoughts in words.

"Yes, the tailors," the more experienced Mr. Pitt went on calmly. "With a new coat for His Highness."

"Ah, a new coat," the Minister of War said, his face turning from red to purple. "In that case we may as well leave ... Cooling our heels here won't ..."

"Sir," Mr. Pitt said in his calm but impressive voice, "you're comparatively a newcomer at Court." The temperamental Prince Regent had been changing his war ministers every six months or so. "Permit an old man to give you a piece of advice. Royalty is like a woman. Guided by their moods, whims, caprices. Let us be wise then, let us be patient. Mr. Brummell promised me to put in a word for us at an opportune moment. Therefore we must wait. The important thing is to get the supplies over to Nelson, and for that we must have the Regent's signature at the bottom of this document sent by Nelson." He slapped a palm at the papers he was holding. "Then the required money will automatically be released from the Exchequer."

The Minister of War mopped his brow, then, heaving a sigh, he said:

"I don't know what we'd do without Mr. Brummell."

There were graceful little satin-upholstered sofas and chairs alongside the walls. But it was against the Court etiquette to sit down while waiting for an audience. And so they stood …

In the adjoining anteroom, an exact replica of the first, including the sunlight streaming in through the tall palace windows, another group also stood waiting. This group, glittering with lavish foreign uniforms, consisted of ambassadors representing the various nations which had formed an alliance against the Napoleonic menace. Since the largest of these nations were Imperial Russia and the Prussian Kingdom, their respective ambassadors, taking precedence over the rest, stood directly in front of the closed door.

The Russian Ambassador, who bore a striking resemblance to his young handsome blond Czar, Alexander I, said to the Prussian Ambassador:

"What in the world could be keeping His Royal Highness so long?"

"Someone mentioned that His Royal Highness is closeted with his tailors," the Prussian Ambassador replied, preserving a perfectly straight face.

"Ah, with his tailors," the other repeated, with as straight a face, since he was as great a diplomat as his colleague.

"His Royal Highness is trying on a new coat," the Prussian Ambassador went on, taking snuff meanwhile from a little treasure of a box, on the lid of which was painted the portrait of his king. And he stretched the snuffbox out invitingly, looking very solemn.

"Ah, a new coat," the Russian Ambassador repeated, like a parrot. And, accepting the offer of snuff, he delicately inserted some first in one nostril, and then in the other.

The two of them then sneezed very loudly, each politely holding a lace handkerchief in front of his face.

The other ambassadors, though they knew what was keeping His Royal Highness, did not dare mention the fact even in the most discreet of whispers, since the countries they represented were not big enough to be called empires. And they bowed very low, as etiquette prescribed, when their two superior colleagues sneezed. The Russian Ambassador and the Prussian Ambassador bowed in return, but not half as low. Then all of them, straightening up, continued their long wait ...

Meanwhile, on the other side of those closed doors, the Prince Regent, surrounded by his courtiers, was trying on a new coat. The trying on of a new coat did not mean just *one* coat. A dozen coats, each of a different color, material, and style, had been brought, and he tried them on, one after another, finding fault with each. Enraged he'd tear the coat off—one could hear the seams ripping—fling it at a trembling gentleman-in-waiting, and shout:

"Tell the chief tailor that he's a fool and a scoundrel!"

The chief tailor, pale and shaking in his shoes, was right there, but the Prince Regent never spoke directly to anyone whom he considered an inferior.

He stood there, tall and gross, the tight white satin breeches accentuating the ugly abundance of flesh about his thighs and stomach. His shirt, of linen so fine as to be almost transparent, had very full sleeves with ruffle-trimmed cuffs, and over the shirt he wore a waistcoat of glistening white brocade. The exaggerated folds of a white silk neckcloth propped his fat florid face, which was framed in the glossy brown curls of a large wig.

He could see in the mirror, besides his own unflattering reflection, everybody who was in the room, and he eyed them with a haughty, suspicious stare. Did they, by any chance, think he was fat? And were they laughing at him? He was very sensitive about his figure.

"Brummell," he suddenly shouted, "where are you?"

"Right here, Your Highness," Brummell's quiet voice replied reassuringly.

The swarming courtiers and tailors had momentarily concealed Brummell from view. But he was standing only a few feet away, a picture of slender elegance in his plain tan coat, fawn-colored breeches, and modest neckcloth. He held his gloves and tall beaver hat in one hand and with the other leaned lightly on a slim ebony cane.

The Prince Regent could now see Brummell in the mirror and he grew somewhat calmer.

"Let's have the next one," he ordered. "And the Earl of Strasford," the Regent added with a spiteful laugh, "will pay the bill."

A more comically senile little figure than the Earl of Strasford, the wealthiest noble in the realm, couldn't have been imagined. Shriveled with age to a ridiculously small stature, the Earl looked like an absurd doll in his old-fashioned courtier's costume of pink and blue satin besprinkled with pearls and diamonds. He carried a bejeweled fan to toy with coquettishly, a lace handkerchief to wave about coyly. His little face under the neat white wig was powdered and rouged and lipsticked; and all of him reeked with perfumes. He lisped, giggled, flirted. Exhausted, however, from standing on his French-heeled slippers for three long hours, he had slyly tiptoed to a chair in a faraway corner and lay collapsed in it as though his doll-joints had become loose.

"Did Your Grace hear what I said?" The vicious irony of that "Your Grace" made even the tailors' apprentices shiver.

Nobody was more tormented by the Regent's bad temper, mean wit, and cruel practical jokes than the diminutive, senile Earl.

"Do I have the honor of being spoken to by Your Royal Highness?" The fantastic doll figure had somehow managed to scramble to its feet.

"*You* will have the honor of paying my tailor's bill," the Regent said. "I owe the scoundrel for two years."

"But … Your Highness … That … that will amount to a fortune. A small fortune!" And with a moan, which somehow resembled the squeak of a stuck pig, the little Earl again collapsed into the chair.

"Brummell! Where are you?"

A courtier explained respectfully that Mr. Brummell had just stepped out into the corridor to speak to someone. The Regent, frowning, began to shove everyone out of his way until he reached the spot from where he could see who it was Brummell was talking with. A row of marble columns ran down the palace corridor, and leaning against one of these columns stood a man wrapped in a black cloak and wearing a broad-brimmed hat. It was Clarissa's erstwhile mysterious stranger, the Rosicrucian. But all the Regent knew, or cared to know, was that it was a man, not a woman, that Brummell was speaking to. Reassured, he strode back to the mirror.

"Well?" the Rosicrucian said.

"He has given no audience to anyone as yet," Brummell said. "If he does, it will mean that he's in a good mood, and then he won't be watching me and I will be in a position to let you know immediately."

"It is the negative information that must be passed on to Lord Nelson as soon as possible," the Rosicrucian pointed out. "He then may manage to stall for time, hold back giving battle to the French fleet on the Nile."

"Suppose we agree," Brummell said, after thinking this over, "that if you don't hear from me by tonight then the answer is negative, and you will so inform Nelson."

"Very well."

"But that's just in case," Brummell added. "There's every indication that His Highness will grant the needed audience."

"Let us hope so."

They parted, the Rosicrucian hurrying away, and Brummell going back in to the Regent.

"One of your artist friends?" the Prince said, smiling indulgently.

Having been helped into another coat, he was turning this way and that in front of the mirror.

"Where is the Princess Royal?" he suddenly demanded. Now he was in a different mood, a mood of power and grandeur. "Am I not supposed to be granting an audience," he gestured pompously, "to somebody or other?"

Brummell stepped forward eagerly.

"Mr. Pitt, and the Minister of War. And the foreign ambassadors." He motioned at the closed doors behind which the two respective groups were waiting.

"Then how do you expect me," the Regent went on in the same grandiose manner, "to make my appearance without a female member of my own family walking beside me as the etiquette prescribes?"

Every rule of the Court etiquette, which in his opinion created an impression of power, he exploited to the utmost. Since the deposition of his young wife, Princess Caroline, the Regent's eldest sister, the unmarried Princess Royal, had been acting as his official hostess, and much as he disliked her he now gave an order:

"Get Her Highness."

But the Princess Royal was already hurrying in with her nervous mincing step. As tall as the Regent, but very thin, with a long neck like a giraffe's, she wore a long gray silk gown trimmed with salmon-colored ribbons. The gray curls, bunched dowdily on top of her head, were encircled with a diamond tiara, and this tiara actually wiggled, the poor woman was so nervous. Since the tailor's arrival she had been standing just outside the door, listening, afraid to go in. She lived in terror of her brother and had developed a permanent chill. Goose-pimples stood out on her lean arms.

Directly behind her came her ladies-in-waiting; a bevy of young pretty girls, all beautifully dressed. The Princess Royal, like any other old maid, was a born matchmaker. By bringing to Court these girls, some of them quite poor, she could encourage their romantic attachments, or find them suitable husbands, provide dowries. Now, after leading them in making a low curtsy to the Regent, she sat down on a sofa and the girls arranged themselves about her in a pretty group. When thus surrounded by youth and beauty, the unhappy Princess Royal pathetically resembled the mythological ass, looking out of a flower bed into which it had wandered by mistake.

The Regent noticed at once, by the way her tiara wiggled, that this stupid sister of his was more nervous than usual and, scowling, he was about to address her. But just then the Duke of Cumberland entered to pay the etiquette-prescribed daily call on his royal brother. Luxuriously attired, languid, a trifle insolent, he was notorious for his passion for women and such sadistic sports as cockfighting and rat-baiting. The careless cruelty of a born sensualist gazed out of his velvety brown eyes, and his beautiful white hands with tapering fingers and long polished nails glittered with fabulous jewels.

Advancing with his indolent walk to the center of the room, the Duke swept the Regent a low bow. Then:

"Brummell, my dear fellow," the Duke again swept a bow.

His third bow included the Princess Royal and all the courtiers present. He then sank into the nearest chair and, so reclining, stretched out a leg to admire its shape. But, instantly bored, he yawned, carelessly and somehow insolently covering the yawn with his effeminate, bejeweled hand.

The Regent's attention, once the ceremony of acknowledging his younger brother's greeting was over with, reverted to the unfortunate Princess Royal.

"What are you sniveling about? Out with it! What's that you're crumpling in your hand? A letter? Trying to hide something from me?"

"I ... I brought it for you to see. It's from that little Swiss doctor ... I'm sure I mentioned him to you. He's an expert on ... on mental sickness. Very famous in Europe he is ... so I persuaded him to come over. And the last time I went to see His Majesty, our poor father, I took him along with me ... Your Highness told me, repeatedly, you didn't care whom ... whom I took with me ..."

"Did I ever say you could take a *doctor* with you when you go to see the old dotterel?"

"What strange words Your Highness uses speaking of our father...." The Princess Royal looked shocked. "Of course, I know you don't *mean* it...."

"Stop sniveling, for heaven's sake, and come to the point! What does the letter say?"

"Such wonderful news, dear brother," the Princess Royal clasped her hands and gazed at the Regent with tear-filled eyes. "This very learned doctor says that father isn't sick at all! That he doesn't have to be confined ..."

"Wonderful news, indeed," the Duke of Cumberland remarked lanquidly, and he laughed.

"Oh, when I think of him in that old summer palace," the poor woman meanwhile went on, "so far away from us all, under guard, not getting enough to eat perhaps …"

"Let me see that letter," the Regent said quietly.

The Princess Royal gave it to him eagerly. Then she gasped to see the Regent stride over to the fireplace, drop the letter—without even glancing at its contents—on the glowing coals, and watch it burn to ashes. Then he went to stand in front of the mirror again. Flicking an invisible speck of something from the coat cuff with a snap of his plump fingers, he said casually:

"The whole medical profession, unanimously, has declared His Majesty, my father, King George III, to be insane. The old man is mentally deranged. And he's been put away. Otherwise I wouldn't have been Regent."

"My dear brother," the Duke of Cumberland said languidly, "everybody knows how very legally it was all done."

If there was a hint of a sneer in the Duke's tone it was lost on the Regent, who thought his brother too indolent to meddle in politics.

"No man in his right mind," he declared, "would have lost the American Colonies. What better proof could there be of how insane my father *was* and *is*."

"Ah, what better proof indeed?" the Duke of Cumberland said.

"But they fought a fair war, Your Highness," the Princess Royal reminded the Regent timidly, "and they won. All they wanted was their freedom …"

The loss of the American Colonies was a sore point with the Regent and his voice rose to a shriek, as very rudely he told her to shut up.

"And," he added, "you better tell that little Swiss doctor of yours to get out of the country, or I'll have him thrown into the Tower, for treason!"

"What a bore," the Duke of Cumberland murmured, and he raised his white bejeweled hand to cover an especially huge yawn.

The Regent barely had time to regain his composure and concentrate his attention on the coat he was trying on, when a door opened and a frail-looking stately woman, wearing a long traveling cape over her pale brocade gown and with a stylish Paris bonnet perched on her ash-blond ringlets, came in swiftly. Unmindful of the general astonishment her unexpected appearance produced, she walked straight to where the Regent stood and sunk down on her knees at his feet. Everybody had recognized her at once, of course. It was the Regent's deposed wife, Princess Caroline. The Duke of Cumberland whistled softly. This might prove quite amusing. Everybody had instantly surmised what must have happened; somebody at Court, probably Mr. Brummell, had promised to arrange for her to see her child, but once on native soil, instead of waiting patiently, she had let her emotions get the better of her and here she was, throwing herself on the mercy of this most merciless of men.

"Your Highness," Princess Caroline's melodious voice rang out clearly in the sudden hush. "Let me see my child. If only for a few minutes ... my baby. My little Charlotte ..."

"Madam," the Regent roared. "What is the meaning of this outrage? You have been legally exiled. Who *dared* smuggle you across the Channel? I'll have them all hanged! I ... I ..." he stuttered. "I'll have *you* placed under arrest ..."

"Your Highness," Brummell said, coming over swiftly, "let me take care of this." And he addressed Princess Caroline, after helping her to her feet hastily, with well-assumed severity, "Madam, I won't have His Highness so unnecessarily annoyed. You shouldn't have come." Holding her by the arm firmly, he marched her to the door. The Princess Royal, as they passed, stretched out her goose-pimpled arms in sympathy.

"My poor Caroline …"

But Brummell wouldn't let the wretched young mother pause for even a second. And once he had her outside the door, he again said:

"You shouldn't have come."

But his voice was kindly now and full of understanding.

"Oh, Mr. Brummell," Princess Caroline dabbed at her eyes with her tiny handkerchief. "I just couldn't help myself. I realize now, it was very foolish of me…. Have I ruined everything?"

"You know how unpredictable His Highness is," Brummell shrugged. "But I'll do my best. Stay at the Countess Argull's, as I asked you to do, until you hear from me. It may take weeks perhaps, so arm yourself with patience. How did you come here?"

"In a hired coach. And I wore a veil." Producing it from under her traveling cape, Princess Caroline draped the long veil about her bonneted head to show him how it concealed her features. "Nobody recognized me. And I told the guards at the gate, and then the palace footmen, that Mr. Brummell was expecting me. They probably thought I was someone from the theater in whose talent you take an interest."

"So long as your presence doesn't become public knowledge … But now, please go."

He watched her hurry away down the columned corridor, then hastened back to the Regent.

"To place her under arrest might create an unfavorable impression," Brummell explained, very seriously, "since the common people have a tendency to sympathize with a mother's feelings. Anyway, she'll be leaving England," which was true enough, except that Brummell didn't specify when that would occur. "I'll see to it personally," which, again, was true, if indirectly so. "Give no more thought to it, Your Highness. An unimportant, silly incident, that's what it amounts to."

The Regent, as usual, had interpreted Brummell's quick action as testimony of Brummell's loyalty to himself and he looked all puffed up with pride.

"You're perfectly right," he said. "It *is* unimportant. And I don't think that any one of my own subjects," he went on, sticking out his chest grandly, "knowing how I feel about the stupid woman, would have dared smuggle her in from abroad. But the French now, they might have had a hand in it, since we're at war with them. Anything to annoy me."

Brummell had counted on the Regent's immense vanity to suggest some such conclusion to him. There would be no investigation started then to track down the real culprits, whose identities were known to Brummell through the intermediary in his employ. He could breathe a little easier.

And trying to create a diversion, and so further draw away the Regent's thoughts from the just-enacted incident, Brummell said, without moving from the spot where he again stood, lightly leaning on his slim cane:

"Did I tell Your Highness that I met a poet this morning, a real poet, a genius? The young man as good as forced his way into my house; I was at breakfast, and he read me his poem. It's about a woman of great beauty, Clarissa. She's been his inspiration."

"A new beauty?" the Earl of Strasford lisped, sitting up, using his bejeweled fan coquettishly, flapping his lace handkerchief about in sprightly senile excitement. "A newly famous beauty in London and I haven't seen her!"

"This Clarissa," Brummell explained, "is not famous as yet. And she has just left London to act in some little theater in the provinces. But the Poet is convinced she'll be back."

"Hasn't he a name, this new discovery of yours, Brummell," the Regent said, "that you call him simply the Poet?"

"That's what the people in the neighborhood he comes from, he told me, call him. And very aptly too, though they don't know it. For with that poem alone he's already *the* poet of our century. One of the immortals. I'm giving him a small stipend."

"Speaking of women, any woman ..." the Duke of Cumberland observed very languidly, his boredom having been pierced by Brummell's mention of a woman's name. "The most important point of a woman's beauty, more important than her breasts, are her buttocks."

Since the Duke was an acknowledged connoisseur on the subject, everyone listened most attentively.

"A woman's buttocks should never be too large, but they must be firm. Like this ..." By cupping his white effeminate hands knowingly, he conveyed quite a vivid picture of that particular part of a woman's anatomy.

The courtiers laughed lustily and the Regent, after laughing with them, said:

"The description seems to fit your new mistress, dear brother."

"Ah, Your Highness is too kind," the Duke murmured, flattered, but already about to yawn again.

"Well, what do you think of this coat, Brummell?" the Regent went on, the incident of Princess Caroline's reappearance wiped out of his mind thanks to the diversion started by Brummell's simple little story. "I can't say I particularly like it."

"I quite agree with Your Highness," Brummell said. "The style isn't quite ..." He bent his head to one side, then to the other, scrutinizing the Regent critically. "Well ... it's not right, somehow. And the material ..." Brummell knew and so did everybody else that the fault was not with the style, or with the material, but with the Regent's figure. He was so gross. "But what about this coat?"

With the tip of his cane Brummell pointed at one of the remaining three coats which lay on the satin-upholstered bench. He beckoned the chief tailor over.

"His Highness will try this one on."

The chief tailor took up the coat very carefully, handed it over to a gentleman-in-waiting, who then approached the Regent and, standing behind him, held the coat out for him to put on. All the Regent had to do was slip his arms into the sleeves. It was a plum-colored coat and had large diamond buttons all the way down the front. The gentleman-in-waiting closed the buttons for him, then, with a bow, stepped back.

"Well ..." the Regent said uncertainly, turning this way and that in front of the mirror.

Perhaps because of the dark color's slenderizing effect, it was the first coat that looked decent on him. And Brummell could say in all sincerity:

"A perfect fit."

"I sort of like it myself ..." the Regent confessed childishly, his florid face creased with smiles of gratification.

"I've never seen a coat that was so becoming to Your Highness."

"Well ... It will do. Yes, I'll keep it. In fact, I'll wear it."

And turning round, the Regent announced, addressing all the courtiers present:

"Gentlemen, Mr. Brummell admires my new coat."

The room was suddenly buzzing like a beehive with flattering exclamations.

"A beautiful coat, Your Highness!" "*Wonder*ful, "Magnificent!" "Lovely, simply lovely!" "*Most* becoming!"

"Merveilleux!" the Earl of Strasford lisped, kissing his perfumed fingertips in senile rapture.

The ordeal was over. Everybody could breathe again. His Highness looked happy. Everybody *was* happy. The moment augured well for all concerned. The granting of audiences to Mr. Pitt and the Minister of War, to the foreign ambassadors, seemed assured. Except that capricious Fate here chose to play one of its unexpected little tricks and so change the course of several destinies.

One of the young ladies-in-waiting surrounding the Princess Royal dropped her handkerchief. And Brummell, since of all the gentlemen present he happened to be standing closest to the group, stooped to pick it up, handed it to its owner. The girl, new at Court, blushing profusely, could barely stammer a polite thank you. How it made the other girls green with envy; to be so singled out by the famous Beau Brummell! That's how they saw it. And that's how, evidently, the Regent saw it. He strode over at once, his face livid.

"Do you find her attractive?" he said to Brummell.

And without waiting for an answer, he pointed at the girl, who was half-fainting with fright:

"Go. I henceforth banish you from my Court."

And he said to the Princess Royal, in that tone of voice which, as everybody knew, meant that his decision was absolutely final, irrevocable:

"Have her sent home, back to her parents, immediately!"

The kindhearted old maid tried to stand up for her protégée.

"But they live in the country, and with no dowry … she'll never meet anyone suitable, she'll never get married."

"So much the better," the Regent said spitefully.

The poor girl now lay in a dead faint, the other ladies-in-waiting hovering about, ministering to her. Little flacons of smelling salts, of cologne appeared. Fans, lace handkerchiefs fluttered.

"Now," the Regent said, turning to Brummell.

And Brummell saw how absolutely beside himself the Regent was, with fierce jealousy, possessiveness, with wounded vanity and pride. His cheeks trembling like jelly, thick lips quivering, and tears of rage welling in his round eyes, he looked like an overgrown fat boy, having a tantrum. A hundred ridiculous, petty accusations gushed out of his distorted-with-passion mouth.

"And you're supposed to be my friend ... The only person I can trust. I'm surrounded by enemies ..."

"But, Your Highness ..."

"Don't argue! Friendship, indeed! Maybe there's no more basis for it than that stupid promise you gave my father, to stand by me. Yes, in my presence, and right here in this very room, before they took him away. I heard the old dotterel babbling something about restraining influence...."

"We were friends for many years before that," Brummell tried to point out mildly. "Don't you remember how we first met? I was in a shop, looking for a neckcloth, and Your Highness came in with two of your gentlemen. You asked my advice in selecting a waistcoat.... And, right there and then, you invited me to dinner.... But the *basis* of friendship, who could explain it? It's a mystery. I, a poor man, a mere nobody ... you, a Royal prince ... And yet ..."

"Now you're trying to make me feel sentimental. But it won't work!" the Regent told him very rudely.

"I'm trying to remind Your Highness that real friendship, such as ours, is a precious thing. Surely ..."

"And as soon as you see a pretty face ... I saw it all. I was *watching* you!"

"The young lady dropped her handkerchief," Brummell explained patiently. "I picked it up and handed it to her. Mere politeness ..."

"The first thing a woman does when she hooks a man is poison his mind against his best friend," the Regent shouted. He was still very angry. "How do I know what's going on in that romantic head of yours? Maybe you're waiting for your *ideal* of a woman. And so much the worse for you! Because you'll never find her. Anyway, my mind is made up!"

Brummell did not have to ask what about. He knew. It happened every time, the usual thing.

"I'm going to take you away from the temptations of pretty ladies-in-waiting," the Regent announced spitefully. "We're going to the country, for a quiet visit, no other guests but us. To Ravisham."

It was generally Ravisham. Because her ladyship was homely, the growing daughters were homely.... Of course, there'd be a governess, but a governess didn't count. A housemaid, for instance, could be pinched and mauled, if she happened to be attractive. But what could one do with a wellborn, virtuous young lady, except despise her for not having a fortune?

"They have the best hunting," the Regent went on. "And besides, as you know, her ladyship is as fond of card-playing as I am, and I may win that famous rope of emeralds she always wears and which hangs down almost to her knees."

"But—Mr. Pitt and the Minister of War. The foreign ambassadors ..." Brummell pleaded.

The Regent didn't even deign to answer. Instead, he began to give orders. A messenger was to gallop to Ravisham to inform the Marquis and Marquise of Trall of the royal visit. The Regent's private coach was to be readied, his luggage packed. A flunky was dispatched to Mr. Brummell's house to bring *his* luggage.

"And Your Grace is going with us," the Regent told the Earl of Strasford.

"But, Your Highness ... What will Nona say?" Nona was the Earl's current mistress, famous for her extravagances.

"She'll console herself with her young lovers," the Regent told him cruelly, "while you go hunting with us. You like riding a horse, don't you?"

The Earl, who as everybody knew was terrified of horses, collapsed into his chair, moaning.

"Her ladyship's porridge-eating husband," the Duke of Cumberland drawled, "knowing her passion for gambling, never gives her any cash. So again she'll be forced to stake her rope of emeralds to match Your Highness' little mounds of gold. Well, I wish Your Highness luck, though I doubt you'll ever win it." The Duke yawned. "When is Your Highness leaving?"

"Right after lunch."

The tailors and their helpers had long since departed. The girl who had fainted had been speedily hustled out of the palace as soon as she was revived.

And now the Princess Royal rose, to place her fingertips on the Regent's outstretched arm. Brummell took his place immediately behind, with the Duke of Cumberland. Then the young ladies-in-waiting in their beautiful dresses. Then the courtiers. A door was flung open into the adjoining apartments, where more courtiers stood waiting around the magnificent table, set with a sumptuous meal. The major-domo, after tapping with his tall mace on the floorboards announced in a thunderous voice:

"His Royal Highness, the Prince Regent!"

And thus ceremoniously, with everyone wearing the hypocritically radiant smile reserved for public appearances, they all filed out and the door closed upon them.

Brummell had not dared send a message to either Mr. Pitt or the foreign ambassadors, and the two respective groups continued to wait long after the Regent's coach, preceded by the mounted guards in their red-with-gold uniforms, and surrounded by yellow-coated outriders, rumbled out of the palace courtyard, bound for Ravisham.

CHAPTER TEN

BRIGHT MORNING SUNLIGHT awakened Clarissa, and at first she couldn't understand where she was. Then it all came back to her, she was at Ravisham, and at the same instant the door opened and Sally came in with the breakfast tray.

"Good morning, Miss Gray."

"Good morning, Sally." Clarissa smiled at the little kitchen-maid in Miss Gray's most gentle manner.

She sat up in bed and Sally placed the tray, which had short legs to it, over her knees.

"The gypsies are gone," Sally announced triumphantly. "I ran over to make sure. And the trollop's rags are gone with them, just as I thought they'd be. No trace of them on the nearby hedge where I left them. So that's taken care of! And Pete," Sally went on, blushing and giggling, "you should have seen the way Pete's eyes almost popped out of his head when he saw me, looking the way I look now, thanks to you, Miss Gray."

The low neckline of Sally's blouse offered an inviting glimpse of her budding young breasts, and the narrow blue ribbon in Sally's hair brought out the rosy color of her small face, now emanating blissful happiness.

"And the first chance Pete gets," Sally chattered on, "he grabs me behind the kitchen door and starts kissing me. But we couldn't stay together long because of all the work that had to be done in preparation for the Prince Regent's visit. Didn't sleep a wink, none of us did, all night. And so many little things still left undone. The place is still in a turmoil. And everybody so *excited!*"

Clarissa, scooping the egg out of its little cup, biting into the crisp buttered toast, and sipping coffee, all very daintily, quite as if she was used to having breakfast in bed every day of her life, said:

"When is the royal party expected to arrive?"

"Not till afternoon."

Which suited Clarissa fine, since there was something she was very anxious to do first thing in the morning. If she managed to slip out of the house, that is.

"There, Sally. I've finished. You can take the tray."

Sally, removing it cheerfully, placed it on the little table, to chatter on:

"The housekeeper went after me something fierce, when she saw me bringing breakfast up to you. But the butler heard her, and he told her to leave me alone. It was all right, he said. And then Mr. Henderson gave orders to Bertha, the gruff housemaid, about drapes and pretty chairs and a rug for your room. You should have seen Bertha's face! I brought your hot water first thing, it's on the washstand," Sally added. "You didn't hear me, you were so sound asleep."

Clarissa, already out of bed, washed hastily, then did her hair, taking pains, in spite of her impatience, to make it very smooth, including the sausage-like curls dangling over her ears. Having put on Miss Gray's camisole and petticoat, she hurried over to where the dresses hung on the row of hooks. And it was when she was about to take a dress down that something caught her eye suddenly, and she saw a tiny bit of paper sticking out of the bare part of the wall there. Sally had just gone out, carrying the chamber pot. It didn't take a moment to investigate swiftly, pull the tight little wad of paper out; there was a small crack in the wall and someone had stuck the wad of paper in to close it, from *this* side, the side where Clarissa stood. Clarissa's predecessor, the genuine governess, had doubtless virtuously closed up the crack to insure privacy for herself, the silly creature.

Clarissa brought her face close to the wall, and by putting an eye to the tiny opening she could see into the adjoining room—mannishly furnished, with big, leather-upholstered sofa and chairs. If she could see into that room, anybody standing on the other side of the wall could see into *her* room. On hearing Sally's returning footsteps outside the door, Clarissa hurriedly replaced the wad of paper into the crack, moved away. As Sally came in Clarissa was getting into the dress, the same plain dark dress she had worn the previous day. Later, she would have to change into one of Miss Gray's summery, white muslin, blue-sashed dresses. The Ogre would probably expect her to, in honor of the royal visitor.

"I was wondering, Sally," Clarissa said, casually, while pinning the cameo brooch on the cambric neckerchief, in front of the bureau mirror, "who occupies the room next to this one? Probably one of the housemaids." Though she knew perfectly well it was no housemaid's room. "On that side," Clarissa motioned at the wall in which she had discovered the crack.

Sally, who was starting to make the bed, paused in smoothing the sheet over the mattress.

"The housemaids have their quarters on the floor above, the mansard floor it's called, right under the roof," Sally said. "And all the male servants, such as footmen and grooms, they're on this floor, but on the *other* side of the servants' staircase. On this side there's only the housekeeper's room; and the butler's, Mr. Henderson's; and yours, Miss Gray. But nobody occupies *that* room, the one you mean," Sally pointed at that wall. "It's what they call a drinking room. The gentlemen guests go there, last thing at night, to drink their liquor. It being on the fourth floor, no matter how late it might be, the gentlemen don't disturb the ladies when they get together there, to drink and talk and tell jokes, smutty jokes, I guess. And His Highness, when he stays here, joins them, before going to bed."

"But isn't there such a thing as a royal suite at Ravisham?" Clarissa said. From Lafonte she knew that every great house had a series of rooms reserved for royal visitors.

"Sure there is," Sally said. "On the second floor, the whole of the right wing. And that's where the Prince Regent will be staying, naturally. And Mr. Brummell, too, and whoever else His Highness brings with him. But next to this drinking room," Sally again pointed at that wall, "there's also a billiard room, and, last thing at night, before having his liquor, the Regent likes to have a game of billiards with Mr. Brummell. And *that* after sitting up half the night playing cards with her ladyship, trying to win her rope of emeralds."

"Her rope of emeralds!" Clarissa said. She was patting a little of Miss Gray's lavender cologne from its flacon onto her wrists and hair and a clean handkerchief. "But they're worth a fortune. Doesn't his lordship, her husband, protest?"

"The emeralds came to her from her side of the family. So *he* has no say in the matter," Sally explained. "She can do anything she likes with them. Pawn them, sell them, give them away, or throw them in a gutter."

"Well, Sally, here we are chattering," Clarissa said, drawing on the black lace mitts and laughing Miss Gray's merry little laugh, "when I should be attending to my duties."

She had no idea, of course, what these duties might be at this hour of the morning—or at any other time, for that matter—but Sally supplied the information, as Clarissa thought she would.

"The schoolroom is on the third floor," Sally said, "next to Lady Sue's bedroom."

"Thank you, Sally."

Clarissa sailed out into the passage and then down the side stairs to the third floor. Right away she could see what Sally had meant about the place being still in a turmoil. A housemaid was hurriedly polishing a doorknob. Another was dusting the railing of the main staircase, a magnificent affair of marble, gilt, and crimson carpeting. A flunky, fully dressed except for his powdered wig, was standing on a stepladder, putting into the chandelier fresh candles, which another flunky, this one in shirtsleeves, handed to him from below. Servants, in one or another degree of undress, were hurrying hither and thither. And so busy were they that none took the least notice of Clarissa. She went into the schoolroom.

The four-year-old Lady Sue, wearing a ridiculously elaborate school dress, was sitting on the floor, a large expensive doll on her knees, and, armed with a pair of large scissors, she was savagely snipping the long golden hair from the doll's head. Clarissa, after closing the door, quietly walked up to Lady Sue, then suddenly taking her by the arm, she jerked her to her feet and over to a chair by the school table. Sitting down on the chair, Clarissa quickly laid the brat down over her knees, lifted her skirt, pulled down her drawers, and, picking up a ruler from the table, she brought it down on Lady Sue's exposed bottom. She kept whacking that bottom with the ruler until the skin turned a bright red color. Lady Sue, taken by surprise, hadn't uttered a sound at first but was by then screaming and sobbing with the pain of it.

"That's for putting little snakes into my bed and big frogs into my washstand pitcher," Clarissa said, replacing the ruler on the table, and then pulling the drawers up over the inflamed posterior and the skirt down.

"I'll tell my mamma," Lady Sue screamed, her homely face dirty and swollen with tears. "I'll tell my mamma ..."

"Oh, no, you won't," Clarissa told her very calmly. "Because if you do, I'll give you to the peacocks and they'll peck you to death."

Nobody had ever said anything like *that* about the peacocks to the four-year-old, and she stared at Clarissa with her mouth wide open, absolutely terrified.

"You hear them shrieking at night, don't you?" Clarissa went on. "That's when they're pecking a little girl to death." Clarissa spoke with great authority. "Any little girl who's been a bad little girl is brought here and thrown to the peacocks. And *I* am the person who throws that little girl to the peacocks. I'm the only person who can *do* it. So, one word out of you to anybody, and ..."

"Oh, no, please—please don't throw me to the peacocks," Lady Sue pleaded. "I ... I will never say anything about it, not to anybody, never, never!"

"And you must always obey me," Clarissa went on severely.

"Oh, yes, yes, Miss Gray. And I love you, I love you!" the shrewd brat cried enthusiastically.

"That's fine," Clarissa said. "Another thing, you must always tell *me* the truth. Understand? Now about Lady Flo. What kind of pranks does *she* play on people?" Clarissa wanted to be fore-warned, in order to have the older brat in her power, as she so obviously now had the younger one.

"Flo doesn't play pranks on anybody," Lady Sue explained eagerly, ingratiatingly. "But she likes to play with the garden-er's boy."

"With the gardener's boy, eh?" Clarissa said. "And where do they play?"

"In the woodshed, behind the kitchen garden. That's where she runs to every morning, before breakfast. And then she comes back, bringing a bunch of radishes, or maybe a stalk of fresh celery, for Mamma, and Mamma is very pleased."

"Fine," Clarissa said, and she got up.

"Mamma said we're to have our morning lessons as usual, because the Prince Regent doesn't arrive till afternoon. So what about my lesson?"

"What lesson?"

"Learning French. Every morning, it's one hour French, and the next hour it's German, and the next Italian."

The tip of the four-year-old's homely nose barely reached the top of the table, but already she wanted to be superior, with all kinds of accomplishments. It was really ridiculous!

"Go and play with your dolls." A corner of the schoolroom was stacked with a variety of expensive toys, the dolls predominating. "But if her ladyship happens to come in, you'll tell her you're having your lesson and that Miss Gray has just stepped out to bring you a glass of water."

And Clarissa hurried out, and by the side staircase descended to the ground floor. Servants seemed to be everywhere, but again her passage attracted no attention whatsoever, they were so busy putting the finishing touches to the tremendous preparations. She found a back door and went outside.

To the right, where rose the high-gabled stables, there was a great deal of activity, the splendid mounts being readied for the prospective hunt. The hounds, who had not been fed their breakfast to make them more ferocious for the eventual kill, howled with impatience, while straining on their leashes. And the mounted figure of the master huntsman, in his bright pink coat, his gilded horn slung over one shoulder, stood out among the score of grooms and stable-hands, busy under his directions.

But the kitchen garden which, enclosed with a yew hedge, stretched on the other side, was completely deserted. This was not the time for anything so prosaic as tending the vegetables. Clarissa, holding up her skirts to avoid soiling them in the dew-covered grass, hurried alongside the hedge and to the woodshed at the end. She pushed the rickety door open and there they were, the eleven-year-old Lady Flo and the gardener's boy—he couldn't be more than fourteen—stretched out on a heap of straw, enjoying themselves, in the shadows. The old shed probably was never used for any practical purposes; the two of them seemed so assured of utter privacy.

Both scrambled to their feet, and stood, wide-eyed with surprise and fear.

"Oh, Miss Gray—please don't tell Mama. Please ..." Lady Flo pleaded. Bits of straw clung to her frizzed hair, and the skirt of her elaborate school dress was badly creased. "If Lord Cavor should hear of it ..."

The vain brat wanted to be married to Lord Cavor eventually, for the sake of his money, social position, title, but she wanted to have a good time before then, and probably afterwards, too.

"I won't tell," Clarissa said, and she laughed. "For all I care, you can go on seeing your boy lover. But I'm in possession of your secret, and I'm going to hold it over you. So I'll expect you to act accordingly."

"Oh, Miss Gray, I'll do anything, anything ..." And, "I love you. I love you!" Lady Flo cried ingratiatingly, enthusiastically, just as the younger brat had done.

"Go to the schoolroom, put a couple of books on your head, and walk the floor, for two hours by the clock," Clarissa ordered.

Lady Flo went. The gardener's boy had already sneaked away. Clarissa followed a path which seemed to lead further away from the house.

The Ravisham grounds, famous for the beauty and formality of their landscaping, were all at the front of the house, but here, in the back, it was simply country, first a meadow with some cattle grazing on it, and then a copse, the path running through it. A rustle, as of someone moving in the underbrush, made Clarissa stop. And suddenly, as if grown straight out of the ground, there was a neat little old woman, a bundle of dry twigs on her back, standing before her. Clarissa at once recognized her from Sally's vivid description. Nellie Harris.

"You just follow this path," Nellie Harris said, surprisingly, "until you come to a big fir tree. Then you turn to the right, and *that* path will take you right to the church and the graveyard. Hee, hee, hee." She had a weird laugh.

Clarissa was reminded of Prickly Gil. There seemed to exist some sort of similarity between Prickly Gil, though she was just a young girl, slovenly, unwashed, and this little old woman, who was so very clean and neat. The same kind of strangeness about them, of weirdness. And didn't they both go to Kenerevy woods, which had such an evil reputation? Anyway, the rumors about Prickly Gil and Nellie Harris were the same.

"Hee, hee, hee," the little old woman laughed again, weirdly.

Then, munching with her toothless mouth, she stared at Clarissa with her sharp little eyes.

"How did you know where I was going?" Clarissa said.

"Oh, I knew, hee, hee, hee. I always know …"

Then, setting straight the fagot on her back, Nellie Harris walked past and was suddenly gone, probably diving into the underbrush to look for more firewood.

Clarissa hurried on. By following the little old woman's directions, in something like ten minutes she was within sight of the village church's spire, peeping out through the green growth around it. And in another few minutes she was standing at the low, crumbling wall which surrounded the graveyard. And outside that wall, marking the limits of the consecrated ground, and only a couple of yards from her, was a freshly made grave, the little mound of earth still bearing the marks of the spade with which the clay soil had been hurriedly pressed into the required shape. How bare it was! And around it nothing but dust-covered weeds, growing untidily, nettles, and clumps of prickly thistle. A piece of a broken-off board had been stuck at one end of the grave, for a marker, and on it was written, in black—tar, probably—just one word—"Clarissa."

What a shock it was to see her own name marking this desolate grave! And yet she had been so impatient to come, see for herself. An irresistible, almost a supernatural force had drawn her to the spot. Now, shivers ran down her spine.

She had to remind herself that it was not she, Clarissa, but Miss Gray who was buried there. And then Clarissa felt quite indignant. Miss Gray had been her friend. Aside from Lafonte, the gentle governess was the only person who had been kind to Clarissa.

She could see in the highly respected graveyard, clustered around the church, some very fine, impressive monuments. It was the fashion to erect tall, heavy monuments, of stone or marble, over the remains of the departed. The living vied among themselves in providing these expensive monuments, as they vied in possessing rich homes, elegant carriages, beautiful clothes, jewels.

Don't you worry, Miss Gray, Clarissa told her mentally. I'll have you moved to consecrated ground, not this graveyard but a better one. And I'll buy you the most expensive monument I can find. When or how I'll manage to do it, I don't know yet. But I will. Just give me time....

And Clarissa was about to turn away.

But a greater shock than seeing her own name on a grave marker was in store for her. A voice, a man's voice, which she knew so well, said:

"I knew you'd come here."

And she saw Slippery Jack, sitting astride the crumbling graveyard wall. He had probably been watching her from behind it, with great amusement, all along. He had exchanged his dandified attire for a patched jacket and plain breeches, to look like a rustic. He had come to kill her, of course. She glanced around quickly. But who would hear her call for help, it was such a lonely spot? And there she'd be found eventually, her throat slashed with the sharp little knife. She was so petrified with fear, she couldn't move.

"I knew you'd come to see how they buried you," Slippery Jack said, his handsome face alight with malicious amusement.

Of course, she had expected him to follow her, find her, sooner or later. But she had never imagined him popping up so soon.

"My good man," Clarissa said. "I'm Miss Gray, the new governess at Ravisham."

Which was just plain silly, of course. She might as well have tried pretending to Dumb Clara, the woman who bore her.

"No wonder you're fooling them all, the wonderful actress that you are!" Slippery Jack stared at her with genuine admiration. "Miss Gray is there," he pointed at the freshly made grave. "And I was here when they buried her early this morning. I and Honest Gregory, and the two gravediggers. And what's more, I formally identified the body, last night, as being Clarissa's, a cousin of mine. Oh, I was quite overcome with grief," Slippery Jack pretended to wipe away imaginary tears, and laughed. "I'm not going to kill you," he added. "There's something at Ravisham which I and Honest Gregory want very much. And you're going to get it for us."

"But ... but how could you know I'd land at Ravisham," Clarissa said, "or even that I left London?"

"You were seen and recognized, taking the stagecoach at the Rose and Crown, by Honest Gregory. You didn't see him, did you? Anyway," Slippery Jack went on, "he told me, as soon as he got back to the Waterfront Tavern. I wasn't going to start after you right away, of course. What with the constabulary on the watch and all, since Carbuncle Joe's capture. But Honest Gregory, who hates to be inactive, was planning to leave London, until things returned to normal. In his parson's garb, and with his cunning, and his acting, he'd get us both out of the city safely, I thought. And he did. He got me these clothes ... And, once outside the city limits, we caught the next stagecoach. I mean, the next after the one you left London in," Slippery Jack grinned at her, very much pleased with himself.

"And Honest Gregory, I suppose," Clarissa said, "had made it his business, as soon as he saw me outside the Rose and Crown, to find out where I was bound for?"

"Naturally. Colchester. And so there we were, sort of combining our aims, I to get you, and Honest Gregory to pull one of his neat little jobs at some great country house that might catch his fancy. But when our stagecoach stopped at the village inn here we heard the gossip about the coach's upset and that a woman, an actress, Clarissa, was killed. So we paid a visit to the local constable. Honest Gregory did the talking. I was the woman's cousin, he said. And we were taken to the shack of a morgue to see the body and it *wasn't* you. Which made me think *you* were up to something. So I pretend grief, and I say, 'yes, yes, it's she, my poor cousin, Clarissa.' And the constable is very sympathetic. Afterwards, Honest Gregory and I talked it over. From the gossips we already knew who else was in the coach at the time of the accident. Miss Gray, for one, the new governess at Ravisham. By putting two and two together, we didn't have a doubt that you had assumed her identity. Honest Gregory then persuaded me not to kill you now. 'You can always kill her later,' he said. 'Meanwhile, she can be of use to us.' So here I am," Slippery Jack said. "And what I want you to get for us is her ladyship's famous rope of emeralds."

"And how am I supposed to accomplish *that,* may I ask?" Clarissa demanded.

"You're smart. You'll think of something. And if you don't …"

"Well, I can't do it today, or tomorrow," Clarissa said. "You'll have to give me time. Besides, there's someone else who knows I'm not Miss Gray, and he's been pestering me. The postilion."

"Saw him at the inn last night," Slipper Jack said. "A young, surly fellow.… So he wants to be paid, does he?"

"I told him I have no money," Clarissa explained, "but he suggested—jewelry."

"Oh, he did, did he?" Slipper Jack frowned, sensing a competitor. "I'll take care of him, don't you worry."

Well, maybe she'd be rid of the postilion, at least.

"Now about those emeralds," Slippery Jack went on. "I'll give you three days …"

"That's impossible," Clarissa said decisively. "I don't know my way about the house yet. Make it a week."

"You expect me to hang around this hole of a village for as long as that?" Slippery Jack was very angry. "The constable here is no fool, he may get suspicious."

After some more bickering, they agreed, at last, that she would come to this very same spot, with the emeralds, Friday night, not later than midnight. Which gave her exactly five days. Slippery Jack then slipped off the low wall into the graveyard and walked away, whistling, between the headstones and the monuments. While Clarissa hurried along the path back to the house.

Inside, now that the preparations for the royal visitor had been completed, the flunkies in their resplendent silk attire, and wearing their powdered wigs, stood here and there along the corridors, immobile as statues. Everyone else had gone to put on his best clothes. Clarissa hurried up to her room. Sally was there, adjusting the newly hung drapes. A soft rug, a couple of cushioned chairs, a lamp with a gay glass shade on the little table ... The butler had kept his word.

"Now, thanks to Mr. Henderson, your room looks as nice and sweet as yourself, Miss Gray," Sally said, with great satisfaction. And she chattered on excitedly. "The Prince Regent will be here any minute now. And Mr. Brummell. Oh, I just can't wait to get a glimpse of Mr. *Brummell!*"

With Sally's help, Clarissa swiftly changed into one of Miss Gray's modest, blue-sashed, white muslin dresses. She pinned the little cameo brooch on the prim neckerchief, smoothed her hair, and patted some of the lavender cologne on the sausage-like curls dangling over her ears. Then, taking Miss Gray's little volume of poems with her to add an authentic touch to the picture of chaste virtue which her role demanded of her, she hurried down to the schoolroom, where her two young charges were waiting for her. They, too, had changed into white dresses, but of silk, and so fashionably made, and with such beautiful long sashes of pink satin! They carried large straw hats, with flapping brims, the pink velvet streamers looped over the crook of their elbows, stylishly. Not that any of it did the wearers any good! They looked more homely, more awkward than ever.

"They're coming. They're coming!" the four-year-old Lady Sue screamed, jumping up and down with excitement.

The older brat rushed to join her at the window. And Clarissa followed. What a splendid sight it was! The royal coach, preceded by the mounted guards in their red-with-gold uniforms, and surrounded by the yellow-coated outriders, all trotting briskly up the long driveway, winding between the sun-flooded, vivid green lawns. Clarissa knew that from every window the housemaids and the flunkies, cooks, kitchen helpers—all who managed to get away from their chores, in fact—not to mention the housekeeper and the butler, were watching the progress of the cavalcade, just as she was watching. The Ogre and her porridge-eating husband would be greeting the guests on the front steps. There, the coach was drawing to a halt.

"The first thing Mamma always does," Lady Flo prattled, "is persuade His Highness to admire the Ravisham grounds. So Mamma said we should go to the rose garden. And then His Highness will just *have* to say how-do-you-do to us. It's against etiquette for children to bother royalty with their presence. But if it's accidental like ... Mamma is very clever."

So downstairs they hurried, and out of the house, and into the rose garden. And in a little while, the Ogre appeared, looking very ugly, in a magnificent gown of white lace, her rope of emeralds hanging down almost to her knees, and bringing in tow proudly the Prince Regent, Mr. Brummell, and the Earl of Strasford. Lord Cavor and Mr. FitzMaurice hovered respectfully in the rear. Clarissa's young charges curtsied. And His Highness duly chucked Lady Flo under the chin, and tweaked Lady Sue's ear, without looking at them; he so hated homeliness.

"Miss Gray," the Ogre introduced Clarissa.

Clarissa curtsied very low to the Regent and he bowed politely. Then she curtsied to the Earl of Strasford. What a comical little figure the Earl was, with his painted little face, his bejeweled fan, lace handkerchief, his senile giggling. Clarissa could hardly keep herself from laughing. She had heard of him, of course, since in the Thieves' Village the Earl's wealth, his profligate habits, and his mistresses were a frequent subject of discussion. And so she even knew the name of his current mistress, Nona. Some said Nona was very uncouth, a gypsy, not even pretty....

And then Clarissa was curtsying to Mr. Brummell. There he stood, manly elegance personified, his gloves and the tall beaver hat in one hand, and with the other leaning lightly on the slim ebony cane. Just as Miss Gray had imagined it would happen. In the rose garden. The peacocks strutting proudly on the green terraces in the background. While within the rose garden a thousand blooms, opened to the sun and to the blue sky, perfumed the air with their delicious fragrance romantically.

Mr. Brummell bowed politely. Just as Miss Gray had said he would. But then he did something which the gentle governess had never expected him to do—unless, deep down in her heart, she had nursed the secret hope that he would do exactly that. He noticed her. He was actually looking at her. Clarissa could feel his suddenly attentive gaze upon her. Out of the corner of her eye she could see his handsome face lit up with a tenderly eager expression. Good heavens, Beau Brummell, of all men, to feel attracted to *me!* And then, immediately, she remembered; attracted not to her, to Clarissa, but to the person she was supposed to be, to Miss Gray.

Her ladyship, with the Regent and the other gentlemen, had left to change into hunting apparel. Mr. Brummell did not care for hunting and he stayed on in the rose garden. It was assumed, since a governess didn't count, that he remained there for the purpose of admiring nature, the scenery, a predilection he was known for.

"Lady Flo and Lady Sue," Clarissa said very kindly, "you may go and walk on the lawns."

"Oh, thank you, Miss Gray. Thank you," the two brats, each having a secret reason to be scared of her, at once piped out ingratiatingly. And, "We love you. We love you!" they cried in chorus, with shrewd enthusiasm.

And much as they would have preferred to stay to stare at Beau Brummell, the object of highest curiosity throughout the nation, away they tripped obediently.

"How they adore you," Mr. Brummell said.

"Ah," Clarissa murmured, "they're so sweet."

Sand-sprinkled paths ran between the rows of rose bushes and here and there stood a stone bench. Clarissa sat down on the one near which she and Mr. Brummell happened to be standing. Demurely, she had seated herself at the end of the bench. She arranged the skirts of her blue-sashed, modest white gown. Her hands, in the black lace mitts, lightly clasped the thin little volume of poems with its pretty cover.

Mr. Brummell, indicating the *other* end of the bench, said:

"May I, Miss Gray?"

And, on receiving her timid nod of assent, he sat down exactly *there*, at the other end, thus establishing the distance required, by good manners, between them. Of about a yard.

"But who could help adoring you?" he at once went on, quite boldly.

"Mr. Brummell, *really*, sir!"

Since even a very bad actress can blush at any proper moment, it was easy for Clarissa to blush prettily, as Miss Gray would have blushed.

Mr. Brummell, at once, was overwhelmed with remorse and apologized profusely.

"No, I insist," he again said, probably encouraged, as he was supposed to be, by her blushes, "who could help adoring you?"

"You are pleased to joke, Mr. Brummell, sir," Clarissa laughed, Miss Gray's merry little laugh.

"What a lovely laugh you have," he exclaimed. Everything about her charmed and delighted him.

"*You,* to notice *me,* a mere nobody, a poor little governess," Clarissa went on. "*You,* who are fawned upon by all the court ladies, every one of them beautiful, gorgeously attired, elegant, accomplished, rich!"

"But I dislike the court ladies," he assured her very earnestly. "They're vain, envious, ambitious, selfish, deceiving, corrupt! It's the spiritual qualities that I admire. Virtue, goodness, honesty ..."

How am I going to get those emeralds? Clarissa was thinking. The problem was starting to worry her acutely. The Ogre seemed to be always wearing her rope of emeralds. Never parted with it. Even right now, in her riding clothes, her ladyship was probably wearing it, tucked out of sight under her mannish shirt ...

"Why are you so silent, Miss Gray?"

Clarissa could feel Mr. Brummell's gaze fixed adoringly on her profile.

"Have I spoken too boldly? Or, perhaps—too soon?"

And not to frighten her any further, he quickly changed the subject, asking her what little book it was she had with her.

Clarissa, her eyes downcast, gave it to him. Both of them, of course, being very careful not to have their hands touch.

"So you love poetry, too!" Mr. Brummell said, looking extremely gratified, even deeply moved.

Mutual interests ...

Are you satisfied, Miss Gray? And I'm going to keep it up, don't you worry, Clarissa promised her.

Mr. Brummell was telling her, meanwhile, a little about himself. Then, in a few humorous words, he sketched the scene which had resulted in the Regent's sudden decision to visit Ravisham.

"So that's what people mean," Clarissa said, "when they say the *usual thing* happened?"

"That's what they mean, yes."

"It's not easy to be a friend of a royal prince, is it, Mr. Brummell?" Clarissa murmured, with a little sigh of sympathy.

"Not at all easy, no, Miss Gray. How understanding you are!"

"And is it true, Mr. Brummell, that you are being constantly watched by … by spies, employed by the Regent?"

"Quite true, Miss Gray. But spies, after all, are just ordinary people. And people generally like me. So … these spies will report in detail some trivia, such as my going into a shop to buy a neckcloth, or where I went for a drive, say. But if it's anything that may prove damaging to me in the eyes of His Highness, then they won't mention it. I know that from experience. They'll *give* their report, yes. In general terms. But they'll gloss over the main issue, drawing his attention instead to something utterly unimportant."

The gay sound of the hunting horn reached them now and again. Sometimes quite near, sometimes distant—thus giving them a vivid picture of the hunting party, galloping over the fields, jumping hedges and fences, the dogs racing on ahead, and all moving in one direction, fast upon the terrified fox.

Every afternoon the Regent went hunting. And every afternoon Clarissa sat in the rose garden with Mr. Brummell. The distance between them on the bench remained the same. Of about a yard. Nothing could be more romantic! They spoke very little. There was no need for words as far as he was concerned, she could see *that*. His glance, smile, the way he watched her with tender eagerness, spoke volumes. And Clarissa, on her part, for Miss Gray's sake, would drop her lashes, or sigh gently, or turn her head a little, in order that he might the better admire her profile.

CHAPTER ELEVEN

ND THEN, SUDDENLY, it was Thursday night, and very late, and she was in her room, waiting for the sound of the gentlemen's voices in the drinking room on the other side of the wall to cease, and for the gentlemen to be gone. Lord Cavor was there, and Mr. FitzMaurice besides the Regent, and probably Mr. Brummell. She could hear the Earl's senile giggling. Every day, on the hunting party's return, the shriveled little Earl had to be taken off his horse, more dead than alive, and carried in, and his valets had to minister to him for several hours before he could stand on his feet again. The Regent thought it a great joke.

Clarissa listened to His Highness' fat laugh, and it sounded the same as it had every night, which meant that he had again failed to win her ladyship's rope of emeralds. Clarissa would get them tonight. Yes, she would go to her ladyship's bedroom and simply take the emeralds. It was well known at the Thieves' Village that wealthy people were very careless with their jewelry. Just dropped it on the bedside table before falling asleep. Or left it on the dresser. Or the jewel box, if they took the trouble to put the valuables there, would have no lock....

The gentlemen were still there, talking and laughing. Clarissa stared at the bare part of that wall, where the crack in it was closed with the tight little wad of paper. But *that* would have to wait.

At last, the voices ceased. The gentlemen were gone. Clarissa let some twenty minutes elapse. Then she lowered the lampwick, tiptoed to the door, opened it softly, and slipped out into the passage. The strip of carpeting deadened her footsteps. All the lights were out, it was so late, and she had to grope her way in complete darkness until she reached the main staircase, where the moonlight from a faraway corridor window gleamed on the railing. Clarissa had two long flights of stairs to descend; the Ogre's bedroom was on the second floor.

Holding onto the railing, Clarissa hurried down the first flight. On the third floor, a flunky, who was supposed to be on duty there, was fast asleep in an armorial chair. She was about to hasten on down, when she suddenly saw another flunky, racing up the stairs towards her. He was fleeing from someone or something, and had lost his powdered wig in the process. And then he almost collided with her. Clarissa grabbed at his sleeve;

"What is it? What happened?"

"The ghost. It's after me." The man's face was ashen with terror. "Out of my way!"

And pushing her aside, he fled on.

The shove he gave her sent her against the marble column at the turn of the stairs, and from behind this column, concealed by it, she could look down. Then her hand went to her mouth, stifling the scream that rose in her throat. There it was—the ghost. All in white, fast-moving. Just as the butler, Mr. Henderson, had described it. Up the stairs it came, in a straight, purposeful line. It had almost reached the column behind which Clarissa stood, breathless with terror, and then it stopped.

And dim though was the slanting ray of moonlight there, Clarissa saw that the ghost had lost a slipper. A bedroom slipper. She could see the bare foot, with its large strong toes, feeling about the stair carpet for the slipper. The foot had found the slipper. Without waiting to see anything more, Clarissa turned and, picking up her skirts, ran. Well in advance of the ghost, and all the way up to the fourth floor; and then, bursting into her room, and holding the door partly open, she waited, peeping out cautiously. Didn't Mr. Henderson say that the ghost always walked the same route? Along this passage and towards the servants' stairs, where it would *disappear.*

And there it was, a shimmer of whiteness at the end of the passage, and moving swiftly nearer and nearer. Clarissa, darting out, grabbed at it with both hands, and with all her strength, and so dragged it into the room. The suddenness of her attack had made it easy. Then, at once, taking hold of the ghost's white raiment, she gave it a pull, and off came the sheet. And there stood the Ogre, in her long-sleeved, high-necked nightgown, with her hair in curlers, and her face absolutely livid with hatred.

"Now, Your Ladyship," Clarissa said, after quickly closing the door and raising the lampwick to illuminate the scene, "let's be frank for a change. You were on your way to visit your lover."

"How dare you ...!"

"The first room on the other side of the servants' stairs is always occupied by Your Ladyship's personal groom." Thanks to Sally's constant chattering, Clarissa had come to know who occupied what room throughout the huge house. "It's through the door of that room that the ghost seems to disappear. For the last fifteen years you've been assuming this ridiculous disguise in order to visit your lovers. Now, if his lordship, your husband, learns of this he might raise the legal question of Lady Sue's and Lady Flo's rights to his fortune, his title. Since they well may be bastards, sired by one or another of your grooms."

"Who—who are you?" the Ogre stuttered, her horselike face the color of chalk. "You're not Miss Gray. You couldn't be the governess. I—I'll expose you—I'll dismiss you ..."

"Oh, no, you won't," Clarissa laughed. "What you *will* do is go right back to your bedroom ... Better wear your silly disguise"—Clarissa flung her the sheet—"and bring me your rope of emeralds."

"You're insane!"

"Do as I tell you," Clarissa said. "How long will it take you? Ten, fifteen minutes? I'll expect you back in fifteen minutes, with the emeralds."

The woman then tried a ruse.

"His Highness has them," she explained. "He won them from me in a game of cards, tonight, just a few hours ago ..."

"Oh, no, he didn't!" Clarissa was certain. "Go and bring me the emeralds. And another thing. I'm going to stay here as long as it suits my purpose. Understand? And you will be very nice and sweet to me, as your silly daughters are now."

"What did you do to them?" the doting mamma was almost in tears with rage. "The way they've been behaving lately, so quiet and obedient. They're afraid of you, that's what it is! What did you do, to make them so afraid?"

Clarissa merely laughed.

"Once I have the emeralds," she said, "you can go to your lover, the groom. He's young and very handsome, somebody told me. Have your joy of him, with my compliments."

The Ogre stared at her for fully a minute. Then she put on her sheet and went out.

In less than ten minutes—so impatient her ladyship was for her lover's embraces—she was back. She threw the rope of emeralds on the table, and they rattled like so many large pebbles scattered over the surface. Then out the "ghost" hurried.

Clarissa, her face flushed with the special excitement that always surged through her veins at the sight of jewels, took up the rope of emeralds almost reverently. How each precious stone glowed and sparkled! She put them against her cheek, then slowly caressed them with her fingers. If she could only keep them, have them for her own! Instead, tomorrow night, she'd have to give them over to Slippery Jack. And then he, with Honest Gregory, would go away, back to London. And Clarissa would be rid of him, for a little time, at least.

Meanwhile, she'd have to wear them, looped several times around her neck, under her clothes. Like this ... Opening her dress, she put the emeralds on. Then, closing the dress, repinning the cameo brooch on the cambric neckerchief, she surveyed herself in the bureau mirror. Nobody could possibly guess she had them on, underneath. And at night she'd wear them to bed with her, under the nightgown.

When, the following afternoon, Clarissa as usual entered the rose garden, she saw Mr. Brummell, pacing up and down the sand-sprinkled path in a state of perceptible agitation. He hurried forward to meet her and at once began to explain. The Prince Regent had decided to go back to London, tomorrow. His fit of jealousy having spent itself, His Highness had become bored with the country pastimes. Besides, his chief interest when at Ravisham, the possibility of winning her ladyship's rope of emeralds, was gone. Strange as it might seem, her ladyship appeared at breakfast without her emeralds. She had sent them away to be pawned; she needed the money. A plausible explanation, since her porridge-eating husband never gave her any cash.

Clarissa daintily smoothed her neckerchief, her fingers feeling for the emeralds underneath.

"We'll be leaving tomorrow before noon," she heard Mr. Brummell say. "Therefore, I can no longer postpone ... That is ... If you will allow me to speak ..."

It was really amusing to see him, the great sophisticate, behaving as nervously as a schoolboy, fumbling with his gloves, stammering.

Her eyes demurely cast down:

"Speak about what, Mr. Brummell?" Clarissa said innocently. Though, of course, she knew what was coming. He was about to declare himself.

She sat down on the bench, *their* bench he called it. Mr. Brummell remained standing. He glanced around, then, boldly, he took the plunge:

"My fate has been in your hands, Miss Gray, from the first moment I saw you. Surely that must have been clear to you all along ... When a man carries an ideal of a woman in his heart, he recognizes that ideal at once. I knew you instantly."

Well, hadn't Miss Gray confided that he was her ideal of a man, even though she had never seen him?

"You understand, of course," Mr. Brummell went on, "that once united we could not remain on English soil, without His Highness inflicting his wrath on both of us. In fact, the wedding ceremony itself would have to wait until we reach Calais. We must leave Ravisham tonight, secretly, of course. The man whom people call my valet, but who is really my only friend, would procure a coach to take us to Dover, arrange passage on ship to cross the Channel. Then, Italy ... Since my personal income is very small, we'd have to live modestly, there may be even hardships ... Dear Miss Gray," he added, after a silence, "do not keep me in suspense!"

"Suppose I were to tell you," Clarissa said. "Well, it's like this. The stagecoach in which I was traveling to Ravisham overturned, and a woman was killed, an actress, Clarissa ..."

"Clarissa?" Mr. Brummell said. "But it *couldn't* be the Poet's Clarissa...."

He told her briefly about his recent meeting with the Poet. So the foolish fellow had achieved his ambition: fame, immortality, and ... no money to speak of! She wished him joy of it.

"According to what the Poet said, *his* Clarissa had a great future before her," Mr. Brummell was saying. "A woman of that caliber doesn't just die, or get killed, since she must live to fulfill her destiny."

"I believe the name Clarissa," Clarissa said quietly, "is a very common one among the theater folk."

"I suppose it is," Mr. Brummell agreed.

"Anyway," Clarissa went on, "a woman was killed. But there were two women, of about the same age, both young, in the coach at the time. This Clarissa. And Miss Gray, the governess. Now, suppose it was the governess who was killed, and that Clarissa, for reasons of her own, took her place. Try to imagine that's what happened."

"It's certainly a difficult thing to imagine," he said, smiling at her, "but, since you wish it, very well. I am imagining it."

"Then it would be Clarissa answering you, wouldn't it?" Clarissa said. "And this would be her answer: 'Thank you for the honor, Mr. Brummell, sir. But love in a cottage couldn't *possibly* appeal to me. What I want is money, plenty of it. So that I could wear luxurious clothes, and have my own equipage, and a rich house, and jewels, especially jewels ... But you can't provide me with anything like that, Mr. Brummell. For the simple reason that, once His Highness finds out—as you just told me yourself— you'll be thrown out of Court, and out of the country, to live in exile, a mere nobody, penniless, perhaps even starving ...!' That would be Clarissa's answer," Clarissa said. "And then what would *you* say, Mr. Brummell?"

"I would say, Miss Gray," he said, smiling at her tenderly, "that in the kindness of your heart, you invented this fantastic little story, to soften the blow of your refusal."

What could one do with such a man!

"And the real reason ...?" he added quietly.

"It's ... my health ... lungs ..."

Weak lungs, consumption, were very much in vogue, and were considered very romantic. One was honor-bound to forego matrimony, no matter how remote the threat of the mysterious, languishing ailment. One simply bowed to fate, and that was all there was to it. And that was how Mr. Brummell took it. He stood, his head bowed, silent.

"Of course, I don't *look* ill, yet," Clarissa hastened to explain, getting up from the bench, smoothing the skirts of the blue-sashed white dress, and patting her demure curls. "But ... the doctors said, in a few months ..."

How brave she was to speak of it so casually, said his admiring gaze.

"Since this is good-by, may I ask one question? Are my feelings fully reciprocated?"

"Miss Gray loves you."

It was the truth, and it made him happy. Modesty, naturally, prevented her from using the first person singular in admitting the fact; that's how he'd see it.

"Thank you, Miss Gray. I will always remember this rose garden."

And, breaking off one of the numerous blooms which perfumed the sunlit air, he gave it to Clarissa, just one lovely rose. She put it between the pages of Miss Gray's little book of poems and closed the pretty volume.

"Good-by, Mr. Brummell."

He bowed, then quickly walked away down the sand-sprinkled path.

After a little while, Clarissa also left the rose garden, and went into the house by a side door. Now that she had accomplished what Miss Gray would have wanted her to accomplish, she could attend to furthering her own immediate plans.

And that evening, when Sally brought her dinner on a tray, Clarissa said:

"Put it on the bureau, Sally. There's something I want you to do for me."

Clarissa was sitting at the little table, under the lamp, writing a note on a piece of stationery which she had procured from the obliging butler. Having finished the note, she read it very carefully, to make sure it was exactly right. It was short and to the point.

Miss Gray, the governess, presents her compliments, and begs the gentleman not to use the drinking room on the fourth floor between the hours of ten and eleven tonight. Miss Gray's room adjoins the drinking room, and there may be a crack in the wall.

Satisfied, Clarissa took up a second piece of stationery and copied the note on it, word for word. Then, on a third piece of stationery, she again copied the note, again word for word. Then she slipped each of the three notes into its matching envelope. And on the first envelope she wrote, "The Earl of Strasford." On the second envelope, "Lord Cavor." And on the third, "Mr. FitzMaurice."

"Now, Sally," Clarissa said. "I want you to deliver each one of these three envelopes to the gentleman it's addressed to." She showed them to Sally. "The Earl of Strasford, Lord Cavor, and Mr. FitzMaurice."

Sally repeated the names, reading them from the envelopes.

"Mind you," Clarissa said. "You must deliver them personally. Give each note right into the gentleman's hands. You know where their rooms are?"

"On the second floor, just outside the royal suite in the right wing," Sally said. "Lord Cavor's and Mr. FitzMaurice's, that is. And the Earl's is the second door *inside* the suite, because he's of the Regent's party."

"Then this is how I want you to do it," Clarissa instructed her. "In about an hour, they'll be coming out of their rooms, after dressing for dinner...."

"That's right," Sally nodded her head eagerly. "They sit down to dinner at exactly eight o'clock. And they don't leave till nine-thirty."

"What a chatterer you are, Sally," Clarissa said. "Here I am trying to make you understand how I want it done, and you keep interrupting me. Not that it's important, really...."

"Don't you worry, Miss Gray," Sally assured her, with a saucy jerk of her head. Sometimes, Sally could be very saucy indeed. "I'll be in the corridor outside their rooms just before they start coming out to go down to dinner. And I'll give the note to the gentleman it's meant for, right into his hands. And what's more," Sally added, "nobody will see me do it, either. You just give me those envelopes."

Clarissa gave them to her. The envelopes were rather small, dainty-looking, regular billets-doux.

"And as soon as they have them," Clarissa said, "you come right back and tell me."

Sally, carrying the billets-doux in such a manner that they were hidden from sight by the folds of her homespun skirt, hurried out.

Clarissa, after moving the dinner tray from the bureau to the table, sat down to eat, with a very good appetite. Excitement always gave her an appetite. And she was more than a little excited.

Would her simple little ruse work? Each of the three gentlemen would doubtless be very much surprised to receive such a note from Miss Gray, the governess, a well-bred, virtuous young lady. In fact, they would be astonished. And, somewhat bewildered, too. But—if she knew men—the mention of the crack in the wall should surely bring them hurrying to the drinking room precisely at the hour designated by her.

She had chosen that particular hour because that was when the Regent took his after-dinner nap. His Highness thus would remain ignorant of the affair. And that meant Mr. Brummell, too, since there'd be no one else to tell him the very droll story. For Mr. Brummell, as Clarissa had already learned from Sally, who had heard it from the gossips in the kitchen, was planning—pleading a headache—to keep to his room, till such time the next morning as he would take his place beside the Prince Regent in the royal coach for the return trip to London. And so, to Mr. Brummell, Miss Gray would always remain the *real* Miss Gray.

"Well?" Clarissa said, as Sally came in.

"Lord Cavor got his note, and Mr. FitzMaurice got his, and the Earl of Strasford his," Sally reported triumphantly. "How funny the shrivelled little Earl is," she at once went on, "with his bejeweled fan, and his lace handkerchief and his giggling. All that paint on his little face, and the way he reeks of perfumes … I'd hate to have him touch me. Brr …" Sally made a face.

"Never mind that," Clarissa said. "Bring me the round tin tub, the one you said I could take a bath in."

"You want me to bring it now? You're going to take a bath?"

"Bring it."

Sally again hurried out. Then she was back with the tin tub. It was only about four times as large as the porcelain bowl on the washstand, and it was shallow, besides. Taking the tub from

Sally, Clarissa placed it on the rug, not quite in the center, but closer to that wall which had the crack. Then, with Sally's help, she pushed the two cushioned chairs well to the side, so there'd be no obstruction between the crack and the tub. The table with the lamp was moved close to the bureau. Now the lamp showered its light straight and full over the tub.

"Now, a pail of hot water, and a pail of cold water," Clarissa directed.

While Sally was gone to fetch them, Clarissa moved about busily, bringing over from the washstand the bath towel, soap in its little dish, and the smaller one of the two water pitchers. As soon as Sally returned, carrying the pails, they filled the tub, mixing the hot and the cold water about evenly to produce a pleasant temperature. Obeying Clarissa's directions, Sally drew the curtains over the window. Clarissa then undressed swiftly, taking everything off, so that when she slipped the wrapper on, Sally handing it to her, there was nothing between it and her bare skin. She took all the pins out of the prim hairdo, with its smooth center parting and the demure, sausage-like curls. A single toss of her head, and her hair fell in a wild mass about her shoulders. Sally gasped at the sudden transformation:

"But ... you are *beautiful!*"

"What time is it?"

The small ormolu clock, with which among other things Mr. Henderson had refurbished her room, stood on the white mantel and it showed ten minutes to ten.

"Get me another towel, Sally."

Not that she needed it, but as soon as Sally's back was turned, Clarissa stepped over to the wall to take out the tight little wad of paper which closed the crack. The tiny opening, she saw with satisfaction, made a perfect peephole. The three gentlemen would see it instantly, since the drinking room was in darkness, while the crack shone with the light from her side of the wall. Dropping the little paper wad, she swiftly moved away—not a minute too soon. They were already there. She could hear their cautious though hurried tread. Who would be the first to reach the crack, put his eye to it: Lord Cavor? Mr. FitzMaurice? The Earl of Strasford?

"Come and help me with my bath, Sally."

And letting her wrapper slip to the floor, Clarissa, proud of the beauty of her body, of its graceful nakedness, stepped into the shallow tub. Sally, using the small pitcher, scooped the water and poured it over her, while Clarissa slowly turned around. Now she would have her back to the crack, then her side, or she'd stand facing it, one lovely arm half raised, as she leisurely soaped that armpit. The gentlemen, evidently, were taking turns at looking through the peephole, and not being very amiable about it. A muffled noise, as of a scuffle, was distinctly audible at times. One of them was breathing very hard; the plebian Mr. FitzMaurice, probably. While the aristocratic Lord Cavor's rising excitement expressed itself in a husky cough. The senile Earl giggled or moaned.

"Isn't it rather early for the gentlemen to gather in the drinking room?" the unsuspecting Sally said. "Usually it'd be after midnight … There, I just heard the Earl giggle."

Clarissa let her chatter.

Then, dropping her voice to a whisper, she said:

"Sally, don't ask any questions now. But just do what I tell you. Go and blow out the lamp, sudden-like."

Sally quickly obeyed. The room was suddenly plunged into darkness. And the three Peeping Toms were thus left at that precise point of kindled desire which demands to be satisfied, no matter at what high cost to the man's pocketbook....

Very patiently Clarissa waited for them to be gone. And Sally, though completely mystified, had enough sense to remain just as quiet. When Clarissa was certain, at last, that the drinking room was once more empty, she stepped out of the tub and over to the wall, stooped to feel with a hand for the tight little wad of paper—she remembered exactly where she had dropped it on the floor, right under the crack—then, finding the crack by the same process, she swiftly pushed the paper wad in, closing the tiny opening. She then told Sally to relight the lamp, adding, as she slipped into the wrapper, that Sally could go now; the removal of the bathing paraphernalia, the cleaning up, could be done in the morning.

And as soon as the door closed on Sally, Clarissa hurried over to the bureau, pulled out the drawer where she kept Miss Gray's satchel, and out of the satchel she took out the rope of emeralds. That's where she had concealed them, knowing that she would have to undress in Sally's presence, while Sally was delivering the notes to the three gentlemen. Now she looped the emeralds around her neck, exchanged the wrapper for the nightgown, and went to bed.

Nobody seemed to be up yet the following morning when Clarissa, wearing Miss Gray's modest, blue-sashed, white dress, and the smooth hairdo, crept softly downstairs and left the house by a side door, making her way to the front of the house, just far enough to be seen by whoever came out onto the terrace through the front door. There was some shrubbery near where she stood, but she kept herself well in view.

The first to appear was the Earl of Strasford. As a rule, he never showed himself before noon, since it took his valets a good four hours to make him look presentable: paint his little face, lace his shrivelled little body into stays, pad him here and there before getting him into his ridiculous costume of pink and blue satin besprinkled with pearls and diamonds, and then perfume him, and then put on the neat white wig to cover the hairless skull, as bare of hair as an egg. The poor senile creature must have risen with the sun, so urgent was his lust, his desire. His bejeweled fan in one hand, and the lace handkerchief in the other, he stood a moment, peering around anxiously, and then he caught sight of her and hurried over, his French-heeled slippers almost making him trip several times, he was so anxious. Already close, he suddenly stopped. For a moment he looked quite confused, bewildered. This obviously well-bred, virtuous young lady ... No, it was inconceivable! Clarissa slowly closed one eye, then opened it quickly. To put it plainly, she winked. The Earl was instantly reassured. His little eyes now ran all over her, like mice. She might as well not have had any clothing on at all!

"It was *you,* last night. It was *you* ..." he repeated over and over. "Oh, so beautiful! Oh ... Oh!" he giggled, moaned.

He got so excited, he dropped his fan. And how his stays creaked as he retrieved it!

"*Anything* ... only come," he begged. "When can you come?"

"A house, equipage, servants, *all* expenses billed to *you.*" Clarissa enumerated her demands, counting them on her fingers very calmly. "And a monthly income of------." She named a sum, higher than was customary.

But it merely inflamed his desire.

"Anything ... anything. Oh ..." He tried to take her hand. "My address in London ..."

"Everybody knows which of the residences Your Grace owns is your *unofficial* residence," Clarissa told him.

The house in which a noble or a wealthy man installed his mistress and where he spent most of his time was called his unofficial residence.

"Come tomorrow ..." the Earl urged.

"You'll hear from me," Clarissa said imperiously, catching sight of Lord Cavor, who had come out through the front door onto the terrace.

The Earl also saw him, and he instantly sneaked away through the shrubbery.

And then it was Lord Cavor, stopping suddenly within a few feet of Clarissa, with the same expression of bewilderment, disbelief on *his* face. Again Clarissa closed one eye, then opened it, in a wink. Reassured, Lord Cavor said:

"My address in London ..." and he told her. His *unofficial* residence, of course.

"A house, equipage, servants, *all* expenses billed to *you,*" Clarissa bent a finger as she enumerated each demand. "And a monthly income of-----." She named the sum.

Lord Cavor's eyes, a monocle stuck in one of them, probed her clothing. His cough was as husky with excitement as it had been last night, when he admired her through the peephole.

"Can you come tomorrow?" he asked. "Mr. FitzMaurice and I will be leaving with His Highness. In a separate coach, of course."

Were they cutting short their stay at Ravisham on her account?

"You'll hear from me," Clarissa said imperiously, catching sight of Mr. FitzMaurice, who had come out through the front door onto the terrace.

Lord Cavor instantly hurried away, also through the shrubbery, as had the Earl. It was really funny! All three men knew that they were rivals for her favors and each tried to save his face, in case he proved to be the loser, by pretending he had not been there to make her an offer.

And here was Mr. FitzMaurice now. Like the two gentlemen before him, he too had stopped, suddenly, assailed by the same doubt. Could it be the same woman actually? And again Clarissa had to wink, to reassure him. Mr. FitzMaurice then began to breathe very hard, just as he had when viewing her through the peephole.

"My address in London ..." and he told her. His *unofficial* residence, of course.

"A house, equipage, servants, *all* expenses billed to *you*," Clarissa enumerated the items on her fingers. "And a monthly income of-----." She named the sum. "And," she added, "since I'm an actress ..."

Mr. FitzMaurice breathed harder than before, with rising excitement. She had been right then, an actress was what he wanted most, since it would be more showy, more public.

"I will expect you," Clarissa went on, "to provide the money for the production of a promising play, a musical preferably, a sure hit. And, of course, to pay for the most gorgeous *costumes!*"

Mr. FitzMaurice, breathing heavily, agreed.

"Could you come tomorrow? Please ..."

"You'll hear from me," Clarissa said imperiously.

And leaving him standing there, gazing after her hungrily, almost voraciously—he was probably very virile, too much so, in fact—she hurried around to the back of the house.

But she didn't go inside. The Regent would be leaving shortly, and according to etiquette those who had had the honor of being introduced to him were expected to be on hand to bid him farewell. The Ogre would send for her to appear, everybody would be there, including the Earl, Lord Cavor, and Mr. FitzMaurice. And Clarissa considered it bad policy to have those three gentlemen see her again as the prim Miss Gray. Once, as they had just seen her, was all to the good. The contrast between Miss Gray and the woman they had looked at through the peephole acting like a dash of spice to their appetite for her. But now it would be wiser to let the *peephole* image of her, alone, and vivid, prey on their minds, increase their desire.

Besides, there was Mr. Brummell. And the real Miss Gray would certainly have avoided letting him see her again after their final irrevocable parting. It would have been much too painful for both. Yes, Clarissa's nonappearance would be understood perfectly by Mr. Brummell, and how he would appreciate the delicacy of her sensibilities!

The deserted kitchen garden, with its yew hedge, seemed like a nice place to hide in. Some gardening tools lay about and there was an overturned wheelbarrow. Clarissa sat down on it and very carefully began to consider the three splendid propositions she had just received. Any woman would have given her eyes away, as the saying went, to get just one of them! And she had three to choose from. It was very difficult to decide. Right away—yes, at once—she would order, from the most expensive dressmaker in town, her first silk gown! But what color? Crimson, perhaps. The Poet had been very definite about it....

Becoming aware suddenly, of the quiet which seemed to have settled over Ravisham, Clarissa, still undecided, got up and went into the house, and up to her room.

Sally was there.

"I've been everywhere, looking for you," Sally said, "when the Prince Regent and Mr. Brummell and the others were leaving. And that was hours ago. Where were you, Miss Gray?" Sally seemed strangely excited.

She had two pieces of news for Clarissa. The postilion had been murdered; he was found with his throat slashed, not far from the village inn. And downstairs, just arrived, and waiting for Miss Gray, was her long-lost brother—such a resemblance to the miniature on the bureau, Sally chattered, except that, of course, he's a man grown now—Captain Richard Gray.

PART THREE

PART THREE

CHAPTER TWELVE

"YOUR LONG-LOST BROTHER, Miss Gray! Think of it!" Sally prattled on excitedly. "Isn't it wonderful? Oh, how happy you must be! Of course, it's a shock, a *happy* shock, him turning up all of a sudden like that, after all these years. But, *please* don't faint, Miss Gray. Please …!"

Sally obviously took it for granted that that was what Clarissa should do, start having a faint. Clarissa, secretly, was just plain scared. Miss Gray's brother! Miss Gray's darling Richard. And now, according to Sally, Captain Richard Gray. Surely, being a brother, he would become aware of the deception immediately. The moment he set his eyes on her, on Clarissa, he would know her for the impostor she was. She could well imagine his indignation, his righteous wrath! Where *is* my sister? What has *become* of her? What have you *done* to her …? He would demand an investigation. Justice. Punishment. Deliberate impersonation was punishable by law. The culprit, if a female, branded on the left cheek with a hot iron, publicly, by the horrible executioner. Clarissa's beauty devastated, her ambitious plans ruined …

Consequently, it was easier than ever for Clarissa to feign the kind of reaction one naturally expected Miss Gray to exhibit on receiving the happy news of her long-lost brother's unexpected reappearance. She gracefully sank into a chair and closed her eyes and looked very much on the point of fainting away—her mind, actually, very busy, trying to cope with this newly arisen problem. While Sally, genuinely concerned, rushed to get the lavender cologne and a clean handkerchief from the bureau drawer. On rushing back, moistening the handkerchief with the cologne, Sally began to apply it to Clarissa's temples, and then to flap the handkerchief about Clarissa's face frantically.

"It's the suddenness of it, *that's* what it is, Miss Gray," Sally repeated over and over, while pursuing her anxious ministrations. "I guess you'd given him up for dead years ago! But there he is, very much alive, and Oh, looking so very handsome, in his uniform, and waiting for you downstairs! There, you've opened your eyes. You *do* feel better, don't you, Miss Gray?"

"My darling brother Richard," Clarissa murmured, in a behoovingly frail voice, and gazing sentimentally towards the miniature on the bureau top.

Why did you have to come back? Why didn't you perish in a shipwreck? Why weren't you devoured by the wild beasts in the African jungle?

"Like I said," Sally chattered on, very much pleased with what she thought was the result of her ministrations, "it was a shock, a *happy* shock. But now *that's* over, you're feeling very happy, aren't you, Miss Gray?"

"Ah, so happy …" Clarissa sighed, ever so gently.

Anyway, she was no longer scared. She had had time to collect her thoughts, and to realize, gradually, the significance of the fact that it was ten years since Miss Gray had seen her brother. Which meant that it was also ten years since *he* had seen *Miss Gray*. And ten years ago Miss Gray must have been a mere child, six years old, seven at the most. It was highly improbable that anyone, even a brother, could recognize the child he remembered in the grown-up young lady into whom that child had been transformed during his prolonged absence. Or be absolutely positive about the recognition. That is, if he, Captain Richard Gray, should have any doubts. And there was no earthly reason for him to entertain any doubts on the matter. At Miss Gray's boarding school, where he had probably hastened immediately on his return to native soil, he must have been informed by no lesser person than the headmistress herself—the highest possible authority—that his sister had been recently installed as a governess at Ravisham. And so, at once, he had traveled posthaste to Ravisham, eager to claim the new governess, Miss Gray, as his beloved sister. Impatient, doubtless, to clasp her in his strong arms. A purely brotherly embrace, of course. Clarissa laughed to herself.

Still ... a brother. Little childhood memories he would naturally expect her to remember. Family secrets, unimportant as they might be, which he would expect her to know of. Pitfalls, stumbling blocks, which she would have to beware of every single instant. One wrong word from her, and he would *know* ... Yes, it was a challenge. A greater, riskier challenge than she had had so far—to her ingenuity, her wits, her acting ability ...

"Oh, Sally," Clarissa said. "I'm really quite excited." And she laughed, Miss Gray's merry little laugh.

"Well, don't keep him waiting then," Sally said, very sensibly.

"Ah, but I must make myself look very nice for my darling brother Richard," Clarissa cried.

And, getting up, she hurried to the bureau mirror, to make sure that her prim hairdo was very, very smooth indeed. The long skirts of the modest white muslin dress had to be patted into smoothness, and the narrow blue sash set straight in the back. Sally helped her.

"You said he was waiting downstairs," Clarissa said. "You mean, in the hall?"

That big barn of a hall, full of drafts, and with those big, ferocious dogs probably sniffing at his boots!

"When a flunky was sent up here, to announce your brother's unexpected arrival," Sally said, "well, since you weren't in your room, Miss Gray, I had to go down and invent some explanation about your nonappearance—I had no idea *where* you got to," Sally put in reproachfully.

"I was in the kitchen garden," Clarissa said, intent on repinning the cameo brooch on the chaste neckerchief absolutely straight, "sitting on an overturned wheelbarrow."

"Now what in the world would you be doing *that* for?" Sally looked her surprise.

"I had something very important to decide, Sally. Out of the three choices offered to me, I had to pick just one. It's very difficult."

"Well, and did you decide?" Sally asked, though completely mystified.

"No, I didn't," Clarissa had to confess. "But maybe now, after I see my brother, I'll have to make a quick decision. Go on with what you were saying, Sally," Clarissa added impatiently.

"Well," Sally went on, "there was Captain Richard Gray, like the flunky told me, standing in the hall, very handsome in his blue-coated uniform ..."

"*Blue*-coated?" Clarissa said, interested in spite of herself. "So he's in the navy."

"Where else would he be, a fine-looking man like that," Sally remonstrated, "except serving under Lord Nelson? Right now, Nelson needs the best men this country has ... Anyway," Sally went on, "there was Captain Gray. And her ladyship was with him. And Lady Flo, and Lady Sue. And the three of them talking to him in a very lively fashion."

Had the Ogre dared tell him of her suspicions concerning Clarissa's identity? Or perhaps insinuate knowingly ...?

"What were they saying?" Clarissa said aloud.

"Oh, singing your praises to your brother. Her ladyship assured him that Miss Gray was a veritable treasure of a governess. And Lady Flo and Lady Sue kept crying out, 'We love her. We love her …' Anyway, after I explained, very respectfully, that you had a terrific headache and were lying down—telling a lie, in other words, I was—but that you'd be down shortly, I heard her ladyship say to Captain Gray, 'Why not wait in the gun room? You'd be interested in our famous collection of firearms, I'm sure. And when Miss Gray comes down, the two of you will meet alone, in perfect privacy, as brother and sister should after a parting of so many years. Ten years, did you say it was?' And Captain Gray said, 'Yes, ten long years.' And then her ladyship went away, taking Lady Flo and Lady Sue with her. And that's where he's waiting, in the gun room, which, as you probably know by now, Miss Gray, is just off the hall. A small room, all of stone and, instead of ordinary windows, with low iron-framed casements."

"How do I look, Sally?" Clarissa said, turning round, and meanwhile smoothing Miss Gray's black lace mitts over her wrists.

"You look very nice," Sally declared. "But you know what, Miss Gray?"

"What is it, Sally?"

"There's no family resemblance between you and Captain Gray," Sally said. "I had a good look at him, and that's what struck me right away. 'No family resemblance, none whatsoever, between the two of them, though they're brother and sister!' I said to myself," Sally declared.

"We used to look a little alike, naturally, Sally," Clarissa explained. "But don't forget that my poor brother has been knocking about all over the world. Privations, adventures, danger … It's bound to show in a man."

And Clarissa, already at the door, turned round:

"Didn't you have another piece of news, about the postilion? Murdered, was he?"

"Found with his throat slashed, he was," Sally at once began to chatter excitedly. "And the funny part of it is, the constable …"

"You'll tell me all about it later, Sally," Clarissa cut her short. "I've kept my darling brother Richard waiting long enough, as it is."

And Clarissa sailed out, into the passage, and then down the main staircase, to the ground floor, arriving in the hall in just the right degree of well-bred breathlessness and demure eagerness which the situation demanded of her role. The door into the gun room was open, and inside, standing with his back to her, was a tall, broad-shouldered man, dressed in the blue-coated uniform, the tight white breeches that went with it, none too clean, she at once noticed; dust on his tall black boots; and the black ribbon with which his dark hair was tied in the back a bit frayed. He was examining a big fierce-looking old-fashioned gun, which he had removed for the purpose from one of the glass cases that stood alongside the stone walls. At the sound of her ladylike footsteps, he turned round, looked up …

Clarissa was not at all prepared for the delicious shock the handsome face of Captain Richard Gray would have upon her. Little shivers of delight ran up and down her spine. She would have swooned, except that she was not the kind of woman to swoon at the sudden sight of a desirable male. It was really ridiculous, the way he made her feel! She was very angry with herself…. Just the same, there was no denying the simple fact that she was glad, idiotically glad, that Captain Richard Gray had neither perished in a shipwreck, nor been devoured by wild beasts in the African jungle. But that, instead, he was standing there, looking quite hale and hearty, in the shaft of sunlight as it streamed through the open casement, his strong tanned hands still holding the silly old gun, while his fine eyes gazed towards her with that daredevil smile she had come to know so well from the miniature on her bureau top. As in the miniature, a lock of his unruly hair fell over the open, well-molded forehead, which, with the rest of the handsome face, and like the hands, was nicely tanned by the man's wanderings in the faraway lands.

"My dear, dear brother!"

Daintily, she had stepped across the threshold. Without any hurry, he put the ancient gun back into its velvet-lined case, then held out his arms. And she tripped right into them.

"My dear, dear sister!"

Naturally, he clasped her to his heart. But Clarissa prudently kept her head bowed so that when the expected kiss came it was implanted right on the center parting of her smooth hairdo. From *him,* even a kiss on the cheek would have been too exciting to bear calmly. She just didn't trust herself.

"But let me look at you properly," Captain Gray cried. What a masterful voice he had! "You don't seem to realize, my dear sister, that when I left England, ten years ago, you were a mere child. And now ..."

Holding her away from him at an arm's length, he observed her. Was laughter still dancing in his eyes, or were they very serious all of a sudden? She dared not look to make sure.

"And now you're a well-bred young lady," he went on gaily. "A perfect product of that boarding school. Don't you ever really smile, or laugh loudly, or maybe weep a little? Why don't you *look* at me? Ah, I forgot," he snapped his fingers and laughed. "That boarding school again. But surely, even that dried stick of a headmistress would allow you to look at your own *brother!* Come," and stepping up very close, he put a hand under her chin and jerked her head up rather roughly. He sniffed at her hair. "What's that? Lavender?"

That foolish Sally had as good as drenched her with the hateful cologne.

"Lavender," Captain Gray went on, very seriously, "symbol of modesty, virtue, purity!"

Clarissa could feel his eyes slipping meanwhile all over her face. Scrutinizing, probing her every feature. He even lifted one of her sausage-like curls to take a good look at her throat there, just below the ear. Then, dropping the curl, he commanded:

"Now, look at me."

With a pretty flutter of her lashes, Clarissa raised her eyes and looked.

What a generous mouth he had! And the vital lips so perfectly shaped, the upper one curling slightly. And, since he was smiling again, she could see the gleam of the strong, white teeth, Strength and pride, or maybe just plain stubbornness, showed in his thrust-forward chin. The golden specks of laughter in the dark eyes made them seem amber-colored. Even his nose was pretty wonderful.

Anyway, Clarissa needed all her self-control to speak with sisterly composure:

"My darling Richard, you haven't changed so very much, really."

He had both his arms clasped about her waist now, but Clarissa, undaunted by the thrilling contact, merely leaned her back against those strong arms, and smiled sweetly.

"How do you know whether I've changed or how much?" he demanded gaily. "Surely, you can't actually *remember* how I looked ten years ago. You were a mere child then!"

"Ah, but I have your miniature."

"Oh, yes, the miniature ..." He seemed surprised for some reason. A troubled look had come into his eyes. But it lasted only an instant. "So you have it?"

"Why, who else would have it but your own loving sister?"

"Yes, of course ... Naturally ..."

That forelock of his! She had an uncontrollable desire to touch it, take it in her hand, and then wind it over a finger, very leisurely. But prudence again restrained the thrilling impulse. Maybe someday she would do exactly that. Hadn't Lafonte said that for an op ... optimist anything was possible, no matter how improbable it might seem at the moment?

"Throughout the long years that you were away, darling brother," Clarissa went on gently, "it's been my most treasured possession—the miniature, I mean. It always stands on my bureau. So that I can see it, first thing on waking up, last thing before I fall asleep."

"What devotion!" Captain Gray laughed gaily. "But then, that was always your strong point, among others. Loyalty, kindness, gentleness. Young as you were. Do you remember the little kitten you always carried around with you? Nobody could part you from it."

"Oh, such a cute little kitten!" Clarissa clasped her hands ecstatically.

"It was black, as I remember. Absolutely black."

"Black as coal! And the fur so *soft* ..."

"Unless it was white. After all, it was *your* kitten," Captain Richard Gray pointed out, smiling down at her. "You should know. And it *was* white. Yes, I'm certain now. White."

"Of course, it was white. How silly of me," Clarissa laughed, Miss Gray's merry little laugh. "The cutest little kitten in the world ... And white. White as snow."

"It's really wonderful," Captain Gray remarked, "how many shared memories the two of us have, you and I!" The circle of his arms, in which Clarissa stood, as if imprisoned, tightened. "Dear, dear sister. Dear ... Polly. Remember how I used to tease you about your first name? You so disliked it. And do you still?"

Somehow one couldn't imagine Miss Gray to have had such a stupid-sounding first name. So utterly incongruous it seemed to the gentle governess' personality. But since her brother said that that's what the name was, then that's what it was.

"Do you still dislike it, dear ... Polly?" Captain Richard Gray repeated, smiling down at Clarissa in the most brotherly fashion.

"One naturally outgrows such childish prejudices," Clarissa said sedately. "But don't you think, my darling Richard," she went on lightly, "it's time *I* asked you some questions? Weren't you supposed to come back only when you'd made your fortune? Lots and lots of money? Enough to buy back the old family home, the estate? Provide a suitable dowry for your beloved sister?"

He suddenly let go of her and laughed.

"I left England a pauper," he said. "And I've come back a pauper. That's why I never wrote...." His immense pride! "Aside from my pay, I haven't a penny to my name."

Clarissa had surmised as much. His uniform looked a trifle shabby. The boots were badly worn. On the nail-studded bench, near the door, lay his hat, a tricorn, adorned by the modest naval cockade. And even from where Clarissa stood, she could see how battered that tricorn was.

"But what about all those mines," she persisted, "the gold and diamond mines in Africa?"

He looked at her quickly.

"So you know ... I mean, you remember about *that?*"

"Why, of course, I remember. Before you left, that was all you talked about!" This particular portion of Miss Gray's confidences having remained vivid in Clarissa's mind, she could recite it almost word for word. "Naturally, I was much too young to understand, then. But you were so enthusiastic...."

"I still am," Captain Richard Gray said quietly.

And suddenly taking Clarissa by the hand, he drew her over to the open casement. In the glow of the starting-to-set sun the famous Ravisham grounds lay spread before them.

"I don't know which is more magnificent, the house itself or the grounds," Captain Gray said. "Anyway, of all the great country seats this realm can boast of, Ravisham is one of the best. And that's the kind of a place I'll own someday."

A dreamer! Just a foolish, stubborn dreamer, notwithstanding his broad shoulders, strong hands, his masterful voice, and the battered tricorn. Unless the hot climate of those outlandish places he had been knocking about in had affected his brain ...

"You see, my dear sister," Captain Gray explained very rationally, "it isn't that I never made any money. I made a lot. And I lost a lot. But some of it I have invested in those gold and diamond mines you just mentioned. Also in several plantations over in the New World, in Virginia. These ventures may end in utter failure. Probably they will. On the other hand, they may make me a very rich man, someday. Rich enough to buy a place as magnificent as Ravisham. Maybe even Ravisham itself."

The man was really demented!

"But my darling Richard," Clarissa reminded him very gently, "no one could ever *buy* Ravisham. Ravisham can be only *inherited*. Whoever inherits the Marquis of Trall's title will get Ravisham."

"There's no male issue. I looked it up in the peerage."

"You mean, the ... the present Marquis"—she had almost said "the porridge-eating husband"—"has no male issue. But there must be nephews, or cousins, even if it's a cousin forty times removed."

Captain Gray suddenly burst out laughing.

"Oh, so you were only joking," Clarissa rebuked him prettily. "What a teaser you always were, and in that you haven't changed! But tell me, how long can you stay? Since you're in service," she glanced at his uniform, "you couldn't have come unless you were given a furlough. And have you seen Lord Nelson?"

"All the women ask me that," Captain Gray laughed, hugely amused. "Every single one of them!"

Women … Probably all of them in love with him, too. And how Clarissa hated them. The forward hussies. The shameless sluts!

"Most of us sailors never get to see Lord Nelson," he explained. "It's a very big fleet. Bigger than the Spanish Armada ever was. And a marvelous sight it makes, even when the sails are down. The masts are so tall and thick. A veritable forest of masts. And when the sails are up and the whole fleet moving, it's simply breathtaking!" Captain Richard Gray grinned at his own enthusiasm.

To *think* that he could be enthusiastic while knowing, only too well, that he might be killed, felled by the enemy's bullets, or the ship blown up by Napoleon's big guns, any minute! The man was really an enigma.

"The name of the flagship, which is Lord Nelson's ship, since he's in command, is *Victory*," Captain Gray went on. "And, of course, the men on it see Nelson daily. He's very democratic. But I'm on another ship. So I've never seen him. As to my furlough," Captain Gray said, "the only reason I could get it was that Nelson is stalling for time. He's in need of supplies, especially ammunition. He can't attack until he gets it. So there the English fleet stands, at one end of a certain stretch of the Nile. And the French fleet, at the other end. Waiting. With a plain telescope we can see them and they can see us."

"But why don't the French attack first?" It seemed to Clarissa that the enemy must be very stupid.

"Because Nelson is a genius," Captain Richard Gray declared with great satisfaction. "He has made his reputation as a tricky strategist. So the French are always afraid he may have some new trick up his sleeve. They'd never dare make the first move."

There! The enemy *was* stupid.

"But why talk about the gruesome war, when I haven't even kissed my dear sister properly as yet," and, laughing, Captain Gray once again swept Clarissa into the circle of his strong arms.

"You still haven't told me how long you can stay," she reminded him, both her hands pressed against his chest to keep that handsome face of his at some distance, at least.

"Only three days."

Only ... A great deal could be found out in three days.

"You seem disappointed, dear sister." His voice and glance were full of sympathy. "But it's quite a journey from Egypt to here, and then back again. Which leaves me with a mere three days, out of my furlough, to spend with *you*. Her ladyship, by the way, has been very gracious. She gave orders to the butler to have me put up in one of the guest rooms. And she told me what a treasure of a governess Miss Gray was, and how fortunate it was that it was not Miss Gray killed in that stagecoach upset, but some other woman, a cheap little actress, Clarissa. Was that the name?"

"Yes," Clarissa said, a fingertip on one of the brass buttons which adorned his shabby uniform. And she added, in Miss Gray's most kindly manner, "The poor soul must have died instantly, her head having struck a stone."

"Why concern ourselves about *her*?" Captain Gray at once said. "Probably a very vulgar person. Deserving nothing better than a quick burial somewhere in unconsecrated ground, since she was an actress … But what *I* am interested in is what happened to your little birthmark?"

"Birthmark?" Good heavens …

"Why, yes. On your throat, just below the ear."

Fortunately, Clarissa remembered which of the cluster of sausage-like curls he had lifted; on the right side of her face. And she now put a hand to those curls.

"That's right," Captain Gray said. "Just below that ear … But I suppose," he at once went on, "there are ways and means known to the medical profession, nowadays, to get rid of such a blemish. And that headmistress of yours probably considered it as such—though it was more like a beauty spot, actually—and she had insisted it be removed. Was the process painful?"

"Not … not at all," Clarissa said. And quite reassured by his manner, she went on boldly, "And it left no mark, as you can see for yourself."

"Yes, I can see that," Captain Gray agreed very soberly.

But almost at once he laughed and, catching her completely off guard, he suddenly kissed Clarissa on the cheek, but so close to the mouth as to rob her of breath. She would have tottered, in the silliest fashion, except that she was still imprisoned in the circle of his strong arms. Then he pushed her aside. He actually *pushed* her.

"What with traveling and all, I haven't had any sleep in the last twenty-four hours," he declared. He stretched himself, yawned hugely. "So I'm going straight up to that guest room, and to bed." He picked up his battered tricorn from the bench by the door. "I will see you in the morning, dear sister. We have three whole days in which to talk to our hearts' content, remember."

And, with these words, Captain Richard Gray marched straight out of the gun room.

Since he was counted as a guest, he would be conducted by a flunky up the main staircase, but there was no sign of him as Clarissa passed it on her way to the side stairs. On reaching her room, she found Sally waiting for her with the dinner tray. Clarissa ate mechanically, her mind busy scanning the just-enacted meeting. Everything seemed to have gone off well. He had been affectionate, gay, he had laughed. In short, Captain Gray's behavior had been that of a man happily reunited, at long last, with his beloved sister. And yet ...

Somehow, Clarissa was not satisfied. Again and again she recalled every detail, examined it, analyzed it, and could find no flaw. And the next instant, something undefinable, something she couldn't put a finger on, would turn her cold with sudden fear.

Sally, as usual, was chattering away. About the postilion. Oh, yes, Clarissa remembered, with no particular interest, the postilion had been murdered. And good riddance ...

"A little knife was found not far from the body," Sally was imparting the details excitedly. "The knife with which the postilion's throat had been slashed. And the constable thinks he may trace the murderer through that knife, because it's sort of peculiar."

Not really peculiar, as for instance in shape, Clarissa knew, visualizing Slippery Jack's little knife. But peculiar in the sense that there was no other knife quite like it in all of England. Slippery Jack had bought it from a Spanish sailor. And it was the foreign make that made it quite unusual, easily recognizable.

"The constable is very angry," Sally went on, "because nothing like that had ever happened around here. And he's given a solemn oath, the constable has, that he'll find the murderer. Even if it takes him months, maybe."

"He'll never find him," Clarissa said.

Though Slippery Jack, at this very moment, was probably hanging about the village inn, right under the constable's nose, as it were. And she let Sally chatter on …

"What's that you said?" Clarissa suddenly asked, quite sharply.

"Goodness me, Miss Gray! Seeing your long-lost brother has certainly made you awful nervous. All I said was that the two strangers who were staying at the inn, one of them a parson and the other a young fellow, his friend, well, they're gone. Left, all of a sudden like, they did. Without even saying good-by to anybody. Both were liked, especially the parson.…"

Honest Gregory and Slippery Jack, frightened off by the loss of the little knife, beating it back to London, to the Thieves' Village, since it was the safest place to hide. Which meant that tomorrow night—Friday night—Slippery Jack would *not* be at the churchyard wall, waiting for her to bring him the rope of emeralds. Clarissa, under the pretense of smoothing her neckerchief, felt for the emeralds, which reposed there concealed, close against her skin. She could keep them then, for the time being, anyway! Also, even if only temporarily, she was once again free of Slippery Jack.

The knowledge helped her to steady her nerves, clear her mind, and Clarissa understood suddenly what it was that had bothered her about Captain Richard Gray. The way he had kissed her! On the mouth. Well, almost. Anyway, it was not a brother's kiss. No man would kiss his *sister* in such a fashion …

"Sally,' Clarissa said, "go and ask one of the flunkies to find out if my brother, Captain Richard Gray, is in his room. A guest room has been assigned to him … That's all I want to know, understand? Hurry now."

Sally hurried out. In something like ten minutes she was back.

"Well?"

"Captain Gray is not in his room," Sally reported. "His bag had been sent up, but Captain Gray ... Well, as a matter of fact, on coming out of the gun room he went straight out through the front door. After asking a flunky the shortest way to the village."

Yes, to make inquiries, find out everything he possibly could about that stagecoach upset and the woman who had been killed. Very discreetly, of course, since he wouldn't want to make a public scandal of something which concerned his own sister, the *real* Miss Gray. Anyhow, he would probably pay a visit to that desolate grave, on the *wrong* side of the old churchyard's crumbling wall. Ah, he would be very indignant, wrathful! Clarissa shuddered at the thought. Most likely, even at this very moment, he was already gloating with anticipation of seeing her being branded by the executioner's hot iron ...

Would he bring the constable over immediately, have her arrested at once? But didn't he say he would see her in the morning? He had been very positive about it. He had plenty of time—three days, *he* thought—in which to gather all the necessary proofs, before he'd spring the trap. She, Clarissa, at one point or another, during that tender meeting in the gun room, had made some mistake, and so bungled her role; while he, the masterful Captain Richard Gray, had played *his* role of an unsuspecting brother to perfection—that's what *he* thought. He needed those three days, and so he was going to go on pretending, in order not to scare her off, not to let her escape, before he was ready. Actually, he had betrayed himself, most flagrantly, by that passionate kiss! Only he didn't know it, the poor simpleton ...

"Sally," Clarissa said, "come back, put that tray down, and listen to what I have to say. It's very important."

Sally, who was already at the door, about to carry the tray with the emptied dinner dishes down to the kitchen, came back, put the tray on the table, and stood before her.

"Sally," Clarissa said, "how would you like being a full-time personal maid to a great lady?"

A sparkle in her honest eyes, Sally asked quickly:

"You mean you could get me a wonderful job like that Miss Gray?"

"No more scouring pots and pans, or washing vegetables, or paring potatoes in the kitchen," Clarissa went on persuasively. "No more being ordered about by the cook, the housemaids, or having your face slapped by the housekeeper. Instead, all you'll have to do is take care of the lady's beautiful gowns. Silks, satins, laces. Maybe do her hair. You're bright, Sally. You'd learn fast. And you'll wear a pretty dress. And your hands will improve in appearance ..."

Sally looked down at her homespun skirt, then at her hands, red and calloused with menial chores.

"I'd consider myself the luckiest girl in the world!" she cried. "But ... there's Pete."

It was really Pete who was indispensable to Clarissa's plans, but she only said, mildly:

"Well, don't you think he must be pretty tired of being ordered about by the head groom? Your Pete is an able, hard-working fellow. He'll be the lady's personal coachman. And he'll have plenty of underlings to order about then!"

"Wait till Pete hears that!" Sally was so excited she clapped her hands. "It sounds like a very rich household," she said shrewdly. "In London, I suppose it is. And the lady must be a very great lady indeed. Who is she, Miss Gray?"

"You'll find out," Clarissa said very calmly, "when we get there."

"We?" Sally was astonished. "You'll be going there too, you mean?"

"Yes, Sally. And we are going *tonight*. We must leave Ravisham secretly, as soon as it gets dark. Nobody must see or hear us. Now don't ask me any questions, Sally. Someday, maybe I'll tell you all about it."

"You always say that."

"Don't be saucy, Sally," Clarissa reprimanded her. And she added imperiously, "It's been all arranged."

"Well ..." Sally seemed undecided. "It does seem sort of strange. As if you're running away ... And just when your brother has come back, too." Sally's face suddenly brightened. "It's your brother, Captain Gray, who must have arranged it all. Of course! Anyway," she added, "I'd do anything to stop being a kitchenmaid."

"And Pete, naturally," Clarissa said, "is only too glad to do whatever *you* want to do."

Sally giggled happily.

"Now, Sally," Clarissa went on, "first of all, I want Pete to get something for me. But the trouble is, the thing I need is probably kept in the constable's office...."

Where else would the constable keep the property of a woman supposedly dead, killed in an accident? Unless Slippery Jack had claimed it, under the pretext of being next of kin, the Poet's valise, containing Clarissa's belongings, would surely have remained in the constable's office.

"It's not an office, really." Sally said. "Just the front parlor of the cottage where the constable lives. He's a bachelor, and the inn is only across the road, and that's where he'd be at about this time, having his supper, at the inn."

"But he'd lock up the place before leaving, wouldn't he?" The inexperienced Pete might well be caught red-handed and, since then he would be unavailable for her purposes, Clarissa was a little apprehensive.

But Sally only laughed.

"Nobody locks their doors around here. Of course, the man who works as the constable's clerk would be there, to keep an eye on things. But don't you worry, Miss Gray. Pete will think of something. He's smarter than he looks, my Pete is. Just tell me what it is you want him to get."

Clarissa described the valise. There was no lock, so all Pete had to do was to lift the metal clasps. Inside, he would find theatrical costumes. Let him thrust a hand in among them and feel for a small package, wrapped in a piece of an old newspaper. It was this small package that Clarissa needed. Pete then should bring it, in all haste, to Sally, after making sure, of course, that he had closed the valise and restored it to its original place. Much as Clarissa longed for her precious costumes and Slippery Jack's money, she dared not run the risk of exciting the constable's suspicions either by having the valise left emptied, or the valise itself spirited away. So there it would remain, probably forever …

"And as soon as Pete is back," Clarissa further ordered, "you come right up with the package—if he succeeds in getting it, that is. We don't have much time, you know, and so many preparations to be completed. So do be quick about it, Sally."

Sally hurried out. And Clarissa, getting up, went over to the window. It was already growing dark. A feeling of impending rain was in the air. Huge, tempestuous-looking clouds were gathering over Ravisham. And the thick leafage of the ancient trees rustled now and again, ominously, as if with approaching storm.

Moving away from the window, Clarissa became active. The few things she had decided to take with her would go into Miss Gray's satchel. Taking it out of a drawer, she dropped in the hairbrush and comb, the little sewing kit with its dainty pair of scissors, a few clean handkerchiefs. No sense in leaving the miniature behind, since it took up so little space. Holding it in her hand, Clarissa gazed down at the handsome features. There was that forelock again! A very high opinion you have of yourself, Captain Richard Gray! She was very, very angry with him. She was about to drop the little picture into the satchel as she had dropped the other things, just anyhow. But miniatures were supposed to be valuable, and it might get scratched.... She rummaged in the drawer for a bit of paper which the gentle governess had used to protect the likeness of her brother. There! And the miniature once again in its original wrapping, Clarissa thrust it into the satchel. The flacon with the lavender cologne, however, could remain where it stood, on the bureau top. Never again, thank goodness, would Clarissa be forced to use the dowdy scent.

But she'd have to keep on the prim white dress she was wearing, incongruous though it would be for her new role. And she'd take with her Miss Gray's short traveling cape, since the night might turn chilly with rain. Clarissa took it off the clothes hook, and laid it on a chair, together with the satchel. Then she sat down in the other chair to wait for Sally.

She knew it would be a long wait, but just as she was starting to worry, Sally came in, looking very proud and excited. Sally had in her hands the small package, wrapped in a piece of an old newspaper.

"Didn't I tell you Pete would think of something?" Sally declared. "He simply walked into the constable's office, and there was the clerk, sitting at the desk, and Pete told him the constable wanted him to come over to the inn, fast. So, of course, Pete being a local man, the clerk asks him to stay there, till he gets back. 'Glad to oblige,' Pete says. And the clerk hurries out.... The only trouble Pete had was finding the valise, since there were a lot of other unclaimed things stored there, on the shelves. But once he found it, it didn't take him a minute. And then, just as he comes out, there's the clerk, crossing the road, hurrying back. Pete slips around the corner, and then he just ran ..." Sally paused for breath.

"And where is Pete now?" Clarissa said, taking the small package from her, putting it on the chair, where lay the satchel and the traveling cape.

"I told him to wait in the passage, outside the laundry room. It's quite a distance from the kitchen, and he won't be seen. And I already had Pete take the few things he owns, and mine, too," Sally reported eagerly, "over to the coach house, and put them in the trap."

Both were evidently immensely excited by the prospect of their new jobs, since it meant bettering themselves.

"But, Sally," Clarissa said, "we can't use the trap. It's open, and if it rains, which it probably will ..."

"Yes, we'll be drenched to the skin," Sally nodded her head sagely.

There was the risk, besides, of Clarissa being seen by some chance passer-by on the highway, and the curious tale of the Ravisham governess, going somewhere at such an hour and in such weather, spread through the village ... But Clarissa didn't mention that.

"All the carriages and coaches I've seen here," she said, "are much too large and heavy. What I need is a small, closed carriage. Is there anything of that description, do you think, Sally?"

"There's only the one the housekeeper and the butler are driven to church in every Sunday."

"Then tell Pete that's the one I want," Clarissa ordered.

"I'd love to see the housekeeper's face when she finds out, come Sunday, that she has to use the trap instead," Sally said, laughing.

"And another thing," Clarissa went on, "we'll have to leave by the back road, of course." It led through the fields and, without coming too close to the village, would bring them out straight onto the London highway. "Have Pete drive up behind that old shed, at the end of the vegetable garden," Clarissa further instructed Sally. "We'll meet him there."

Sally again hurried out. Clarissa quickly put on the short traveling cape, took up the satchel. She could hear the first drops of rain knocking on the roof. Then a sudden gust of wind closed the window with a bang. Sally came in, wearing some kind of a short coat, badly worn.

"You can carry this," Clarissa gave her the newspaper-wrapped small package. "Now don't drop it."

"Why should I drop it?" Sally said, with a pert jerk of her head, as was her habit.

"Shh ..."

"Shall I put the lamp out?" Sally asked, in a whisper now.

"No," Clarissa decided. "Leave it."

A light in the room would give the impression that its occupant was in it. And by the time the lamp went out, for lack of oil, she would be several miles away. Clarissa gave a last glance around.

"I see you left no note, for her ladyship, I mean," Sally whispered. She had evidently expected to see a note pinned on the bed pillow. "Some kind of explanation ..."

"I'm leaving that to Captain Richard Gray," Clarissa said rather grimly.

Let him!

"And now, Sally ..."

Clarissa tiptoed to the door, opened it, let Sally through first, and softly closed the door behind them. Very, very quietly they made their way to the back stairs, the servants' stairs. Then crept down the four long flights, and into a dark passage. There they had to stop. From the direction of the kitchen, all aclatter at this hour with the dinner preparations, someone was walking along the long, well-lighted corridor, no further from where they stood than a half a dozen yards. And then they saw a flunky, resplendent in his silk attire, and with a big powdered wig on his head, go by majestically, bearing aloft an enormous silver-covered dish.

Once he was well out of sight, Clarissa gave Sally a little push to hurry on, show the way. After crossing the corridor, they had to traverse several dark passages until, at last, a door was reached in the back of the house. Outside it was just starting to rain harder, and a streak of lightning suddenly zigzagged across the sky. Then a tremendous clap of thunder shook the earth under their feet. Sally squealed.

"Don't be silly!" Clarissa hissed.

And, grabbing Sally by the hand, she pulled her on, against the pressure of the wind. The nearby treetops were swaying madly in the forceful gusts. The footpath, which ran alongside the vegetable garden, was still dry, however, and Clarissa moved on swiftly, making Sally precede her by a series of impatient pushes and prods. Between the occasional flashes of lightning, the night was black as pitch, and the outlines of the old shed, at the path's end, were barely discernible. But there it was. And just behind it stood the small closed carriage, with Pete, all bundled up against the wet, on the box. Just as Clarissa, jerking the carriage door open, got in, followed by Sally, the rain suddenly came down in torrents.

"Goodness gracious!" Sally expostulated, hastily pulling the door shut.

The small carriage was already in motion. With the rain lashing the windows, it was very snug inside. Sally hadn't dropped the package, after all. There it was, the newspaper wrapping just a little damp. Clarissa placed it beside her on the seat. But the satchel she kept in her lap. She draped the traveling cape closer about her, and leaned against the comfortable cushions. But they were still within the confines of Ravisham. Only when she knew, by the accelerated pace, that they had come out onto the highway, could she really relax. She was leaving Ravisham! But it was useless to try to get a last glimpse of it; nothing could be seen through the tumultuous downpour.

Oh, well … And she composed herself for sleep. She *had* to have a good night's sleep. To look her very best in the morning. The dawn would wake her long before they reached London, and she would have plenty of time to prepare herself, in every way, for her new role.

CHAPTER THIRTEEN

S O SOUND WAS Clarissa's beauty sleep, however, that when she awoke, marvelously refreshed, the city of London was already well in sight—an impressive jumble of rooftops, with the spires and towers rising into the cobalt-blue sky, and the bridges that spanned the river Thames glistening in the sunlight.

The small, enclosed carriage, moving along at a brisk pace, had just reached the tip of a little green hill, and Sally was drawing her head in from out the window after bidding Pete, on his driver's box outside, a cheery good morning.

Clarissa sat up, threw off the traveling cape, and at once began to get ready. First—the emeralds. Since from now on, in keeping with her new role, her neck and breasts would always be generously exposed, the rope of emeralds had to be concealed elsewhere instead of on her own person.

"Sally," Clarissa said, "turn around. And yes, better close your eyes, tight."

Sally obeyed.

Clarissa unpinned the cameo brooch which held the neckerchief so primly together at her throat, slipped the emerald rope over her head, and dropped it into the satchel.

"You can turn round now, Sally."

Before snapping the satchel shut, Clarissa took out the little sewing kit with its dainty pair of scissors. Certain drastic changes had to be made in the dress she was wearing—Miss Gray's modest white muslin. Even without the neckerchief, which Clarissa now pulled off, tossing it aside impatiently, the gown was disgustingly unrevealing at the neckline. Manipulating the scissors quickly, dexterously, Clarissa began to cut it down, snipping the unwanted material away, until her breasts were half-bared. This accomplished, she made use of the insipid blue sash by arranging it in quite a different manner. Very tight, and high under the breasts, so that their roundness and firmness appeared to be pushed out invitingly by the bodice, now extremely décolleté.

There was nothing she could do with the skirt, which was all *wrong* ...! But at least it was long enough to make her look taller than she really was and full enough to billow enticingly when she moved. And there was the petticoat. Wonderful possibilities in a petticoat. That is, for a woman who *knew* how to handle this provocative piece of feminine apparel ...

But those ugly narrow sleeves!

"Take the scissors, Sally," Clarissa ordered, handing her the scissors, "and cut off the sleeves. Right here, at the shoulder. Go on, don't be afraid. Cut!"

Sally, though amazed, mystified, gloomily disapproving, started to cut. First she snipped off one sleeve, then the other. And now Clarissa, raising her lovely bare arms, hastily removed all the pins from her smooth hairdo, throwing them out the window by the handful. That particular stretch of the London highway was suddenly strewn with hairpins ... Her abundant hair rippling down to her shoulders in lustrous waves and silky ringlets, Clarissa at last opened the small, newspaper-wrapped package. It was her make-up, of course. When packing her "costumes" into the Poet's valise, back in the Poet's garret, she had carefully gathered together the few items of her precious make-up and had wrapped them in this scrap of an old newspaper, so that the costumes wouldn't get smeared inadvertently, and here were these items, intact. The box of homemade powder, rouge in its crude little container, bits of charcoal for darkening the eyes, the Green Perfume—what remained of it—in its peculiar tiny flacon, and the piece of a broken mirror.

"Hold it for me, Sally."

And, Sally holding the mirror, Clarissa briskly rouged her cheeks, applied powder, reddened her lips, drew the charcoal over her eyelids. The *tiniest* drop of Green Perfume behind each ear and in the hollow of her breasts ...

"I hope you know what you're doing," was all Sally said, her honest eyes full of doubt, as she sniffed at the lusty scent suspiciously.

Clarissa laughed.

"How do I look?"

"You look like a harlot," Sally told her bluntly. "A beautiful and radiant harlot," she added grudgingly.

"*Courtesan* is a politer word, Sally," Clarissa pointed out.

Swiftly wrapping the make-up into a package, she again entrusted it to Sally's keeping. The snipped-off sleeves, the scattered-about shreds of snipped-off muslin were swooped up, thrust under the seat cushion, together with the discarded neckerchief. The poor little cameo brooch went into the satchel. All this in sudden haste and excitement. For they had already entered the colorful city, the wheels rumbling over the cobbles of the narrow, crooked streets. The noise, the bustle, the cries of old London were all about them. Sunshine there was, and sudden patches of black shadows, too, cast by the overhanging upper stories of the crowded dark houses. From a steeple, somewhere nearby, the chimes rang out: eleven o'clock. Which explained why only the wagons and carts were abroad. A gentleman's carriage was almost never seen until after noon. The nobility and the wealthy would now be at their toilette, a complicated ceremony of being dressed for the day, while sipping hot chocolate brought in by a pretty maid in silk cap and gown, or a valet in brilliant livery.

"Tell Pete," Clarissa instructed Sally, "to keep straight on till he catches sight of a gilded spire, the Prince Regent's palace. It serves as a sort of landmark, that gold spire," she explained. "Nobody could possibly miss it! As soon as Pete sees it," Clarissa went on, "he must start watching the street signs for the one that says Grosvenor Square. He's to turn into it, and just drive on. I'll tell him where to stop."

Sally put her head out the window and, raising her voice, relayed the order.

Quite soon, the din of the streets grew more subdued. Then all sounds seemed to cease. They had entered the aristocratic Grosvenor Square.

"Goodness gracious!" Sally ejaculated. "What fabulous mansions! And one bigger than another …"

"Tell Pete, the one with the portico of marble columns. That one. That's the one," Clarissa, remarkably cool, pointed it out to Sally.

Sally again relayed the order.

In a few seconds the small, enclosed carriage would come to a stop … Born and bred in the Thieves' Village, the ownership of every one of the great mansions was no secret to Clarissa. And how often, in her brief shabby skirt and torn blouse, she used to loiter hereabouts at night, looking up at the brightly lighted windows to catch a glimpse of the bejeweled, beautifully gowned women, the richly attired indolent men. And now she'd be actually entering such a mansion.

"Now, Sally," Clarissa said, "you're coming with me. And no matter what happens, you just stay as near me as possible. Understand?"

The carriage had stopped. Clarissa jumped out, and ran up the steps. Immediately, a resplendent flunky appeared, and tried to bar her way. But with a great presence of mind, Clarissa simply walked on, very fast. The flunky, astounded, turned, followed her inside hastily. And Sally slipped in after him.

"His Grace, the Earl of Strasford, is expecting me," Clarissa proclaimed boldly, standing in the middle of the imposing entrance hall, while a dozen flunkies, including the one who had failed to stop her, stood about, dumfounded, gaping. "Announce me!"

Clarissa purposely spoke in a very loud voice. A magnificent stairway, carpeted with red velvet, led to the second-floor landing, which ran all around like a narrow balcony. And in one of the rooms there, on that floor, the senile diminutive Earl was probably busy at his toilette, was being put into his ridiculous costume of pink and blue satin by his valets. If she made enough noise, created a commotion, the sounds of it all might reach his ears, arouse his curiosity. Senile men, as a rule, were full of petty curiosity.

"Announce me! Well, didn't you hear what I said? Have you lost your wits, fellow?"

A flunky, more somberly dressed than the others, of gigantic stature, and wearing a gold chain about his neck—the major-domo—stepped forward now. Clarissa turned upon him.

"Announce me," she shouted. "You fool!" She stamped her foot. "Lout!"

A thin, angular woman suddenly appeared on the landing above, near the top of the stairs. Though it was close to noon, she still had her nightgown on and over it she had flung some kind of a wrapper, in a hurry. Her long black hair, very coarse, hung about her olive-skinned face in slatternly disorder. That would be Nona, the Earl's current mistress, who was said to be a gypsy. Instantly, at sight of Clarissa standing down below in all the radiance of her young and vital beauty, the gypsy woman sensed potential competition, a danger, a menace to her own supremacy. Furious, the olive color of her face greenish with fear, and a bony hand clutching at the stair rail, she screamed to the major-domo:

"Throw her out! Throw her out, I tell you!"

Clarissa laughed, her arms akimbo.

"We'll see *who* will throw *whom* out!"

The gypsy woman wailed piercingly. Then, quivering all over with rage, stumbling in her nightgown, and again screaming, "Throw her out! Throw her out, I tell you!" she came running down the stairs.

On the landing, several flunkies appeared. And then the Earl of Strasford himself. He had not quite finished his complicated toilette and was wearing only the satin breeches and the silk shirt, trimmed lavishly, ridiculously, with lace. But his little face had been carefully powdered, rouged, lipsticked, and the neat white wig set securely in place. His bejeweled fan in one hand, a lace handkerchief in the other, he peered over the banisters down at Clarissa and suddenly gave a little squeal of senile delight.

"It's *you!*" he cried. "So you have come!"

Supported on either side by a flunky, he descended the magnificent stairway. Then, walking mincingly on his French heels, he approached Clarissa and stood very close.

"You ... You!" he repeated, his little eyes running over her neck and breasts, exposed by the bodice, over her bare arms, like mice.

Giggling, all out of breath with excitement, he collapsed into a cushioned chair.

"Yes," Clarissa said, standing before him, her head high. "I have come. But I'm going right out again, I promise you, unless this ... this creature"—she stretched an arm out quickly, to point with an accusing finger at the gypsy woman—"leaves immediately!"

The scrawny gypsy, her face ashen with fear, was at once beside the Earl's chair, taking his tiny wrinkled hand, drawing it shamelessly inside her nightgown, and baby-talking to him in the most disgusting fashion.

"My big strong Bowwow won't let his little Nona be insulted, will he? Remember how little Nona always makes her Bowwow happy. Oh, so happy...."

To keep her hold on the aged Earl, the slut doubtless practiced some kind of perversion. Such was the rumor, anyway. And Clarissa now was ready to believe it.

"*Bowwow?*" Clarissa said, raising her eyebrows delicately.

"She calls me that," the Earl explained, "because I remind her of a very large, ferocious dog."

So the gypsy woman thought herself very clever, did she, by thus flattering the poor man's vanity, so obviously, so grossly.

"But what a coarse name to give Your Grace!" Clarissa exclaimed. She seemed indignant.

"Coarse?" the Earl repeated anxiously. "Do you really think so?"

"I certainly do," Clarissa said very decidedly. "You, who are so petite, so fragile, so ... so *exquisite*. Like a French figurine of the finest porcelain! *I* am going to call you my little Peewee."

The childishly obscene implication of the word delighted the Earl's senile sense of humor, as Clarissa knew it would.

"Hee, hee, hee ..." And quite overcome with giggling, he moaned, "Oh ... oh ..." He flirted with his fan, flapped his lace handkerchief about.

"My little Peewee," Clarissa cooed. And coming close to the side of his chair, she placed a fingertip behind the Earl's ear, and drew the fingertip up and down, lightly, tickling him there.

"Oh ... oh ..." And squealing, the Earl collapsed in his chair.

"You slut!" the gypsy woman shrieked.

And she threw herself at Clarissa, her clawlike hands outstretched for Clarissa's hair. But Clarissa was ready for her. By quickly jerking a knee up, she caught the desperate woman right in the stomach.

"Ouch!"

Dazed with pain, the once-powerful mistress of the Earl of Strasford's unofficial establishment sank to the floor, groaning, babbling lugubriously. Clarissa at once grabbed at her hair, twisting it, long and coarse as a horse's tail, around her own wrist, and so pulled the miserable woman swiftly along, and to the front door. It was already held open by the gigantic major-domo, who, being experienced in such situations, had guessed by now the Earl's secret preference.

Clarissa pushed the gypsy woman out. Then, slapping the palms of her hands one against the other smartly, as much as to say, That's that! she sailed imperiously back to the Earl's chair.

"Oh dear ... Oh dear," he murmured. "Is she really gone?"

His relief was obvious.

The strange ways of the gypsy woman had happened to catch his fancy, but he had grown tired of her ... And now she was banging with her fists on the door, while screaming curses, threats, demanding her things, her clothes.

"Making a scene right on my own doorstep, and with only a nightgown on and that wrapper.... The neighbors are probably looking," the Earl confided nervously. "What will people think of me? Do give her *something*," he implored.

"Very well," Clarissa said.

And she turned to the major-domo.

"Have one of the footmen throw a few of her things in a bag and take the bag out to her, around through the back door. And he's to tell her that if she persists in annoying His Grace constables will be summoned, and she will be arrested for breaking the peace."

"Yes, madam," the major-domo said respectfully, and he bowed very low.

"And another thing," Clarissa added. "How many footmen are there in all?" Since the flunkies would be now *her* flunkies, she preferred to call them "footmen."

"Twenty-five in all, madam."

"I will need at least four more," Clarissa declared calmly. Not that she really needed them, but simply to make an impression, assert herself.

"Yes, madam," the major-domo's bow was lower, more respectful than before.

Another sign of her triumph was the fact that several footmen, as Clarissa was quick to notice, had already managed to slip away, in order to spread the news of the change in the Earl's establishment among the tradesmen. To notify the drapers, dressmakers, milliners, perfumers, jewelers, upholsterers, carriage designers. The installation of a new mistress meant new orders in every line of merchandise. In no time now, all these people would be pouring into the house.

Meanwhile, the exciting tidings had reached the servant staff and, from behind the various doors around, heads peeped out: housemen, kitchen help, valets, chefs, grooms, stable-boys, all eager to get a look at the new mistress. Not a single woman among them. That was always the rule in an "unofficial residence." Only menservants.

"Shoo!" Clarissa said.

And all the curious heads instantly disappeared.

The pounding on the front door had ceased, the gypsy woman, scared by the promise of constables, having sneaked away, probably sniveling with rage and horrible disappointment. But where was Sally?

Sally had found herself a seat in a faraway corner. And now, at Clarissa's nod, she came over.

"My little Peewee," Clarissa said. "This is Sally. My personal maid."

Naturally, a mistress was expected to have her maid. As to the gypsy woman's own maid, the frightened creature, without waiting to be thrown out, had doubtless fled the place at the first rumor of her employer's sudden downfall, in order to escape a thrashing from the servants, who bore her many a grudge....

Sally, trying not to laugh—the senile little Earl was so *funny!*—bobbed him a curtsy, while he murmured, vaguely polite:

"Ah, yes ... yes. Nice girl ... nice."

"Sally," Clarissa said, "you can go and tell Pete now to drive straight into the stables, and then go into the kitchen and make himself at home. Then come back. I may need you."

"All right," Sally said.

"Now, Sally," Clarissa at once corrected her, "let's try to be a little more chic about it. From now on, unless we're alone, you must say 'madam' to me. Let me see how well you can do it. Say, 'Yes, madam.' "

"Humph!" Sally said. Then she added grudgingly, "Yes, madam."

"That's better!"

"But where *is* the great lady," Sally whispered, tugging at Clarissa's skirt and so drawing her a trifle aside, "the one Pete and I will be working for?"

"You silly child," Clarissa laughed. "I'm that great lady, naturally."

"Humph!" Sally again said, her nose in the air.

Then off she went to relay Clarissa's order to Pete.

"But I don't even know your name," the Earl of Strasford confided, taking Clarissa's hand, fondling it.

"It's Clarissa."

"Clarissa! But I've heard that name mentioned before ... Why, of course, by Mr. Brummell. Who is the Poet's patron. *The Poet's* Clarissa?"

"The very same one, yes."

"The famous new beauty!" Highly excited, the Earl imprinted a series of drooling kisses along her arm, from the wrist to the elbow. "How peeved the Duke of Cumberland will be! Every time a new beauty appears in London, the Duke of Cumberland gets her first. But now *I* will be the first to have *you*. I can't wait to show you off." He giggled delightedly. "I will give a ball, of course. How soon can you be ready, my dear?"

Without giving it much thought, Clarissa said negligently:

"Oh, in about a week."

"Then I will have the invitations sent out tonight," the Earl announced. "Everybody will come! The Prince Regent never misses the presentation of a new mistress. And even Mr. Brummell, though he's been looking rather sad lately, nobody knows why, will be curious, I'm sure, to see his Poet's Clarissa in the flesh!"

Tired out with talking, with excitement, the Earl of Strasford, breathless, sank back in his chair and rested briefly. Then, a look of cunning on his painted little face, and with a glance around to ascertain that the flunkies standing about were out of earshot, he pulled at Clarissa's arm, forcing her to bend down, close, and confided, surprisingly:

"So you are *not* Miss Gray."

"No, of course not."

"And you never were Miss Gray."

"Of course not," Clarissa again said.

"Fooling them all at Ravisham, fooling her ladyship." He giggled maliciously. "But," the Earl went on, "when I watched you taking your bath through that peephole, right away I *knew* you *couldn't* be Miss Gray."

And looking highly pleased with himself, with his acumen, he began to flirt with his bejeweled fan, flap his lace handkerchief about.

"I'm glad *that's* settled," he then confided, but very seriously now, anxiously. "Because if you were Miss Gray, there'd be the family to reckon with."

"Family? What family?"

"A proper young lady like Miss Gray always has a family. A father, an uncle, or maybe a brother, popping out, all of a sudden, to make trouble. Demand satisfaction for seducing the girl. Call me to a duel … Imagine! Why, I'd be killed instantly.… Haven't used my pistols, my sword, for years."

Clarissa found it hard not to laugh. The ridiculous, dried-up little man was actually shaking with fear.

"But I'm Clarissa," she said.

"Oh, yes … yes. Of course. Thank you for reminding me, my dear." He pressed her hand gratefully. And since Clarissa was still bending over him, very close, pretending eager solicitude, he took a peek inside her bodice. "Dear me …" he squealed. "And how exciting you smell," sniffing at the Green Perfume avidly. "Really … My head's going round.…"

"The tradespeople, madam," the gigantic major-domo announced.

And he flung the front door open wide, letting them in.

There was a regular swarm. With ingratiating bows, keeping their greedy eyes lowered in simulated humility, they surrounded Clarissa, and jostling each other for a place of vantage, they began to display their merchandise. Soft jewel-colored velvets, glistening silks and satins, shimmering brocades, gauzes fine as cobwebs and as transparent as glass. Some of the rich stuffs had been brought in whole bolts, and these the drapers' green-aproned apprentices unrolled with a practiced flourish. While the shorter lengths of material—more precious, more rare, more expensive—were spread out knowingly by the dressmakers' young girl helpers.

Proffered for inspection were feathers of brilliant hues, or gold and silver braid, gold lace; various perfumes in their little sample flacons; lotions, pomades, lip salve made by famous experts and subtly scented; all sorts of trinkets, each worth a laborer's pay for a year's back-breaking drudgery. And then there was jewelry: rings, pendants, bracelets, necklaces, pins—rubies, amethysts, sapphires, emeralds, diamonds, all sparkling, glowing …

With someone holding a hand mirror, Clarissa, inwardly terribly excited, but outwardly perfectly calm, tried on a diamond necklace; just laying it briefly against her petal-smooth skin, then giving it back with a pretty pretense of capricious indecision. Everybody clamored for her attention. "Please have the kindness, madam, to feel the texture of this beautiful material," a draper pleaded. "And the primrose-yellow color, madam! How becoming it is to Madam's hair and complexion!"

"Try on this glorious feather, madam," another implored. "Nothing so imparts stateliness to a woman as a feather! Though, of course, madam is naturally stately … That goes without saying. Still, to enhance madam's loveliness …"

Clarissa tried a long, curled plume against her hair. Gasps of admiration punctuated the din around her. With the help of a perspiring dressmaker, she held a length of gleaming violet satin against her generously exposed breasts. "How becoming to madam! Madam will be a sensation!" Every time she tried something on, there was awed admiration. She could trust no one.

Very carefully, shrewdly, guided by nothing but her own inborn taste, she proceeded to make her choice of materials, explained patiently how she wanted the dress or cloak or bonnet made, stating precisely every detail of trimming and ornament. It all took a long time. At last, a definite selection was made.

Of the countless things she had ordered there were four dresses which she especially liked. In her mind's eye she saw them very clearly. A so-called carriage dress of pale blond brocade, like Princess Caroline's gown, and fashioned in a similar style. A theater dress of brilliant green velvet, with slashes of purple silk in the short sleeves, and the daringly low-cut bodice trimmed with flounces of lace. Then, the dress which she would wear when accompanying the Earl to such places of entertainment as gaming houses, cockfights, bear baitings, and the intimate, exclusive brothels that were currently in vogue. Innocently azure in tint, but of the sheerest gauze, that particular dress promised to be almost insolent in its boldness. Clarissa laughed to herself.... And then, equally important, there was the crimson ballgown, of very stiff silk. Remembering the Poet's advice, she had made her choice of that particular color with special care—a brilliant, luscious crimson.

Yards and yards of this crimson silk were to go into the making of the skirt, she once again reminded them all. They looked dubious.

"We beg to contradict madam ... A full skirt ... Whoever heard of such a thing? Completely out of fashion!"

"I know what I want," Clarissa told them.

They tried to persuade her to forego the strange notion. A big, full skirt! When everybody wanted their skirts made narrow, no more than five yards wide, that is, around the hem. They had madam's interests at heart, the future of their businesses depended on madam's success; therefore ... "madam would be making a terrible mistake. So unfashionable ..."

"But I'll *make* it the fashion! You stupid people," Clarissa shouted at them. "Don't you understand? Once I wear it, it will become the *rage!*"

And, willy-nilly, they had to acquiesce with her demand.

"Everything must be finished within a week," Clarissa further commanded. "And delivered Saturday at noon, precisely!"

They were astounded. Then they laughed. Madam was joking, of course. For an enormous order like that only a little week! Impossible! Did madam realize how many thousands and thousands of little stitches would have to be set, one by one, to make the seams in the skirt of that crimson ballgown *alone?* The sewing girls would go blind....

"That's the dress I'm going to wear at the ball," Clarissa pointed out.

Her positive manner seemed to indicate that the date for this momentous event had been already set, and the invitations sent out and accepted.

Well, she had told the Earl she'd be ready within a week, and she wanted him to know, right at the start, that if she said something she really *meant* it. Or he might get the idea that she was just a silly little scatterbrain, something any man could shove around. It had been very foolish of her, of course, to promise any such thing. But there it was ...

"Considering the size of the order, madam," a dressmaker said, "the time limit is really fantastic. But ..."

The forthcoming ball was as important to all these people as it was to Clarissa. If Clarissa was a success, they would have not only her patronage, but the patronage of all the rich women, some of them quite respectable wives, or even titled ladies, who would be anxious then to ape her in everything she did.

"We'll have to hire extra sewing girls, a hundred maybe...."

"Hire two hundred sewing girls. Hire three hundred...." Clarissa waved a hand airily. She had won a point very important to her.

And, turning to the jeweler, she said:

"Let me see that necklace again."

Besides the necklace, Clarissa selected a pair of diamond earrings to match, some rings, and a few bracelets.

And now she had to attend to the upholsterers, and to the men who made drapes, and so forth ... The talk and the excitement of all the people around her was starting to give her a headache, and she was terribly hungry besides, having had nothing to eat since the previous night. But, the major-domo leading the way, and with the Earl mincing on his French heels by her side, and the trades-men following in a crowd, Clarissa had to make a long tour of the luxurious ground-floor rooms. Sometimes she would stop, and everybody instantly standing still, she would say:

"Yellow satin here ..."

"Wall panels, too, madam? Besides the drapes?" The anxious upholsterer had his little slate and the crayon ready, to put it all down.

"The wall panels also, naturally. And plenty of gilded mirrors ..."

Try as she might, she could see no possibilities for improve-ment. Everything was so magnificent. But it was evidently expected of her to make some changes in the place. They all hung on her every word.

And so she moved from room to room, the white muslin skirts billowing with the swing of her lovely swift walk. There are women who can make even a cheap cotton petticoat seem to rustle with all the allure of rich silk. And Clarissa was such a woman.

The diminutive Earl, trying to keep pace with her notwith-standing his high heels, giggled delightedly.

"Already she's spending my money as if it were water," he exclaimed. "One might think she was a royal mistress, instead of having a mere Earl of the Realm for her protector."

He was immensely flattered.

The major-domo now led the way back to the entrance hall, and then upstairs to the second-floor landing and into the bedroom, which had been occupied by the gypsy woman only a few short hours ago, though now it was already Clarissa's. The slatternly habits of Clarissa's predecessor had left their chaotic imprints all over the place. The satin hangings of the big bed were spotted, and torn. One shoe, its buckle broken, lay on the rug, while feminine garments were strewn about on chairs and the pretty chaise longue.

Sally had shrewdly made friends with the flunkies, who had shown her the mistress' room, and was already busy trying to bring order out of chaos.

"With your permission, madam," Sally said very importantly, bobbing a curtsy to Clarissa, and managing to keep a straight face while doing it, too, "I will give the creature's rags to the footmen to sell. They told me they know a dealer in secondhand clothing. She's a very old woman who goes by the name of Granny, and she resells the clothes to the prostitutes, which is exactly what the things deserve, seeing to whom they had belonged!"

Granny ... It was certainly a small world. But Sally, who naturally had no inkling that Clarissa might have had acquain-tance with any such a harridan as Granny, went about her busi-ness of picking up after the gypsy woman quite unperturbed. One after another she threw belongings to a flunky, who carried them away, in an untidy heap. The flunkies, as was the rule, were paid a certain percentage of any monetary business transacted by the mistress. Those who had been first in notifying the trades-men, for instance, would receive from those worthies at least ten, maybe fifteen percent of the sum of all orders. A mistress thus was a source of ceaseless profit to the servants of an "unofficial residence."

"And you should see the *filth* in the kitchens," Sally whispered. Cockroaches everywhere."

"Sally, I'm absolutely famished," Clarissa whispered back.

Sally's small honest face was at once full of sympathy.

"You poor thing! Why, of course, you haven't had any break-fast. While Pete is still putting it away, down in the kitchen ... And I had a hot mutton pie and several small beers and oysters."

And stepping over to the Earl, bobbing him a perfunctory curtsy, Sally said, with just a shade of justifiable indignation in her brazen little voice:

"Begging Your Grace's permission ... But madam should eat now. Madam is somewhat fatigued ..."

"Of course ... of course ..."

There was instant commotion. The tradesmen, looking quite crestfallen at the sudden dismissal, began to leave in a crowd. They were told to come tomorrow.

"But *you* I won't need," Clarissa said to the group of shoe-makers, the best in London. "I have a man who always makes my shoes."

"And who may *that* be?" they retorted, angry, disdainful.

"A Mr. Davey."

"Never heard of him!"

"Well, Mr. Davey will be making all my shoes," Clarissa told them. "And *that* will make him famous!"

They went, grumbling.

But there was still the carriage designer; an elderly indi-vidual wearing a shabby leather jacket and corduroy breeches.

Clutching his portfolio of sketches, he had hovered anxiously, and now he was almost in tears with disappointment.

"Come tomorrow," Clarissa told him graciously.

And so he too left, at last, looking a trifle happier.

"Madam will be served in my bedroom," was the Earl's order to the major-domo.

And he led Clarissa there, through the door connecting the two bedrooms.

From a gilded coronet, attached to the wall high above the headboard, the gold-colored velvet swept down in rich folds to form a magnificent canopy over the enormous bed, which stood on a dais. The bed itself was very high, consisting as it probably did—it looked luxuriously soft—of numerous feather mattresses, piled one over another, and topped with several mattresses of pure down. The innumerable down pillows were covered with gold-colored silk, to match the spread, which was decorated with rows of heavy gold tassels. The arrangement of the pillows made it quite clear that the bed was for two. However, the time hadn't come for *that* yet.

The raised bed was at one end of the large room. At the other end there was a round table, already set for a tête-à-tête repast, and with some cushioned chairs drawn up to it. Clarissa languidly sat down.

"At last we're alone," the little Earl exclaimed. In a very sprightly manner he appropriated the chair next to her own and, taking her hand, started to fondle it.

But several flunkies came in, bringing silver-covered dishes. One of the flunkies shook out a large napkin and, standing behind the Earl, tied it under his chin. Another poured ruby wine into tall glasses. Then they left.

Clarissa felt her nostrils dilating at the tempting odors that rose from the steaming food. There was some kind of a plump bird, partridge probably, stuffed with something very tasty, truffles most likely. She had heard of truffles from Lafonte.... Tender mushrooms swimming in a rich sauce. A meat pie, the crust of which promised to melt in one's mouth. And small individual tarts filled with the rarest of fruits: peaches, apricots, pineapple.

But the Earl was again trying to fondle her.

Does the old fool expect me to romp in bed with him on an empty stomach? Clarissa thought indignantly.

She shook a finger at him playfully.

"My little Peewee mustn't be naughty," she cooed. "Little Peewee mustn't be so impatient...." She administered a slap to the pawing hand.

The slap, though seemingly so gay, must have caused him considerable pain. For he squealed most comically. Then, visibly cowed, he promised to be patient.

And Clarissa, without bothering to figure out which knife, fork, or spoon should be used for what, began to eat, using her fingers instead. Blinded as the Earl was by desire, he wouldn't notice anything amiss, she knew. And she was right. When she at last had finished eating, and had wiped the grease off her mouth and fingers with her napkin, he hastened to compliment her on her table manners.

Then he placed a hand on her knee. His old man's kisses made a little trail along her bare arm from elbow up to the shoulder. Smiling roguishly, she put a finger behind his ear, tickling him there. Suddenly she sprang to her feet, and ran around the table.

"Catch me, little Peewee. Catch me...."

Giggling, thinking it to be some kind of preliminary game, the Earl set off after her with his mincing little steps. Round and round the table they went.

"Catch me, little Peewee...."

Sometimes, laughing gaily, provokingly, she let him almost catch her. But not quite ... Clarissa wasn't playing any games.

The question of the Earl's age, how much strength there was still left in him, had occupied her mind, while she ate, in the most businesslike fashion. There was a very ancient saying which, back in the Thieves' Village, Black Moll, for one, never tired of quoting to her girls:

> If around the table
> Five times an old man
> Can run,
> Then a girl needn't fear;
> She won't be hanged.

For should a man give up the ghost while in bed, the girl would be held responsible, and hanging was the punishment. The crude verse was based on centuries of experience, and Clarissa had implicit faith in its wisdom.

"Catch me, little Peewee!" Out of the corner of her eye she watched the senile Earl, while she gaily ran around the table ahead of him.

He had lost his bejeweled fan and his lace handkerchief. His breath came in short painful gasps. He was getting tired. She could see that his little face, in spite of all that powder and rouge, was turning a ghastly white. Still he persevered. The neat white wig all askew, his diminutive arms outstretched, and the silly napkin flapping under his chin, he came mincing after her. There he almost caught her....

Suddenly, with a little thud, he fell, and just lay there, sprawled on the floor, motionless, like some ridiculous doll. He had run around the table exactly four times.

She hurried over and crouched beside him. Her first thought had been that he was dead. She placed an ear to his chest. No, he was breathing. His eyes were open but he couldn't see her, she could tell. He was in a faint. Clarissa, rising to her feet, stood a moment, thinking the situation over.

To call the servants was out of the question. They might accuse her of being the cause of the Earl's utter collapse. Again she looked down at him. He was so small. He couldn't be very heavy. She hurried over to the bed. She had to go up the two steps of the dais in order to pull the bedclothes aside. Then, hurrying back to the Earl, she stooped very low, thrust one arm under his shoulders, the other under his knees, and so lifted him. He was no heavier than a child. Clarissa carried him to the bed, laid him down, got rid of the silly napkin tied about his wrinkled neck. His eyes were closed now, and his breathing sounded better. But he seemed to be having some kind of a chill. She drew the bedclothes over him.

Then she walked back to the other end of the room and sat down in a chair.

A good romp in bed was not for *him,* definitely! The Earl would simply expire, Clarissa was certain of it now. In plain words, he'd be dead. And then where would she be? All her plans ruined … What a predicament! What *was* she to do? *How* should she handle the senile little creature henceforth in order to keep her hold on him through his constant desire for her, and yet, at the same time, prevent him from … well, doing something foolish, which would bring on an apoplexy, and cause his death? A predicament it certainly was! Clarissa stamped her foot and clicked her tongue with chagrin. She had never expected to find herself in such a strange predicament.

"I can be of service to madam," a quiet voice said suddenly.

Besides the door connecting the Earl of Strasford's bedroom with her own, there was another door, which probably led into the Earl's dressing room. And at that door now stood a man of pleasing appearance, with a small black mustache on his upper lip, and wearing a valet's brilliant livery.

CHAPTER FOURTEEN

"AND WHO ARE *you?*" Clarissa asked.

The small black mustache on the man's upper lip quite intrigued her.

"I am His Grace's chief valet, madam."

Clarissa now noticed that while the other valets—whom she had already seen—wore breeches of green satin and jackets of yellow silk, this man's livery was entirely of green satin. His shoe buckles, instead of being plain silver, were gilded. And on his left sleeve he wore the Earl's crest, embroidered in gold thread.

"You speak with an accent," Clarissa told him bluntly. "And you don't look like a valet."

The man smiled slightly under his black mustache and replied quietly:

"I happen to be French, madam. And … I was born a count." And then he added, "Madam is very observant."

Meanwhile he kept staring at her with calm inquisitiveness, deliberately sizing her up. Making Clarissa suddenly aware that both her hair and gown had become disarrayed during the just-enacted scene with the Earl. She straightened her bodice, gave a shake of her head to set the lustrous, abundant waves and ringlets back in place. The exercise of running around the table had heightened the natural radiance of her lovely face. Her partly-bared breasts heaved slightly, becomingly. And her eyes sparkled with energy and bold spirits.

"A count!" Clarissa repeated, amazed.

"Will madam excuse me for just a moment?" the chief valet said.

And walking over to the bed, he bent over the Earl to examine him. Then, as quietly, he came back.

"His Grace will be perfectly all right now," he told Clarissa reassuringly. "The Earl sometimes gets these spells, when very excited, that is.... The Earl is far more advanced in years than people think. And he is very feeble. As madam has just discovered for herself."

Had the man seen it all, then? Was there perhaps a secret panel in the wall somewhere, through which he had watched her, Clarissa, the new mistress, from the very first moment of her entering the room with the Earl, his employer?

The chief valet was stooping down to pick up the Earl's bejeweled fan, the lace handkerchief. After placing them on the table, he stationed himself a little away from Clarissa, and said:

"Madam is surprised to see a genuine count working as a menial, wearing a valet's livery? But the explanation is very simple. I am an *émigré*."

"An *ém ... m ... émigré?*" Clarissa repeated slowly, meanwhile putting away the new-found word in the back of her mind, as was her habit, for future use. "And what is *that?*"

"When Louis XVI, the last rightful king of France, perished in the Revolution, most of the French aristocracy had to share his fate. And my parents, the Count and Countess D'Este," the chief valet said quietly, "were among those who died a martyr's death on the guillotine."

He means that they had their heads chopped off, Clarissa told herself. That much she understood.

"I was very young then, and my mother's personal maid, who came from a peasant family," the chief valet went on, "managed somehow to carry me away and hide me in her native village.

Then she smuggled me out of France, across the Channel into England, to London. And so I grew up an *émigré*. That is, a person of noble birth who is forced to live in exile."

"You mean, you can never go back?" Clarissa was surprised. "Back to your own country, to France?"

"Not until Napoleon is conquered. Napoleon is nothing but a *vile* usurper, whose ambition is to be the ruler of the whole world!"

"I've heard him called the Beast," Clarissa said importantly, recollecting the word used by the Rosicrucian.

"And justly so! Anyway, that very kind woman, my mother's maid," the chief valet resumed his story, "at once found work as a laundress, and she took care of me. Then, when I was old enough, she placed me in the Earl of Strasford's service, as an under-valet. But the Earl took a liking to me, and he soon raised me to the status of a full valet, and then to that of chief valet. I've been with the Earl all of ten years.... And everybody here calls me François."

"And is that why you have this little mustache, François?" Clarissa said. "I mean, because you're French?"

"Madam doesn't approve of a mustache?" François stroked it with a finger reflectively.

"On the contrary." After all, the fellow was rather handsome. "I approve of it wholeheartedly," and Clarissa smiled at him, roguishly.

Did he smile back brazenly? Clarissa couldn't be quite certain, on account of that mustache of his. His manner, however, was perfectly respectful as he said:

"Madam mustn't think that I have bored madam with the details of my personal history for the mere sake of hearing myself talk. I had a definite purpose. Which was, to make madam understand how I came to have in my possession ... *this!*" Suddenly producing something from about his person, and holding it out, for Clarissa to see—a tiny vial, filled with a dark, brownish liquid.

"I suppose is a draught of some kind," Clarissa said calmly, masking her surprise, and trying not to show the sudden interest she felt.

"A draught which is *unique* in the universe," the chief valet François corrected her gravely. "The formula of this draught," he explained impressively, "has been in my family since Madame Pompadour bequeathed it to a relative of ours. Eventually, my mother's trusted maid was the only person living who knew the formula. She passed it on to me.... Now, please listen very carefully, madam. For this is important." And François went on, "Madame Pompadour, the famous mistress of Louis XV ..."

"The one who had his head chopped off?"

"No, no ... That was another Louis. The one who had Madame Pompadour was Louis XV, his grandfather ... Madame Pompadour, as I was saying, had this marvelous draught made for her by her personal physician. *At the time* when Louis XV, her protector, had grown very feeble with age. *As feeble as the Earl is now.* In other words, Madame Pompadour was faced with the same problem which now confronts *Madame* Clarissa," and here François made Clarissa a little bow.

"But what does the draught *do?*" Clarissa said, staring at the tiny vial, held between the fingers of the chief valet's tantalizingly extended hand.

"It induces sleep. A perfectly normal, wholesome sleep. But, of course, that's not its principal value, since there are other draughts which achieve the same purpose. The *unique* value of this precious draught is something quite different. It makes the person receptive to suggestion. The suggestion, however, must concern a subject very agreeable to the person. Does madam follow me?"

"Well ..."

"Let me give you an example," François said quickly. "Suppose I were given this draught. I immediately fall asleep. Then, after a certain period of time, depending on the number of drops administered, I awake. And, just as I awake, somebody says to me, 'François, you must be very happy. You've been on a visit back home, to your own country, to France! Oh, what a lucky fellow you are!' And I will *believe* it. I will be *convinced* that that's exactly what has happened to me. Because it's something that's agreeable to me, something that I desire very much, a dream." The chief valet gestured with his free hand expressively.

And before Clarissa could say anything, he at once went on:

"But ... suppose that same somebody said to me instead, 'Eh, poor François! You've been tried by the Revolutionary Tribunal and you're condemned to the guillotine. Yes, your handsome head will be chopped off. Eh, what an unfortunate fellow you are.... ' *Then* I wouldn't believe it. I'd know it was a lie. Why? Because it's something not agreeable to me, something I do not desire," François again gestured with his free hand quickly. "It is only when the *suggestion,*" the chief valet held up a finger triumphantly, "concerns something the person wants very much, something he greatly desires, that the person is gladly receptive to it, and believes in the truth of it implicitly! *That* is the magic power of this unique draught. Now does madam understand?"

"I think I do," Clariss said. "And it's nice of you, François, to help me out in my dilemma," she added negligently. And, very blandly, she put out a hand for the tiny vial.

"Ah, yes. This precious draught would be of great advantage to madam, wouldn't it?" François said. "*If* she had it ..."

The tiny vial had disappeared, François having imperceptibly secreted it away somewhere about his valet's livery.

"I see what you mean," she said. "Naturally, you expect to be paid for this little service."

François shrugged.

"A mistress never *pays*," he pointed out quietly. "A mistress merely looks the other way, when a servant of an 'unofficial residence' has a chance of making a little additional profit."

"And in this particular case," Clarissa said, "how do you plan to make this little additional profit for yourself?"

"It's very simple." And the chief valet explained. "His Grace, the Earl, has become rather careless with the money he happens to have on hand. Golden coins, silver ... He's gotten into the habit of leaving them lying about, on chairs, on tables, dropped on the floor. With Madam's permission, I will deem it my duty to pick up these forgotten coins, and put them in my own pocket."

"And, I suppose," Clarissa said, "they'd add up to quite a tidy little sum at every day's end, these forgotten coins, wouldn't they?"

"Oh, yes." François was perfectly frank about it. "A sum, in fact, equivalent to my year's wages. Quite a worthwhile sum."

"Which," Clarissa said, "I could very easily put in *my* pocket. Probably that's what the gypsy woman, Nona, did. Appropriate the money ..."

"The gypsy woman was stupid," the chief valet was quick to point out. "She was overgreedy. Nobody here had ever offered to do her any kind of a service. But madam is clever, she is shrewd. It would be a pleasure to be of service to madam."

It was all very flattering. Clarissa especially enjoyed hearing herself addressed as "Madam." Of course, an owner of a brothel was also called "Madam." Still ... François made it sound most flattering, important....

"And I suppose," Clarissa said, "you'll be putting that money away with the rest of your savings, François. You don't look to me like a person who'd be spending his money foolishly."

"Ah"—François gave a deprecative little sigh—"nothing can be concealed from madam."

"What are you saving it all for, François?"

"To open a little business of my own, eventually, madam. A hairdresser's shop. It is the ambition of every *émigré* in London to own a small business, in whatever line the *émigré* happens to excel."

"And you consider yourself qualified, François, for a hairdresser's establishment? After all, it's one thing to take care of the Earl's wigs, and apply all that paint to his wrinkled little face, and quite another to bring out the beauty of a woman's hair...." Clarissa spoke carelessly, on purpose. It was as she had thought: this François could be made use of, in more ways than one.

"There's nothing I don't know about the care of the ladies' hair," François declared proudly. "My mother's maid was famous at the court of Louis XVI for the marvelous coiffures she produced, some of them so complicated and enormous that they measured three feet in height and as much in width, and that mass of curls covered with powder, and topped with, say, a copy of a ship, masts and all ... Ah, madam may well laugh. But such was the fashion. And those monstrous hairdos were works of art! Well," François went on, "that devoted woman taught me everything she knew. And she predicted that I'd make my fortune, some day, as a hairdresser."

Clarissa, who was still highly amused at the thought of those impossible hairdos—no wonder most of those ladies lost their heads on the guillotine!—said:

"I guess I may as well look the other way, as you suggested, while you're picking up those coins His Grace leaves lying about so carelessly."

"Then it is agreed," François said eagerly.

The tiny vial, filled with the dark, brownish liquid, instantly made its reappearance. Holding it carefully between thumb and forefinger, the chief valet said:

"But first, let me show madam how to administer this unique draught."

And coming close to the table, he took up the wineglass which the lust-tormented Earl had left almost untouched. François expertly poured most of the contents back into the crystal decanter, which stood right there. When a very little of the ruby wine remained at the bottom of the glass, he set it down. Then he removed the little stopper from the tiny vial and, holding the vial at an angle, he let the dark, brownish liquid very slowly trickle out, form a drop, and so fall into the wine. Then, another drop …

"If eight hours of restful sleep are required," François said, "three drops are sufficient."

"But … how do I know it isn't, maybe … poison!" Clarissa said, suddenly filled with misgiving. "Why should I be trusting you?"

"You're trusting me, madam," François said very coolly, while letting one more drop, the third, fall into the wine, "because madam has no choice. Of course, to trust anyone, especially a perfect stranger, as I am to madam, is always a terrible risk. But I think taking risks is nothing new to madam."

And Clarissa had to agree with him.

"There," Francois said. He replaced the stopper in the tiny vial. "Now, please watch."

Nothing had happened to the small amount of wine at the bottom of the glass, as yet. The presence of the three drops of the dark, brownish liquid had caused no change in it—the ruby color was as clear as before. But suddenly, as Clarissa looked on, fascinated, it began to fizz, the black foam rising almost to the brim of the glass. Then, the foam gradually disappearing, but the contents still expanded, the mixture slowly turned opaque. After remaining so a few seconds, it began to settle down to the bottom. And then, suddenly, the queer opaqueness was gone; the little bit of wine in the glass was again a clear ruby color. Looking at it, nobody could have guessed that anything had been added to it, that it had been tampered with.

Clarissa, made somewhat breathless by what she had just seen, put her hand out for the tiny vial, and this time François gave it to her. Clarissa quickly put it away, inside her bodice.

"And now," François said.

He took up the glass and, carrying it, he hurried over to the bed's dais, Clarissa moving swiftly at his side. She followed the chief valet up the two steps and stood beside him, close to the canopied bed.

The Earl, though breathing regularly, seemed to be lying there in some kind of a coma. François, bending down, thrust a hand under his head, raised it, and bringing the glass close, forced the wine through the painted lips. Clarissa heard the sound of swallowing made in the Earl's throat.

François then withdrew his hand from under the helpless head, letting it drop back on the pillow. After giving the emptied glass to Clarissa to hold, he neatly straightened the white wig, which was all askew, and smoothed the bedclothes. And the two of them then hurried back to the other end of the room.

Clarissa set the empty wineglass down on the table. And the chief valet said:

"His Grace will sleep now till morning. And madam can go and have a good night's sleep in her room, in her own bed. Ten minutes or so before the Earl awakes," François went on, "I will come and rouse madam's maid—Sally, I think her name is, I heard the valets mention it...."

And, Clarissa nodding affirmatively, François continued:

"I'll rouse Sally. And Sally then will awaken madam ..."

The complicated way of simply getting her up seemed awfully silly to Clarissa. But she at once understood the wisdom of it. What possible business could the chief valet have with her, Clarissa, the Earl's mistress? While if he sneaked in to say something to Sally, well.... He must have taken a fancy to the mistress' perky little maid. That would be the harmless interpretation. Since, doubtless, nothing passed unnoticed here. Everybody spying on everybody else, everybody envious ...

"And madam then will hasten back," François went on, "to this bedroom. I advise madam to wear her most becoming nightgown."

"Well, I haven't got one," Clarissa told him. "Aside from a short traveling cape"—which probably was still lying there, on the seat of the small, enclosed carriage, where she had left it!—"all I have is this dress I'm wearing right now."

"But, of course ..." François was very polite about it. "The extensive wardrobe madam had ordered this morning won't be ready for several days.... Well," and stepping back a few paces, holding his head bent to one side, he scrutinized the dress Clarissa had on critically. "Let's see ... Hmm ..."

Then, coming back quickly, he gave instructions;

"Slash it open all the way down in front. And make it loose.... Throw away the blue sash. And pick out all the stitches which gather the dress at the waist ... It will then resemble a peignoir, which madam can handle with great advantage for herself, by knowingly concealing or revealing her beauty, as she sees fit."

How surprised Miss Gray would have been if she could see the changes made in her modest white muslin! Now it was to be a peignoir....

"That's not a bad idea," Clarissa conceded aloud.

Given time, she would have thought up something similar, but it never did a woman any harm to let the man think himself the cleverer of the two. Feed their ego, and you'll always get the better of them eventually, was Clarissa's motto. Still, it was really funny that François, considering he was a man, should display such a keen intuition about feminine apparel....

"Wearing a peignoir, then," the chief valet went on, "Madam will hasten back to this bedroom, and ... But, probably, I don't have to tell madam what she should do, once she's here."

And he escorted Clarissa to the door connecting the two bedrooms. Holding it open, he added:

"Madam forgot her satchel."

He had the satchel in his hands, having picked it up from the chair where Clarissa had deposited it during the tête-à-tête repast with the senile Earl. Throughout the busy day, whenever forced to relinquish her hold of the satchel—as, for instance, during the scramble with the gypsy woman—Clarissa, every time, had instantly retrieved it. But now she *had* forgotten it.

"Madam probably has something very valuable in the satchel." And, for the first time, François grinned broadly under that small black mustache of his.

"I'll ask you to mind your own business," Clarissa hissed, snatching the satchel from him.

And, as she flounced out, very haughtily, she heard him chuckle softly, before he closed the door after her.

Sally had worked hard at tidying up the room. Not a trace of the gypsy woman's slatternly habits remained, and it looked quite different, almost luxurious. And Sally had dozed off in a big chair close by the grate, in which a cozy coal fire was burning to ward off the penetrating rawness of the dense London fog outside. On the big dressing table, fitted out with a profusion of mirrors, lay spread out the diamond necklace and the other jewels which Clarissa had selected that morning. How their glow and sparkle dominated the room!

Hurrying over, Clarissa laid her fingers on the diamonds greedily, tiny pricks of sensual delight running up and down her spine, as she caressed the cool precious stones. Taking up the necklace, she laid it against her throat, and stared at her reflection, which was repeated over and over again in the numerous mirrors of the dressing table. Then, dropping the necklace, she picked up the matching earrings and held them to the lobes of her ears.

She had to bring all her will power to the fore to tear herself away. Scooping up the jewels, she put them in a drawer and quickly pushed it shut. She had things to do ... First of all, the tiny vial with the precious draught. Taking it out of her bodice, Clarissa very carefully put it away in the satchel, among Miss Gray's clean handkerchiefs. Then, producing the little sewing kit, she took up the dainty pair of scissors ...

Sally had awakened from her doze and was staring at her.

"You're not going to start cutting at that dress *again!*" Sally said, horrified.

Clarissa boldly slashed it open, all the way down. Then, slipping it off her shoulders, and sitting down on the velvet-covered bench, the slashed dress in her lap, she took out of the sewing kit two needles.

"Take this needle, Sally," Clarissa said, holding one out, "and start picking out the stitches from *that* end of the waistband, while I'm doing the same from *this* end."

"Well, I never!" Sally said.

But she took the needle, seated herself close, and obediently set to work. In no time, all the little stitches were out, and the dress, no longer gathered at the waist, was transformed into a tolerable likeness of a peignoir. Clarissa tried it on in front of the mirrors—really, it made her *dizzy.* All those mirrors ... each one attached to the dressing table at a different height, and at a different angle. She could see herself *en face,* in profile, she could see her back, all at one and the same time!

And Sally, meanwhile, said:

"That short traveling cape you left in the carriage ... Well, Pete brought it to the kitchen with him, thinking I'd take it to you. But while we were eating breakfast a ragged beggar came to the door, and I told Pete to give the cape to the beggar. Considering the number of rich dresses and other things you've been ordering for yourself this morning," Sally said, with a toss of her head and a smirk, "I figured you wouldn't need that shabby little cape."

Clarissa wasn't interested. The "peignoir" deposited on a chair, she had removed her petticoat, the camisole, and the hideous drawers, the latter such an indispensable item of her former role as a demure governess, but quite out of place, thank heavens! in her present role. And now, absolutely naked, Clarissa stood beside the big bed. Though, in contrast to the Earl's, this one did not boast of a dais, it was ever so much higher. More mattresses ... Which explained the presence of a little ladder, leaning against one side.

"Sally, come and hold this silly ladder. So I don't break my neck climbing the stupid thing."

Sally, giggling, hurried over, and she held the ladder firmly with both hands, and Clarissa nimbly climbed up the few rungs and fell into bed. The gypsy woman, for all her slatternly ways, had been no fool when it came to her own comfort, Clarissa observed, as with a little gurgle of pleasure she snuggled against the down-filled top mattress, the down pillows. Sally pulled the bedclothes over her. But if Sally had to make use of the little ladder in order to do that, Clarissa wouldn't have known it, for she was already fast asleep.

When she awoke, it was to hear Sally's disgruntled voice saying:

"This fellow François, who says he's the chief valet, woke me up, and he told me to wake *you* up. I've been shaking you these last five minutes...."

It was broad daylight. And the sun, very bright after the night's dense fog, was sending its shimmering rays into the room.

With Sally's help, Clarissa got down from the bed. Then she snatched up the "peignoir" and, wrapping it swiftly about her naked body, she hurried into the Earl's bedroom. There the heavy curtains were still drawn across the tall windows, shutting out the daylight, and the lamp, lit the previous night by the flunkies, was still burning, and François stood at the faraway door, which led into the Earl's dressing room. He had been waiting to see Clarissa come in. And now, without saying a word, François left by that door, closing it behind him.

Clarissa hurried over to the bed, and very quietly and swiftly got in under the covers. The Earl was sound asleep, even snoring a little. François, excellent valet that he was, had changed the Earl's clothes. Without disturbing the wholesome sleep induced by the unique draught, François had relieved his employer of the French shoes, the satin breeches, the lace-trimmed shirt, the white wig. The diminutive Earl now had on an old-fashioned nightshirt and a nightcap with a long tassel.

Clarissa prepared herself for the moment when he would awaken. She let the "peignoir" slip down alluringly from one shoulder. By passing a hand through her hair quickly, she gave the lustrous tresses a tumbled appearance. She didn't have to wait long. François' timing, indeed, was almost perfect.

The Earl opened his eyes.

"My little Peewee," Clarissa at once cooed at him, "how you tired me out…. Ah, never, *never* have I been loved with such a passion, such a … with such intensity. I'm completely exhausted. Have pity on your poor Clarissa. No more, I pray you, no more …"

The Earl sat up with a jerk, the long tassel of his nightcap flapping about comically.

"Eh? I tired you out, did I? Is that what you said?"

"He *asks* me that," Clarissa sighed. She glanced around, as if appealing to the world in general to bear witness to this … this injustice. "Why, you kept bothering me all night long! My little Peewee was cruel, positively cruel. Making love, making love …"

"Making love, eh?" He giggled, immensely pleased.

"All night long …" Clarissa again said.

"Hee, hee, hee …" The Earl rubbed his hands with glee.

Then he looked down at Clarissa. Her lovely hair spread over the pillow, her eyelids heavy, drooping, the luscious red lips parted, one breast bared, she presented a ravishing picture of languid, love-exhausted womanhood. The terrible fear with which the Earl had had to live for the last twenty years, the fear of impotency, was suddenly, unquestionably allayed. To regain his manhood, to have proof of it, had been his most cherished desire, a dream…. He would have given all his wealth to be convinced on that point. And now this beautiful young woman, lying beside him, was actually exhausted, completely spent, the poor thing, because of *him.*

"Hee, hee, hee …" The Earl giggled, sitting there in the cano-pied bed, wearing that ridiculous tasseled nightcap. "And do you know," he suddenly confided, "I'm not tired at all. In fact I feel wonderfully rested. As if I've slept eight hours, at the least."

"Well, you did doze off now and then," Clarissa conceded. "While your poor Clarissa didn't get a wink of …"

"But most of the time I just kept at it, eh? Eh?"

"You most certainly did!"

"Hee, hee, hee …" The Earl again giggled. "But," he then confided, "I don't remember François coming in to undress me. Or François putting this on me instead," he looked down at his nightshirt, and felt with a hand for the nightcap's tassel. "I don't remember it at all."

"How can you say such a thing?" Clarissa hastened to reproach him, "Why, you told me to call the chief valet, and I did. I mean I … pulled at the bell cord"—there was probably a bell cord *somewhere*—"and he came in, and undressed you, and put your nightshirt and the nightcap on."

"Well, that is as it should be," the Earl said. "And François must have called your little maid in, to help *you* undress, and take your clothes away, and give you this bewitching thing"—he placed a hand on the peignoir—"to wear instead. Very becoming to you, my dear. I suppose my forgetfulness about it all," he declared with conviction, "is just another proof of how preoccupied I was with … with making love." He thrust out his dried-up little chest importantly.

"May I go now, please, and get some rest?" Clarissa pleaded, in a very small voice, pathetically.

"I didn't mean to tire you," the Earl said politely. "I … I guess I just don't know my own strength." He giggled happily. "Certainly you may go. But I will get dressed. Please pull that bell cord."

So there *was* a bell cord. Clarissa found it, a wide brocade ribbon, dangling from among the velvet folds of the bed canopy. By lifting a hand languidly, she managed to give the ribbon a little pull.

"And I will drink my hot chocolate with you," the Earl went on graciously, "while you're making your toilette, at your dressing table, my dear."

Whenever the bell cord was pulled, the little bell would start to tinkle in the Earl's dressing room, where it was François' duty to keep constant vigil. And now François entered, in answer to the summons. Treading softly, he went first to draw back the curtains, then to extinguish the lamp. Then, coming over to the bed, he made a low good-morning bow to the Earl. François was very careful not to look straight at Clarissa, and Clarissa was very careful not to look at him. The two of them had never spoken to each other privately. That was the idea ...

"And if Your Grace permits me to make a personal remark," the chief valet said respectfully, "never have I seen Your Grace looking so well!"

The Earl beamed.

"I may as well tell you, François," he confided, "that I have never felt better in my life! But we have to thank Mistress Clarissa for it. She has me rejuvenated. Positively rejuvenated!"

And he proudly pointed with a finger at Clarissa, who, having gotten out of the bed, seemed to totter with fatigue as she clasped the trailing peignoir about her.

Then, the Earl urging her kindly to go rest, she very becomingly tottered to the door and out.

Henceforth she wouldn't have to worry about the Earl suddenly getting another apoplexy and dying on her, ruining all her plans. Every time, from now on, as soon as she saw him become overexcited by her beauty, her nearness, she would manage somehow, undetected, to add a few drops of the unique draught to the little amount of wine and coax him to drink it. On the pretty pretext, perhaps, of having herself drunk most of the wine from *this very same* glass and wishing him to finish what still remained on the bottom. *Her* lips had come in contact with this wine, and now *his* lips would come in contact with it.… The old fool would be sure to fall for something like that.

And from now on, every night, like last night, she'd leave him, fast asleep in his canopied bed, and go to have her beauty sleep in her own room. And every morning, like this morning, a few minutes before he was to awaken, she would hasten back to his bedroom and get under the covers beside him, and then pretend she'd been there with him the whole night—with the most gratifying results to his ego.

That problem off her mind, Clarissa now could concentrate her thoughts on preparing herself for the forthcoming ball, which was to decide her success as a mistress before the luminaries of London's wealth and fashion. Among the countless purchases she had made the previous morning, in addition to ordering her extensive wardrobe, there were scores of various beauty aids— body lotions, pomades, creams, salves. And now Sally was told, as soon as Clarissa was back in her own room, to bring all these precious items forth, out of the corner cupboard where the purchases had been placed, and to assemble them on the dressing table, at which Clarissa had hastily seated herself, tingling with anticipation.

"This fellow François," Sally said, taking the gilded stoppers out of the crystal lotion bottles, removing the tops of the costly porcelain containers, full of pink-colored, fragrant creams, "the chief valet. He doesn't look like a valet to *me*."

Clarissa, busy rubbing a musk-scented pomade on the skin of her bare arm, said loftily:

"I wish you wouldn't show your ignorance so, Sally. François is an *émigré*."

"And what is *that*?"

When Clarissa briefly explained, Sally said:

"I knew there was something funny about him! I *knew* it, the minute I saw the little black mustache that he wears on his upper lip!" Then, her inquisitive nose close to the beauty cream, as she opened yet another pretty container, she exclaimed, "Goodness gracious, how lovely all this stuff smells!"

But Clarissa was frowning. She had expected so much from these expensive beauty preparations, *because* they were expensive, and made by famous experts, out of rare ingredients, and now she was disappointed. The rouge salve, for instance, which she had carefully sampled by spreading a little of it on the back of her hand, wasn't half as smooth as the rouge she used to make back in the Thieves' Village, out of the juice of red berries, with a bit of lard added for a base. Evidently, just because a thing was terribly expensive it didn't mean that it would be excellent, or even passably good. Any other woman would have been swayed by the mere fact of an article's costliness, and foolishly, without thinking, she would have decided in its favor, but Clarissa refused to be taken in.

She had Sally bring her the package containing her old make-up and patiently compared the two rouges. Yes, the rouge in the crude little earthenware container was unquestionably superior. There was little left of it, however, and she would be too busy, probably, to make a fresh supply herself. But there were venders in London, as Clarissa well knew, who went from door to door, selling inexpensive homemade beauty preparations. A poor vender like that might, quite conceivably, come to the door of the Earl of Strasford's "unofficial residence," the back door, naturally, on the chance that a flunky would buy a little pot of rouge, or a box of face powder, to give as a present to his inamorata, who worked as a maid in one of the rich homes nearby. I will tell Sally to be on the lookout for such a vender, Clarissa told herself.

But the expensive hand lotion was really very fine. It was scented with the fragrance of some strange, exotic bloom, and, as Clarissa spread it gently over her hands, she was amazed at the velvety smooth texture and the lovely whiteness which the skin instantly acquired. A pair of loose cotton gloves came with the lotion. One was supposed to put them on, over the lotion-saturated hands, before retiring for the night. The purpose of the gloves was to protect the bedclothes from getting soiled and, what was more important, to prevent the beneficial emollients from evaporating. Clarissa knew, of course, through hearsay, that the great ladies always slept with such gloves. And now *she* would be doing so—preposterous as the idea was!

All in all, Clarissa was satisfied. Even the profusion of the dressing-table mirrors no longer irritated her. Having become used to seeing her radiant reflection repeated over and over again, at various angles, she could now understand the practical wisdom of such an arrangement, and was quite enchanted by it. Anyway, the idea of the mirrors had been no product of the gypsy woman Nona's slatternly brain. Some other, former mistress was responsible for it. And, since the dressing table, luxurious though it was, showed signs of much usage, that must have been many years ago. Some lovely young girl, as young *then* as Clarissa was *now*, who had once inhabited this room, at the time when the Earl was neither old nor senile, but in the prime of life …

"Hee, hee, hee, my dear." The dried-up-with-age, diminutive Earl giggled, coming in, a bejeweled fan in one hand, a lace handkerchief in the other, and dressed fantastically for the day in his old-fashioned costume of blue and pink satins, besprinkled all over with pearls and diamonds.

He seated himself, and hot chocolate was brought in. And Sally, bobbing a curtsy every time, served it to them, poured in delicate porcelain cups with gilded handles. Clarissa took a sip, and it was delicious. She had never tasted hot chocolate before. The poor people couldn't afford even plain cocoa.... Clarissa drank two cups. The Earl's little eyes were focused on that part of her "peignoir" where the transparent muslin veiled her breasts. He giggled, flirted with his fan, flapped the lace handkerchief about. However, the preparations for the forthcoming ball soon claimed his presence. He had to give orders, consult with the gigantic major-domo. He excused himself.

The bustle of these preparations had been resounding throughout the great mansion since early morning, at times reaching Clarissa. And now, once again reminded of how little time there was actually left till the night of the momentous event, and how much there was still to be done, she said to Sally:

"I want you to deliver a message to Mr. Davey, an old friend of mine. Now listen carefully, Sally ..."

Mr. Davey was to start, instantly, making two dozen pairs of shoes for Clarissa. Mr. Davey had her precise measurements. Each pair of shoes was to be of a different color. She was leaving the choice of colors to his discretion. Also the choice of materials—brocade, velvet, satin, silk. But one pair, to be made of crimson satin—to match her ballgown, only Clarissa didn't mention this in her instructions to Sally—this particular pair of shoes must be delivered Saturday morning, positively.

"You'll have no trouble finding the house," Clarissa said. "It's in a little side street, just off the main thoroughfare, which starts not far from the embankment and the bridge there," Clarissa supplied the name of the thoroughfare. "Once you find *that*," Clarissa said, "just ask anybody where Flaxy, the boy with the trained dogs, lives. Everybody there knows Flaxy. He's on the ground floor. And Mr. Davey lives on the second floor. Now go, Sally. And hurry."

Sally was about to hurry out, but Clarissa called her back.

"Before you go," Clarissa ordered, "find François, and tell him to come here. Can you do that?"

"I'll get hold of him, don't you worry," Sally said.

And she hurried out.

In a very little while the door opened softly, and François entered. After closing the door, he quietly came over.

"Sally told me," the chief valet said, "that I'd find you alone, madam."

"François," Clarissa said, turning to him as she sat there at the dressing table, "I want your advice."

François was all attention.

"What should a woman do," Clarissa went on, "to make herself look different? *Quite* different!" No, she was putting it very badly. "You see," Clarissa tried to explain, "among the guests at the ball there will be someone who has seen me before, who ... who knew me ..."

She was thinking of Mr. Brummell, of course.

"Does madam mean, perhaps," François said, "that she does not wish that *someone* to recognize her?"

"Oh, there's no danger of *that!*" Clarissa was absolutely convinced of it. She laughed; the idea was so absurd.

And she was right.

The gentle governess, Miss Gray, the very proper young lady who always kept her eyes demurely downcast, whose face was so clean and sweet, whose modest, even somewhat shabby clothes were faintly redolent of lavender cologne. Miss Gray, with her gay little laugh, her pretty little volume of poems. And her *so*-smooth hairdo, the part *so* exactly in the center, and the sausage-like curls bunched dowdily over the ears.

Miss Gray, and ... and the Earl's new mistress, Clarissa? A woman of singular beauty, yes, but coarse, vulgar, as one expected her to be. A woman whose abundant hair rippled down to her shoulders, whose face was bright with paint, who laughed loudly, whose voice was just a little harsh. And whose eyes always looked at a man boldly, invitingly …

What possible connection could there be between the two of them? No such revolting thought would ever enter Mr. Brummell's romantic mind.

"Madam means, perhaps," François said, stroking his mustache reflectively, "that this *someone* will be the only person among the guests who has seen her before?"

"A few of the others have also seen me before, but I'm not worried about *them!*" Clarissa said.

As Miss Gray, she had been introduced, back at Ravisham, to the Prince Regent, and to Lord Cavor, and Mr. FitzMaurice, all of whom would be present at the ball. But these gentlemen had barely noticed a mere governess, they wouldn't even remember how Miss Gray looked. While Mr. Brummell … well, he loved Miss Gray. And a man in love was apt to be supersensitive. After all, it was not the *real* Miss Gray, but Miss Gray as impersonated, flawlessly, by Clarissa, who had captivated Beau Brummell's fastidious heart. Therefore, wasn't it possible, just faintly possible, that on seeing Clarissa again, no matter how vastly different she'd *look* and *be* this time, he might be … not exactly reminded, but made vaguely disturbed? That was the word—disturbed. Something about this woman, Clarissa, something quite indefinable, something he couldn't put his finger on, would disturb Mr. Brummell, by suddenly bringing to his mind the image of the gentle governess, Miss Gray, with a vivid, refreshing force.

It was this possibility that was now making Clarissa just a little nervous, as she sat there, staring at François eagerly for advice.

"To be perfectly frank, madam," François said, "the situation, which seems to perturb madam, is not at all clear to me.

"The situation is extremely unusual, François," Clarissa said. "Besides, I express myself so badly. Let me put it this way. What feature of a woman's appearance, would you say, it apt to remain most vivid in a man's memory, a man who is in love, romantically? What is it about a woman, a girl, or even about a very proper young lady, let us say ... What is it about her that identifies her, instantly, in a man's mind?"

"Why, the color of her hair, of course," François said.

"I was thinking of that," Clarissa said slowly, staring at her reflection in the mirror.

"Madam has beautiful hair," François said. "It would be a crime to change the color."

And coming closer, standing behind Clarissa, François put a hand on a strand of her rippling hair, and lifting the strand he passed his sensitive fingers through it, feeling the texture.

"Not *change* the color," Clarissa said. "Just lighten it, perhaps, a very little. So that in the light the hair will gleam just slightly auburn. What do you think?"

"It can be done."

"Would it take long?" Clarissa was all eagerness. "Could you do it right away?"

"First, I have to send a flunky to the apothecary's shop to get the necessary ingredients," François said. "I will explain to the man that I need them for the new experiment I'm making on the Earl's wigs."

Clarissa nodded approvingly.

"Naturally, I wouldn't want anyone to so much as suspect even ..."

"The secrets of a woman's toilette," François said, "must never be known to the world."

And he hurried quietly out.

In something less than fifteen minutes, he was back, bringing with him several little bottles and a small china dish. He set
it all down on the dressing table. Then, after pouring the contents
of the bottles into the dish, he briskly stirred the mixture, which
had a purplish cast to it. Since the dyeing of human hair was
almost unheard of, an art known but to a few and then practiced
secretly, the preparation had all the fascination of mysterious
alchemy to Clarissa. She was just a little scared. But she had to
go through with it. In order to keep the romance between Miss
Gray and Mr. Brummell quite intact, perfectly safe, if you please!

François had brought a big towel with him, and he now
wrapped it about Clarissa's shoulders, arranging it close to her
neck in the back, under her hair. Then, he set to work with a little
brush.

"Nobody will ever guess," he once more reassured Clarissa.
"There will be a difference in color, but so imperceptible. People
will merely think that madam has just washed her hair, and then
used maybe a new pomade of some kind. And yet the difference
will be there, exactly the way madam wanted to have it."

When François, at last, pronounced himself satisfied, Sally
suddenly burst in.

"What a lovely person Mr. Davey is," Sally at once began to
chatter. "I didn't see Flaxy's dogs, but I heard them barking. All
but scared the wits out of me, they did!" Sally, obviously, had
enjoyed herself. "François helped you wash your hair?" she asked
Clarissa.

François had quickly gathered his paraphernalia into a small
towel and he now stood ready to depart. But there was a knock
on the door. Clarissa looked towards the chief valet swiftly. The
Earl ...? Then she glanced about the room. A corner was parti-
tioned off by a drawn-across curtain.

"François," Clarissa whispered, and pointed at the curtain. He could conceal himself behind it, she meant.

But François shook his head.

"Madam should know," he said, "that His Grace never knocks on a door. His Grace just walks straight in. Besides, he's busy looking at the gold plate from which the guests will eat their supper after the ball."

The knock was repeated.

"Who is it?" Clarissa asked, raising her voice.

"It's the major-domo, madam. The man who designs carriages is here to see madam. And the tailor who is making the livery for madam's personal coachman ..."

"Oh, Pete will love *that!*" Sally cried, and she clapped her hands.

Clarissa ordered her to be quiet, but Sally burbled on.

"The crimson satin shoes," she belatedly announced, "will be delivered early Saturday morning."

Well, Clarissa could depend on Mr. Davey. But what about her ballgown of stiff crimson silk with its daring décolletage and full skirt? Those stupid dressmakers ... Clarissa suddenly put a hand to each of her temples with a gesture bordering on despair. She had a terrible feeling that nothing would be ready in time for the decisive event, her presentation as a mistress. Nothing would be ready. Nothing ... It would be a complete fiasco! She was certain of it....

PART FOUR

CHAPTER FIFTEEN

BUT, AS IT GENERALLY happens in such cases, everything was ready and in perfect order by the time the important night arrived.

And Clarissa, wearing her crimson ballgown, stood at the top of the magnificent stairway and looked down at the glittering throng of the Earl of Strasford's guests, assembled in the imposing hall below. She had paused there, in the full blaze of the chandeliers, for just a moment before going down.

The radiant beauty of her face was enhanced by the lovely rippling hair, which shone with auburn gleams in the light. While the fleshy tints of her smooth bare shoulders and the generously exposed breasts stood out with vivid lusciousness.

A strange little hush had fallen upon the assembled guests. All heads were upturned in her direction. Lorgnettes, quizzing glasses, monocles were held glued to the greedily curious eyes. They had all come here to appraise, to criticize, to find fault. And now they were dumfounded. She wore jewels, of course, the more jaded connoisseurs observed. Yes, very fine diamonds. And something green ... emeralds? But even they, the jaded ones, knew that such trifles as priceless jewelry did not matter in the *least,* that personal adornments, in this particular case, were absolutely *unnecessary.* The woman's natural beauty outshone the glow of precious stones.

When the gathered company understood this, the momentary hush of awed amazement was suddenly broken. Giving way to gasps of admiration, exclamations of homage, spontaneous applause. In fact, all these men, titled, wealthy, famous, all richly dressed, debonair, arrogant, were so carried away by their feelings that they forgot their good manners and behaved a little wildly. But some of them had brought their beautifully gowned mistresses with them, and the poor women were ready to burst into tears with envy, rage, and hatred. They bit their lips, tore their wisps of handkerchiefs to shreds, and secretly cursed this new mistress of the Earl's, this Clarissa, whom, a mere half-hour ago, nobody had ever heard of!

Clarissa, meanwhile, began to come down the stairs slowly. With one hand she held up her full skirt, raising it just enough to show the tip of a crimson satin shoe. In the other hand she gracefully carried a long black ostrich plume, her closed fan. Her head up, a smile on her lips, she came down the magnificent stairway, at the foot of which the Earl stood, waiting for her.

Then, taking her by the hand, he led her forward, and proudly presented her:

"Mistress Clarissa!"

She was at once surrounded. In fact, the men, led by the Prince Regent and the Duke of Cumberland, as good as mobbed her. In a well-bred sort of way, naturally. She was ogled, showered with compliments, sweet nothings were whispered in her ear by the younger fops. Clarissa smiled, laughed, said something witty. And when a man's remark happened to sound over insolent, or just plain obscene, she would gaily, coquettishly, give the man's face a little slap with the tip of her swaying black ostrich plume. Her overwhelming, instantaneous success made her eyes sparkle. Already, in such a ridiculously short time, she was as popular with all these wealthy, important people as she had been with habitués of the Waterfront Tavern.

Resplendent, white-wigged flunkies, bearing silver trays on which stood crystal goblets filled with bubbling champagne, moved among the guests. And the Poet, who was of course present, having come with Mr. Brummell, his patron, unceremoniously snatched up one of these goblets, and raising it aloft, he cried triumphantly:

"To Clarissa!"

Everybody immediately took up the proclaimed toast, with enthusiasm.

"To Clarissa!" "To Clarissa!" "Clarissa!" they cried, holding the short-stemmed glasses out to her, and then emptying them in a gulp.

The Prince Regent, his gross thighs encased in white satin breeches, and wearing his favorite plum-colored coat with large diamond buttons, said to Clarissa, his eyes bulging slightly, as he stared at her bodice:

"Mistress Clarissa, it actually amazes me that we had not had the pleasure of admiring you till now. Where have you been hiding your so very ravishing charms, pray?"

And extending two fingers of his pudgy hand, he patted her cheek approvingly.

"Your Royal Highness."

Her crimson ballgown rustling, she gracefully sank down in a very low curtsy.

Clarissa's private thought was that His Royal Highness had put on weight since the short time back when, as Miss Gray, she saw him in the rose garden at Ravisham. The poor man was really getting fat.

"Ouch!" Clarissa suddenly said.

Somebody, very expertly and painfully, had pinched her behind. She turned, and it was the Duke of Cumberland, very handsome, richly attired, indolent, his long-fingered effeminate hands covered with jewels.

"A very nice pair of buttocks you have, Mistress Clarissa," he drawled, his velvety eyes smiling insolently into hers. "Why hide them under this big skirt? That's why I had to pinch them, to find out just how shapely and firm they were."

Laughing, Clarissa gave him a little slap with her black ostrich plume. A courtesan, a mistress, could take such liberties with royalty. And the royalty loved it. Who else would dare to slap their faces for them but a loose woman, a harlot? And so they enjoyed the novelty of it.

"But I was admiring the emeralds you're wearing," the Duke of Cumberland added casually.

Yes, Clarissa was wearing her ladyship's emerald rope.

At the very last moment, when already fully dressed for the ball and observing the effect in the mirror, she had suddenly decided that her costume of scarlet gown and the diamond jewelry lacked something, just a *little* something, to make it absolutely perfect, striking. A touch of contrasting color, green preferably, was what the outfit seemed to cry for. And taking the emeralds out of the satchel, Clarissa had put them on quickly, twining the sparkling rope twice around her neck, and then arranging the two green strands to rest on her breasts, just below the diamond necklace. Ah, what a difference! Yes, she would wear the emeralds. She would *always* wear them. Of course, they'd be recognized and there would be talk, questions. But she'd fabricate some kind of plausible explanation. Her ladyship would never dare claim her emerald rope because of the knowledge Clarissa had about her groom-lovers. And the tiny vial, containing the unique draught, Clarissa would also always carry on her own person, concealed in her bodice. The reckless decision thus solved the problem of having to lug the shabby satchel around with her constantly.

"Strangely enough," the Duke of Cumberland now went on, his indolent voice very casual, "these emeralds, which you wear so prettily, Mistress Clarissa, remind me of the Marquise of Trall's famous heirloom."

"Yes," the Prince Regent said, a quizzing lens at one eye, as he stared at the emeralds, "if I wasn't convinced, as probably everybody else is, that *nothing* on earth would make her ladyship part with her heirloom, I could have *sworn* it was the identical emerald rope."

"But didn't Your Royal Highness know," Clarissa said innocently, "that there were *two* ropes made, exactly identical? Surely Your Royal Highness is more or less familiar with the histories of all the great heirlooms in existence. There were *two* emerald ropes made. Abroad somewhere. Yes, France, I think it was. And the family's name was D'Este, if I remember correctly."

"Wasn't it the old count D'Este," somebody in the group surrounding Clarissa said, eager to display his knowledge, "who had been the first to lose his head on the guillotine?"

"That's quite true," the Prince Regent said importantly.

"Anyway, this distinguished family," Clarissa went on, "had these *two* emerald ropes made to their specific order. And one, eventually, came into the possession of her ladyship's family."

"That stubborn mule of a ladyship," the Prince Regent broke in crossly, "always *was* secretive about the origin of her emeralds. And now I understand why. *Her* rope wasn't the only one made, as she claimed!"

"And the other emerald rope," Clarissa went on quietly, "was bought by a very wealthy British merchant. And he gave it to—*me*—" Clarissa put a fingertip to the green stones sparkling on her breasts—"as a little token of—of his friendship."

Clarissa was merely repeating the story she had had to invent, in a hurry, to satisfy the Earl's curiosity, when the Earl, before going downstairs to greet his guests, came into her room to admire her gown and, on seeing the emeralds, asked her about them. While making up the story, the name D'Este had suddenly popped into her mind, and she had used it. For the life of her, she couldn't remember where she had heard such an unusual name before! Until the Earl confided gossipingly that François, his chief valet, who was an *émigré*, though few people knew about it, had been born a D'Este, and that probably it was the same family, since they were known for their jewels before the Revolution. Why, of course, François, Clarissa had then told herself, he *did* mention the name to her....

And now it seemed to give weight, plausibility to her fabrication, as the little story was circulated among the guests.

"Did you know, there were *two* emerald ropes made," one guest said to another. "You don't say!" the other answered. And he added, very much indignant, "The *audacity* of her ladyship, claiming to own the only one in existence!" And there were those who bragged, "Oh, I've heard the story before." The irony of it was that the guest in question had indeed heard it. But in this very room and just a few minutes back, something he didn't want to admit for fear of showing his ignorance. The probable identity of the wealthy merchant, so discreetly mentioned by Clarissa, was also discussed with interest. "Probably Samuelson," some declared with conviction. The Prince Regent's gaudy pavilion at Brighton had been financed by the millionaire Samuelson. This very dignified merchant never showed off a mistress, but he would seek out some unknown young beauty in the provinces, and would keep her with him for two or three nights, in dead secrecy, and then let her go, after rewarding her with a gift of fabulous price."

But in the Duke of Cumberland's velvety eyes there was a humorous twinkle.

"What are you laughing to yourself about, you wicked man?" Clarissa demanded.

Bringing his sensual mouth close to her ear, the Duke whispered:

"It amuses me to think that my princely brother will never get the emeralds from her ladyship after all, no matter *who* wins in their little game of cards!"

And the Duke of Cumberland and Clarissa laughed together. The fact that the Duke didn't believe her clever little story had instantly established a most delightful secret bond between them. And Clarissa was thrilled. This very handsome and luxurious Highness never left her side. Of course, he *would* stand a trifle behind her, so that, now and then, he could pinch her in the buttocks.

"Go and bring Mr. Brummell over," Clarissa said to the Duke, "and introduce him to me properly."

"Yes, I've noticed," the Duke drawled indolently, "that our Beau Brummell has been watching Mistress Clarissa with a peculiar interest, since the very first moment of her appearance amongst us."

And they both looked to where Mr. Brummell stood, a little away from the glittering throng, a picture of quiet elegance.

The Duke of Cumberland, to reach Brummell, had first to push his way through the crowd of fops that milled around Clarissa. They were all in the spacious ballroom now, and couples were starting to glide over the gleaming parquet to the strains of the musicians' violins. A gavotte, or was it the polonaise ...? And though Lafonte had taught Clarissa the gracefully intricate steps of both these fashionable dances, she said, "No, later perhaps," to all the men, and waved them all away.

Mr. Brummell stood before her. He bowed. And Clarissa, at once, purposely, for his benefit, displayed an outrageously vulgar set of manners. First of all, she ogled Mr. Brummell boldly, like the harlot she was. Then, she said "Ouch!" though the Duke of Cumberland had *not* touched her this time.

"You wicked man!" Clarissa cried. "My bottom must be all black and blue with your pinching, I'll swear!"

And she slapped the Duke's face smartly with her black ostrich plume.

Mr. Brummell, Clarissa noticed with satisfaction, could not help but wince at the nasty crudeness of her behavior. Her arms akimbo, Clarissa threw her head back and laughed loudly. Then, very rudely, she told the Duke of Cumberland to go away and dance with somebody. Chuckling to himself, the Duke departed. And Clarissa and Mr. Brummell were suddenly alone.

"I saw you staring at me," she told him bluntly, "and I wondered what the reason could be."

"Surely," Mr. Brummell said politely, "Mistress Clarissa's beauty is reason enough."

"Ah, but that was not the reason," Clarissa parried. And she went on quickly, "Perhaps—perhaps I *remind* you of someone?"

Mr. Brummell glanced at her brightly painted face, and he slowly shook his head.

"That's quite impossible," he said quietly.

And he kept looking at Clarissa, now and again, and a slightly perturbed expression would come into his fine, thoughtful eyes. Something about her seemed to disturb him. I must settle it for him, once and for all, Clarissa told herself.

And she suddenly said, speaking very slowly, "I wonder what she's like."

"Who?" Mr. Brummell said, his voice strangely low.

"I'm supposed to be, well—clever about such things," Clarissa told him. "And when I saw you staring at me from a distance, I had a feeling, I *knew*, I was *positive*, that you were actually thinking of—of a certain young lady who is very dear to you, whom you ... love. And I hope, Mr. Brummell, you don't mind me mentioning it so bluntly."

"Strange enough," Mr. Brummell said, "though I've never spoken of it before to anyone, and—and though nobody knows about it, of course ... I ... I don't mind it at all, coming from you. When I first saw you coming down that stairway, I had the strangest feeling ... As if I'd known you before somewhere. Which is, of course, impossible!"

"*Absolutely* impossible," Clarissa said.

"A woman of such singular beauty as you," Mr. Brummell said, "surely would be recognized instantly by any man, if he had so much as caught a glimpse of her before."

"And what woman could ever forget Beau Brummell, if he had so much as said a single word to her before?" Clarissa cried, swaying her black ostrich plume about flirtatiously.

"Just the same," Mr. Brummell went on, after giving her a little bow, "I'm glad you understood the cause of that strange feeling which I had ..."

"A woman's guess, that's all it was," Clarissa said. "It's really very simple."

Mr. Brummell's fine brow cleared, the perturbed expression in his eyes giving way to a slight smile. He gazed straight at Clarissa, but did not really see her, as Clarissa could tell. The sentimental fellow, at that very same moment, was imagining himself back at Ravisham, in the rose garden, reading poetry from the pretty little volume to Miss Gray, the gentle governess.

"But, surely," Clarissa said, "the young lady in question couldn't have refused Mr. Brummell's honorable devotion? Surely, the young lady must reciprocate Mr. Brummell's selfless affection?"

Mr. Brummell, thus unwillingly recalled to prosaic reality, passed a hand over his brow. And then he said quietly:

"She does me that honor, yes."

"Then why isn't she *here?*" Clarissa demanded. And with a great show of astonishment, she glanced around, as if expecting to see the aforesaid young lady, actually in the flesh, and probably keeping her demure distance somewhere on the fringes of the gay, glittering throng before them. "And you're alone, instead," Clarissa went on gently, "and looking quite sad ..."

"Circumstances were against us."

"Ah ... Cruel, selfish parents, no doubt!"

"No," Mr. Brummell said. "Miss Gray ..."

"Is that her name?" Clarissa pretended bright interest. And, quite as if she had never heard the name before, she repeated it, to fix it in her mind, presumably, "Miss Gray ..."

"Miss Gray is all alone in the world," Mr. Brummell went on. "Except for a brother, who left the country many years ago to seek his fortune in other lands."

Well, Mr. Brummell had no way of knowing that the long-lost brother had suddenly returned.

"Then the only other possible obstacle," Clarissa said, "would be the—the state of health."

"Yes. Her lungs, you know ..." Mr. Brummell explained quietly. "The doctors told Miss Gray that it was a matter of only a few months, perhaps ... And so, naturally, our parting had to be final, irrevocable. We don't even correspond...."

Which explained why Mr. Brummell could take it for granted, as he evidently did, that Miss Gray was still at Ravisham, and looking after those two horrible brats, Lady Flo and Lady Sue.

Clarissa, as she stood there, with Mr. Brummell before her, shook out her big skirt, making the crimson silk rustle provokingly. With one white hand—*white,* thanks to that expensive lotion and the gloves worn ridiculously while asleep—she set straight the jewels which sparkled and glowed at her throat and on her daringly exposed breasts. Then she gave a little shake with her lovely head, to make fall into place the lustrous waves and silky ringlets of her hair that rippled down to her bare shoulders. And then Clarissa said:

"Mr. Brummell, now that I know all about it, I wonder even more what she's like, this young lady, this Miss Gray. In appearance, I mean. Would you say, for instance, that she's about my height?"

Mr. Brummell looked Clarissa over, from head to foot. Then, after making the necessary comparison very carefully in his mind, he said decisively:

"Miss Gray is taller. Oh, yes definitely, quite … Taller by two, three inches, I would say."

Fancy that, Clarissa told herself. So I've grown *shorter* by two, three inches, in the last couple of weeks. Aloud she said:

"I see." And she went on, "There's just one other little thing, Mr. Brummell. If you *pardon* my curiosity, if you don't find it offensive to your *sensibilities*. After all, who am I? *What* am I? A mistress, a vulgar creature …"

And it was there and then that Beau Brummell produced one of his spontaneously created, famous bon mots.

"No woman is ever vulgar," he said, and he bowed very low to Clarissa. "A woman is either very beautiful … or, if she's not that, then she is very, very charming."

How gallantly he could say such things! No wonder all the ladies adored him.

"Then you won't mind," Clarissa went on, "my asking you … what is it that you remember first about this Miss Gray's looks? I mean," Clarissa said, "when you think of her, what particular feature of her appearance stands out with special clarity?"

Mr. Brummell considered. Then he smiled, and said:

"Why, it's her hair, I suppose."

"She has lovely hair?"

Mr. Brummell didn't seem to hear the question.

"It's dark, for one thing. None of this brilliance, these auburn gleams," he waved a negligent hand at Clarissa's hair. "And she has the *smoothest* of hairdos. Even the few curls that dangle over the ears are smooth...."

That horribly dowdy hairdo! Those sausage-like curls, bunched together so tight! And he was in rhapsodies about it. The blindness, the strange aberration, the phenomenal loyalty of romantic love! Well ... Laughing to herself, Clarissa gave it up.

Her numerous admirers, besides, were once again milling close around her. Obeying her caprice of enjoying a little tête-à-tête with Mr. Brummell—-something every woman naturally craved for—they had politely placed themselves beyond earshot, but now they had swarmed back. The Poet was the first to reach her side, however. With a triumphant shake of his unruly locks, he declared, conspiratorially:

"Wasn't I right in saying you should be robed in crimson?"

And away he hurried, impatient to get back to his garret, and his everlasting scribbling.

And then suddenly it was Mr. FitzMaurice, with his quizzing glass, and Lord Cavor, with his monocle, each at one side of her. Throughout the evening she had been aware of the pair of them, portly, richly attired, ogling her avidly from a distance. No danger of recognition *there*, she had at once decided. And with good reason.

As the governess, Miss Gray, she had been below their notice. Then, when in answer to the little note from that demure creature, they saw, through the peephole, a woman completely naked, taking a bath.... Well, *that* was proof enough she couldn't be the *real* Miss Gray, wasn't it? And if somebody, an impostor, was fooling her ladyship, so much the better! None of *their* concern, anyway. They must have had a good laugh about it, at her ladyship's expense.

As to their present failure of connecting Clarissa, the Earl of Strasford's new mistress, with the woman they had watched through the peephole ... Well, Clarissa wasn't taking a bath *now*, she wasn't *completely* naked. But, instead, splendidly gowned, shining with jewels, surrounded, courted. The conviction that they were viewing her for the first time was written all over the smug faces of the pair of them.

And now there they were, Mr. FitzMaurice and Lord Cavor, whispering advantageous offers into Clarissa's ears. The stupid fops were still in search of a mistress. And they didn't realize how recently they had already propositioned her, Clarissa, once before. But this time they raised her price considerably, the villains! Because she was a success. Some of her glory would rub off on *them*, they thought. Should Mistress Clarissa find herself without a protector, they whispered. The Earl's advanced age ... anything might happen ... apoplexy ... any day ... quite *soon*, maybe....

Clarissa thanked them prettily. Promised to keep them in mind.

She saw that the guests were standing aside respectfully.

"I am dancing this polonaise with Mistress Clarissa," the Prince Regent said.

It was a distinction His Royal Highness had never previously conferred on anybody's mistress. He was in a very good mood. Not a woman in the room who wasn't a harlot; which meant there was no fear, as the Regent well knew, of Brummell suddenly finding someone to attract him.

Taking Clarissa by the hand, the Prince Regent led her out onto the gleaming parquet, to the strains of violin music. Like all people inclined to stoutness, or already quite stout, he was surprisingly light on his feet. Even Lafonte, Clarissa thought as she gracefully followed her partner's intricate figures, would have approved His Royal Highness' performance.

Altogether, Clarissa so thoroughly enjoyed herself that later she had only a hazy recollection of when precisely the guests began to leave, in what order, and how did it happen eventually that she was in bed, at last, and falling asleep.

On arising quite late the next morning, Clarissa put on a peignoir, a *real* peignoir, made of lace. The partition curtain in the faraway corner now bulged with the dresses which, finished and delivered, hung on the rows of hooks there. Sitting down at the dressing table, Clarissa sipped her hot chocolate, brought in by Sally, who looked really nice in her new silk cap and gown. Sally had never had a silk dress in her life, and she tittered constantly, and in the silliest way, with the sheer excitement of it. Then Sally hurried over to the windows to draw back the curtains. And suddenly she gave a cry of astonishment.

"Goodness gracious! There's quite a crowd collected outside. And they're all staring up at our windows. Now what could it be? Maybe the house's on fire and we don't know it!"

And Sally seemed quite ready to start rushing about in a fright, waving her arms and screaming for help. But Clarissa merely laughed:

"That shows what a country bumpkin you are, Sally. Of course, there's a crowd," Clarissa said very calmly. "I expected there would be. All those people you see collected outside are here for a very simple reason. They're waiting to catch a glimpse of *me*," Clarissa said, leisurely sipping hot chocolate.

"And why should they be wanting to do *that?*" Sally demanded.

"Because I'm famous now, you silly goose," Clarissa said. "News travels fast in London. Probably by the time the people had had their breakfasts this morning, in their homes, or in the taverns, there wasn't a body left who hadn't heard of the success I made with all those fops last night! My name, Clarissa, is on everybody's lips by now," Clarissa said.

"Humph!" Sally said.

"And naturally, the people are curious to see for themselves what I, the famous new beauty, look like," Clarissa went on. "That crowd outside has been gathering for hours, I wouldn't be surprised. They've all been very patient, knowing that I'll be going out somewhere eventually, since a mistress, as a rule, makes it a point to show herself the morning following her presentation. And so they're waiting to see me come out and get into my carriage. Send a flunky to tell Pete to bring it around," Clarissa ordered. "And take out my carriage dress. The one of pale brocade. And don't forget to lay out the accessories I selected. The little bonnet matching the gown. And the long blue gloves. And, yes, the tiny ruffled parasol. Since the sun is so bright."

The crowd, when Clarissa at last appeared, hailed her by name. Plain folk, most of them, they took pride in her success. A young fellow, wearing an apprentice's leather apron, shouted, quite beside himself with joy, "Good luck to you, Mistress Clarissa!" And they all discussed her aloud among themselves, unceremoniously. "She's a beauty, no mistake!" "See the bonnet she has on? Straight from Paris, I bet!" A shawled housewife, with a market basket on her arm, cried shrilly, "The gown she's wearing must have cost the old Earl a pretty penny!" And they all roared with laughter, at the Earl's expense.

Clarissa, smiling graciously, stepped into the elegant landau which the Earl had put at her disposal while her own personal carriage was being made. Reclining against the cushions, she opened her tiny parasol. Sally sat on the bench facing her. A flunky jumped onto the step attached at the back of the carriage, to ride there standing like a statue. Another flunky took his place on the box beside Pete, who, very much aware of the brilliant livery he was wearing, kept grinning all over his homely yokel's face. And so, in great style, and with the crowd running after the carriage, Clarissa set off to do a little shopping.

Not that she needed anything particular. But it was gratifying to have the shopkeepers meet her everywhere with low bows. To buy some costly trinket and not care *how* costly it was. To be stared at by the other customers with curiosity, with flattering envy. "Is that *she?*" "Is that Clarissa?" "*You* know—the Earl of Strasford's new mistress." And, on coming out, to see a new crowd already collected around her carriage.

When darkness settled over the city and the fashionable places of amusement started to blaze with lights, the Earl took Clarissa around with him everywhere, showing her off. And wherever she appeared she produced a sensation. At the theater, or opera, the people in the pit stood up the better to see her as, beautifully gowned, bedecked with jewels, she entered the Earl's gilded box. Nobody paid heed to the performance on the stage, but all the opera glasses instead would be fixed on Clarissa.

The other mistresses, every time, seemed ready to faint with envy and helpless rage. "Look at her!" they whispered to one another. "This Clarissa! She may as well have no bodice on at all!" "Shameless hussy!" "Slut!" And the miserable women would be so overcome with hatred and frustration that one or another of them would suddenly go off into hysterics and would have to be carried out bodily, while the public tittered.

The Court ladies, though decorously immobile, were just as envious. They watched Clarissa from behind their fans with hard, cruel eyes. "My dear," they would say one to another, their thin lips barely moving, "what can the men possibly *see* in her? Such a coarse, vulgar creature. So flamboyant!" But the Princess Royal, her tiara wiggling, as it always did when her brother, the Prince Regent, happened to be present, was heard to ask, while looking towards Clarissa with warm interest, "Who *is* that very beautiful woman?"

And even at the cockfights Clarissa's appearance always stole the show. Instead of watching the little cocks peck each other to a blood-dripping death, the audience stared at Clarissa. Her slightest movement, glance, turn of the head was watched with avid curiosity. To whom did she give her lace shawl to hold, or her fan, or her little flacon of perfume? The Green Perfume.

"Mistress Clarissa," the Duke of Cumberland would drawl, ready to yawn with boredom though their select, pleasure-seeking little group had just come in, "let's go and see the dancing bears."

The Duke was generally in the group of fops surrounding Clarissa. Of course, first of all, there would be the diminutive Earl, in his blue and pink satin costume, besprinkled with diamonds and pearls, his painted little face beaming with pride. And then the Prince Regent, the tight white breeches accentuating the grossness of his figure, and his eyes coldly haughty under the brown curls of his big glossy wig. To be seen constantly in the company of the famous new beauty, Clarissa, increased his own popularity, or so the vain Prince thought. And with the Regent, naturally, there would be the quietly elegant Mr. Brummell.

To be near Clarissa, since she was the only person who knew about his secret attachment for Miss Gray, seemed to ease the romantic fellow's loneliness and heartache. It was very seldom that Mr. Brummell could find an opportunity to actually speak of Miss Gray, because Clarissa was always so surrounded. But Clarissa, when unobserved, would give him a little nod, implying understanding, sympathy. And Brummell thus gained solace from being in her presence.

And always—standing or walking, as the case might be— right behind Clarissa, there would be the luxurious Duke of Cumberland, carrying Clarissa's lap dog. Every mistress was supposed to have one; it was the fashion. And the Duke had personally procured the lap dog, a fluffy roll of honey-colored fur, for her, declaring:

"No, it won't be a nuisance to you. Because I'll always carry it for you, I promise!"

Clarissa had laughed in disbelief. The indolent Duke burdened with a lap dog, as if he were a footman!

But there he always was, carrying the pretty little animal in the crook of his silk-clad arm.

And so they all went to see the dancing bears, a great novelty at the time.

As soon as the swarthy trainer began playing a little tune on his flute, the two great bears stood up on their hind legs and starting waltzing about awkwardly, the heavy chains that dangled from their nose rings clanging loudly. Everybody knew how the bears had been trained. On a floor of iron, gradually heated to redness from below. Howling with pain, the beasts would rear, and then would try to remain in an upright position, while hopping from one hind paw to another in the attempt to escape contact with the hot metal that burned their soles. And the trainer, meanwhile, would be playing that little tune on his flute. And now, on hearing that selfsame music, up they rose and danced. The memory of the pain they had endured was sometimes so vivid with them that suddenly a tremendous howl would issue out of their husky throats.

But everybody stared at Clarissa, including the swarthy trainer himself. A short, stocky man, with matted hair which gave him a wild appearance, he kept looking towards her with his dark intense eyes, while playing his flute. And when Clarissa, about to leave, had almost reached the door, the man was suddenly right there, speaking to her.

"The casket, lady. I have the casket for you.... It's small. But made of rare, precious wood. And the clasps are of brass ..."

His voice was thick with some foreign accent. Spanish, perhaps. Or Portuguese. The great bears, Clarissa had heard somebody mention, came from the Himalayas.

"What was the swarthy knave saying to you?" the Duke of Cumberland said.

The trainer had slipped away at his approach, and Clarissa hastened to lie glibly:

"Oh, some gibberish or other. I couldn't make out a single word of what the man said."

Privately she was intrigued, mystified by the incident. But the Duke of Cumberland, satisfied by her explanation, began to enthuse about a very exclusive brothel, newly opened. And there their pleasure-loving group gaily went to have supper. Very young girls, with not a stitch on them, and looking like a garland of flowers, danced around the guests seated at the sumptuous table. And Clarissa, flattered by the compliments the men showered on her, forgot about the bear trainer, and about the small casket with brass clasps which he was so anxious to give her.

Never had the nation known such reckless gaiety as during the reign of the Prince Regent. Nobody seemed to know that there was a war going on. Or perhaps everybody wanted to forget the war. Forget the menace of the aggressor Napoleon. And the fact that almost all of Europe was already in his grasp. And forget about their own British fleet, forced into inaction, standing idle in the faraway, unknown waters of the ancient river Nile. But what everybody wanted to blot out of their minds most of all, especially the poor people, was the lonely figure of Lord Nelson, pacing the deck of his flagship *Victory,* as he still waited for the needed supplies ...

CHAPTER SIXTEEN

CLARISSA, ON COMING HOME with the Earl, swiftly undressed with Sally's help, put on a peignoir of pink tulle, richly flounced, and was about to hurry to the Earl's bedroom when, suddenly, sounds of some kind of commotion, coming from the hall below, reached her. Voices of the flunkies arguing with someone. And a man's loud voice, which struck Clarissa as strangely familiar. She hastened out onto the landing and looked down over the banister.

And there, standing at the foot of the stairs, struggling with the flunkies, was a tall broad-shouldered man, wearing the blue naval uniform. The uniform was a trifle shabby. And that's how Clarissa knew who it was, before the man raised his head. Or maybe she would have known him instantly anyway. Captain Richard Gray.

Just as she was about to turn and run, he saw her.

"Clarissa!" he shouted.

Two flunkies hung on him bodily. Captain Richard Gray suddenly flung them off, and then he started up the stairs in a rush, taking two, three steps with each leaping stride.

Clarissa ran. She ran straight to the Earl's bedroom, her thoughts in a whirl with fear. Captain Richard Gray had called her Clarissa—which meant that she had been right, back at Ravisham, to think that he knew instantly, the moment she so demurely tripped into the gun room, that she was not his sister, Miss Gray, but somebody else, an impostor! All that sly talk about the childhood memories shared ... The little kitten Miss Gray was supposed to have loved so dearly when a child. The tiny birthmark, a mere beauty spot, on Miss Gray's delicate neck, just under the right ear. And Miss Gray's first name—Polly, of all things! What nonsense ... pure invention! It had been nothing but a *test*.

And his suspicions confirmed by the wrong answers Clarissa gave him, Captain Richard Gray had hurried to the village to find out about the details of the stagecoach mishap. Directed to the spot where the woman killed in the accident had been buried in such haste, hastening there, he saw the name Clarissa, painted with tar, on the crude piece of board which marked the desolate grave in the unconsecrated ground, where weeds and nettles grew, collecting dust.... Since the demure creature in the gunroom was not his sister, then it was his sister resting here. While the impostor was this Clarissa, a cheap little actress.

Wrathful though he was, he had bided his time, getting all the evidence needed. Then to London in haste. To find the brazen hussy who had dared to impersonate Miss Gray.

And here he was, come to demand justice. He had probably brought several constables with him to arrest immediately the hateful culprit.

Clarissa, on running into the Earl's bedroom, didn't stop, but ran on to where the Earl sat in a cushioned chair beside the small table on which had been placed, as usual, the decanter with the ruby wine and two crystal glasses.

"Don't let them take me," Clarissa cried. "It's Captain Richard Gray ... Miss Gray's brother.... And, of course, he has the constables with him ... Your Grace, protect me," sinking down to the floor before him in a hasty curtsy.

"Gray? Captain Gray?" the Earl said, sitting up in his chair with a jerk. "Miss Gray? Her *brother!*"

Captain Richard Gray was already in the room and striding towards them.

"You see?" the Earl said to Clarissa. "Didn't I tell you some member of the family would be sure to pop up? Either a father, or an uncle ... making trouble ... duel ... and now it's your brother ..."

And jumping out of the chair, the Earl, looking smaller than ever with fright, ran half around the chair and then tried to hide himself behind it.

"But I'm *not* Miss Gray!" Clarissa cried. "The constables. Your Grace must send them away!"

And the flounced hem of her pink peignoir trailing over the rug, she hastened to step back, away from Captain Gray, who looked so flushed, and disheveled, and altogether furious, as she thought.

"What constables?" Captain Richard Gray said. And he, too, raised his voice. "What are you talking about?"

The two of them seemed to be speaking at one and the same time. Both angry, excited. Interrupting each other. And neither listening to what the other was saying.

The Earl came out from behind the chair.

"Thank you for reminding me, my dear," he said to Clarissa. "Of course, you're not Miss Gray. But for a moment there I was all confused! Thank you."

He reseated himself in his chair, and then he was busy retrieving his lace handkerchief, and his bejeweled fan, and shaking out the handkerchief, and opening the fan to cool his painted little face, which had gotten quite warm from all this excitement. And while the Earl was doing all this, Captain Richard Gray, suddenly and surprisingly, winked at Clarissa. And a very expressive wink it was. Now you leave it all to me, the wink said. Let me handle the situation in my own way ...

Some new trick of his, Clarissa told herself. Did he actually think that she would ever again fall for any of his despicably sly machinations? The idea was fantastic!

She stood close beside the Earl's chair, and looked very haughty.

"What's this about constables?" the Earl said. "Young man, how dare you!"

"Your Grace," Captain Richard Gray said, sweeping him a most respectful bow.

The tricorn, held in one strong, rough-looking hand, was adorned with a naval cockade. Just as Clarissa remembered it. And Captain Gray didn't look so very furious, she could see that now. If he had appeared somewhat flushed and disheveled from the flunkies' brutal handling, he had managed to make himself presentable by now. The jacket of the shabby uniform sat straight and well on his tall, broad-shouldered figure. And his hair was smooth enough, though that forelock of his fell, as usual, over the fine, open brow.

"If Your Grace will allow me to explain," Captain Richard Gray went on, his loud voice ringing through the room. "There's been an unfortunate misunderstanding...."

"I very distinctly heard her say," the Earl pointed with his bejeweled fan at Clarissa, "the word 'constables'!" And he flapped his lace handkerchief about to emphasize his great displeasure.

"Mistress Clarissa," Captain Gray said, now sweeping *her* a most respectful bow, "whose beauty has made her famous. And whose name, on that account, is on everybody's lips ..." Trying to flatter the Earl. Only it won't do him any good! "Mistress Clarissa," Captain Gray went on, "on catching sight of my uniform," he placed a hand on the brass buttons with which his jacket was closed, "probably, er ... mistook it for that of a constable. You know how women are," Captain Richard Gray appealed to the Earl, as one man to another, "always jumping to conclusions."

"Now, my dear, that was very foolish of you," the Earl said, turning to Clarissa. "Anybody seeing this fine young man would have known that he was wearing the uniform of our ... our glorious fleet. Yes, Lord Nelson's fleet!" And in the attempt to look patriotic, the Earl tried to thrust out his dried-up little chest.

"So that's how this unfortunate misunderstanding occurred, you see," Captain Gray went on easily.

What an incredible liar the man was, Clarissa thought, indignant. And why did he keep looking at her peignoir? Perhaps she had made a rent in it, while fleeing—at the sight of him—from the landing? No, there was no rent in the peignoir.

"You mean," the Earl said, "there are no constables?"

"No," Captain Richard Gray said. "Of course not."

"Of course not," the Earl repeated. "The idea!"

"The idea is ridiculous," Captain Gray said. "Absolutely ridiculous!"

"Fantastic! As if anyone would dare bring them into *my* house!"

"No one would dare do such a thing," Captain Gray assured him solemnly. "No one. Nobody!"

"I should say not!"

"Certainly not!"

"No ... no constables?" Clarissa said, in a very small voice.

Captain Richard Gray turned to her. And though he kept his face serious, his eyes, under that forelock of his, were full of laughter.

"No," he said.

"Not ... even *one* constable?"

"Not a single one. No constables at all. None. There!"

"Then why are you here?" Clarissa cried.

"Yes," the Earl said. "Why are you here? You haven't explained that, young man. Have you?"

Captain Gray explained it very simply, easily, with a comically assumed grace and a lot of respectful bows. Clarissa had a suspicion that he was enjoying himself tremendously. Being on a furlough, and finding himself in London—so ran his innocent little story—he had felt it his duty to pay his respects to the Earl of Strasford, the greatest noble of the realm, member of the Council of State....

"Hmm ... hmmm ..." the Earl said importantly.

Not having an appointment, however, Captain Richard Gray went on, he was stopped by the footmen.

"That is as it should be," the Earl said.

But he was determined, Captain Gray continued hastily, to pay his respects, and ... and so here he was. A very low bow.

"A most commendable attitude," the Earl announced. "I commend you, young man. I commend you."

And since all the inns and the hostelries were filled to capacity with the fighting men hurrying back from their furloughs, Captain Gray went on, he was confident the Earl would find it convenient to put him up for the night. All the nobles were being very helpful that way ...

The impudent liar! Now Clarissa was certain he would be thrown out without more ado.

But the credulous Earl, fearful of being outdone by his peers, said:

"Naturally ... Of course!" And his good mood quite restored by Captain Gray's shrewd flatteries, he began to flirt with his fan and flap his handkerchief about and giggle.

"You know," he confided, "all I do at the Council of State is have a nap. Hee, hee, hee."

Then the Earl turned to Clarissa:

"Please pull the bell rope for François."

That was the one that dangled from the velvet canopy of the raised bed. To reach the bed, Clarissa had to walk past Captain Richard Gray. And he whispered quickly, as she came close:

"I'm leaving tomorrow to rejoin my ship. Clarissa ... I must talk to you."

She gave no sign that she heard him. And walking back, after a good tug at the bell rope, she made a little detour so as not to pass him. How could she trust such a man! Besides, it would do no harm to get him worried a bit. But was he worried? Not in the least! Every time he knew himself to be unobserved by the Earl, Captain Gray would grin at her, in the most brazen manner, his teeth gleaming very white against the sea-tanned skin of his handsome face.

"François," Clarissa said, as the chief valet entered, "this is Captain Richard Gray. His Grace wishes him to stay overnight. Escort him to a guest room. And do make sure that the bed is *very comfortable.*"

As she spoke the last two words, Clarissa looked straight into the chief valet's eyes, a significant stare in her own.

"Very good, madam," was all François said.

And he conducted Captain Gray out, and quietly closed the door.

Clarissa, at once seating herself gracefully on the arm of the Earl's chair, began to coo at him sweetly:

"My little Peewee ..."

Placing a fingertip behind his ear, she tickled him there.

"Hee, hee, hee ..." The Earl giggled senilely.

His little eyes running all over her transparent pink peignoir, like so many mice, he put a hand on her knee. Clarissa let him fondle her for a while. But when she saw him getting overexcited, she ordered him to get into bed.

And giggling happily with anticipation, the Earl, as usual, eagerly complied.

Clarissa took up the decanter, poured the ruby wine into the crystal glass, and drank from the glass leisurely. When only a little of the wine was left on the bottom, she set the glass down. Then, standing with her back to the canopied bed, she swiftly produced the tiny vial from inside her bodice, removed the little stopper, and let the unique draught trickle down into the wine, drop by drop. Only instead of the customary three drops, Clarissa this time made it six drops. The Earl, besides sleeping the whole night through, would sleep most of the following day, too.

After watching the mixture on the bottom of the glass fuzz swiftly up to the brim with a black foam, and then turn opaque, and then, settling down, regain the wine's original clear ruby color, Clarissa carried the glass over to the bed.

"Now my little Peewee must drink what's left of the wine in my glass," she declared prettily.

Accustomed to interpreting this nightly ritual as a fanciful preliminary to long pleasurable hours dedicated to the gratification of his lust, the Earl, as usual, was highly delighted. Taking the wineglass from her hand eagerly, he gulped the ruby-colored mixture down hastily.

"There!" Clarissa's smile was full of promise, as she took the emptied glass from him.

One minute, his painted little face was giggling up at her. The next, he had sunk back on the pillows, and was asleep, snoring slightly.

Clarissa carried the glass back to the table, set it down. François would wash it out later, when he came to undress the Earl, put him into his nightshirt, exchange the neat white wig for that ridiculous nightcap with its long tassel…. And, thinking this, Clarissa hurried through the connecting door into her own bedroom.

Sally, of course, wasn't there. Every night Sally would sneak out of the house to join Pete in the hayloft over the stables for a few hours of love-making. And now Clarissa's first thought was that the room was empty. But, no; François had understood her implied command perfectly. A man's blue jacket with brass buttons decorated a chair. And the shabby tricorn with the naval cockade had been flung onto her dressing table and now lay there, incongruously, among her pretty bottles and jars. While from the top of the very high bed the sole and heel of a man's heavy boot protruded impudently. Very sure of himself was Captain Richard Gray! Hadn't even bothered to remove his dirty boots. The leather of the visible sole, Clarissa noticed, was worn very thin, almost to a hole.

And now he was asleep. And he had probably broken the little ladder, climbing it to stretch himself full-length on the down-filled top mattress. She'd find one of the rungs split, Clarissa was sure of it. But hurrying over to the little ladder she saw that no harm had come to it. Using one hand to hold on with, and with the other holding up her pink peignoir, she scaled the ladder with the nimbleness of frequent usage. And then she lay beside "darling Richard" and, her chin propped on an elbow, looked down at him. Many a woman would have envied the brute's beautiful eyelashes. The collar of his shirt was open and Clarissa could see his pillar of a neck, as nicely tanned as his face.

Captain Richard Gray suddenly opened one eye. Clarissa, taken by surprise, tried to look haughty, angry, disgusted, but failed. And both his eyes open now and brimming with laughter, he said, mockingly accusing:

"Confess now, you thought I was asleep. If you don't, I'll immediately bring the constables over!"

"Never mind *that*," Clarissa said. "You do owe me an explanation." And pushing his hands away, and clutching her pink peignoir about her—when he wasn't looking at her face, he was looking at the peignoir—Clarissa went on. "How could you have been so sure, the first time you saw me, in that gun *room*, back at Ravisham, that I wasn't Miss Gray, that I wasn't your sister? After all, she was but a child when you left."

"You adorable little fool!" Captain Richard Gray said. "Why, a man has a way of knowing, when he looks at a woman, what she is to him. As soon as I saw you, tripping so demurely into that gun room, all I wanted to do was take you in my arms, like this," and Clarissa was suddenly in his arms, enveloped, imprisoned, as he demonstrated. "And," Captain Gray went on, "to kiss you, like this," and he began to demonstrate.

"No man would want to do that to his sister, now would he?" Captain Gray demanded, when he stopped demonstrating for a second.

"No, I suppose not," Clarissa agreed, and she sighed with great satisfaction.

And then his mouth was suddenly pressed hard against hers. And ... Well, for a long time, there was no talk between them.

Afterwards, her head snuggled against his shoulder, Clarissa said:

"So there never had been any little black kitten?"

"No," Captain Gray said.

"Not even a little *white* one, maybe?"

"No. No kitten of any description whatsoever!"

"And the little birthmark, like a beauty spot, which Miss Gray was supposed to have had, just under her right ear," Clarissa went on. "That was another invention of yours, Captain Richard Gray, wasn't it?"

"Didn't take me a second to make that one up!" Captain Gray said. And very proud of himself he sounded, the way he said it.

"And then," Clarissa went on, "that name—Polly, of all things! That's what made me suspect, later, that you were just testing me. That," Clarissa said, rubbing her cheek against the smooth hardness of his shoulder "and ... and the way you kissed me."

She didn't mind the smell of the sea which clung to his clothes, even to his skin. The smell of the strong sea spray, lashing the deck of a ship. *His* ship ...

"The way I kissed you was good," Captain Gray declared. And he kissed her again, just to show how good he had been at it even that first time. "But inventing such a wishy-washy name for my sister was a stupid mistake on my part. Didn't sound right, did it? Because it doesn't suit a personality such as hers was, I suppose."

"But, what actually *was* Miss Gray's first name?" Clarissa said. She had been curious to know it for so long. And now she would find out.

Captain Gray didn't answer at once. And then he said, quietly:

"Lucinda."

"Ah, that's better," Clarissa was all approval. "Lucinda Gray. Now it sounds absolutely right. Perfect!"

"She was such a gentle, loving thing as a child...."

Naturally, it worried him to think that he had returned just a little too late to see her grown up.

"You would have found her the same, as a person, if you saw her when I knew her," Clarissa told him reassuringly.

And then they were both silent for a while, thinking of the gentle governess.

"And so, whatever the reason," Captain Richard Gray went on, his voice loud and gay once more, "my adorable little fool got scared of having her clever impersonation discovered, and she ran away. Her ladyship, and the rest of them, knew nothing about it till the following morning. Plenty of excitement you caused them, believe me! Miss Gray gone. And the kitchenmaid, Sally. And one of the grooms, Pete. And a small, enclosed carriage found missing. The three of them must have fled in it sometime during the night."

"While everybody was in the kitchen, preparing dinner," Clarissa said. And she laughed, remembering her flight in the downpour from Ravisham.

Who would have thought it possible then that she would be lying in bed, as she was now, so very cozily with "darling Richard?"

"And so, there I was, left to do all the explaining to her ladyship," Captain Gray went on. " 'Miss Gray,' I told her very calmly, 'has probably been summoned unexpectedly to the bedside of her great-aunt, who lives in Scotland. The old lady must have been taken very ill.... And that's why Miss Gray had to leave in such a hurry.' "

"I remember your sister mentioning a distant relative of some kind," Clarissa said, "a great-aunt, yes. And does this great-aunt really live in Scotland?"

"For a change, I was telling the truth," Captain Gray laughed. "I thought it would be safe to mention it, since Scotland is so very far away. Not that her ladyship showed any eagerness to find you. In fact, she seemed rather relieved at your going, for some reason."

Clarissa laughed to herself. And Captain Gray, quite unaware of her secret amusement, went on:

"And then I thanked her ladyship for her hospitality, and I went to get my traveling bag, and I walked out of that great stone pile of a house, past the peacocks strutting on the terraces, and along the endless driveway that curves so splendidly between the vivid green lawns. And so out through those enormous iron gates, guarded by the stone lions bearing the ancestral shield of the Marquises of Trall. But when I reached the road that was to lead me to the inn in the village, I turned to look back at Ravisham. All I could see was the forest of its ancient trees, with a chimney or two showing far beyond. And I said—yes, I spoke right out, aloud—'When I return, it will be as your owner. *I'll be the master!*' "

"Oh, come now, you're not going to start *that* again," Clarissa remonstrated. "Considering the worn condition of your boots, and the shabbiness of your uniform, it's not even funny!"

"Ah, but there's always the future," Captain Gray pointed out, laughing. "And the future is always wonderfully different! If the investments I've made in those gold mines in Africa, and in the plantations in the New World, in Virginia, ever pay off ...'"

"I know," Clarissa said mockingly, "you'll have such a lot of money that you'll buy Ravisham." The man was really demented on the subject! "But do go on," she prompted him eagerly. "So you went to the inn in the village, and ..."

"And there I stayed."

"But you told me, that time, you could stay only a few days—three days, wasn't it?" Clarissa was frankly surprised. Horrified, in fact. "And that was several weeks ago! And your furlough ..."

"Did I say I could stay only a few days?"

"Oh, so that was a lie, too!"

"Well, probably I was interested in seeing how you'd react to that one," Captain Gray said, grinning at her. "No, I was not pressed for time as far as my furlough was concerned," he went on seriously. "Besides, there was something very important that I had to do. And so ..."

"Something very important?" Clarissa frowned, trying to guess what it could have been.

"And so I stayed on at that inn," Captain Gray went on, unmindful of the interruption. "What I had to do had to be done with a great deal of care. And it all took time. For one thing, I had to wait for a moonless night."

"Oh," Clarissa said. She was beginning to understand.

"It had to be pitch dark, for my purpose," Captain Gray said. "Since I couldn't afford to be seen. Or to have any one suspect what it was I was doing. There are laws, strict laws, about those things.... And then I had to find the men to help me carry it off successfully. To look for them among the local people might have caused talk, aroused suspicion. So I made several trips to Sudbury ..."

A market town about seven miles distant from the village of Wickhem St. Paul's, Clarissa was quick to recollect.

"And in that busy little town," Captain Gray continued calmly, "I at last found four husky fellows whom I deemed worthy of my trust. And I swore them to utter secrecy. And I gave them most of the money I had. And then, at the dead of night, I met them, as prearranged, at that desolate spot, beside the grave there. They had brought a wagon with them, and the necessary tools, pikes and spades. And we set to work. We had to be quick, and yet not make any noise. And it was so dark we had to feel our way about. We spaded away the earth that made the little mound, and then we dug into the ground, deeper and deeper, till the coffin was reached. We lifted it out very carefully, and carried it and placed it in the wagon, and covered it with straw. And two of the men at once drove away with it. To Halstead."

"And where is that?" Clarissa said.

"It's a small place, not far from London. My people used to own a home there. I thought my sister might have mentioned it to you."

"Miss Gray spoke about your old home, yes. But she didn't give a name to the place. Is it a village?" And remembering Miss Gray's enthusiasm about her childhood home, Clarissa added, "Probably, a pretty village."

"Well, the scenery is supposed to be very fine," Captain Gray conceded. "Anyway," he went on, "I gave to one of those two men a letter I had prepared beforehand. Addressed to a solicitor in Halstead, an old friend of the family. He was to arrange immediately for a proper burial, in the churchyard there. And, by now, that has been done."

"And the empty grave?" Clarissa said.

"The other two men and myself," Captain Gray said, "we hurried back to fill it up. And we built up the little mound, giving it the required shape with the backs of our spades. The very elements, fortunately, seemed to have been in league with us. For it rained the next day. And the wet, doubtless, obliterated whatever traces of tampering there might have been left. As to the broken weeds and nettles that we couldn't avoid trampling on, that might have been done by the rain. And by the wind, which generally seems to accompany the rain in those parts."

"And the marker?" Clarissa said. "The marker with my name painted on it so horribly, with tar!"

"I had to put it back," Captain Gray admitted. "The absence of that marker would have certainly attracted attention, made the gossips curious. *Who* had removed it? And *why*? And that might have led to a closer observation of the ground, with most undesirable results.... So I put it back. Making it as secure as it had been before. And there it must remain."

Goodness, Clarissa thought, I seem to be leaving mementoes of myself all over the country! Her old brief skirt and the torn blouse gone with the wandering gypsies. And her "costumes," in the Poet's valise, destined to repose forever on the shelf of unclaimed possessions in the cottage-office of the Wickhem St. Paul's constable. And the short traveling cape given away to a beggar, and *he* going off with it heaven alone knew where to. And now her name on the crude marker of that empty grave. Were all these things good omens? Clarissa wondered. And if not, what did they all portend?

"But don't let's waste any more time," Captain Gray said.

And he tried to draw her back into the circle of his strong arms.

"Wait," Clarissa laughed. "First answer me this question. How in the world could you have been so sure that the famous new beauty, Clarissa, and the Clarissa whom you were looking for, were one and the same woman?"

"Ah, there I was taking a chance," Captain Gray boasted, "of being thrashed within an inch of my life by the Earl's flunkies, for my impudence. But when the stagecoach carrying me to London stopped at the Rose and Crown, and I went into the tavern, there was all this talk about Clarissa. The latest new gown this Clarissa was seen in. And how the Duke of Cumberland always carried her lap dog for her, as if he were a common footman! And the latest compliment which the Prince Regent had paid this same Clarissa. And how even Mr. Brummell seemed attentive to her ... 'Clarissa?' I said to myself. 'Could it be my Clarissa? It doesn't seem possible!' And leaving my traveling bag at the Rose and Crown—which shows how unsure I was it'd be *you*—I went to find out. It wasn't until I saw you, looking down over the banister, that I could be sure.... But didn't your hair used to be of a darker shade?" he added, admiring it.

"Oh, it's just some new pomade I used after washing it," Clarissa said.

"And now it shines with auburn gleams. Most becoming, I must say," and he again tried to take her in his arms.

"Wait!"

"Wait *again?*"

Clarissa, raising herself on an elbow, put out her other hand and placed a fingertip on "darling Richard's" forelock. It was so exactly like the forelock represented in the oval miniature of him. And, besides, from the first moment that she beheld him in the flesh—a man grown, Captain Richard Gray—she had wanted to touch it.

"You witch!"

And this time the Captain did not have to wait.

Much, much later sleep overcame them both....

And then, a shrill "Yap, yap, yap," was what Clarissa awoke to. What a nuisance that lap dog was! Always being stepped on by somebody. And now it was rushing around the room, just a roll of fluffy, honey-colored fur, yapping at the top of its tiny lungs. "Yap, yap, yap!"

"Sally! Come and take it away immediately!"

Clarissa suddenly realized that Captain Gray was no longer lying beside her. She was alone. Down from the bed Clarissa came in such haste that this time she did make a rent in her pink peignoir.

"Sally!"

"Now don't get excited," Sally said, coming in. "He's not gone, as you seem to think by the looks of you. He's right in the next room, standing in front of your washstand mirror, shaving. I had to borrow François' razor for him. And it was he—Captain Gray, I mean—who had stepped on the poor little angel," and picking up the lap dog, Sally began to caress it with the silliest ardor, until it stopped yapping.

Then Sally put it on a cushioned chair, and coming back, standing close to Clarissa, she said:

"I must say! When I came in and saw the two of you in bed together, you could have knocked me down with a feather!"

"Pshaw!" Clarissa laughed. "Captain Gray is not my brother."

"You mean, *you* are not Miss Gray," Sally said. "Don't you think that much was certainly getting pretty obvious to me, the way you've been behaving, since we left Ravisham? Miss Gray, indeed! Why, Miss Gray was such a lovely person. She was *modest!*"

"But you've never even seen her," Clarissa pointed out, highly amused. "You only saw me *enacting* the role of Miss Gray."

"Well, the way you *enacted* it showed me what a lovely person she was. Miss Gray was a *lady!*" And Sally, taking up a flounced petticoat of Clarissa's which lay on the chaise longue and was probably in need of ironing, marched out of the room, her nose in the air.

Captain Gray, freshly shaved, hurried in from Clarissa's dressing room, buttoning his jacket.

"Why did you have to get up so early?" Clarissa complained, as he took her in his arms.

His forelock, as it brushed her cheek, felt a trifle damp from the cold water he had used for his brisk ablutions.

"I have to go out and make a purchase," Captain Gray said, his mouth against her throat.

"You're going to buy something?" Clarissa was at once consumed with curiosity. "Will it be expensive?"

"Very expensive, I'm afraid. And I want you to come with me to help me make the selection. So hurry now and get dressed."

Clarissa needed no urging. She ran behind the curtain to seek among her costly wardrobe for something suitable to wear.

She chose the simplest gown she had, a so-called morning dress, of sprig muslin. A petticoat of yellow silk, to match the tiny rosebuds of the delicate sprigs … She could hear Captain Gray making noises of impatience as he strode up and down, waiting. Throwing off her peignoir, Clarissa dressed quickly. Then she rummaged among her vast supply of various-colored shoes for the pair she wanted. Of green satin. She found them, put them on. A bonnet, with streamers of violet velvet, caught her eye. And snatching it up, she ran to the dressing table to put it on. But, suddenly remembering the emeralds, she dropped the bonnet and ran to the bed instead.

"*Now* what?" Captain Gray demanded, as Clarissa swiftly climbed the little ladder.

"I forgot my 'beads.' "

During the night he had complained that her "beads" scratched his chest. Just because she wore the emeralds around the house he had taken it for granted that they couldn't be *real*. And laughing to herself, Clarissa had removed the emeralds and thrust them under the pillow.

Now, having retrieved the "beads," she wound them twice around her neck, dropping the dangling ends inside her bodice. Then she put the bonnet on. And very pretty she looked in it, and in the simple gown, the yellow petticoat showing provokingly with her hurried movements.

"Now I'm ready," she announced.

"At long last, you mean." Captain Gray laughed.

Then he followed her to the door, which brought them out onto the servants' stairs. After waiting a few seconds to make sure that no one was about, Clarissa led the way swiftly down the narrow stairs, and along a dark passage. She had never been in that part of the mansion before, but she knew from Sally's chatter the whereabouts of a side exit. And here it was. And so Clarissa and Captain Richard Gray slipped out of the house, unobserved, and walked into the street.

The day was simply glorious. The sky a perfect blue. And the sunlight golden. Captain Gray strode along swiftly with his big stride. It made Clarissa laugh how fast she had to walk to keep up with him. The passers-by smiled at them. Everybody seemed to know that they were lovers. And the Captain, stopping a food vender, bought a meat pie for Clarissa, and some freshly baked sweet potatoes for himself, and they ate with a great appetite, while standing on a corner in a little crowd of simple, noisy folk. And then the two of them hurried on. *Where* was he going ...?

Captain Gray turned in through a rickety gate and Clarissa, as she followed, held up her skirts because of the whitish dust that covered the ground. A man was working with a chisel and a hammer on a slab of rough stone, and the huge yard around was stacked full of monuments. And every one of them worth a small fortune, Clarissa thought. And she was duly impressed. Even a little awed. The cost of it! But then to some people it was a matter of the greatest importance. Or so she had heard from Lafonte. If they happened to be poor, they'd pawn or sell whatever valuables they had left, or even mortgage their homes, in order to provide the deceased relative with a monument.

"What about this one?" Captain Gray asked eagerly.

And it made Clarissa feel very proud to have him seek her advice as, walking side by side, they made a little tour of inspection.

The monument he eventually chose with her help was a very simple one. Needle-shaped, gracefully tall, of gleaming gray marble, it stood on a base of rough stone.

"I think Miss Gray would have been very pleased," Clarissa said approvingly.

There would be no elaborate inscription. Just the name. And the two dates. The short span of time between the dates was eloquent enough in itself.

"But isn't it terribly expensive?" Clarissa asked cautiously.

"How can a pauper like myself afford such a thing, you mean?" Captain Gray said quietly. "You're right, I couldn't have afforded anything like it! But I sent a letter to my great-aunt in Scotland, asking her to forward the needed sum of money to the solicitor in Halstead. And I also wrote to him. And he will take care of everything."

"Is she rich then, your great-aunt in Scotland?" Clarissa asked.

Grinning with amusement at the expression of lively curiosity on Clarissa's lovely face, the Captain said:

"No, she's not rich at all. But she will sell the few pieces of jewelry she has still left, and borrow the rest of the money."

And then Captain Gray called the stonecutter over and showed him what had been selected, and the two of them began to talk terms, the man agreeing readily that the payment would be made on delivery. And next they discussed the nature of the soil in Halstead. It seemed that a certain period of time had to pass to allow the earth to settle down permanently before the monument could be set up. When all the details were thus arranged to Captain Gray's satisfaction, he shook hands with the man, and then he and Clarissa quitted the place.

"But when will it be set up?" Clarissa said eagerly, as they walked along the street swiftly. She had a very definite reason for asking. "Will somebody let you know?"

"The solicitor, of course, will write me, care of my ship, at once."

"And then, would you write to me," Clarissa said, "and let *me* know?"

Once the simple monument was set up, Clarissa then could pass the information on to Mr. Brummell. He had a right to know, at last. First, very gently, she would break the news of Miss Gray's passing away, at the home of some distant relative where Miss Gray, it seemed, had gone to from Ravisham, when the languishing disease took a sudden turn for the worse. Clarissa would be vague as to details; it just happened that she heard the sad story from somebody reliable. And Mr. Brummell, since he had been expecting to hear of the gentle governess' demise sooner or later, would take it all very quietly. And the sentimental fellow probably would pay a visit to the respectable old village churchyard in Halstead. And it would please him to see, as he lingered there reading the name and the two dates, how properly everything had been done. And thus the romance would be rounded out, made complete, perfect. As Miss Gray would have wished it to be.

"Promise to let me know, immediately," Clarissa insisted. "About the setting up of the monument, I mean. Promise!"

"Very well, then," Captain Gray said. "I promise."

Clarissa wished she could tell him the true reason for her anxious interest. But not even to Captain Gray, to Miss Gray's adored brother, to "darling Richard," could she reveal the secret of Miss Gray's beautiful romance. Of that Clarissa was certain. For once again, as several times before, it seemed to Clarissa that she could almost see Miss Gray, a finger at her gently smiling mouth, urging Clarissa to secrecy. Yes, it was Miss Gray's own precious secret. And so it must remain, as far as the world in general was concerned.

"But why are we hurrying so?" Clarissa cried, aware suddenly that she was getting a trifle breathless in trying to keep up with Captain Gray's swift pace. "Goodness!" she laughed.

"Because I have to catch the stagecoach which leaves the Rose and Crown in exactly ten minutes."

"So soon!"

"Unless you want me to be court-martialled," Captain Gray laughed. "And since we're at war, as likely as not they'd shoot me with great ceremony, at dawn, right there on deck, the minute I'm back."

But they were already entering the busy colorful square and there, in front of the inn, was the stagecoach, about to leave. Captain Gray dashed forward. And Clarissa hurried after him. She saw him dive first into the inn, for his bag. Then he reappeared with it, and dashed for the coach. It was full inside, and he had to climb onto its roof, also crowded, mostly with men in uniform.

And there Clarissa stood, in a knot of coarse-voiced housemaids, frowsy housewives, and big awkward milkmaids, come to see their husbands or their sweethearts off to the fighting lines. Rubbing shoulders with such stupid females! What foolishness. What utter foolishness! The man was a pauper. And what was even worse, a silly dreamer. But her hand fluttered upward, to wave to him, to "darling Richard."

He was looking down, searching for her. Suddenly he saw her. He grinned and waved his tricorn. The impatient horses tore forward. And away rolled the coach, in a little cloud of dust, the wheels rumbling over the cobbles.

Clarissa suddenly felt very much alone. He was gone. It would be months probably before she saw him again. How she would miss him! And gradually it dawned upon her that she loved the man. She might as well admit it—she loved Captain Richard Gray. She loved him dearly. She'd do anything for him, go with him anywhere. The memory of his kisses thrilled her, made her spine tingle.

Moving like a sleepwalker, unconscious of the jostling crowd, Clarissa quietly left the noisy square, and wandered up the street. Since the Earl, thanks to those three extra drops of the unique draught, would be sleeping till evening, she still had the better part of the afternoon at her disposal. And she suddenly remembered the trainer of the dancing bears. He had a small casket to give her, he had said. She could go to him now, it would be a diversion. The Arena, as the place was called, was not far away, and Clarissa hurried there.

On reaching the old building by a back alleyway, she at once saw the swarthy trainer, who, broom in hand, was sweeping animal-smelling refuse over the threshold of the iron-reinforced door. He turned round at her approach, immediately recognized her, in spite of her simple gown and bonnet, and said quickly:

"It's a good thing you came today. Tomorrow would have been too late!"

"Why—too late?" Clarissa said, surprised. "What do you mean?"

"Because tomorrow I would have to give the casket away to someone else."

"To—whom?" Clarissa said.

But he wouldn't explain. Instead, giving her to understand by a gesture that she should wait, he leaned his broom against the wall and, after a quick glance around, disappeared behind the heavy door.

Almost instantly, however, he was back, with the casket. And Clarissa was disappointed; the casket looked quite ordinary. True, the dark wood it was fashioned of was smooth with age, and the brass clasps were pretty, and they shone. Otherwise, there was nothing remarkable about the casket.

"It's yours now," the trainer said. And he at once thrust the casket into Clarissa's hands. "It will bring you good fortune. Your wish will come true, your dearest wish...."

"Has it some magic powers then?" Clarissa exclaimed.

And, holding the casket, she raised the lid. But it was empty. She snapped the clasps shut. Then, by running her fingers over the surface, she quickly examined the casket for a secret opening, maybe a secret bottom. But there was none.

"It's empty now," the trainer said. "But the *means* of obtaining your wish will be *inside,* eventually. Yes, you, or someone else, will put something in the casket. From time to time, the contents will be changed. But, sooner or later, *whatever* it happens to contain will become the *means* of making your wish come true."

Her *wish* ...? The one about Captain Richard Gray, maybe? And Clarissa bombarded the swarthy foreigner with questions. But he would tell her nothing more.

"You have the casket; now go. Go!" he said over and over again.

What an unpleasant character! Something sinister about him, Clarissa decided, as she began to move away. But the man suddenly hurried after her. Placing one grimy hand on her arm, and bringing his dark-skinned face very close, he said quickly, anxiously:

"There's a condition attached, remember."

"A condition?"

"Certainly! As soon as your wish comes true, you must give the casket away. At once!"

"But ... to whom?"

"You will know," the man told her mysteriously. "An inner voice will tell you. It is all *predestined*.... My inner voice commanded me to give the casket to the most beautiful woman in

London, so I gave it to you. The important thing is to give it away, remember. Or great misfortune will befall you ... But go now. Go!"

He released his hold on her arm, and gave her a little push, and Clarissa was glad to make her escape. Carrying the casket, she hurried away without glancing back once.

CHAPTER SEVENTEEN

T O SPEED HER RETURN to Grosvenor Square, she moved along the comparatively empty residential streets. But on turning into one of them she suddenly stopped and stood there on the corner, on the pretense of retying her bonnet streamers, while holding the casket under an arm.

Drawn up at the curb stood a heavy black carriage, and out of it there had just emerged two tall, very thin men, dressed in somber black, and with long faces, the color of wax. Alike as two peas, both had silver shoe buckles, and wore small black wigs. Unaware of being watched, they crossed the sidewalk and went up the steps of a narrow brick house, where all the blinds were down to protect the furniture and the carpets from being faded by the sun, they were so stingy, the "two dry sticks," as Clarissa privately called them.

They were the great-nephews of the Earl, and his only heirs. On Clarissa's first memorable visit to the opera several of the fops had hastened to point them out to her. The Earl had out-lived his immediate family, and only these two great-nephews remained, and they would probably outlive him. Clarissa had had a good look at them on that occasion. And they had been very much aware of her, though they pretended not to see her, the hypocrites! But she had caught the gleam of vicious venom in their pale-lidded eyes, and it had sent an icy shiver up her spine. How they hated her! For spending the Earl's money, which they regarded as already their own. The more she spent, the less they'd have left to inherit! And since then, every time she had happened to catch sight of them, at some brilliant social function, or in a fashionable street, she'd feel this chill of fear seize her, as it did now, while she watched them being let into the house by a silent manservant. So that's where they resided, the "two dry sticks!"

And she couldn't stop shivering till she reached Grosvenor Square and the Earl's mansion. Then she slipped in through the side door, and waited there, to make sure no one would observe her using the back stairs. Any one of the flunkies might be in the pay of the great-nephews, to spy on her. How happy it would make them if they could learn something with which to slander her to the Earl! She hurried up the stairs and into her room.

She placed the casket on the dressing table, then removed her bonnet, tossed it aside, and throwing herself into a chair, kicked off her green satin shoes. The excitements of the day had tired her out. But Sally came in and at once began to harangue:

"Where on earth have you been? I was getting worried. There's this grand affair the Earl is taking you to tonight, and you know the *hours* it takes you to get dressed! And you missed having your hot chocolate ..."

"Bring it to me now," Clarissa ordered, "and for goodness' sake stop chattering!"

"Who's chattering, I'd like to know?" Sally stooped to pick up the shoes off the floor. "I'm only talking sense. Captain Richard Gray is very nice. But his boots are badly worn, and his uniform is shabby, and he hasn't got a penny to his name! So you better forget about him. Not that I, or anybody else, have to tell you *that!*" Sally said, with a toss of her head and a smirk.

Little do you know! Clarissa thought. But she preserved her silence.

Sally took the shoes behind the curtain, to replace them on the shelf there, and coming back with Clarissa's peignoir, went on:

"I suppose you'll be wearing the new dress tonight. Yellow velvet and gold lace ... Well, it's certainly magnificent. But a new dress as expensive as that every time you go out! I wouldn't be surprised if you land yourself in the debtors' prison, and that pretty soon. And then, what will become of Pete and me?"

Sally, besides being naturally saucy, was frequently now just plain impudent.

"Oh, yes," she added, "there's the cosmetics vender, waiting downstairs."

"That's fine. There's very little left of the homemade rouge we got from him last time," Clarissa said, slipping out of her simple muslin gown, with Sally's help, and putting the peignoir on.

She then removed the emeralds and laid them down on the dressing table, and Sally instantly made her customary remark, which Clarissa always ignored.

"They still look like her ladyship's emeralds to *me*," Sally said. "In spite of the story you spread around about *two identical* ropes having been made originally!"

And with hardly a break, Sally went on:

"This vender is not the same one you bought from before. This is another vender. And a very engaging fellow he is," Sally tittered. "He first came in the morning, while you were out, so I told him you weren't up yet, and for him to come later. And now he's back."

"Well, have him come up," Clarissa said, "when you bring my chocolate."

Sally hurried out. And Clarissa, taking up one of the pretty jars with which the dressing table was crowded, began to spread the rich fragrant cream over her neck and face. When Sally came in followed by the vender, Clarissa could see them reflected in the many mirrors. Sally came right over to set down the tray with the graceful chocolate pot, and the cup and saucer. While the vender stayed by the door, waiting to be ordered to come closer. Because of the confusing arrangement of the mirrors, and the distance at which the man stood, and Clarissa's utter disinterest, the fleeting impression she received was merely an over-all picture of a vender, any vender. Breeches and shirt of some kind, a bright bandanna around the neck, and carried on the head, protected by a padded skullcap, the lid-covered tray containing the merchandise."

"Oh," Sally said, "a casket! Where did you get it?"

The fact that the sharp-eyed Sally had failed to see the casket until it was right in front of her nose, as she poured out the hot chocolate, showed what an ordinary-looking object it was.

"Never mind that now, Sally," Clarissa said. And she motioned into the mirror at the vender, to come over.

Then, taking the filled cup on its saucer from Sally's hand, Clarissa sat back in the silk-cushioned chair. She raised the cup to her lips, was about to take a sip of the aromatically steaming contents, and ... almost scalded herself. The vender's face, Slippery Jack's face, was staring back at her from the mirror, malicious laughter in his eyes.

She had been expecting him to show up sooner or later, of course. Still, the sudden sight of him was quite a shock. Clarissa waited a moment. Then, very calmly, she took a few sips of the hot chocolate.

"You can put your merchandise over there," she then told him, for Sally's benefit, and pointing at the chaise longue.

Slippery Jack, Clarissa had to admit, made a very handsome vender. And he managed to balance the vender's tray on his head most successfully. He now lifted it down, and deposited it on the chaise longue. Then, removing the padded skullcap, thrusting it into his pocket, he just stood there, waiting for further orders, as a vender should.

Clarissa, meanwhile, swiftly took stock of the situation. It was Sally, back at Ravisham, who had brought her the news of the postilion's murder, and of the disappearance from the village inn of the two strangers, a likable parson and his friend, the young rustic. But Sally had been merely repeating the gossip she heard in the kitchen; she had never laid her eyes on either Honest Gregory or Slippery Jack. No, Sally and Slippery Jack had never seen each other before.

And the way the two of them now behaved made it very obvious, Sally tittering, and Slippery Jack grinning—a saucy maid flirting with the engaging fellow whom she thought to be a vender. Maids always flirted with venders.

So far, so good. Clarissa wanted to have every fact clear in her mind. There was the matter of the little knife, of a peculiar shape, Slippery Jack's little knife—found on the scene of the crime, and now in the possession of the village constable. She mustn't forget about that. Not that Clarissa had any particular plan in mind. Slippery Jack, she hadn't a doubt, had come to get the emeralds. She would give them to him and he would go away. But it was her principle to be prepared for any emergency that might arise. Well, she was prepared.

The first thing to do, however, was to get rid of Sally's presence.

"Sally," Clarissa said, setting the chocolate cup down on the dressing table, "when the sewing women delivered the new dress, did they also bring the scarf?"

"The scarf?" Sally said. "What scarf?"

"Why, the scarf that goes with the dress, naturally! Don't tell me they forgot to deliver the scarf!"

"Well, it's not *my* fault," Sally, at once, began to defend herself. "There was no scarf with the dress, that's all I know!"

"Then you must go to the dressmaker, right away, and get it," Clarissa said. "It's most important. I can't wear that new dress tonight without the scarf. The whole effect would be ruined. Go on. Hurry!"

Sally, though unwillingly, went.

And once the door closed on her, Slippery Jack's manner changed. Grinning insolently, he moved about with his catlike walk, examining the rich appointments of the room. The expensive material of the drapes made him whistle. He kicked at the gorgeous rug to see how thick it was.

"You're fixed pretty nicely here, aren't you?" he said.

Then he pulled up a chair, and lolled in it, while grinning at her derisively.

"Of course, you came for the emeralds," Clarissa said calmly.

And picking up the emerald rope, which lay glittering beside the delicate cosmetic jars and bottles, she gave it to him.

"Don't think I didn't spot it as soon as I came in!" Slippery Jack bragged.

Nothing escaped him, nothing would ever escape him, and she had better remember that!

Holding the emeralds in his strong nimble fingers, he examined each priceless green stone.

"I suppose you were surprised I failed to show up with them the night we agreed on—Friday night, wasn't it?" Clarissa said lightly.

She knew, of course, that previous to the night she mentioned he had already taken to his heels, for fear of being traced through the little knife he had dropped on the scene of the postilion's murder. But she had to pretend utter ignorance of this fact, since otherwise he would understand that she also knew about the murder.

"I got the emeralds, as you see," she went on. And then she explained, lying glibly, "But ... a housemaid saw me, coming out of her ladyship's bedroom. So, of course, I had to leave right away. And I did."

"And what day was that?" Slippery Jack asked casually. A little too casually.

He was naturally trying to find out whether Clarissa had had time to have heard about the discovery of the postilion's body, and of the finding of the little knife with which the victim's throat had been slashed ... And should he find out that she had stayed at Ravisham long enough to have learned these two facts then he'd know that—aside from Honest Gregory, who had been with him at the time, but whom Slippery Jack trusted implicitly—Clarissa was the only person who knew positively the identity of the murderer. And then, of course, Slippery Jack just couldn't afford to let her live even another hour, a half-hour ... He would strangle her right there and then, if she gave the wrong answer.

"Wednesday it was," Clarissa said. She had actually left Ravisham on a Thursday. "Wednesday, in the afternoon." The postilion was murdered Wednesday night. "And I made my way straight to London, and here. Since the Earl, while he was at Ravisham with the Prince Regent, happened to notice me, and he made me this advantageous offer, and so ..." And Clarissa, as she spoke, hoped she wasn't talking too much, or too quickly, or too casually.

Slippery Jack, fortunately, cut her short.

"Never mind that! So it was on a Wednesday you left?"

"That's right."

"You're sure?"

"Of course I'm sure! Wednesday afternoon it was," Clarissa declared. And she asked quickly, pretending sudden curiosity, "Is it important?"

"Of course it's not important," Slippery Jack said.

And he at once assumed utter indifference to the subject.

But he believed her assertion, she could see. And since he had no way of checking up on its truthfulness immediately, the danger was over and she was safe, for the time being anyway. Her palms were wet with nervous sweat. She was glad she had used that cream on her face, or he would have noticed the drops of perspiration glistening around her hairline. And taking up a soft white cloth, she passed it over her hands and forehead, as if removing what traces of the cream there still remained.

Slippery Jack, perfectly relaxed now, rattled the emerald rope in his hands, admiring it. Then, reluctantly, he put it back on the dressing table.

"Aren't you taking it with you?" Clarissa said, feigning extreme astonishment.

But she knew he dared not. If caught and searched, the emeralds would be yet another proof of his presence in the vicinity of the crime.

"As you like," Clarissa said. "You can come for them some other time."

Slippery Jack was again glancing around with shrewd appraisal.

"The Earl must be giving you a very handsome allowance," he said, grinning.

"Oh, so-so," Clarissa said.

Slippery Jack named a sum, and it was very close to the actual monthly amount she was being paid.

"Well," he then went on, his grin broader, more insolent than before, "you'll be giving me half of what you get, every month."

"That's out of the question. There're all the dresses I have to pay for myself, and a lot of other things ..."

Not that she was proposing to let Slippery Jack get even a penny of the money. She had already decided what she would do in respect to *him*. But she pretended to bargain.

"To be constantly beautiful means extravagant clothes," Clarissa argued sensibly. "And unless I am beautiful the Earl may get tired of me and throw me out. So it's as much to your benefit as mine for me to have some money for current expenses."

"Well, there's something to that," Slippery Jack had to admit. "All right then, we'll make it a third of the sum, instead of a half. And when is your next allowance due?"

"The day after tomorrow," Clarissa told him, though it wasn't due for another three weeks. "The Earl sends it up to me with the major-domo in the morning. A small bag full of guineas."

Slippery Jack's eyes sparkled at the thought of all that gold.

"Then I'll be here the day after tomorrow," he announced, "to get my share."

His share, indeed!

"You don't have to come here," Clarissa protested mildly. "I was planning to go down to the Thieves' Village, anyway. And I'll bring you the money there." She didn't want him to think that it was most important for her to have him pay her another visit.

"Well, you wouldn't find me there," Slippery Jack said.

"Oh?" Clarissa was genuinely surprised. The safest place for him to hide!

"I went there once or twice," he went on, "just to keep abreast of the latest London news." That's how he knew all about her sudden success, and where to find her. "But most of the time I wasn't in London, anyhow."

Was he lying, or had he been actually roaming about? Doing *what?* The way he kept looking at her, his eyes full of malicious laughter, as if he had something up his sleeve concerning her, something unpleasant for her ...

"Very well, then," she said. "I'll have the money ready for you the day after tomorrow. And you be here about three in the afternoon."

She expected him to get up, take up his vender's tray, and go.

But he continued to loll in the chair where he sat and grin at her. Always a bragger, he was dying to brag to her about something.

"What amuses you so?" And pretending unconcern, Clarissa began to brush her lustrous hair, gleaming with auburn highlights.

"You'd be surprised if you knew," Slippery Jack laughed gleefully.

"Surprise me then!"

"Well," Slippery Jack said, "only yesterday I came back after paying a little visit to—Halstead."

Privately, Clarissa was struck with amazement and a sudden anxiety. But not a muscle of her face moved as she asked mildly:

"And what's so wonderful about *that?*"

"Doesn't the name, Halstead, mean anything to you?"

"Never heard it before," Clarissa declared flatly.

"I thought Miss Gray would have mentioned it to you."

"And *why* should Miss Gray have mentioned it to me?"

"Because Halstead happens to be the name of the place where she was born, where her family used to have their home, that's why!" Slippery Jack said.

"Obviously, you made it your business to procure this piece of information, in some manner or other," Clarissa conceded calmly, thus giving credit to his wits in order to mollify him. "You were interested, then?"

"*Interested?*" Slippery Jack snarled. "Only a fool wouldn't have been interested! Certainly I was interested. Why, to that kind of people, a respectful family, to have one of them buried in unconsecrated ground is a matter of shame, a terrible disgrace, a blight on their name! So I had that piece of information to give them," Slippery Jack explained, and he laughed. "They'd be glad to pay me, exorbitantly, to know where the grave was, so that they could remedy the disgraceful situation, change the place of burial. That's how I figured. And then they'd be paying me year in, year out, for the rest of their lives, to keep my mouth shut about it having ever happened!"

"Blackmail, you mean," Clarissa said.

"Call it what you like," Slippery Jack shrugged.

"Well, I didn't know Miss Gray had any relatives," Clarissa said, and she went on brushing her hair very calmly.

"There was bound to be somebody," Slippery Jack pointed out. "And that's what I set out to discover. I already had something to serve me as a lead, from having listened to the gossips at that village inn. All excited they were because of the stagecoach mishap, and talking about the governess who, as they thought, escaped being killed. So what did I learn about Miss Gray? Very little. She was traveling from London. And she was just out of a boarding school. Well, that was enough for me. How many such boarding schools, I mean for gentlefolk, are there in London?" Slippery Jack demanded.

"Oh, not more than a dozen, I suppose."

"So all I had to do," Slippery Jack said, grinning at the simplicity of it, "was start making the rounds of them, with my story. And that's exactly what I did, just a few days ago, as soon as I was able to shake Honest Gregory off. Didn't want him cutting in on this, which he'd surely have tried to do if he knew about it. But I kept it strictly to myself."

"You had to invent some story, of course, as a pretext for seeking the information you were after. I understand that," Clarissa said. "And I suppose," she then went on, conversationally, "at every one of those boarding schools you asked to see the headmistress?"

"Naturally. And with the first, and the second, and the third—all of them very strict-looking old ladies—I drew a blank. But the fourth one I saw said, 'Miss Gray? Oh, yes. And what can I do for you, young man?' And then I told her my pathetic little story," and here Slippery Jack grinned in appreciation of his own histrionic talents. "How my poor dear mother, who was in service with the Gray family, gave me away as an infant to be brought up by foster parents, who took me with them to another part of the country. But now that the foster parents were dead, I wanted to find my real mother. Very little information I had as to what's been happening to her all these years. But I did remember that the daughter of the family she worked for, Miss Gray, had been placed in this exclusive boarding school, and maybe she could tell me something. So, please, could I see Miss Gray? And very humbly I behaved, you may be sure," Slippery Jack added, grinning.

"And the headmistress then told you," Clarissa said, "that Miss Gray was no longer there."

"And very sympathetic the old lady was, too. Miss Gray left quite recently, she said, to take up her position as governess at Ravisham, the seat of the Marquises of Trall. And I said, 'Oh, dear! that's much too far away. I couldn't afford such a journey ...' The way I figured was," Slippery Jack explained slyly, "that the headmistress was bound to mention the name of the place Miss Gray came from, sooner or later. And sure enough, no sooner had I finished my disappointed tirade about Ravisham being much too far away, than the old lady said, very sensibly,

'Of course, Halstead is quite close. So why don't you go straight there, young man? And maybe the former neighbors of the Gray family could tell you something about your poor dear mother ...' And that's how I found out the name of the place, Halstead," Slippery Jack said, and he laughed.

"So you went there," Clarissa said.

"The very next day. Which was the day before yesterday," Slippery Jack said. "Got a free ride in a farmer's wagon that was going that way. Took less than two hours to get there. Well, Halstead is just a small village. And the people there, old-fashioned friendly folk, are very proud of the scenery around ... So right away, but most discreetly, I started making inquiries about the Gray family, while still talking about my poor dear mother. And you can imagine my surprise when I was told, quite simply, that, only a few days back, Miss Gray had been buried in the little graveyard that sprawls around the old stone church there. Now what do you think of that!"

Clarissa stared at him as if speechless with astonishment.

And, satisfied with her reaction, Slippery Jack went on:

"But they spoke of it quite simply, as I already said. Seems like her lungs had never been very strong, and they just took it for granted that that was the reason of her sudden passing away. *Where* it happened, nobody seemed to know, and they weren't curious, either. Since it was her *brother* who had sent the coffin on to Halstead, for the solicitor, an old friend of the family, to arrange a proper burial. The brother, naturally, would know all the details, and that was enough to satisfy anybody. It made everything look perfectly normal and right."

"Her ... brother?" Clarissa said, and she raised her eyebrows slightly.

"Miss Gray didn't mention having a brother?" Slippery Jack said.

"Not that I remember … After all, we were only a few hours together in that stagecoach," Clarissa pointed out. "But do go on. This is beginning to sound really interesting."

"You bet it's interesting!" Slippery Jack agreed, significantly emphatic. "And this is how it must have happened," he went on. "The brother, whose name is Captain Richard Gray who is serving under Lord Nelson, returns to England on a furlough and, right away, goes to Ravisham to see his sister. Well, in one manner or another, he finds out the truth; that it's not some cheap little actress, Clarissa, who was killed in the stagecoach accident and is burried in that desolate grave, in the unconsecrated ground, but his own sister, *Miss Gray.* And how he found it out was probably very simple. Anyway," Slippery Jack boasted conceitedly, "didn't take me a minute to explain *that* to myself!"

"You mean, her ladyship suspected me of not being the real Miss Gray all along?" Clarissa suggested helpfully.

"Quite possible. Or when she missed her emeralds, and somebody might have seen you taking them … Didn't you tell me, a while back, that a housemaid as good as caught you in the act?"

"Oh, yes, that horrible housemaid," Clarissa said.

"I figured something like that must have happened," Slippery Jack argued triumphantly. "And so her ladyship told Captain Gray that she had been taken advantage of by an impostor, and he secretly investigated and was convinced that that impostor had changed places with his sister! And then, in great secrecy, he dug up the grave. Arranged for the coffin to be conveyed to Halstead. Covered up the empty grave. And hurried away to rejoin his ship. But he'll be back, sooner or later," Slippery Jack said, and he chuckled, "and I'll find him, and tell him what I *know.* First, that he tampered with a grave. Which is a crime punishable by law. And second—and this he'll like even less—that his sister had been buried in unconsecrated ground. And to keep my mouth shut, Captain Gray will be paying me for the rest of his life!"

"Is he rich then, this ... this Captain Gray?" Clarissa said.

"The family had had financial reverses, and the Captain had been abroad for years, trying to make his fortune. I don't think there are any other relatives.... Anyhow, that's all I could find out," Slippery Jack explained. "After all, I had to be careful how I asked questions."

At least, he had failed to find out about the great-aunt in Scotland, Clarissa told herself.

"But Captain Gray has his pay," Slippery Jack went on. "And small though it is, it'll be something for me. As a starter. Later, if he happens to make some money, I'll be getting more."

"Well, I must say," Clarissa said, with an assumed air of grudging admiration, "you've been very clever about it all. No wonder you're grinning all over your face!"

Slippery Jack laughed.

"Oh, that," he said. "I keep thinking about that empty grave. Nobody knows it's empty. But it is. And the marker bears your name. I'm sure the marker was carefully replaced, not to arouse suspicion. And so the grave stands there. As if ... waiting for you," he added, grinning maliciously.

"I'm not superstitious," Clarissa said with a shrug. "But you better go now. My maid will be coming back any minute."

"Listen to her talk," Slippery Jack appealed to the world in general. "My maid ..." he mimicked her. "How grand we are!" Envy of her tremendous success made him bristle with hatred.

Clarissa hastened to mollify him.

"You haven't done so badly yourself," she said. "The steady income you'll be getting from this—what's his name—this Captain Richard Gray!"

The reminder restored Slippery Jack's good humor. He got up, pulled the vender's padded skullcap out of his pocket, replaced it on his head, and, walking over to the chaise longue, took up the vender's tray. Where did he get his disguise? Clarissa wondered. Probably by luring a real vender into a dark alley, strangling the unsuspecting fellow, then stripping the still-warm body of the clothing.

"I'll expect you the day after tomorrow then," she said. "I'll have the money ready."

"You better!" Slippery Jack said, already balancing the vender's tray on his handsome head in a very authentic manner.

Sally suddenly burst in, talking as she entered.

"You never ordered any scarf to go with that dress! The dressmaker was positive, she told me, you never did!"

"Never mind that now, Sally," Clarissa said crisply. "And you don't have to show the vender out," and Clarissa turned to Slippery Jack. "You can find your way, can't you, vender?"

"Down the back stairs, sure, mistress," the pseudo-vender answered humbly.

And grinning at Sally, who held the door open for the engaging fellow, so she could titter at him, he went out.

"Tell François I want him here right away," Clarissa ordered, as Sally, having closed the door, came over.

"He's supposed to do your hair *after* you have your bath," Sally protested.

"Do as I tell you! Go on!"

"Always something!" Sally grumbled.

But she hurried out.

Clarissa ran to the window. Concealed behind the curtain, she looked down into the street below. It appeared to be empty. Suddenly, she saw Slippery Jack. The pseudo-vender was already half a block away. And any moment now he'd be turning the

corner into a little lane that would take him out of Grosvenor
Square. There, the pseudo-vender was gone all of a sudden, having rounded the corner....

And behind her, François' voice said respectfully:

"Madam needs me?"

"François," Clarissa said as, turning away from the window,
she hurried towards the chief valet. "I want you to hire a small
coach, with the fastest pair of horses they can supply you with,
and go to the village of Wickhem St. Paul's. It's near Ravisham."

"I know which road to follow," François assured her quietly.

"You will get the village constable out of bed," Clarissa went
on. "And you will give him this information: you know the identity of the person who is the owner of the little knife which had
been used to slash the postilion's throat. The name of that person
is Slippery Jack."

As Clarissa paused briefly, François, who had listened attentively, nodded, to signify that he would convey the message word
for word.

"You will also tell the constable," Clarissa then went on,
"that the day after tomorrow, at three o'clock in the afternoon,
Slippery Jack will be in Grosvenor Square. Masquerading as a
cosmetics vender, he will be seen coming out of one of the mansions there."

"Not any *particular* mansion?" François said. "I quite understand. Madam does not wish to be involved."

"The constable wouldn't be interested, anyhow. All he wants
is to get his man," Clarissa said. And she continued with her
instructions. "You will then offer to have the constable drive
immediately to London with you. And once in London, he'll
contact the constabulary here, and working together they'll
have their spies stationed all over Grosvenor Square the day
after tomorrow. The spies, naturally, will be in disguise. One as a

footman, perhaps. Another as a street sweeper. Still another as a washerwoman ..."

Everybody in the Thieves' Village knew how the constables worked when setting a trap. And Clarissa could visualize it all very clearly.

"But surely," François suddenly said, "you wouldn't want them to grab this man, Slippery Jack, right in the immediate vicinity? He might then suspect you of having had a hand in his apprehension! They should follow him and grab him on the way, in a busy street, where there are shops, people...."

"And that's exactly how it must be done," Clarissa told him. "All you have to do is indicate to the constable that a personage of a very high rank wishes it so. Just infer it, by your manner. Be importantly mysterious. I'm certain you'll be splendid at it, François. And no constable would dare take the risk of displeasing a titled personage. But you should wear something different, of course," Clarissa added, glancing at the chief valet's luxurious livery of green silk with the Earl's crest embroidered in gold on the sleeve.

"I have my street clothes," François explained. "A very simple but dignified outfit. And when does madam wish me to start on this journey?"

"As soon as the Earl and I leave for this grand social affair where he's taking me tonight. It will probably last till dawn, and you might be back by then. If you ride fast enough. It would be wiser if the Earl had no inkling of your having absented yourself."

"I'll make those horses gallop there and back!" François promised, a fist clenched, as if already laying the whip mercilessly on their rumps.

"One other thing." Clarissa had suddenly remembered something. "I'll have no way of knowing how it all comes out, I mean the day after tomorrow ... unless you meet with that constable right afterwards. At some place where you go to habitually, François."

"The hairdresser's establishment."

"Then have the constable come there, to tell you exactly what happens. Make it a condition with him, *before* you start giving him the information he's so anxious to get—the identity of the postilion's murderer. Do you understand, François?"

"I understand perfectly," the chief valet assured her.

The two of them went over the whole plan once again, swiftly, to make certain that no detail had been forgotten. And, this done to Clarissa's perfect satisfaction, she suddenly said:

"But you'll have to loan me some money, François."

Because of her extravagances, the magnificent allowance the Earl paid her would be all spent in less than a week, and it was very seldom that she had any cash on hand. Besides she was constantly up to her ears in debt, to the tradesmen, the bankers, money-lenders. But she could depend on François to loan her the money she needed, from the savings he so patiently accumulated.

And now Clarissa named the considerable sum which she had promised to give Slippery Jack the day after tomorrow.

The chief valet's reaction was respectfully noncommittal.

"Madam always repays a loan, eventually," he said. "First thing, the day after tomorrow, she shall have the necessary amount. This man, Slippery Jack, is probably ... blackmailing madam."

"Something like that. And you might have caught a glimpse of him, from that window, if you had been here a bit sooner, François. Not that it matters. When Slippery Jack comes up for trial, one of the rats will identify him."

"One of the *rats?*"

Clarissa explained briefly. The lowest caliber of pickpockets went by that name. Utter weaklings, they couldn't endure

the slightest form of torture. And would instantly turn inform-
ers when shown the rack. Several of them were generally kept on
hand by the London constabulary, in case some specific information or identification was called for.

And that's whom Slippery Jack, when caught, would suspect
of betraying him—one or another of the rats, Clarissa told herself, her fingers tugging at the flounce of her peignoir nervously.

"Madam is very much upset," François observed discreetly.

"Naturally I'm upset."

"But not on her own account, solely. That's what I meant,"
François explained, and he spoke slowly, quietly. "Perhaps there
is danger of somebody else being threatened, also. A certain person who has become very dear to you, madam. Whom you …
love. And perhaps, this certain person is none other than …
Captain Richard Gray."

Clarissa did not deny it.

"François," she said, "I'm afraid. Terribly afraid!"

François tried to soothe her agitation.

"Let us hope that madam's bold plan will be crowned with
success," he told her.

And on this reassuring note, François hastened out.

And that night, at the brilliant social affair, Clarissa, as usual,
was the most beautiful and the gayest of all the mistresses present. Inwardly, she was all on edge with suspense and anxiety. But
when at daybreak she returned home with the Earl, there was
François, pretending to be straightening the magnificent counterpane on the raised bed. It had rained most of the night, and
the chief valet's face glistened slightly with wet. The collar of his
livery, into which he had had to change in a hurry after his secret
journey, was not properly closed. He had only just come back.
And before leaving Clarissa alone with the Earl, he managed to

give her an imperceptible nod: Everything progressing according to plan, so far!

There was the whole of the next day, and the night following, to worry through somehow. And then suddenly it was the day of the appointment. Would Slippery Jack show up? Anything might happen, at the last moment, to prevent his coming. He might simply change his mind, decide to come at some other time. Or, sensing danger, he might slip out of London. Or suppose he changed his disguise? This possibility had not occurred to Clarissa before, and now it plagued her. But he wouldn't have had time for that, surely! And his greed for money would outweigh his natural caution ...

At the hour agreed upon, Sally ushered in the pseudo-vender. Clarissa had the little leather bag filled with coins ready, and when Sally's back was turned she passed it over quickly to Slippery Jack, and he slipped it into his pocket. Then she bought a pot of home-made rouge from him, declaring, for Sally's benefit, that the color this time was exactly right!

At last, he left. Clarissa hurried to the window. Again from behind the curtain she watched the street. And soon she saw Slippery Jack. Balancing the vender's tray on his head, he hurried along. But in the opposite direction to the one she had seen him going the previous time. Slippery Jack, evidently, was taking his own precautions. And where were the spies? Well, naturally, they were not supposed to be recognizable as such. So maybe that street sweeper, busy at the curb, was one of them.

The man didn't even turn his head as the pseudo-vender passed him. After a while, however, the street sweeper entered a house. And then, through the gateway of the same house, a carriage, with four white-wigged footmen in attendance, rolled out and on, following the direction that Slippery Jack had taken.

Clarissa could no longer see him; he was gone from view. And then the carriage disappeared.

It was not until several hours later that François came to her, bringing the news. That it was good news was written all over François' face, including the little black mustache which adorned his upper lip, and which now seemed to twitch with excitement. And as soon as Clarissa had sent Sally out of the room, on some pretext or other, the chief valet announced:

"They got him!"

François then repeated what the constable, jubilant with victory, had told him on meeting with him at the hairdresser's establishment.

"They grabbed Slippery Jack near the market place. He put up quite a struggle. But they clapped the irons on him. And he was hustled off to jail."

The constable couldn't say exactly when Slippery Jack would be called up for trial. He was certain, however, of the eventual sentence—to be hanged at Tyburn.

Clarissa had her own unpredictable ways of expressing her feelings. It was an integral part of her charm. And François, as he ceased speaking, was not in the least surprised to see her suddenly walk over to the door, open it, and call down the back stairs:

"Sally! Get my milk bath ready."

Since the Empress Josephine, Napoleon's wife, following the example set by Cleopatra, started to bathe in milk, the milk bath had become the fashion among the notorious ladies. Clarissa didn't particularly enjoy getting into the tub full of cow's milk. It was so sticky! But this time she didn't mind it at all. Here she was, washing her beautiful body with milk, like a queen. While Slippery Jack had to bear the inconveniences of a smelly jail cell.

But the important thing was, of course, that he'd never have a chance now of bringing his scheme, in respect to Captain Richard Gray, into being. Captain Richard Gray, who strangely enough, didn't even know of Slippery Jack's existence, and who consequently could have no suspicion of the danger that threatened him from that quarter.

PART FIVE

CHAPTER EIGHTEEN

ETE DROVE THE small enclosed carriage—which used to convey the housekeeper and the butler to Sunday morning services, back at Ravisham—half across London, and into a dark side street, and brought it to a stop there.

Clarissa said to Sally, sitting beside her inside:

"Wait for me here."

And getting out, she walked away swiftly, after casting a quick glance around. A plain dark mantle concealed her rich dress, a piece of veiling covered her hair, and she wore a little black mask to hide the vivid beauty of her face. She might have been a lady of quality hurrying to a secret meeting with her lover. And the modesty of the equipage which had brought Clarissa here would make its presence equally un-noticeable to a casual passer-by.

The familiar stench of the Thames struck Clarissa's nostrils as she hastened across the deserted thoroughfare, and a heavy fog all but obliterated the Thieves' Village further on. She made her way between the shacks, and towards the faint glimmer of light that marked the Waterfront Tavern. Then she was at the door, pushing it open ... She walked in.

And there they all were, sitting around the tables, eating and drinking, throwing dice, arguing in loud voices or roaring with laughter. Ugly Frank, Take-the-Road Timothy, Black Moll, Maggoty Jane ... Everybody. And, of course, the gray-haired, distinguished-looking, frail Lafonte, and the ragpicker Dumb

Clara, who had the tools of her trade, a long stick with a hook and a sack, right there with her. Even from a distance Clarissa could tell that the tin mugs before them were empty of liquor, for lack of money.

Before anyone had time to observe her entrance, Clarissa, having swiftly removed her little black mask, was already standing beside Lafonte, her hand on the man's shoulder.

"Clarissa!"

By then everybody saw her, and they all jumped up to rush over, surrounding her. She threw back her mantle to show them her magnificent dress, her sparkling jewels, and laughed at the expressions of their faces. "Well! *Well ...* " they all exclaimed. "Clarissa! *Our* Clarissa. What a wench!" They were all immensely proud of her success, but the remarks they made were naturally full of derision.

And Dumb Clara said, with a jerk of her toothless head in the battered but still coquettish velvet bonnet:

"How very grand we are! Oh, dear me! Yes!"

"You old bitch!" And Clarissa slapped her on the back so hard that Dumb Clara almost fell off her chair.

The rotund proprietor, at Clarissa's signal, had hastened to fill the two tin mugs with the best liquor his tavern could supply. And now, as Clarissa threw a couple of gold coins on the table, he was making her many an obsequious bow.

"Abandoning your poor old mother ..." Dumb Clara whimpered, tipsy, as usual, after the first few sips of gin.

The others were teasing Clarissa about the senility of her protector, the fantastic diminutive Earl. Did he have his bejeweled fan with him when romping in bed with her? some wanted to know. Clarissa laughed with them all. They *were* glad to see her. Especially Lafonte.

"Let me look at you!" he commanded.

And Clarissa had to remove her dark mantle, and take the veiling off her hair, and stand at a little distance before him, in all her splendor, and then turn round slowly, until he was perfectly satisfied.

"I knew you'd make good!" the once-famous dancing master said, his faded eyes moist and the frail hands tremulous with emotion. "With your beauty and talents, all you needed was the right kind of setting."

And the rosy-cheeked proprietor kept reminiscing excitedly:

"Remember, Mistress Clarissa,"—now he addressed her as *Mistress!*—"how you used to dance, right on that table there," and he pointed, "in your brief shabby skirt, and kicking up your legs so very high ... And look at you now! A great lady, and no mistake!"

"Liquor for everybody," Clarissa ordered, this time flinging a handful of gold on the table.

And while the shouting and guffawing company was being served, she resumed her mantle, wrapped the veiling over her hair, and glanced around for Prickly Gil. But they thought she was looking for Slippery Jack. Naturally, there was no way for the recent news to have reached her, moving as she did now in the most elite circle of London's high society, they told her. Besides, there was never any fanfare about the capture of such a one as Slippery Jack. They thus alluded to his low standing as a common felon, of the cheapest variety. Even among his own people Slippery Jack was distrusted and disliked.... Yes, Slippery Jack was in jail.

"Oh," Clarissa said.

And while she duly expressed surprise, and even sympathy, she watched their coarse faces for some possible indication that they suspected her of having had a hand in Slippery Jack's capture. Terrible was the punishment dealt to whoever happened to betray one of their own. So terrible that Clarissa pushed the thought away. The victim's body, or what was left of it, afterwards thrown into the Thames, under the bridge, where the river ran deeper and the current stronger.

But they were all grinning at her, and raising their mugs or tankards to her, in apparent good-fellowship. And somebody said:

"Well, most of us expect to be caught, sooner or later, and end at Tyburn, dangling from the hangman's rope."

And they spoke no more of Slippery Jack.

She had gotten the information she came to procure—Slippery Jack was in jail still, and wouldn't be called up for trial for several months evidently, as usually happened because of the crowded court calendar—and Clarissa was satisfied. Her other reason for coming was to seek out Prickly Gil. And there she was, sitting alone as was her habit, and staring into a corner, as if she could see something in the shadows there. On hurrying over, Clarissa saw that the weird girl was big with child. Carbuncle Joe's child. Under the coarse shift, Prickly Gil's bulging stomach had a strangely pointed shape.

"Prickly Gil," Clarissa said, pulling up a chair and sitting down, her silk skirts rustling richly. "I need your help."

The light of the flaming hearth logs fell on Prickly Gil's bare feet, giving them a queer shape. Like ... a goat's? Clarissa wondered, remembering the rumors.

"You gave me Carbuncle Joe," Prickly Gil said. "You might have had him yourself, but you arranged it so that I got him instead, remember? Therefore, you can ask my help. What is it?"

"Well," Clarissa said. "There's a man I know, and he ..." She had a handkerchief in her hand, and as she spoke she began to twist and pull the scrap of fine cambric with her fingers, quite unaware of what she was doing. "He, this man, I mean ... Well,

I'm just a plaything to him. That's it! Off he went again, to rejoin Lord Nelson's fleet," Clarissa explained, "and I may never see him again!"

"You mean, there are other women he's interested in?"

"Hundreds of them, I'm certain. And I just happen to be one of many. A plaything!" Clarissa's fingers pulled at the handkerchief frantically.

"And the man's name?" Prickly Gil asked, watching her.

"Oh," Clarissa said. "Do you *have* to know his name?"

"Since it's not just any man, but a particular man, naturally his name must be known to us. Otherwise, how can the secret powers single him out?"

"Single him out?" Clarissa repeated. She felt very stupid, and a little afraid, too.

"You wouldn't understand even if I tried to explain," Prickly Gil told her, not unkindly. "Let me hear the man's name," she ordered.

"Well," Clarissa said. And then she came out with it, "Captain Richard Gray."

"The name has a propitious sound," Prickly Gil decided, after saying it to herself several times over, her thin pale lips barely moving. "A person with a name like that should have luck on his side frequently," she prophesied mysteriously. "But as far as you're concerned," she stared at Clarissa worriedly, "that's another matter. There's a problem here. Captain Richard Gray is evidently very attractive to women. And that means, of course, that you have that many secret enemies."

"Maybe if I could just see him again," Clarissa pleaded. "But this war might be going on for *years*. And the trouble is, he won't be allowed to come back until it's over! That's the Prince Regent's latest edict. No furloughs till Napoleon is conquered! So probably I'm asking for the impossible," Clarissa added. Having torn the handkerchief to shreds, she was now busy rolling up the remains into a tight little ball.

"It will be difficult, yes," Prickly Gil agreed quietly. "The plans and movements of some of the historical personages may have to be changed. In such a manner, of course, as to make them think that they are merely following the dictates of their own free will."

Clarissa wanted to ask which of the historical personages the weird girl had in mind, but dared not.

"Nothing is impossible to the Master," Prickly Gil said. "Something may be accomplished, perhaps. A week from today, come to the Kenerevy woods," she went on. "Be there half an hour after midnight. The moon will be in partial eclipse. And this will hold the tides in suspense. All the waters in this section of the world will be temporarily stilled. It will be a great night for us. The Master will let it be known who the Chosen One is. Every six months, if the Master finds someone worthy, he shows the Chosen One to us."

Clarissa had several questions to ask. To what part of the Kenerevy woods was she to come? The woods—the place was always referred to in the plural, for some reason—were said to be almost impassable because of the dense growth, entangled brambles, and other natural obstacles, and besides they stretched for miles.… And would Prickly Gil, or somebody else, perhaps, meet her, to show the way?

But the girl, after smoothing the unsavory shift over her queerly shaped enlarged stomach, was again staring into a corner. And Clarissa could get nothing more out of her. So she rose to go, and suddenly saw, clutched in her hand, the tight little ball which once had been her pretty handkerchief. Feeling very much ashamed of herself, she hastened to drop it into the small velvet bag which she carried with her, and to pull the drawstring which closed the bag. Then, after stopping on the way to bid good-by to Lafonte, Clarissa left the Waterfront Tavern.

And exactly a week later, and at the appointed hour, she found herself within sight of the Kenerevy woods. A broad meadow had to be crossed to reach the place, and she followed the little path which, starting at the roadside, ran through the low grass, wet and glistening with the night dew. Behind her and at some distance, the city of London shone with its many warm lights. But all around her here there was nothing but this faint, sickly moonlight. What was it Prickly Gil had said—partial eclipse ...? And probably that explained it. The moon remained invisible, yet there was enough of its vague, reflected shimmer to make out the looming mass of misshapen trees towards which she hurried.

She had told Pete to put up the small enclosed carriage in the yard of an inn which, frequented by coachmen, was on a busy street, and for him and Sally to spend the few hours of waiting in the taproom. Sally, though extremely curious, had learned not to ask any questions. But Clarissa, to keep her true destination a complete secret, had had to walk the rest of the way, and now she was somewhat fatigued.

She stepped in among the ghostly trees. The misty moonlight barely reached here, and there was the dense growth of brambles and the lower branches to cope with. Resolutely, Clarissa pushed her way on. Sometimes it was so dark that she could hardly see the little path which, without breaking off, still ran on as if showing her the correct direction. A gnarled bough threatened to graze her cheek, and then a bramble scratched her ankle painfully. She could feel a few drops of blood oozing out. The dampness, the cold, and especially the weird mistiness around made her shiver.

And then, suddenly, everything was nice and cozy and quite ordinary. She had entered a spacious clearing and there were people, just plain, everyday people, standing about in groups, or sitting on the ground and on the tree stumps, and talking and laughing among themselves, and Prickly Gil met her, saying:

"You're just in time. We're about to begin."

Begin what? Clarissa wondered.

A pleasant little fire was burning at the other end of the clearing and she thought of going over to warm her chilled hands, but Prickly Gil was introducing her to the women who happened to be standing nearby, some of them young and even pretty. And then a little old woman, very neat, came up, and Clarissa recognized Nellie Harris.

"We've met before, haven't we?" Nellie Harris said, smiling at her as at an old friend.

A man who occupied a neighboring tree stump rose politely so that Clarissa could sit down and, thanking him, she did so. The tree stump was thickly overgrown with moss and made a very comfortable seat. And recollecting the rumors which according to Sally existed in Wickham St. Paul's as to the means of transportation employed by Nellie Harris, Clarissa, choosing an opportune moment, said to her conversationally:

"It's quite a long journey from where you live, isn't it? You probably had to get up very early in the morning."

"Well, I've just arrived."

"Oh?" Clarissa said.

"Doesn't take but a few minutes to get here. Or anywhere else, for that matter."

"Oh?" Clarissa again said.

The poor thing was doubtless touched in the head, and not just slightly, either. No wonder the villagers had tried to stone her out from amongst them!

But Nellie Harris had something to say to her, too.

"There's been a change there," she confided, enigmatically. "But then it's no news to you, of course."

"What change? Where?"

"Why, that grave near Ravisham. It's empty now, eh? Yes ..."

Clarissa, though startled, quickly controlled herself.

"Ah, go along with you," she told her, laughing. "As if you could know anything about it!"

"We know. We always know ..."

The fire at the other end was starting to burn brighter. Most of the men present were gathered there, doing something, probably feeding wood to the flames. And Clarissa saw now that the fire was not built on the ground, but was burning in the niche of a low stone structure, which resembled a crude altar of some sort. And tied to a sapling close by stood a small white animal, yes, a young goat. The whole gathering, in fact, looked suddenly and horribly different. She had thought that they had all come here wearing just their everyday clothes and didn't notice that every one of them, whether man or woman, wore over the ordinary attire a black one-piece garment. But now that there was more light from their altar fire, and they had let down the long loose sleeves, previously rolled up, and had put the voluminous hoods up over their heads, they all looked weirdly alike; she couldn't tell the sexes apart.

They had also removed their shoes, and the numerous bare feet, as the hooded black figures moved about busily, went plop, plop, plop, against the bare ground. Some of them were forming a single-file circle in the center of the clearing. Others, in pairs or threes, were starting some kind of a dance around that circle. And Prickly Gil was giving everybody something to drink out of a little cup. Stopping in front of Clarissa, she refilled the cup with a pleasant-smelling liquid from a steaming small pot which she carried around with her.

"Drink this," Prickly Gil ordered, handing the little cup to Clarissa.

"Is it … a potion of some kind?" Clarissa asked.

But the girl merely repeated her order. And Clarissa obediently drank. The warm, thick liquid had a surprisingly nice taste to it. Instead of being bitter, as Clarissa had expected, it was maybe just a trifle oversweet.

"Is there anything I'm supposed to … do?" she asked, returning the cup.

"You are a friendly outsider," Prickly Gil explained. "Friendly outsiders do not take part in the ritual. Your presence here fulfills your obligation."

Evidently Clarissa, as an outsider, was the last to drink of the potion. For Prickly Gil now put both the pot and the cup away into the nearby underbrush. Then she let down the long, loose sleeves of her black overgarment, put the voluminous hood up over her head, hurried away. And Clarissa, from where she sat, could no longer distinguish her from the others.

By then everything was in motion. Those who formed the circle moved round faster and faster. And those who danced around them in pairs and in threes, were flinging themselves about with such speed that it made Clarissa dizzy just to see it. The whole of the clearing was one mad whirling mass of hooded black figures, the long sleeves flapping, the backs arched grotesquely. And they were chanting something. At first, it was this chanting, with only here and there a little cry, or shriek, flung out suddenly. And then the cries and the shrieks, multiplying speedily, merged into one ceaseless piercing scream, which all but drowned the bleating of the white goat. The weird ecstasy having reached its peak, the little knot of figures which had stayed by the stone altar was slashing the goat's throat open. And Clarissa caught a glimpse of the slender hoofs, jerking once, twice.… Then the flames hissed as blood was poured over the fire.

And they all threw themselves down on the ground, and pleaded:

"Master! Master!"

"Give us the sign, Master!"

"Let us see the Chosen One, Master!"

"Aye, give us the sign. Show us the Chosen One, O Master!"

They went on like that ... And, really! the way they rocked themselves, and crawled on their bellies, while imploring, made the spectacle somehow sickening.

Suddenly somebody shrieked, "The Chosen One!" and pointed upward.

Clarissa had leaned her head against the trunk of the tree behind her and she could see the sky, misty with moonlight. There was something strange about the arrangement of the clouds there. And then she realized that it was not just ordinary clouds, but a cloudlike etching of something, no ... of someone, and she suddenly recognized Carbuncle Joe. He appeared immense, his figure covering half of the sky. Otherwise, he looked exactly as she remembered him that night at the Waterfront Tavern, the night before he was hanged. Gallantly attired, in tall boots, white breeches, blue coat trimmed with silver, the ornamental sword at his hip and in his coarse hand the tricorn, also silver-trimmed. Naturally, the hangman's rope now dangled from around his neck. But the ugly face, under the lavishly powdered hair, was in no way distorted. And even the horrible, purplish carbuncle on the side of his cheek seemed to leak, as it had leaked when he had been alive.

For a moment, the apparition stood there, vividly clear. Then, as Clarissa, paralyzed with horror, stared, the image grew dim, receded, became as if dissolved among the clouds ... And when she dared to look again, even the clouds were gone and there was only the misty moonlight. While everybody in the clearing now was positively wild with joy, shrieking something about the given "sign," and the "Chosen One." And it was no use telling herself that their reaction didn't prove anything. That they also, like herself, had drunk of the potion, and the stuff probably made one see things. And that she, Clarissa, had been tired besides. Yes, she must have dozed off.... But all these private arguments were useless. She was covered with sweat, shaking all over, her teeth chattered.

The altar fire, meanwhile, had gone out. The weird noises gradually subsided. The hooded black figures were now engaged in other kinds of excesses. Clasping one another obscenely, rolling on the ground. Orgies were supposed to be an integral part of the so-called Sabbath. A few of the figures were quite small. Children ...? Maybe there was truth in the rumors that incest sometimes occurred during their ritual....

Clarissa could never remember afterwards how she left the clearing, and then made her way out of the Kenerevy woods, to eventually rejoin Sally and Pete at the coachmen's taproom.

"Where in the world did you go?" Sally cried. "You're as white as a sheet! And there's a rent in your mantle, and your shoes are stained with the wet, and your hand ... yes, it's scratched!"

Not until the privacy of her own room was reached did the strange fear leave Clarissa. But in the morning, she immediately began to wait—for something to happen, as the result of Prickly Gil's mysterious intervention. Days passed, however, and nothing happened. Clarissa armed herself with patience, and to ease the poignancy of waiting she tried to give her attention to such things as—her collection of jewels. It made her laugh to think that she was actually collecting jewels, as a *hobby*. But it came about in this way.

At one of the fashionable gatherings, Mr. Brummell, drawing her aside, begged her to help arrange a meeting between the

Princess Caroline and her child. Since the Prince Regent was adamant in his refusal to grant the deposed wife the necessary permission, Mr. Brummell explained, she, Clarissa, was the only person who had the power of making the long-awaited reunion a reality.

"I ...?" Clarissa said, astonished, flattered. "But how *could* I ...?"

"You have influence with the Earl," Mr. Brummell reminded her. "And if His Grace and everybody concerned will act according to the plan I have prepared, we might get away with it."

He then described his simple plan. And Clarissa that same night explained it to the Earl, who at first, however, refused very flatly to be a party to such a dangerous undertaking. He'd be thrown in the Tower, beheaded ...! But when Clarissa, gracefully perched on the arm of his chair, placed a finger behind his ear to tickle him there, while she cooed, "My little Peewee ..." The Earl began to giggle, and suddenly gave in.

And the very next morning His Grace set off in his crested coach for the house where the child, with her special staff of servants, was kept strictly incommunicado. He would let it be known that he had come to take the neglected little princess out for a short drive in the country, and the servants wouldn't dare say nay to so powerful a noble ...

Clarissa, meanwhile, in her own luxurious coach, drove to the Countess of Argull's house, to fetch the mother. The pair of beautiful bays had barely stopped in front of the narrow gate in the garden wall, when Princess Caroline, heavily veiled, emerged, hurried over, got in, took the seat beside Clarissa, and the equipage instantly drove on. The timing so far had been perfect.

"You're being very kind, madam," the Princess murmured, dabbing at her eyes with her wisp of a handkerchief.

The stately slender woman wore the same gown of pale brocade which Clarissa remembered so well. But she had failed to recognize Clarissa. The curtains were drawn over the coach windows, as a precautionary measure, and in the half-light all Princess Caroline could be aware of was the richness of Clarissa's attire, and the glitter of Clarissa's jewels.

The Earl's coach was the first to reach the lonely spot, on a country road, and shaded with big trees. And now Clarissa's drew up alongside of it. There were no witnesses but the liveried Pete and the Earl's trusted personal coachman. The latter immediately helped the pretty little girl out of one coach and into the other, right into the mother's extended arms.

"Mummy! Mummy!"

"My little Charlotte! My baby …"

To let the two of them have privacy, Clarissa took a little walk. The Earl, she knew, would keep track of the time by his fat gold watch. When Clarissa returned, the time was up, but neither Princess Caroline nor the little Princess Charlotte could be made to part from each other. At last, the struggling child was placed beside the Earl. Clarissa hastened to resume her seat beside the weeping mother. And the two coaches, each following a different road, drove swiftly back to London.

"You've been *most* kind," Princess Caroline murmured, pressing her tiny handkerchief to her eyes, and then trying to smile. "Well, I have something for *you* … Clarissa. Yes, I recognized you suddenly," she went on, "as you stood out in the road there, in the sunlight … I should have known you instantly, of course, because of the Green Perfume. Remember, I advised you then to use it always? And now I have another piece of advice to give you." And, producing out of her bag, which matched her pale brocade gown, a pair of diamond earrings, holding them suspended in her hand, Princess Caroline explained. "As everybody knows, I have very little money now. I have to economize.... But before misfortune struck me, I used to amuse myself by collecting jewelry as a hobby. Never thinking that a day might come when I would have need of it in an emergency, such as this one. So why don't you, Clarissa, now while you're so prosperous, start collecting jewels? And let this," she put the diamond earrings into Clarissa's hand, "be the first item of that future collection of yours!"

And every time Clarissa persuaded the Earl to arrange a meeting between the mother and child, Princess Caroline, as they drove back, would press yet another valuable jewel into Clarissa's hand. The precious stones were always flawless and—if they happened to be rubies, or emeralds, or sapphires, instead of diamonds—of the purest color. The little collection grew. And Clarissa could have increased it considerably by adding a diamond necklace or two which she received from the Earl, except that His Grace kept a strict check on all his jewel gifts. Still, she managed, from time to time, to put aside a brooch, or a bracelet, a pendant—some of the smaller pieces, which he couldn't *possibly* miss—and then add them to her collection.

Clarissa kept it in the drawer of her dressing table. Until she suddenly remembered the small casket given to her by the trainer of the dancing bears. She went looking for it, and behind the curtain which concealed her extensive wardrobe, on a shelf there, stood the casket, the brass clasps shining. She brought it over to the dressing table, opened it. And it was full of ribbons! That's what Sally had been using the casket for. Clarissa swiftly pulled the ribbons out, transferred the jewels from the drawer to the casket, closed the lid, snapped the brass clasps shut.

"There!" she said, very much satisfied.

Certainly a much more suitable receptacle for her little collection, this casket.

And then Clarissa called for Sally, and had her summon François, and, though it was broad daylight, she put on her crimson ballgown, and François fixed her hair in a way quite unusual for Clarissa, with the gleaming auburn curls gathered high on either side of her graceful head, à la Empress Josephine.

"I want the beauty of your face to be fully revealed," the artist had insisted.

Clarissa was due at his fashionable atelier to sit for her portrait. It was the same famous artist who had recently immortalized the haughty grossness of the Prince Regent, and the simple elegance of Beau Brummell, on life-size canvases. But hers was to be smaller. Down only to the waist.

"We will leave the rest to the imagination of the beholder!" the painter had explained with a magnificent gesture.

The portrait was already the talk of London, and when it was completed the Earl would have it installed in his best drawing room.

"But someday," the artist had predicted privately to Clarissa, "it will be displayed in a museum!"

My portrait in a *museum!* Clarissa didn't really believe it.

But the sittings, like her little collection of jewels, eased the strain of waiting for Prickly Gil's promised assistance to bring some tangible result. Nothing had happened so far.... And when Clarissa thought of the many miles that separated her from Captain Richard Gray, she knew what it meant to despair.

CHAPTER NINETEEN

O N RETURNING FROM the sitting, Clarissa was surprised not to find Sally waiting to help her out of the crimson ballgown. Irritated by the girl's strange absence, she hastened to undress and slip into a peignoir of pale blue cashmere. And Clarissa shivered as she wrapped herself in its soft warmth. Was there a draft somewhere? Probably sitting in that high-backed chair for the temperamental artist had tired her out … She felt chilly and somehow tense. And she was about to make herself comfortable on the cushioned chaise longue when the door, which led onto the landing of the main staircase, suddenly flung open and, in the most unconcerned manner, the Rosicrucian walked in. How the unexpected sight of his tall dignified figure in the well-remembered black cloak and the broad-brimmed hat made her jump!

"Do not be alarmed," the Rosicrucian said calmly.

And closing the door, he sat down on the bench beside it, leaned his back against the wall, and crossed his arms.

"No one will disturb us," he added, his piercing gaze bent on Clarissa, on her beauty, and the contours of her figure accentuated by the soft material of the trailing peignoir, approvingly.

"But—anyone may come in!" Clarissa pointed out. Yes, and find her talking to a mysterious stranger in her bedroom! "A flunky, with a message from a tradesman, maybe. Or, François, the chief valet. He's to do my coiffure for the evening. Or even the Earl himself! Since I dare not lock my door …"

"Naturally," the Rosicrucian agreed quietly. "Being a mistress, you cannot afford to lock the door. For no matter how innocent the reason, it would give rise to some slander most injurious to you in the eyes of your protector."

"If you had at least worn some plausible disguise," Clarissa went on, not listening.

She didn't know that she was walking the floor swiftly, at times kicking at the train of her peignoir when it got in the way, and even stamping a foot—she was so angry at this inconsiderate intrusion. What did the man want of her? The last time they met, he had mentioned the possibility of calling upon her to render him some kind of service, and the reward she would receive for it. Well, she certainly didn't need him now! What possible reward could match what she already had: position, luxury, rich clothes, jewels? Pshaw! she'd say to his reward.

"Members of our secret organization," the Rosicrucian said quietly, "never have recourse to disguise. All our actions are open and straight-forward."

"Then I don't understand," Clarissa parried, "how it is you were not stopped by all those flunkies down in the hall!"

"It was arranged that the hall would be empty at the moment, the flunkies pursuing their normal duties elsewhere during that brief period of time," the Rosicrucian stated simply. "There is no dwelling in the world we cannot enter, at will, be it the humblest hut, or the most exalted palace. And do so unobserved, if our purpose requires it."

Well, that time at the Waterfront Tavern, with all the doors guarded by men heavily armed, his means of entry had been just as mystifying. Except that not to be seen hadn't been in his plans then.

"You mean, there's someone here, in this house, who is a Ro ... a Rosicrucian, like yourself?" Clarissa asked, curiosity getting the better of her temper.

"I am not at liberty to say," the Rosicrucian said.

"Who could it be ...?" Clarissa nibbled daintily at the rosy nail of her little finger, as she wondered, frowning.

"I am not at liberty to say," the Rosicrucian repeated. "I told you we won't be disturbed, and it is the truth. But to satisfy your curiosity as to how such a thing can be prearranged, I will give you an example. You mentioned François, the chief valet. Well, at the last moment he won't be able to find the lace-trimmed shirt which the Earl is planning to wear this evening. And looking for that shirt will delay François' coming here to do your coiffure. And so it will be all along the line, seemingly normal little occurrences like that preventing each person from entering this room until I'm gone. And Sally, by the way," the Rosicrucian added, "had a message from Mr. Davey that he has a fresh supply of the Green Perfume, and since you have hardly any of it left Sally immediately hurried there to fetch it."

Which explained Sally's unusual absence. Clarissa was really amazed.

"You knew ... of Sally's existence? And ... about Mr. Davey?"

"Since you're the woman who is to render this service to us, naturally you've been kept track of, and whoever comes in contact with you is known to us. But we musn't waste time," the Rosicrucian went on. "Stop your pouting, Clarissa. And your angry pacing about. And sit down. Here," with a mere glance indicating a chair which stood close to the bench on which he sat.

There was something about the man's personality that made Clarissa hurry over and sit down, as told. Then, realizing that she had actually obeyed his command, something she had had no intention of doing, she instantly assumed a haughty pose, and said, imperiously:

"I am a very busy person now. Therefore, I'll beg you to excuse me. I really have no time...."

Something resembling a smile passed over the Rosicrucian's strong aquiline features, as he sat there, wrapped in his black cloak, immobile, his arms crossed, his eyes a faint glitter in the shadow cast by the broad-brimmed hat. He regarded her thus, in perfect silence, for a long minute.

"No time to hear what I have to say," he then said quietly, "even if it concerns all those ships, standing inactive in the Nile? Lord Nelson's fleet?"

"Ships ... the fleet ...?" Clarissa said in a very small voice.

"The service you're about to render us concerns the future movements of the fleet," the Rosicrucian explained, matter-of-factly. "And will directly affect Lord Nelson's plans, and his ... personal life."

The plans of some of the historical personages might have to be changed ... wasn't that what Prickly Gil had said, among other things? Or was the Rosicrucian's unexpected visit, and this little matter of a service he had in mind for Clarissa to render him, a mere coincidence?

He was still speaking, however:

"As I told you before, you'll be amply rewarded."

The reward! The payment for her trouble ... There was only one thing she wanted, and that's what she'd ask for! She'd demand it, yes. But she mustn't let the Rosicrucian guess how suddenly all excited she was inside. For probably she'd have to bargain with him to achieve her ends.

And leaning back gracefully in the cushioned chair, and after leisurely arranging the folds of the blue cashmere about her becomingly, she said loftily:

"I may consider your proposition. Tell me what it is you wish me to do."

"Before I explain that," the Rosicrucian said, "I want to ask you two questions. And the first one is—have you ever heard of the name, Lady Hamilton?"

"Lady Hamilton ... Lady Hamilton ..." Clarissa repeated slowly. "No, never heard of it. Which proves that the woman, whoever she might be, can't be so very well known! For in the exalted circles where I now circulate," Clarissa pointed out with pride, "famous persons are always talked about."

"Quite true. And certainly very few people have heard of Lady Hamilton as yet. But we happen to know that great fame is her destiny. That her name will go down in history. And you, Clarissa, will be responsible for it."

"Why should I make some other woman famous?" Clarissa demanded jealously.

"Because otherwise you couldn't gain your own ends. It is frequently so in this world, Clarissa," the Rosicrucian told her. "While we're striving to achieve some purpose, we unwittingly are instrumental in assisting others to achieve *theirs*. If the purpose is not the selfsame one, of course."

"Well, I think that's very unfair," Clarissa said. "But do go on. What's the other question?"

"Do you know anything about mushrooms?"

"Mushrooms!" Clarissa was astonished.

"Yes, mushrooms. As edibles, as a dish."

"Oh! Well," Clarissa thought it over. "All I know is that people sometimes die after eating mushrooms."

"Quite right. When the so-called wrong ones are picked. Would you be able to tell them apart from the other kind? If you saw mushrooms in their natural state. Growing, I mean."

"I wouldn't even know how they grow, or where," Clarissa said. "I'm city-bred. Sally, now, she was born in the country. She'd probably know about such things.... But what can mushrooms have to do with this Lady Hamilton?"

"A great deal, in this particular instance. But about that, later. I will now give you a brief survey of the remarkable woman's rise in the world, which is insignificant at present."

And the Rosicrucian did so, in a few well-chosen words.

Emma, the future Lady Hamilton, started as a waitress in a tavern. Romney, the painter, noticed her there, and took her to his lodgings, and she served as his model. But a young fop, Grevile, saw her posing in the nude, and Romney, who was afraid that his infatuation with Emma would interfere with his career, passed her on to him. Then, Grevile, finding himself in financial difficulties, sold her for the sum of five thousand pounds to his uncle, Lord Hamilton, the British ambassador at Naples. The girl's loveliness, however, so bewitched the elderly man that he married her, and now she was Lady Hamilton. She also succeeded in completely charming the Queen of Naples, and the Queen now was absolutely enamored of her ...

"If Lady Hamilton were to tell the Queen of Naples to jump off a cliff," the Rosicrucian said, "the Queen would jump, and that's all there is to it!"

"Is she so very beautiful then, this Lady Hamilton?" Clarissa asked eagerly.

"She is lovely to look at. And she has great charm. A pale blonde, with a porcelain-like complexion, she always wears a gown that is flowing in style, semi-transparent, and with a gauze scarf about her slender neck, the ends floating as she moves. To some people she is nothing less than a ravishing vision, something quite celestial! And among them ..." and here the Rosicrucian paused significantly, "is Lord Nelson, himself."

"Oh," Clarissa said. She was beginning to understand. "Lord Nelson is in love with her, and Lady Hamilton is attracted to him, but they're not lovers yet! How can they become lovers while at Naples?" Clarissa went on, her eyes sparkling at the clear picture she now had of the situation. "With the Queen, jealous of Lady Hamilton, right there. And Emma herself, probably, fighting her infatuation for Lord Nelson, because she's afraid to lose everything she has achieved: title, money, social position ... Lord Hamilton being the ambassador," Clarissa added, "Lord Nelson has to call on him, from time to time, on business of state, and that's how he met Lady Hamilton, and how they go on seeing each other...."

"The principality of Naples, though a very small country," the Rosicrucian explained, "is an important member of the alliance against Napoleon, yes. Because of its geographic position."

"Well, they'll never become lovers, Lord Nelson and Lady Hamilton," Clarissa went on, "unless they're given the chance of seeing each other somewhere else, and in completely different surroundings!"

The Rosicrucian nodded approvingly at her acumen in such matters, and Clarissa said:

"You have some particular place in mind? And would it be here, in England?"

"Yes, and the place is suitably pastoral. Merton, it's called. The ownership of the cottage has already been secured. And the little garden, full of flowers, overhangs a small inlet. Lord Nelson would be able to anchor his flagship, *Victory,* within view of the house, telescope's view, that is. And he'd then be rowed over, right up to the steep path which leads into the garden. Altogether, an ideal spot for our purpose. But surroundings alone are not enough," the Rosicrucian pointed out impressively. "You are supposed to be the owner of that cottage, Clarissa. You'll be the hostess."

"What do you mean ... hostess?"

"First of all, you will transform the place into a love nest. I'm leaving all the details to you. The interior is rather drab ... And then you will grace it with your presence. And that is the most important part of my plan. For it will create the turning point in the relationship of those two future lovers. Your presence. Because you're that rare type of woman, Clarissa, who, besides inspiring love for her own person, also produces what is known as the *atmosphere of love.* It's like an invisible aura exuded by your vital personality. That's why I selected you, Clarissa."

"That night down at the Waterfront Tavern?" Clarissa asked.

"I watched the reaction of the coarse company for whom you danced," the Rosicrucian explained. "And how they all started making love to one another within a minute of your appearance ... The effect you had on those rough people, Clarissa, convinced me that Lady Hamilton would be no more able to resist the stimulus of the atmosphere of love than they did. That, forgetting all practical considerations, she would become Lord Nelson's mistress."

"And once they're lovers, once she's his mistress," Clarissa cried, "Lady Hamilton will procure from the Queen of Naples whatever it is you *want* her to procure for you own *purpose!*"

"Our purpose is world peace," the Rosicrucian said. But he allowed a slight smile to pass over his strong features in appreciation of Clarissa's quick wits and her surprisingly correct deduction. "Yes, the Queen of Naples has a great stock of military supplies, and Lady Hamilton will ask her to have them transported to Lord Nelson's fleet, and Lord Nelson then will give the long-awaited Battle of the Nile to the French. If he wins it, half of the work in conquering Napoleon will be accomplished!"

"And when am I supposed to go to—Merton—that's the name of the place, isn't it?—and prepare the love nest?" Clarissa demanded.

"Lord and Lady Hamilton will be arriving at Merton Sunday morning. The invitation, in your name—a fictitious one, of course—was accepted some time ago. And the bait was old china, *objets d'art*. Lord Hamilton is insane about them. Which was why he eagerly consented to be a guest at the house of a perfect stranger. A crate of very fine pieces has already been delivered at the cottage. And you, Clarissa, will arrange them becomingly in a small corner room there, the study. And that's where Lord Hamilton will spend most of his time. Caressing the figurines, the miniatures ... It's an obsession with him."

Clarissa listened attentively. And then she said:

"But to have everything prepared by Sunday morning! Today is Thursday...."

"Its short notice, I know. But we had to take advantage of the leave Lord Hamilton has been granted from his duties at Naples. That's what brought him and Lady Hamilton to London."

"I just don't see how I can possibly manage," Clarissa complained.

"You'll manage," the Rosicrucian told her, very curtly.

"Well ..." Clarissa temporized. "And what about Lord Nelson?"

"He will reach Merton later the same day. Where the Hamiltons go, there goes Lord Nelson. It has been so for some time. Not that his naval chores don't come first with him, always. One must give him full credit for that."

"There's just one thing I don't quite understand," Clarissa said. "Lady Hamilton's husband, won't he be—well—sort of in the way?"

"Lord Hamilton's attitude is decidedly strange," the Rosicrucian admitted. "He can't but be aware of the situation, that Lord Nelson is courting Lady Hamilton to make her his mistress, yet the three of them are on the friendliest terms. Some people try to explain it by saying that Lord Hamilton is a hero worshipper, he worships Nelson, can't conceive of him doing something he shouldn't.... Anyway, he's not the person who could ruin our little scheme. Ignore him. So long as he has those precious pieces to handle and play with, he'll be perfectly satisfied. And here's the money, Clarissa, for the necessary expenses," the Rosicrucian added, producing from under his cloak a large leather purse and handing it to her. "You will also find inside a list of instructions I jotted down on a piece of paper: what road to take for Merton, and so forth.... You will leave tonight, before midnight."

"Tonight!" Clarissa gasped. "But the Earl! What am I to do about *him?* I can't just walk off ...!"

"That has been taken care of. The Earl by now has received from his personal physician an order to depart immediately to take the waters at Bath. Which means that your and your guests' sojourn at Merton can last a whole week."

"How you think of everything!" Clarissa marveled. And then, suddenly remembering something: "But what about ... mushrooms? And how do *they* fit into your project?"

"I was coming to that. There's only one person who can ruin our secret organization's carefully prepared plans," the Rosicrucian explained, "and this person is Mrs. Cadogan, Lady Hamilton's mother. A very common woman, fiercely grabbing. She hates Lord Nelson, and would do anything to prevent Lady Hamilton from becoming his mistress, since the affair, once it's known, may rob Mrs. Cadogan of her own comfortable position."

"And is she going to be there, too, this ... Mrs. Cadogan?"

"She has attached herself to her daughter like a leech, and Lady Hamilton has to take her around with her wherever she goes. Besides, Lord Hamilton has quite an affection for Mrs. Cadogan. Altogether, our little scheme would have been quite hopeless, on account of this horrible woman. Except that we were lucky to discover that Mrs. Cadogan loves to eat mushrooms. So try to get hold of all the recipes you possibly can for preparing a savory dish of mushrooms. And have them served to Mrs. Cadogan, in one form or another, two, three times a day. It's her weakness," the Rosicrucian pointed out shrewdly, "and once you know a person's weakness, you have that person in your power. Mushrooms have an instant effect on Mrs. Cadogan. She becomes drowsy and soon falls into a long sleep. And then, naturally, she can't interfere."

"But where will I be getting such a quantity of mushrooms?" Clarissa wanted to know.

"Not far from the cottage there's a thicket, and it's full of mushrooms. But be sure you pick the right kind," the Rosicrucian warned her. "And there's another thing," he went on. "If our little scheme proves completely successful, Lord Nelson might wish to acquire ownership of the place, the scene of his conquest of Lady Hamilton. Besides, he's been long separated from his wife, and hasn't had a home of his own for years—as you probably know." Well, everybody knew *that*. Lady Nelson was said to be an awful prude! "So at the very start, Clarissa, you let drop a hint that you're planning to sell the cottage eventually. And when the time comes I will see to it that proper documents are drawn up."

And the Rosicrucian, rising, about to leave, added quietly:

"As I told you before, you will be amply repaid for this service you are about to render us. What is it you wish?"

Here it comes! And Clarissa also rose. And her head high, she prepared herself. To bargain …

"Well," she said. "There's a man I know, and ... he's serving under Lord Nelson. So there he is, with the fleet ... miles away ..." She had started resolutely enough, but the awful anxiety was making her fumble with the words. And her voice sounded very small as she struggled on, pleading almost. "So maybe, a furlough ... a *special* furlough, could be ... arranged?"

"Captain Richard Gray," the Rosicrucian informed her, "has been recently transferred to Lord Nelson's ship, *Victory*. More recently, Captain Richard Gray has been raised to the position of a personal officer, a sort of bodyguard, to Lord Nelson. Which means that he must always accompany Lord Nelson. And *that* means, that whenever Lord Nelson comes to Merton to see Lady Hamilton, Captain Richard Gray will come also."

Clarissa was so surprised that she simply fell into the chair, and stayed there, speechless. When her wits at last returned to her, she saw that the Rosicrucian was gone.

And she didn't even have to bargain! She just couldn't get over it.

And then Sally came in, with the little bone flacon which Mr. Davey had had refilled with a fresh supply of the Green Perfume. And in the wake of Sally, François entered, to inform Clarissa that the Earl was immediately leaving for Bath. The Earl sent his compliments, and begged her not to feel lonesome during his absence ...

As soon as the door closed on François, Clarissa began to move about swiftly, issuing orders, counterorders—she was so terribly excited:

"Sally! We're going shopping. But first, help me dress!"

"Shopping!" Sally said. "At this hour of the day! They'll be starting to close soon ..."

"Not if we're already *in* the shop! That's why I'm hurrying so, silly! Hook me up in the back ... Now you were born in a cottage, Sally. What would you buy to make the interior look very, very nice?"

"Why, crisp white curtains, for one thing," Sally said, while she struggled with the hooks of Clarissa's dress. "And maybe some flowered bedspreads. And small hooked rugs are good to put on the floorboards."

"That's what we'll shop for, then! But first, run down to the kitchen, Sally, and tell the chef to give you all the recipes he has for cooking mushrooms. And, yes, Pete is to bring the small enclosed carriage around to the linen draper's, right away, and wait for us there."

"Recipes ... mushrooms ..." Sally repeated, amazed. "Goodness gracious! What next?"

But she hurried out, to return in a few minutes clutching a little sheaf of grease-stained paper scraps in her hand: the recipes. Clarissa took them from her and thrust them in the corner of the bag which she had hastily packed with the few dresses she had decided to take with her to Merton. And now, radiantly beautiful with happiness, Clarissa quickly donned a bonnet, put on a pretty shawl, and with Sally carrying the bag, the two of them crept down the back stairs, and then left the house by a side door, and hurried to where the shops were.

The shopping took some time, however, for Sally saw so many things which she insisted were *necessary* in a cottage. As, for instance, copper pots and pans for the tiny kitchen. And hemstitched towels for the bedroom washstands ... But, at last, and in accord with the Rosicrucian's instructions, before midnight, Clarissa was in the carriage, with Sally beside her, and on the road to Merton. The excitement and the haste had tired her out, though pleasantly so, and she slept all the way. And when she awoke, the sun was just starting to shine from the pure blue sky, there was a pleasant little breeze, and Pete was holding the carriage door open. Clarissa jumped out.

What a lovely spot was Merton! Everything vividly green. Lambs cavorting in one meadow. Another covered with daisies. And in the shadow of the low hedges, yellow primroses growing, and bluebells, the petals drenched with dew. Clarissa looked around for the thicket—because of the mushrooms, for Mrs. Cadogan—and it wasn't a stone's throw away, the mist of early morning veiling the young trees. And right by the roadside stood the cottage, the thatched roof showing above the flowering shrubs that clustered in front.

Clarissa, followed by Sally, hurried through the rustic gate and around to the back, where the small garden, bright with flowers, overhung the sparkling blue water of the inlet. That's where the pleasant breeze came from. A steep little path led down to the narrow stretch of the sandy shore below.

The interior of the cottage, however, as Clarissa hastened to enter it, was a shock to her. Drab? It was just plain unlivable! Peeling wallpaper, the windowpanes dark with grime, dust everywhere, cobwebs … Clarissa was in despair.

"Now don't you worry," Sally told her. "What the place needs is a good scrubbing. Then a coat of white paint for the woodwork. And some new wallpaper. Blue lover's-knots and pink roses would be nice for the bedrooms.… And I'm sure Pete could find a dozen young fellows in the village who'd be glad to do the work if you pay them well," Sally said, while already rolling up her sleeves and tucking up her skirt to start the scrubbing.

In less than half an hour, the long-uninhabited dwelling was abustle with mad activity. Hammering, the clang of paint pails, the thud of furniture being moved about. Clarissa went about swiftly, supervising, directing, hurrying everybody. She had the crate of priceless figurines opened, and with her own hands arranged them in the study, a small corner room just off the little hall. The harpsichord was moved at her order into a larger room, where there were some pretty cushioned chairs, gilt-framed pictures on the walls, and a very decent rug. Lady Hamilton, doubtless, was very particular about *décor,* and Clarissa was most anxious that the woman beloved of Lord Nelson would find nothing to criticize.

By Sunday morning, however, everything was ready. And the cottage inside looked positively transformed! Truly fit now to be a love nest. The bedrooms, thanks to the new wallpaper, as gay as the flower garden outside. Sunlight lay in golden patches on the waxed floorboards. The white woodwork glistened. All the windows were open, and the breeze from the blue inlet billowed out the crisp white curtains. Sally had been sent to pick the mushrooms in the thicket, Pete was laying the table for lunch downstairs. And Clarissa put on the sprig muslin gown, the one she had worn when accompanying Captain Richard Gray to select a suitable monument for his sister's grave in Halstead. There was something special about wearing a dress which a man might conceivably remember as having seen the woman wear before. And her yellow petticoat rustled with anticipation as Clarissa took a last hasty look at her radiant face in the little mirror, which had a quaintly slim black frame.

Then she walked from room to room, sprinkling in each a few drops of the Green Perfume. The crowning touch to her work of preparation. And Lord Hamilton's chaise, bearing himself, Lady Hamilton, and his mother-in-law, Mrs. Cadogan, arrived soon afterwards. Pete, wearing his coachman's livery minus the coat, which lent him a tolerable resemblance to a bona fide footman, opened the door, and then ushered the guests into the room with the harpsichord, where Clarissa graciously received them.

"Madam, how do you do?" Lord Hamilton said.

And he gave her a low bow, while Clarissa curtsied.

Lord Hamilton, though short and with a paunch, had an ambassador's dignity about him. And he was well dressed, with lace at the throat and wrists. But his broad face had a queer pallor, and he was strangely absent-minded.

His mother-in-law, Mrs. Cadogan, was a stout woman in a purple silk dress, with a frilled white neckerchief, and a frilled white cap perched high over her coarse reddish hair. Flame-colored ribbons ornamented the cap, and she carried a fan of matching satin, minutely pleated. What an atrocious color combination: flame and purple! She had sailed in first, her shrewd little eyes, set like a pair of currants in a suet pudding, which her face resembled, running all over the room. And, at once, she drew a pudgy finger over the surface of a little table, testing it for dust. But there was no dust. "Humph!" Mrs. Cadogan said. And, looking very disagreeable, she sat down in the best chair.

It was at Lady Hamilton, however, that Clarissa stared, with lively curiosity and sincere admiration. A lovelier woman she had never seen! Slender, with a small piquant face, and the pale blond curls gathered on top of her graceful head, Lady Hamilton wore a flowing white gown of semitransparent material, and a gauze scarf about her pretty neck, the ends of the scarf floating as she moved. No wonder Lord Nelson thought her a celestial-like, ravishing vision!

Clarissa hurried forward to greet her, and she and Lady Hamilton curtsied to one another. Then Lady Hamilton, giving her hand to Clarissa, said, while she smiled graciously:

"I'm so glad you invited us!" And, lowering her voice, she added, "And that you also invited ... Lord Nelson."

Clarissa gave the exquisite fingers a quick little squeeze of sympathy and encouragement.

But Mrs. Cadogan's sharp ears had caught the name so hateful to her—Lord Nelson—and, her stout face turned the color of beets with anger, she instantly demanded:

"Is that man coming here, too?"

"Now, now, Mother," Lord Hamilton attempted to pacify her. "Lord Nelson is the greatest hero England has ever had. His friendship to myself and Lady Hamilton is an honor to us. Of course, he's coming. You know he always tries to join us wherever we happen to be staying!"

Lady Hamilton, made nervous by the belligerent woman's suspicious stares, moved away softly to stand beside the harpsichord, while Clarissa hastened to say:

"Mrs. Cadogan, do you like mushrooms?"

At the mere mention of the food she craved, saliva actually trickled down Mrs. Cadogan's plump chin.

"I'm asking," Clarissa explained innocently, "because I happened to come across some recipes for cooking mushrooms. And that gave me the idea to order a savory dish of them, among other things, for lunch."

Mrs. Cadogan's little eyes glittered greedily.

"When ... when is lunch?" she asked, breathing hard.

"Lunch won't be served, naturally, until after Lord Nelson arrives," Clarissa told her sweetly.

Then she saw Pete appear briefly in the doorway. It was the signal he and Clarissa had agreed on beforehand. Pete had stayed outside, right above the inlet, on the lookout for Lord Nelson's flagship, *Victory*. And now the ship had been sighted on the horizon.

Clarissa, picking up a telescope from a window sill on the way, hurried her guests out into the garden. Sally had found the telescope in the kitchen cupboard, and Clarissa had her place it on that window sill conveniently. And now, on reaching the garden's edge, standing there with the blue water sparkling down below and the breeze whipping up her skirts, Clarissa politely handed the lens to Lord Hamilton.

With a pompous air of an expert, the Ambassador to Naples raised the telescope, directing it straight at the ship which, visible to the naked eye, still had its white sails up.

"There, they're just starting to let the sails down," Lord Hamilton reported. "I can see the sailors on the masts, busy there like so many monkeys.... I suppose that's as close to the shore as the ship could go. And there's Lord Nelson himself, standing at the deck rail, and, yes, *he's* holding a telescope, too, and looking straight at us. Of course, he can see us all, and the cottage behind us, as plain as I can see him! And by Lord Nelson's side stands an officer, his personal officer doubtless, a fine-looking young man. But now several sailors are lowering a boat, and the two of them are about to be rowed over. So what about taking a look for yourself, Emma, *ma chère?*" Lord Hamilton said, ready to pass the telescope on to his lovely wife.

But Lady Hamilton hesitated, and she threw a piteous glance at Clarissa, the meaning of which Clarissa instantly understood. Lady Hamilton was afraid that a close view of Lord Nelson would so affect her that, unused as she was to handling the lens, she might somehow fumble with it, drop it suddenly, perhaps, and so betray her true feelings right in front of her domineering mother and her pompous husband.

Quickly, Clarissa came to her aid.

"May I have a look first, please, Lord Hamilton?"

And he had to give the telescope to Clarissa instead.

Having watched Lord Hamilton manipulate the instrument, Clarissa had no trouble in using it herself. Almost instantly she had the ship's deck brought unbelievably close. Lord Nelson looked exactly as he was depicted in the drawings, lampoons, and patriotic posters which Clarissa had seen displayed proudly throughout London.... But she shifted the telescope a bit to the right, and the tall, broad-shouldered figure of Captain Richard Gray sprang into vivid focus. His tricorn set jauntily on the back of his handsome head, he was grinning all over his deeply tanned face, in answer to some observation of Lord Nelson's, evidently. The breeze out there, on the ship, was stronger than in the cottage garden, and "darling Richard's" forelock was blown about. Clarissa, as she looked, felt her pulse quicken. She could have looked forever.... But he was about to follow his illustrious superior into the rowboat, and Clarissa had to relinquish the telescope to Lord Hamilton, who considered it his duty to watch the national hero's approach to the shore.

How amazed Captain Gray would be to find her there! Clarissa thought, laughing to herself, as she waited. But he'd be shrewd enough, she knew, not to show his surprise in front of her guests.

At last, the small boat, with rough-looking sailors at the oars, drew up alongside the narrow stretch of sand down below, and Lord Nelson stepped out, and with a swift glance upward, at Lady Hamilton—naturally, he was aware only of her, of his beloved Emma—he hurried up the steep little path, followed by Captain Gray.

"My Lord Nelson," Clarissa said, and she gave him a low curtsy.

After all, it was quite a thrill to be bowed to by the great Nelson himself!

The merciless discipline of the fleet to which he had been subjected all his life now stood Lord Nelson in good stead. Despite Lady Hamilton's presence and the consequent turmoil of his passionate feelings, he was able to go through the motions of politeness with admirable smoothness. And what charm of personality he had! It made certain tragic facts about his appearance pass almost unnoticed: the black patch over one eye, the empty pinned-up sleeve.... The Battle of Calvi and the Battle of Teneriffe were responsible for the two disfigurements, respectively. Otherwise, of fine height, firm of body, powerfully alert in the expression of his weather-beaten face, he made a lasting impression on anyone who had the privilege of seeing him so close.

He hastened to introduce Captain Richard Gray. And Clarissa, trying not to laugh, had to curtsy to "darling Richard," with great ceremony. There had been a moment when Captain Gray, on seeing her, looked sort of taken aback. But he had quickly rearranged his features, and he could bow to her now very seriously.

"Emma!" Lord Nelson was heard to say. Then, correcting himself, "Lady Hamilton," he said. And he offered her his arm.

As if merely obeying the rules of politeness, Lady Hamilton took it. And thus, with his beloved Emma beside him, Lord Nelson led the way to the cottage. Mrs. Cadogan and Lord Hamilton followed. And Clarissa found herself bringing up the rear with Captain Gray.

"You witch!" he exploded, as soon as the others were out of earshot. "How do you manage these things?"

And then she was imprisoned in his strong arms, and kissed on the mouth, on the throat.... She had to tear herself away.

"Later," she promised. "But tell me," she added, as they hurried on. "Weren't you astonished? To see me here, I mean."

"Well, maybe ..." Captain Gray temporized. "On the other hand, I was sort of prepared. The way I, a poor insignificant individual, was suddenly transferred to Lord Nelson's flagship. And then, on top of that, assigned to be his personal officer ... Well, I told myself, Clarissa must have had a hand in this!"

He was joking, of course. But they had reached the cottage, and now hastened in after Clarissa's guests.

Lunch was immediately served, with Pete waiting on table. Something Sally had categorically refused to do, because of Lord Nelson's presence. It would make her so nervous, Sally had insisted, she'd be sure to spill the soup down the great man's neck, or otherwise disgrace herself. But she would do the cooking. It wasn't for nothing she had slaved as kitchenmaid all that time at Ravisham!

And now Clarissa had to admit that Sally had truly surpassed herself. Everything tasted delicious. And Sally was just as successful with the dish of mushrooms for Mrs. Cadogan.

"Oo ... Ah ... Uhh ...!" Mrs. Cadogan moaned her delight, while gorging herself with heaped spoonfuls of sautéed mushrooms.

The rich sauce besplattered her frilled neckerchief, dripped on her purple silk dress, and stained the tablecloth. She munched, hiccuped. And, savoring the taste, she rocked herself sensuously, the cap with the elegant ribbons all askew on her disheveled head. The spectacle of Mrs. Cadogan eating mushrooms was really disgusting! But fortunately nobody paid her the slightest attention.

Lady Hamilton, her lashes lowered, was listening to what Lord Nelson, seated beside her, whispered to her. While Lord Nelson was too busy courting her to be aware of anything *but* his lovely Emma. His head bent at an angle so that he could watch her piquant face continually, he spoke to her eagerly, flatteringly.... And he kept picking up her napkin, which—as Clarissa suspected, amused—Lady Hamilton kept dropping on the floor on purpose, out of sheer coquetry.

CHAPTER TWENTY

I T WAS TIME, however, Clarissa decided, to gratify Lord Hamilton's strange craving for the *objets d'art,* and so liberate Lady Hamilton from his meddlesome surveillance. The Ambassador to Naples, since the very first moment of his arrival, had been glancing around anxiously, wondering *where* the promised treasures were kept. He fidgeted, scratched his wig, perspired.... And now that lunch was over, Clarissa, rising quickly, said:

"My Lord Hamilton …"

And she swiftly led the way to the cozy study.

At the sight of all the little pieces, Lord Hamilton's eyes bulged with excitement. And grabbing off the shelves as many of them as he could carry in his arms, he at once sat down at the table, to start caressing the exquisite lines and surfaces with his sensitive fingers.

Closing the door upon him softly, Clarissa hurried back to the other guests.

"My Lord Nelson …" she said.

And she led the way to the room where the harpsichord stood.

Clarissa had discovered long ago that if one spoke briefly, briskly, and without offering any explanation, people generally obeyed, quite automatically. And so it was now. Lord Nelson and Lady Hamilton had followed her, the lovely Emma at once going over to the harpsichord. Music was one of Lady Hamilton's many cultural accomplishments. With Lord Nelson leaning an elbow on the pretty instrument, Lady Hamilton, having seated herself, touched the ivory keys, and began to sing gently.

How *right* they look together, Clarissa thought, admiring the picture they made.

And she hastened to leave them, and went to take a peep at Mrs. Cadogan. Mrs. Cadogan was still eating her mushrooms— she'd had several helpings—though with lessened exuberance. A state of stupor was gradually starting to steal over the glutton's gratified senses. Clarissa, well satisfied, hurried away.

"Well?" Captain Gray said, on meeting with her later in the passage. "How is it going?"

He had guessed the serious purpose of her machinations, and tried to keep out of her way, not to distract her.

"Preliminaries," Clarissa explained crisply. "I'm letting them get the preliminaries over with in the harpsichord room."

Captain Richard Gray threw his head back and laughed.

"It's just that seriousness makes you utterly adorable!" he then said. "But haven't I seen you wear this dress before?" he suddenly added.

He *did* remember it....

But she wouldn't let him detain her, and again hurried away, and to the door of the harpsichord room. Opening the door a crack, she looked in.

Lady Hamilton had trailed over to the window, to stand there against the rose brocade of the drapes, a color that so enhanced her delicate beauty. And Lord Nelson had followed her, and he now stood very close to his Emma. Never had he dared to stand so close to her before. For the simple reason that he had never had a chance even to be alone in the same room with Lady Hamilton, since at the prudish court of the Queen of Naples such liberties were unheard of. And there'd be the Queen, fiercely jealous of Lady Hamilton, and in cahoots with Mrs. Cadogan, who'd always be right there, like a hateful toad, watching.... But now, away from the Queen of Naples, away from her slandering courtiers, and with Mrs. Cadogan miraculously absent, Lord Nelson, the poor man, was growing positively bold.

I'll give him a little more time, Clarissa decided. And closing the door softly, she stole away.

But when after a short interval she again took a peek at the pair, Lord Nelson was actually holding Lady Hamilton's hand while, his face aglow, he whispered something into her rosy ear. The preliminaries, Clarissa judged, had reached the point when the whole matter might be clinched successfully if privacy of a more intimate nature was speedily provided.

And Clarissa quickly walked in.

"My Lord Nelson, if I may now show you the arrangement of the upstairs rooms.... And Lady Hamilton's advice, of course, would be invaluable."

What the advice was to be about, nobody knew or cared. The two of them automatically followed as she led the way up the narrow stairs, and into the best bedroom.

"I think you'll find everything in order...."

Dusk was starting to fall outside the cottage. Clarissa swiftly lit the lamp, drew the curtains.

"The bed is very comfortable." She straightened the counterpane on the huge fourposter.

As she moved about briskly, nonchalantly, a conscientious hostess, Clarissa addressed all her remarks to Lord Nelson. Naturally, the room was for *his* use, his *alone,* her manner seemed to indicate. All the appointments, however, pointed to the expectant double occupancy. A woman's dressing table had been placed between the windows, with a long mirror over it. And graceful feminine knickknacks stood about.

"Your valise, Lord Nelson, is right here," Clarissa said. But next to the large valise near the door, there was a smaller one, with Lady Hamilton's initials on it. "Oh, they've brought Lady Hamilton's valise here, too!" Clarissa laughed easily. "By mistake, of course ... Those stupid servants!"

And without pausing in her swift movements about, she approached the washstand and, stooping, opened the little door, as if merely to ascertain that the big chamber pot, with violets painted on the cover, had not been omitted among other comforts for her guests. Clarissa had put it there herself while getting the place ready. And now both Lord Nelson and Lady Hamilton could see the chamber pot very plainly.

"No need for you to leave the room," Clarissa observed lightly. And closing the washstand, moving away, "Nobody will disturb you," she murmured reassuringly.

And then Clarissa swiftly left them and hurried downstairs and to the kitchen to see that Sally had tidied everything up. Sally was not there, but she had left a candle burning in its pewter stand on the clean stove. As Clarissa took up the candle, Captain Gray came in. She placed a finger to her lips, and, motioning him to go with her, crossed the little hall to the study door. When she pushed it partly open, she saw that Lord Hamilton had fallen asleep in the big chair. Cradled in his arms lay one of the statuettes, a starkly naked woman sculptured in detailed miniature.

Closing the door softly on Lady Hamilton's husband, Clarissa walked swiftly on, to take a look at Mrs. Cadogan. The horrible woman was snoring lustily, her head slumped on the table beside the plate emptied of the sauced mushrooms.... Clarissa hurried on, and up the narrow stairs, followed by Captain Gray, who tried to tread quietly in spite of his heavy boots. A thin line of light showed under the door of the best bedroom. Was the faint sound she heard the creak of the big fourposter? Clarissa wondered, as she listened intently. Then the line of light under the door suddenly went out.

Clarissa, smiling to herself, tiptoed away and down the passage to the door of Sally's room, at the furthest end. Light showed from under the door here also, but the sounds from within were more audible. Sally's suppressed titter, Pete's muffled laugh. And then the light shining from under that door went out, too, and just as suddenly.

Clarissa moved away, and to the door of the room she had selected for her own use. And Captain Gray, following her in, took the candle from her and placed it on the little table by the side of the big bed. Then he gathered her into his arms.

In the dark passage outside, the line of light showing from under their door went out after a while as suddenly as it had on two previous instances ...

Love reigned supreme in the pretty cottage. And it was so every single night. In the mornings they all rose very late. Meals had to be prepared, eaten, and household chores attended to. And Clarissa and Captain Gray would sometimes accompany Sally to the thicket to pick mushrooms for Mrs. Cadogan. But Lady Hamilton, careful of her exquisite complexion, never ventured out. She no longer dropped her napkin for Lord Nelson to pick up. On the contrary, it was *she* now trying to please *him*. And, once, Clarissa, eavesdropping at the door of the harpsichord room, where Lord Nelson spent the daylight hours with his Emma, heard her say:

"The Queen of Naples has all the supplies you need, Horatio!"

Lady Hamilton, naturally, now called Lord Nelson by his first name, Horatio, when alone with him.

"The Queen has a deep attachment for me," Lady Hamilton went on. "So all I have to do is ask her to have the supplies transferred to your fleet! The Queen is always harping on patriotism, and she will think I'm merely being patriotic."

"My love, if I win the Battle of the Nile," Lord Nelson told her, "the credit for saving England from Napoleon should all go to you!"

And then suddenly it was Sunday again; the week was up, Lord Nelson had to hurry back to his ship, the Hamiltons back to Naples. And Clarissa, after closing up the cottage, went back to London and Grosvenor Square, with Sally and Pete.

Paradise Merton, Lord Nelson was to write in his diary, in which he put down all his thoughts while away at sea. *Happy, happy* days ...

The arrangement was, however, that whenever possible, that is between battles, he would return for a short stay at the cottage, and that Lord and Lady Hamilton would be invited, too, of course. And this Nelson was able to do many times. Every few months, henceforth, Clarissa was notified by the Rosicrucian, through a beggar woman who would come to the back door of the Earl's mansion, seek out Sally, and mumble—such-and-such a date—while Sally handed her alms. And then Clarissa, on the date so specified, would make the trip to Merton to open the cottage, prepare everything for the guests' arrival. And once again the joys of reunion for Lord Nelson and Lady Hamilton, for Clarissa and Captain Gray. A week of undisturbed bliss. And then farewells, the parting, good-by, good-by ... till the next time. Sally, at least, Clarissa would think enviously, never had to part with her Pete.

Meanwhile, Slippery Jack, as Clarissa learned on one of her regular visits to the Thieves' Village, had been brought up to trial, and had been sentenced to be hanged at Tyburn. The news was exactly what Clarissa had expected, and she was satisfied. Captain Richard Gray, she could now tell herself, need never know of the danger he had come so close to being threatened with. She felt secure, safe. Consequently, what eventually occurred came as a double shock ... The date for the execution of the court's sentence having been set officially, her next visit to the Waterfront Tavern fell within a few days of the scheduled hanging. But ... the jailer had been paid, the rough company hastened to inform her, and the jailer would pretend to the authorities that the convicted man had managed to escape. Aye, Slippery Jack was to be secretly let out.

Clarissa could scarcely believe her ears.

"You may well be astonished," Ugly Frank said. "We seldom bother with anyone as insignificant as Slippery Jack. He's no credit to us. But Honest Gregory, here, insisted we get him out."

"Well, it wasn't *much* the jailer could demand for Slippery Jack," the pseudo-parson pointed out mildly. "The little money we had to pay didn't break us!"

The explanation sounded plausible enough. Except that Clarissa would never have imagined it possible that anyone would be ready to part with even a *penny* to save the neck of someone as odious as was Slippery Jack! And her instant suspicion was that Honest Gregory, doubtless, had his own very shrewd reasons for wanting to have Slippery Jack freed, and on the loose.

But she swiftly controlled her secret agitation, and appraising the unexpected development realistically she suddenly discovered its reassuring aspect.

"There'll be a price on Slippery Jack's head, anyway," she reminded them all calmly. "And he will be recaptured very quickly!"

Honest Gregory, however, had another surprise for her.

"Well, naturally, we have to get him out of the country," he said. "In fact, it's all arranged. The hanging has been set for Monday, but the jailer is to let Slippery Jack out Saturday night, as soon as it gets dark. Because about an hour later one of the hulks will be leaving the Thames. And the captain of the hulk can smuggle Slippery Jack in among the prisoners condemned for transportation to the Colonies. So Slippery Jack won't even stop here to speak to any of us, but will hurry straight alongside the river to the spot where the embankment begins. There's a bridge there, and under that bridge a boat will be waiting, with the hulk captain himself in it, along with the rowers, to personally receive the payment. Which is generally an exorbitant sum of money. And since we couldn't possibly raise the amount ourselves, even if we wanted to," Honest Gregory added mildly, "you, Clarissa, must provide the money and bring it there."

He had been counting on her doing exactly that. Honest Gregory was so absolutely convinced that it was in her own interests to have Slippery Jack out of the country that he expected her to be perfectly willing—no, *eager*—eager to provide this exorbitant sum of money! He hadn't a doubt about it. And the awful part of it was that, of course, he was right.

"If you hadn't come here tonight," Clarissa heard him say, "I would have paid you a discreet little visit at Grosvenor Square. To inform you about it."

But what made him so *certain?* What did he *know?* Clarissa wondered, staring at him.

He specified the hour at which she'd be expected to bring the money. And then he named the sum. And it was an exorbitant one. François, Clarissa knew, couldn't afford to lend her even half of the amount. She'd have to pawn her best diamond necklace, and then live in trepidation of the Earl missing it, asking her questions....

"It's a lot of money," she now tried to protest.

"You bring it!" Honest Gregory told her curtly.

What *did* he know? Did he actually suspect her of being responsible for Slippery Jack's capture ...? But the pseudo-parson's face was, as usual, inscrutable.

Clarissa rose, moved away.

"What has so upset you?" the old Lafonte stopped her, as she tried to hasten past. "Clarissa, you look pale!"

"It's nothing. Nothing ..."

She could see that Prickly Gil was trying to attract her attention, and she hurried over to the weird girl. Prickly Gil's stomach had grown enormous, parturition was obviously expected very soon, while the stomach's queer shape suggested that the child would show some horrible deformity at birth.

"I want to thank you, Prickly Gil," Clarissa told the girl kindly, "for helping me."

"I know," Prickly Gil said. And probably she did know, in some unaccountable way, all about Captain Gray, and Lord Nelson, and the cottage at Merton. And how the combination of purely personal events there would affect the course of history. "Great is the Master's power.... But what I called you over for," the strange creature went on, "was to warn you that next time, if you need help, you should seek out Nellie Harris, in the Kenerevy woods, at the moon's last quarter, in case ... I'm not available."

All pregnant women naturally had their fears ... And Clarissa hastened to say something encouraging.

"Oh, the child will be born, and alive. I can feel it moving." Prickly Gil smoothed the unsavory shift over her frightful stomach. "But I must please the Master."

"Whatever do you mean?" Clarissa said, amazed.

"I must please the Master," Prickly Gil repeated quietly.

And not another word would she add in explanation.

Clarissa quitted the tavern. Then, on reaching home, she immediately had Sally summon François and entrusted him with the pawning of the diamond necklace, the chief valet assuring her that he'd get for it the amount of money she so desperately needed.

And the first hours of darkness of the appointed day found her hurrying towards the waterfront, to that part of it where the bridge spanned the fog-shrouded Thames. The plain dark mantle concealing her dress, her hair hidden in the wrapped-around veiling, and wearing her small black mask, she had cut straight across the deserted thoroughfare, and then it was just a short walk to the embankment. On reaching it, Clarissa stood there a moment, listening. But not a sound disturbed the damp stillness. The fog was so dense she could barely make out the hulk's dark shape further up the river. While down below the water glistened dimly, where it was free of the black shadow cast by the bridge. Was the boat from the hulk already there, waiting, invisible in that shadow? It seemed to her she could feel its presence.

And as she hurried down the little slope that led from the embankment to the water's edge, there was a faint splash of oars and she saw the boat gliding out of the shadow and moving towards her. The men in the boat had been on the lookout for her in compliance with Honest Gregory's instructions and now as the boat touched the bank the hulk's burly captain stood up and addressed her:

"You brought the money?"

Clarissa had put the two little leather bags containing the gold coins, which François had received in exchange for the diamond necklace, inside the velvet drawstring bag which she always carried with her on her secret expeditions, and she now showed it to him, clearly indicating that yes, the money was here.

"I was told a woman would bring it," the burly man said, and he grinned. He had no wig, but wore some kind of a cap on his bushy hair, while his men had bandannas tied on their heads.

And they all looked like regular brigands. "So I guess you're that woman. Well, let's have it then," and he held out his hand for the money.

"Not so fast," Clarissa told him. "The man you're to take with you isn't here yet."

She kept glancing in the direction from which Slippery Jack was supposed to appear. Bypassing the shacks of the Thieves' Village which lay at some distance heavily veiled with the fog, he would be making his way close along the river edge. But there was no sign of him …

"Oh, he'll show up," the hulk captain said. "I know Slippery Jack. I've seen him around. You don't have to wait, mistress. Let me have the money. And I'll start counting it…."

"You'll have the money when he gets here," Clarissa said.

"Time is precious," the burly man again tried to persuade her. "Every minute counts. This is a dangerous game, trying to smuggle someone as should be hanged out of the country. And we'd all be paying with our lives for it, if caught. Including yourself … But there he is," the hulk captain said, pointing.

Clarissa had already caught sight of Slippery Jack. And though he was still at some distance and notwithstanding the darkness and the fog she had recognized him instantly by his catlike walk. He was walking very swiftly, almost running.

"You can have the money now," Clarissa said.

And quickly opening her velvet bag, she took out first one, and then the other little leather bag, packed tight with gold, and gave them to the burly man. For a moment he held them on the palm of his big hand, weighing them. Then he said:

"Well, it's about the right amount, I guess."

And she could go. He wouldn't detain her by counting the money. He was in a hurry to get back to his horrible hulk safely; as soon as Slippery Jack had reached the boat and jumped in, that is. And Clarissa, without looking back, hurried up the little slope, and along the embankment. The bridge was on her right. To the left, within a few minutes' walk, lay the thoroughfare. And she was about to turn in that direction …

"Aren't you going to say good-by, at least?" a voice said in her ear, and then she heard a laugh, Slippery Jack's laugh.

Instead of getting into the waiting boat, he had run on after her, with his swift noiseless tread. And now he had caught up with her.

"Let me pass!" For he was pushing her onto the bridge.

"Let me *go!*" And she tried to twist herself free.

He was quicker, however, and she was suddenly pinned against the low parapet. At the thought of the swift current in that particular spot down below, her eyes seemed to stand out of her head.

"So it was you who betrayed me!" Slippery Jack snarled.

He *knew!* It was something Clarissa had never expected. Maybe Honest Gregory did have his suspicions, after all, and had communicated them to Slippery Jack when visiting him in jail. Or maybe Slippery Jack had deduced the truth through sheer intuition.…

His hands were at her throat. For an instant, she knew the horror of suffocation.

Then, strangely, she could breathe again. The hands that had been strangling her had slid down her neck and were tearing at her bodice. She had taken the precaution of removing all her jewels before starting out. But she had forgotten about the emerald rope. She never parted with the emeralds. When not wearing them openly, she would conceal them inside her bodice, securing them there with a pin. And Slippery Jack, pushing his body against hers, had become aware of the hidden jewels. And greed was his undoing.

For she could struggle now. She struggled fiercely. And wrenched herself free. Except that he still kept his grasp on the emerald rope, was pulling at it. And then she pushed him, with all her strength. The pin that held the gems snapped, and Clarissa saw the gleam of the emeralds in Slippery Jack's outflung hand. But he had lost his balance, and suddenly toppled over the parapet. She heard his scream. And then, a little splash …

She started to run. Disheveled, her bodice torn, her skirts tripping her, sobbing with fear, she ran all the way, across the deserted thoroughfare, and then along the crooked little side streets. She had lost a shoe and didn't know it. Her nice mantle had a big tear all down the front. And so, looking almost demented, she reached the dark alley, and the small enclosed carriage which she always had wait for her there, with Sally inside, and Pete on the box.

Clarissa wrenched the door open, jumped in.

"Go. Go! Hurry!"

Pete's whip lashed the horse's rump and it tore off at a gallop.

The emeralds! She'd never see them again. There they'd stay, at the bottom of the river Thames. The current, which was swift under the bridge, would carry a drowned man's body away with it. But the emeralds would sink instantly, just like ordinary pebbles do. And Clarissa bewailed their loss.

Her ladyship's emerald rope had been something special to Clarissa. It had brought her luck, or so she believed. She had the same superstitious feeling about the emeralds, in fact, as Slippery Jack had always had about his little knife.

Only later did the thought occur to her that, actually, she could never be certain that Slippery Jack had indeed perished that night. There was the hulk captain and his men waiting in their boat close by. They must have heard the drowning man's scream and might have gone to his assistance. Thrown him a rope, perhaps. And then taken him to the hulk with them, and so eventually to the Colonies, to live up to their part of the bargain. On the other hand, since the money had already been paid, they might not have bothered, but, instead, might have rowed away swiftly, brigands that they were.

CHAPTER TWENTY-ONE

W HEN THE NEWS of Lord Nelson's victory over Napoleon's fleet in the Battle of the Nile reached England, the whole nation went wild with joy. The city of London was instantly thrown into a commotion of preparations for the reception of the popular hero, whose arrival was expected any day. And even at the gaming house secretly patronized by the Prince Regent, the talk was all about Nelson, *our* Nelson, *great* Nelson! He was at the peak of his glory. And it was there, around the roulette tables, with the gorgeously attired harlots looking over the shoulders of the fops, as the latter spun the wheel of fortune, that the name of Lady Hamilton was first mentioned publicly, and fatefully linked with Lord Nelson's, as a choice bit of scandal.

Clarissa, wearing a daring green-striped gown, and with red, green, and yellow ostrich plumes nodding from her glittering headdress, moved away from the gamblers and, unobserved, slipped into the little sitting room adjoining. Almost immediately, Mr. Brummell hastened in after her. She sat down in a chair, arranged her rustling skirts becomingly, and he stood before her, leaning slightly on his ebony cane.

"It's very kind of you, Mistress Clarissa," Brummell at once said, "to let me speak to you."

"I could see by the way you tried *not* to look at me while we were in that noisy crowd around the roulette tables," Clarissa said, "that you had something to tell me."

"Yes," Brummell said. And after glancing towards the door, to ascertain that the Prince Regent had not followed him, he added, lowering his voice, "I'm going to Halstead again. I thought you'd be interested."

The poor fellow! She was the only person he could talk to about Miss Gray, and how sincerely he appreciated it.

As soon as Clarissa learned from Captain Gray, during one of their stays at Merton, that he had been informed by the old solicitor that the simple monument had been set up over Miss Gray's grave in the little churchyard at Halstead, she had hastened to tell Mr. Brummell the brief story she had so carefully devised. Drawing him aside at a gay social gathering, she explained that, quite by chance, she happened to have heard a *certain* piece of news—who the person was she heard it from, she couldn't remember. She was such a scatterbrain! But the person was most reliable, of this she was certain. Evidently, a close friend of Miss Gray's relatives ... Yes, it was about Miss Gray.

And having thus prepared Mr. Brummell, Clarissa then related to him in a few words how Miss Gray's languishing ailment having taken a turn for the worse, the gentle governess had to leave Ravisham and move in with relatives—Clarissa wasn't quite sure who the relatives were; and, purposely, she made it all a little vague, thus lending plausibility to her invention. Anyway, these relatives took wonderful care of Miss Gray, until the end, which had been most peaceful and quite painless. And since the family used to have their home in the pretty village of Halstead, there the burial had taken place. And Mr. Brummell would have no difficulty in finding the grave, because of the monument. The person Clarissa had the information from mentioned the existence of a monument. The name would be on it. And Clarissa then told him Miss Gray's first name.

As Clarissa had expected, Mr. Brummell took the sad news quietly, having been forewarned for some time by his prior knowledge of the governess' frail state of health. While to know, at last, Miss Gray's first name, Lucinda, touched his romantic sentiments deeply. And, naturally, he almost immediately paid a visit to Halstead. This would be his second visit there.

"Of course, I'm interested," Clarissa now said, and she smiled at him encouragingly. "But the last time we had the opportunity to exchange a few words in private, we were interrupted just as you were about to describe the monument. So do tell me now, did you like the monument?"

"It's lovely," Mr. Brummell said. "Lovely." And a light came into his handsome face and a smile into his fine eyes. "Very simple. And in the best of taste. I couldn't have wished for anything more suitable."

He was gazing down at her, politely attentive to her every word, but of course he didn't see her. Mentally he was standing before that monument, in the churchyard at Halstead.

"And the name, I suppose," Clarissa said, "is cut in the stone."

"It's cut on the base of the monument," Mr. Brummell said, "which is of rough stone. The rest is plain gray marble, rising gracefully in the form of a thick stubby needle. The lines are very classical."

Yes, that was the monument she and Captain Gray had selected that day in the stonecutter's yard.

"And, I suppose," Clarissa said encouragingly—he so wanted to talk about the place—"there are trees. Probably there are some trees?"

"Very fine trees," Mr. Brummell said. "Several old elms, and a few tall poplars. The leafy branches give a pleasant shade. And underfoot, it's mostly moss.... I walk between the ancient headstones, to reach her grave," Mr. Brummell went on, "and then I stand there for a while ... admiring the monument."

He paused and was silent.

"Yes ..." Clarissa said, gently prompting him.

"Because, standing there," Mr. Brummell explained, "it somehow helps me to see her the way I remember her, in the rose garden at Ravisham. Wearing that white muslin gown, with the modest neckerchief and the pale blue sash. Her dark hair so smooth, parted in the center, and gathered in curls over the ears." He again paused. "And she had such a gay little laugh," he then added, smiling happily. And again he was silent. "She always carried a little book of poems with her. It had a pretty cover, I remember," Mr. Brummell said. "You see, she loved poetry."

"And when you gave her a rose," Clarissa said, trying to please him by making the picture complete, "just a single rose, breaking it off from among the many blooms around, she put it between the pages of the pretty volume."

The words were hardly out of her mouth when Clarissa suddenly remembered that Mr. Brummell had never told her *that* part of it. And she was horrified, thinking she had ruined everything ... But so lifelike, evidently, had she made the personality of Miss Gray while impersonating the gentle governess at Ravisham, that nothing could ever shake Mr. Brummell's conviction that it was the *real* Miss Gray he had known and loved, and had been loved by in return. For all he said now was:

"So I have told you even *that*?" and he smiled at Clarissa gratefully for letting him so freely confide in her.

"Why, how else would I have known about it?" Clarissa said calmly.

But he wasn't even listening.

"And so I stand there, and I see her very clearly," Mr. Brummell went on, speaking quietly and smiling. And then he tried to explain it, by saying very simply, modestly, "She was my ideal. And it's not every man who is fortunate enough to meet his ideal."

Well, and wasn't that exactly what Mr. Brummell, Beau Brummell, had been to Miss Gray? Her ideal, though she had never seen him.

"Therefore," Mr. Brummell went on, "I consider myself the most fortunate of men, and a very happy one ... as I stand there, admiring the simple monument."

Clarissa had accomplished what she had set out to accomplish. Miss Gray's secret romance was now made complete, perfect. And so it would remain. She owed it to the gentle governess. But for Miss Gray, she might never have known her adored brother, her "darling Richard," Captain Gray. And now the debt had been paid. It made Clarissa very happy.

"And then I leave the churchyard," Mr. Brummell continued quietly, "and I get into my cabriolet, and I start back for London ... It's only a couple hours' drive," he explained. And after a slight pause, he added, "But, naturally, I'm followed by the spies."

"Spies?" Clarissa said.

"Yes," Mr. Brummell said, "spies in the pay of His Royal Highness. As everybody knows, I'm being continually spied on, even if it's something as harmless as going into a shop to buy myself a new neckcloth."

"Yes, of course," Clarissa hastened to say. For a moment she had forgotten about the Prince Regent's terrible jealousy, about his spies.

"And these men," Mr. Brummell went on, "have to give a report to the Prince Regent, afterwards. *Where* I went, *whom* I happened to see, *what* I said; every detail is reported to him by them. It is their duty."

"But everybody likes you, Mr. Brummell," Clarissa pointed out. "Surely they wouldn't tell him anything that would make him ... *angry* with you? Somehow, they'd manage ... well, to make a favorable impression on him, as they've always done in the past."

"They've been very considerate of me, yes," Brummell agreed. "And I know that this time they will do their best to protect me. By omitting certain details in their report, about my trip to Halstead. *Where* exactly did they see me there? Doing *what?* That they will not tell him, I grant you. But they'll have to supply him with such information as the name of the place, of the village, in order to make it appear absolutely *unimportant.* After all, I have absented myself from Court not infrequently before, for the sake of solitude in some country spot. And I do appreciate beautiful scenery."

"And the Prince Regent will think that *that's* why you go to Halstead!" Clarissa said.

"Yes, but how long will he think so? He might get suspicious, decide to check up on me personally, secretly follow me there ... And once he sees me in that churchyard, standing before that monument ..." and Mr. Brummell, as he said this, looked genuinely worried.

"But, surely," Clarissa said, and she was really amazed, "surely the Prince Regent couldn't be jealous of someone ... no longer living? Jealous of a woman who is already ... *dead?*"

"Nobody knows His Royal Highness as well as I do," Brummell explained quietly. "His abysmal vanity, his awful possessiveness, his cruel capacity for revenge ..."

And then, suddenly, Brummell ceased speaking, and was silent. For the Prince Regent himself came in, with the Earl of Strasford, the Duke of Cumberland, and several other courtiers, all of them talking excitedly about the reception for Lord Nelson, who, as they thought, would reach London on the following day. But Clarissa, listening, was very much amused. For it was to Merton that Nelson would be coming *first!* Only, of course, it was a secret.

And late that same night she set out in her customary manner for Merton. And in the morning, while the dignitaries with pomp and ceremony waited in London to give Lord Nelson an overwhelming ovation, the Prince Regent fuming at the delay, the flagship *Victory* was sighted on the horizon by Pete from the cottage garden that overhung the sparkling blue water of the inlet.

"It's your shabby uniform I've been meaning to speak to you about," Clarissa was saying several hours later as she sat in her cottage bedroom with Captain Gray. Downstairs, in the harpsichord room, Lady Hamilton, as usual, was singing for Lord Nelson, while accompanying herself expertly on the pretty instrument. "Your shabby uniform is really a disgrace," Clarissa said. "And don't tell me that Lord Nelson's is almost as shabby," she hastened to add. "That's no excuse, Captain Richard Gray!"

"Well, it's like this," Captain Gray said. "We are at war. And when there's a war, that's when one has a chance to make a real fortune. Overnight! A man goes to bed a pauper, and when he gets up he's rich. Fabulously rich! The wealthiest man in the kingdom!"

Next, he'd be talking about how he'd be buying Ravisham! The man was truly demented on the subject … But aloud, Clarissa said:

"You mean you're saving your pay to make another investment?"

"Yes, and you don't have to be so ironic about it, just because my former investments weren't successful," Captain Gray said. "That's exactly what I *am* doing, putting away every single penny of my pay. Except for a few unavoidable expenditures, of course."

Would *women* come under that category? Clarissa wondered. All those loose, scheming women, waiting to prey on someone like Captain Gray in every foreign port....

"My pay being what it is," Captain Gray went on, "it'll take me several years to save the needed amount. But we'll be still at war then! So ..."

"You mean this investment you're thinking of," Clarissa said, "depends on the war?"

She might as well humor him, he looked so serious about it.

"Certainly, it depends on the war."

"And how is that?"

"Because of the war contracts."

"War contracts?"

"Guns, bullets, which the government orders to be made in great quantities. Of course," Captain Gray explained, "only a *multi*millionaire could get such an order. And then he'd become as rich as Croesus! That's why they're all bidding for this new war contract, men like Mr. FitzMaurice, I mean. Probably you've heard of Mr. FitzMaurice."

The brilliant social gatherings, which Clarissa had to attend with the Earl almost every night, seldom lacked Mr. FitzMaurice's presence, or that of Lord Cavor, since the two appeared everywhere together. And only the previous week, the portly pair of them had been whispering flattering offers into Clarissa's ear. But there was no need to make any mention of *that* to Captain Gray, Clarissa decided.

"Mr. FitzMaurice?" she said. "Of course, I've *heard* about him. He owns mines in Africa, diamond mines. Doesn't he?"

"And some gold mines, too," Captain Gray said. "And that's where this investment, this chance of a lifetime, comes in."

And then, very calmly, he explained:

"To get this war contract, Mr. FitzMaurice must show a lot of money on hand, hard cash. But most of his fortune, as is always the case with very wealthy people, is tied up in various enterprises. So ..." and Captain Gray paused triumphantly, "he's selling some of his mines!"

"Oh," Clarissa said.

"Naturally, they're not *working* mines. No digging has been done on them yet. But he's letting them go for a song! Very cheap. Fantastically cheap!"

"But if there's been no digging done at all," Clarissa tried to point out, "how can anybody know what's *in* the mines? Maybe instead of diamonds, or gold, there's nothing but rock and ... and a lot of dirt."

Captain Gray, however, merely laughed.

"A FitzMaurice mine," he announced, "is a mine which *must* have either diamonds, or gold, in it. That's a well-known fact. Mr. FitzMaurice is famous for it. He's supposed to have the magic touch. But the funny part of it is," Captain Gray said, and he laughed, "you'd never guess who tipped me off to it!"

"You mean that the proposed sale of those mines," Clarissa said, "is a matter of great secrecy?"

"Certainly! Don't ask me why, the reasons are too involved. But that's how big men conduct their business. And if it hadn't been for Lord Nelson ... *He* it was who tipped me off! Now what do you think of *that?*" And the Captain grinned all over his face, triumphant. "Somebody passed the information on to Lord Nelson," he explained. "People are always trying to help him make sound investments. But, the trouble is, when it comes to money he's no better off than I am!"

"His pay is bigger than yours, surely," Clarissa pointed out.

"All of his pay goes to that frigid wife of his. They've been separated for years, but now because of Lady Hamilton, the wife is starting to make demands on Lord Nelson, threatens him with scandal. He has no choice but to hand his pay over to her, every penny of it!"

"And that explains why his uniform is almost as shabby as yours."

"And why he couldn't buy one of those mines. But instead, and right away, he said to me, 'Captain Gray, you've been very obliging. And I want to do you a good turn. Buy it. Buy several of those mines, if you can. I know you have no money. Start saving your pay. You'll make a fortune, young man!' Now wouldn't I be a fool," Captain Gray said, "not to follow his advice?"

"Well ..." Clarissa said. She was not at all convinced. Far from it. There was something of a dreamer too about Lord Nelson, just as there was about Captain Gray. Maybe all men who did their fighting on ships were like that. Adventurous. Easily carried away ... However, it would take Captain Gray a very, very long time to save the needed amount of money, and by then every one of those FitzMaurice mines would be snatched up! *If* they were, indeed, as promising as he believed them to be ...

And Clarissa suddenly jumped up, and hurried to the bureau, and pulled a drawer out, and took out the casket which contained her little collection of jewels. Sitting down on the floor quickly, with the casket beside her, she pressed the brass clasps open, raised the lid, and began to take the valuable jewels out, one by one.

Captain Gray came over and squatted on the floor beside her.

"What pretty trinkets you have," he said.

And very patronizing his voice sounded!

"Yes, they *are* pretty, aren't they?" Clarissa said.

She was examining a small diamond necklace to make sure that each stone was held securely by the intricate gold setting. Sometimes the stones got loose, and then she had to go to the jeweler to have them made secure again. After thus examining every item separately, she'd put it in her lap, and now her lap held a little heap of beautiful jewels.

"But where are your green 'beads'?" Captain Gray went on. "You seemed to have been very much attached to them. Why, you even wore them to bed with you, I remember."

"I ... I lost them."

"You mean, you mislaid them?"

"I dropped them ... in the Thames."

"Oh, well, I suppose the clasp broke."

"Probably, yes."

"Very pretty sparklers," Captain Gray went on. "I think women buy such sparklers at the fairs, don't they?"

And he smiled at Clarissa indulgently. He *actually* thought she was amusing herself by looking at cheap, trashy trinkets, the kind some stupid housemaid might buy for herself, for a few shillings, at a *fair!* Well!

"But they are probably becoming to you," the Captain said. "Why don't you put them on?"

Well, he had never seen her in all her glory. For that was what jewels did for a woman, glorified her beauty. And Clarissa began to put them on. All the rings, necklaces, pendants, brooches—she put them all on. And since there was more than one pair of earrings, she used the extra gems for hair ornaments. Then she crossed her arms and looked at him.

"Goodness!" Captain Gray said. "On you the sparklers look almost real!"

"*Almost!* Is that what you think?"

"Truly, you look like some beautiful idol, bedecked with jewels."

"I may not be an idol," Clarissa said, "but I *am* bedecked with jewels!"

"Why, of course. These are diamonds, and these are sapphires, and here are some rubies...." And as the Captain said this, he placed a finger every time on the precious stone in question, little guessing how correctly he was naming the "sparklers." And he laughed.

"They *are* diamonds, *and* sapphires, *and* rubies!" Clarissa told him.

"Well, isn't that just what I said? Of course, they are!"

His tone was even more amused than before. And he had actually laughed! Clarissa had been annoyed, but now she was suddenly very angry. She thought a moment. Then, very quietly, she said:

"Please get that broken-down valise of yours out of the cupboard; it's on the bottom shelf. And bring it here."

"Why, what would you want with it?"

"Please bring it."

With a shrug, Captain Gray got up, went over to the cupboard, took the valise out, brought it over, and deposited it on the floor, in the specific spot Clarissa pointed at with a finger, imperiously. He then, smiling amusedly, resumed his squatting position beside her. He could see that she was enraged about something—women were the strangest creatures!—and he was trying to humor her.

"The day after tomorrow," Clarissa said, "Lord Nelson is going down to London to be acclaimed at the celebration of the Battle of the Nile. And, of course, you are to accompany him."

"And after the celebration," Captain Gray said, "we won't come back to Merton, but we'll have to journey directly to board the flagship, *Victory,* attended by all the dignitaries. And I suppose the beautiful court ladies will be coming with us," the Captain added judiciously. "Part of the way, anyhow."

Two days was all they'd have together at Merton, this time, and yet he could think of the beautiful court ladies, to whom he would be introduced, of course, and who would be fawning on him probably, the sluts!

"As soon as you get to London," Clarissa told him coldly, "ask Lord Nelson's permission to absent yourself for about an hour, and go to Bond Street, and find this jeweler there," and she named the jeweler. "You'll see the name on the shop sign. And ask him how much these ... these 'sparklers' are worth!"

"What are you doing?" Captain Gray cried, astonished.

For swiftly, angrily, Clarissa was suddenly stripping herself of the jewels, the rings, pendants, earrings, brooches. She tore them off, one after another, tossing them into the broken-down valise.

"That jeweler will tell you the *truth.* And then, maybe, you'll stop laughing at me. 'Sparklers,' indeed!" Clarissa cried, all out of breath. "And he will *beg* you to sell them to him. And then you can buy yourself a FitzMaurice mine. Several of those silly mines, probably. There!" And she banged the the lid of the valise shut and turned the key in the lock.

Then, jumping up, grabbing the valise by the handle, she carried it to the cupboard, tossed it on the shelf, closed the cupboard door with a gesture of finality, and came back, her eyes flashing.

"And I don't want to hear another word about it," she announced. "You just do what I said, please!"

"Of course, I'll do it, if that's what you want," Captain Gray said, trying to pacify her. "But ..."

"Not another word about it, I told you."

And picking up the casket, which still stood there on the floor, empty, Clarissa hastened to close the lid, snapped the brass clasps shut, and put the casket away in the bureau drawer.

"Not another word!"

"You're right. Why waste time," Captain Gray said, grinning.

And he took her in his arms. And then Clarissa very quickly forgot about the casket's pathetic emptiness....

But not long after her return to London, Sally came to her, holding the casket in her hands, and said:

"I see you had sense enough, at last, to give your nest egg of jewels to someone for safekeeping. I always thought it was mighty careless of you, leaving them in this casket, which has no lock, what with the thieving flunkies around and all. And then taking the casket to Merton with you, when there are highwaymen just waiting to rob the helpless travelers on the lonely road at night. Is it to François you gave the jewels to keep for you? The chief valet is such a reliable person, despite that funny little mustache of his," and here Sally paused, to take breath and to titter. "Or is it Mr. Davey who's keeping your nest egg for you? That's the only two people I could think of, when I saw that the casket was empty of the jewels."

"Sally," Clarissa said, "it's no business of yours who I gave my nest egg to for ... for safekeeping. Really, the way you keep poking your nose into matters that don't concern you ..."

"Goodness gracious!" Sally expostulated as usual. "You don't *have* to tell me. If you don't *want* to. The important thing is that I know now that it's safe! If anything happens, well, there're the jewels to fall back on. You'll sell them, and we won't have to starve ... And I can use this casket to keep ribbons in, like I did before," Sally added, and she looked very pleased about it. "It makes a very nice receptacle for ribbons, this casket does, indeed."

And Sally turned to go, but then came back and said:

"I forgot to tell you, the cosmetics vender was here this morning."

"The cosmetics vender?" Clarissa said, sitting bolt upright suddenly in the chair.

"But I knew you had enough rouge," Sally went on, "so I sent him away."

"Was it ... was it the same vender," Clarissa asked, and she succeeded in making her voice sound almost calm, "who came here last time?"

"Well, no," Sally said, "this vender was quite a different fellow."

"Are you sure?"

"Why, of course, I'm sure. I'm not blind, am I? The other vender, the one you mean, he was such an engaging fellow. The way he grinned at me," Sally tittered. "But this one ..." And she made a face. "He had freckles on his nose, and he was *uncouth*. But I told him to come again in a couple of weeks, because by then you'd be needing more rouge."

Of course, it couldn't have been Slippery Jack! Clarissa told herself. How stupid of her to have been so frightened, even for a moment! Hadn't she seen Slippery Jack perish in the Thames, the current being so strong there under the bridge from which he had toppled, the gleaming emeralds clutched in his outflung hand? But the dark fog-steeped scene vivid in her mind, she suddenly remembered the presence of the hulk captain and his brigand-like men in their boat nearby. They *might* have come to the drowning man's assistance ...

And so she would never know. She would never be quite certain.

CHAPTER TWENTY-TWO

Everybody at the Thieves' Village, however, took it for granted that Slippery Jack, by now, was far away in the Colonies. And Clarissa, on her brief visits to the Waterfront Tavern, would shrewdly pretend that she thought so, too. But after a safe period of time had elapsed, she once asked Honest Gregory, casually:

"Do you think Slippery Jack will be—coming back, someday, in the future?"

"Well, they generally return, eventually," Honest Gregory said.

Clarissa watched him as he spoke. What did he actually *know*? But the pseudo-parson's face, as usual, told her nothing.

And to change the subject, she hastened to ask after Prickly Gil. Clarissa had noticed the weird girl's absence, and even before Honest Gregory could answer her question she sensed that something terrible had happened. Perhaps the child had been born a monster, or Prickly Gil had died in giving it birth.

"The child was born perfectly normal," Honest Gregory said, "and it lived. But then, afterwards, Prickly Gil ... strangled it. Yes, in the market place, near the Rose and Crown, it happened. Prickly Gil used to go there to pick the pockets of those big gawky milkmaids. And very good she was at it, too. Anyway, she was instantly apprehended, brought to trial almost immediately, and the following day taken to Tyburn. There was nothing we could do for *her*," Honest Gregory explained, "since the law regards infanticide as the most hideous of crimes. And the Lord Chief Justice himself sees to it that the condemned female pays the penalty."

Infanticide, Clarissa thought. The word, indeed, had a horrible sound.

But the news of Prickly Gil's end had neither surprised nor shocked Clarissa. Everybody had always somehow expected something like that happening to the weird girl, and Clarissa would have soon forgotten all about it, except for a certain unforeseen occurrence.

She was sitting at her elaborate dressing table, sipping her hot chocolate, when Sally suddenly burst into the room and, wringing her hands dramatically, wailed:

"Save me! Save me!"

"Why ...? What ... what is it?" Clarissa asked, astonished.

But Sally, instead of trying to explain, flopped down on the floor and, in the most foolish fashion, hid her head under Clarissa's peignoir.

Clarissa had to set her cup down and then take Sally by the shoulders and shake her, and make her get up. But when Sally, speechless with fear, pointed at the window, Clarissa hurried to it, drew back the curtain, and gasped.

Bonfires! Bonfires in the daytime! It could mean only one thing. Yes, the red-coated soldiers were throwing little bags of sulphur into the blue-tipped flames, while the thick white smoke spread the acrid smell close to Clarissa's window. Smallpox! The city was being menaced with an epidemic of the dreaded disease....

Clarissa immediately dispatched Sally to François, with an order for him to look up in the almanac when the moon would be in its last quarter. According to Prickly Gil, that was when

Clarissa could seek out Nellie Harris in the Kenerevy woods. The moon would be in its last quarter, Sally announced on coming back, in exactly two weeks to the day! Clarissa spent the harrowing period of waiting virtually barricaded in her room. The windows tightly shut and the curtains drawn against the polluted air outside, and the food for her and Sally sent up from the kitchen and left outside the door. Fear made her imagine that her skin itched, and every few minutes she would consult her hand mirror, expecting to see the dreaded tiny red spot suddenly show itself, threatening her beauty. Clarissa and the hand mirror remained inseparable during those two weeks. She took it to bed with her, so that on awakening from the selfsame nightmare, screaming, she could look at herself right away, and then sob out her relief ...

Altogether, the ordeal of waiting had so unnerved Clarissa that she was a little late in reaching the Kenerevy woods on the night appointed. As she walked through the trees, made ghostly by the mist and the faint moonlight, and into the clearing, she saw that the hooded black figures were already moving in a single-file circle in the center there. She heard their weird chanting, while other similar figures were starting to dance around them. But everything was exactly as it had been the other time. The crude stone altar with the little fire burning in it, and the knot of the hooded black figures preparing something there; and the young white goat stood tied to a sapling nearby.

Suddenly a small black-robed figure was before her, the neat though toothless face of the little old woman peeping at her out of the folds of the hood.

"Nellie Harris," Clarissa said. "I came here because ..."

"I know, I know," Nellie Harris told her. "You're afraid to lose your beauty through disfiguration. Such a flawless skin you have ... To see it suddenly pockmarked, think of it! Petal-smooth it is now, I bet. And what a pleasure for a man to touch ..." And extending a clawlike hand, the little old woman held it against Clarissa's cheek lingeringly. "But it could become coarse, and ugly," Nellie Harris went on, removing her claw and chuckling, "and full of tiny pits, left by the sores that had been scratched, wouldn't it? The lovely skin, I mean. And the men wouldn't like that at all, would they? No, they certainly wouldn't! And that's why you're here."

But she wasn't really hostile or malicious, maybe just a bit envious, as any old woman would be of someone who was young and beautiful.

"Well, we'll see what we can do," Nellie went on, "since you're a friend of Prickly Gil's." And, handing Clarissa a little cup filled with thick brown liquid, she added, "Drink this."

Clarissa drank the potion obediently, returned the cup, and Nellie Harris hastened to rejoin the dancing, chanting throng of hooded black figures, becoming indistinguishable among them. And then the desperate bleating of the goat pierced the air. They were slashing the creature's throat open. The altar fire sputtered as blood was thrown on it.

"Give us the sign, Master! Show us the Chosen One. The sign, O Master!"

They had all flung themselves prone on the ground, and crawled and writhed there, pleading ecstatically:

"The Chosen One, Master! Show us the Chosen One!"

Clarissa leaned back against the tree trunk behind her. She felt drowsy, and there was an oversweet taste in her mouth left by the potion she had drunk. The sky she stared at looked exactly as it had the other time: veiled with the mist and only faintly moonlit. The clouds there seemed to be arranging themselves in a very strange pattern.

And suddenly, once again, Clarissa saw Carbuncle Joe. His gallantly attired figure looked immense, taking up half of the visible sky. Just as it did the other time. Except that Carbuncle Joe was not alone now. Prickly Gil was with him. The hangman's rope dangled from around the girl's neck exactly as it dangled from around Carbuncle Joe's. He had his arm about her. While clasped in Prickly Gil's thin arms lay the child she had strangled.

Like a little family ... The togetherness rendered the apparition a more terrifying aspect, somehow. And yet it was touching, too. It made Clarissa cry....

The disease never reached the proportions of an epidemic. The fatalities, of course, had been numerous, while many people were left disfigured for life with pockmarks. And among these was one of the mistresses. When Clarissa heard about it she was really shocked. Because, after all, it might quite easily have been she, Clarissa herself, instead of the other woman, who was just as young as Clarissa, and who had been, so very recently, beautiful, gorgeously dressed, pampered, admired ... And now, because of her pockmarked face, she was a miserable creature, unwanted, shunned, fated to end in the gutter ... But it *might have been Clarissa, instead.* Only it *wasn't!* The thought inspired her with a sense of triumph.

And another triumph awaited her when she again saw Captain Richard Gray at Merton.

"Those 'sparklers' ..." were Captain Gray's first words, as Clarissa, preceding him into her bedroom at the cottage, turned around and faced him, her head high. "They were real! And the jeweler you sent me to immediately gave me such a fine price for them that I was able to buy not one but two of those FitzMaurice mines."

"Well, maybe you won't laugh at me any more then," Clarissa said. "Maybe you'll be treating me with a little more respect, henceforth. 'Sparklers …' " she mocked him. "Silly cheap trinkets some frump of a woman can buy at a fair! As if I were a—a housemaid. Yes, a stupid housemaid!"

"Well, I've known some very charming housemaids," Captain Gray said, grinning at her. "And I think you'd make a very pretty one. But let me tell you about the mines. The fine bunch of native laborers out there, in Africa, will be starting the digging, as soon as the local manager of the mines receives my letter of instructions, and …"

"Not another word!" Clarissa told him, and she gracefully put a hand over his lips. "I don't want to hear anything about it until … until you make a fortune, yes, a *fortune,* out of those mines."

As if he ever would! Probably, instead of the gold and the diamonds, the mines, when dug up, would prove to hold nothing more than rock and a lot of dirt. And that's how a man like Mr. FitzMaurice amassed his fantastic wealth. By preying on the credulity of such foolish dreamers as Lord Nelson, and Captain Gray. Taking good money for something he knew to be absolutely worthless …

"Not a word, until then," Clarissa ordered. "Promise!"

Taking her in his arms, Captain Gray duly promised.

And he was to keep his word.

PART SIX

CHAPTER TWENTY-THREE

CLARISSA WAS AWAKENED in the middle of the night by the sounds of commotion coming from the Earl's bedroom. Throwing back the satin quilt, she swiftly climbed down the little ladder from her bed, high with piled-up mattresses, grabbed her peignoir off a chair, and, clasping the peignoir about her naked body, hurried to the connecting door, pushed it open, and then stood stock-still with amazement.

The room, brilliantly illuminated by extra lamps and candelabras, hurriedly brought in, was full of people. Partly-dressed, frightened flunkies running to and fro aimlessly, or standing about, gaping. And the several doorways crowded with other manservants, including even the chef with his tall white hat, which he had put on through sheer habit, in the horrible excitement of the moment. Towels, torn sheets, water pitchers, shallow pans, some filled with water, others empty, were very much in evidence, on chairs, on small tables, on the floor, their presence adding to the general confusion. While around the canopied bed, the three hastily summoned physicians, in their gray-haired wigs—the gray hair symbolizing their indubitable knowledge—were very busily employed, doing something with the Earl. And François, in his green satin livery, was there helping them.

"His Grace had a seizure," a flunky, who happened to be standing nearest to Clarissa, said in answer to her gasp of incredulity and horror.

"His *second* seizure in the last twenty minutes," somebody else said.

The news had spread with lightning-like speed throughout the great mansion, and they had all rushed here to find out just *how* ill the Earl was. One thought took precedence in the minds of all; should the Earl die, and his heirs, the two great-nephews, immediately step in, what would happen to *them,* the servants? There was not a single individual in the place who hadn't been robbing the Earl, in one manner or another. And the great-nephews, naturally, would have everybody's personal belongings searched right away, and the gold coins, or silverware, or some priceless bric-a-brac discovered, the culprit would certainly hang for it. No mercy could be expected from the new heirs. Such was the reputation of the two great-nephews.

The shock of the Earl's sudden illness had so overwhelmed Clarissa that she simply stood there, unable either to move or speak. And, as if in some bad dream, she heard a flunky say to another:

"I'm leaving! I'm taking my things and *leaving,* right away!"

"You'd be a fool to act so rashly," the other argued. "His Grace has had these seizures before. He might recover again, probably *will.* And once you leave, he'd never take you back! You know how touchy these nobles are about what they call loyalty to their person. And where would you find a job as easy as it's here? Eat all you want, no work to speak of ... Why not wait and see, the way I'm doing?"

"Because it might be too late then, that's why. And I'm not taking any chances, not *me!*"

And off that flunky went.

The fact that they had talked in their normal voices, not caring whether Clarissa heard them or not, was enough to bring her to her senses. The impudence of it! And the gigantic major-domo, she suddenly noticed, was actually sitting in a chair, *sitting* in her presence! So that's how little they thought of her already!

And with a cry of, "Your Grace, I'm here. Your Clarissa is here!" she rushed towards the canopied bed.

But before she reached the dais, one of the physicians had hastened forward and down the dais' two steps, and grabbing her by the arm, he pushed her back roughly.

"You musn't come too close to His Grace," he told her. "Because of your beauty, your proximity will excite him, and in his weakened condition such excitement might prove fatal to His Grace."

The elderly physician, notwithstanding his professional dignity and the symbolic gray-haired wig, had the glint of a satyr in his little eyes as they explored Clarissa's half-nakedness with the liveliest appreciation.

"You can't keep me away from His Grace!" Clarissa screamed, struggling. "You can't! You *can't!* You ... old *goat,* you!"

Then she saw François hurrying over, and turned to him, bombarding him with questions. The chief valet hastened to draw her aside.

"Yes, this was His Grace's second seizure," he reported swiftly, lowering his voice. "But it wasn't as bad as the first one. He's so much better, in fact, that the physicians expect him to regain consciousness.... I couldn't leave His Grace's side," François added, "or I would have come to madam to tell her."

"Oh, I quite understand," Clarissa said. "But what I want to know is your own opinion of the Earl's condition, François. Do *you* think he will recover?"

"If I thought there was no hope of recovery ... well, I'd be leaving, right now," the chief valet said, "before the two great-nephews step in. And I'd be advising you to do the same."

But Clarissa was remembering the conversation between the pair of flunkies which she had overheard, and she made her decision right there and then.

"I, personally, will wait till the very last minute," she said. "After all, the 'two dry sticks,' the great-nephews, can't get here *that* fast, no matter how close to the mansion they might have stationed themselves to await further developments. I mean, once the Earl is ... well, once anything *happens* to him, I'll have time to leave, while the 'two dry sticks,' the great-nephews, are hurrying over."

"They might get here faster than you think," François pointed out. "For all we know, they may already be in the house...."

The idea had never occurred to Clarissa, and she could only gape at him, petrified at such a possibility.

"Let in secretly," the chief valet went on, "and into one of those drawing rooms downstairs, maybe, and waiting there now. If someone here is in their pay, that is. Any one of the flunkies, or ... even the major-domo himself, perhaps."

The gigantic major-domo was still sitting in the chair, in the pose of an old and trusted retainer, genuinely distracted by the sudden illness of his beloved employer.

"The big lout dares to sit *down* in my presence," Clarissa hissed, indignant, scared.

"It does look suspicious, doesn't it?" François agreed. "As if the fellow has reasons to be convinced that madam's reign here is almost at an end. Well, I've never trusted *him*," the chief valet declared.

The horrible significance of the situation as it would affect her, personally, struck Clarissa anew, and she wrung her hands.

"Oh, François, what am I to *do?*"

"As I already told madam, His Grace is about to regain consciousness. The joint opinion of the physicians is very optimistic.

Unless His Grace has a third seizure, he will recover. He's had these attacks before, you know," François reminded her. "And if the illness progresses normally, all the Earl will need is a few days' complete rest. And, so long as the Earl lives, madam is second only to him in importance here. Therefore, my advice to madam is to go and put on her richest dress, bedeck herself with jewels, arrange her hair most becomingly. And then to hurry back, and … assert her authority."

"You're right!" Clarissa said. "Absolutely right!"

And she hastened to her room, to be met there by Sally, white-faced with fear and bursting with a hundred questions.

"Is the Earl … *dying?* Oh, it'll be the *end* for *us!* Oh, what are we to *do?* What *can* we do?" Sally wailed.

"The first thing *you* should do is take a good hold of yourself," Clarissa told her. "The Earl is not dying—not yet, anyhow. But, of course I must be ready for any contingency. Bring me that dress of violet silk, the one trimmed with creamy lace. And shoes to match … Now stop gaping at me in that stupid way, do you hear? And do as you're told! Hurry!"

And flinging off the peignoir, Clarissa, stark naked, sat down at the dressing table, to hastily dab on rouge, powder, to darken her eyelids, rearrange her hair becomingly, all of which didn't take a minute. Then, Sally having brought the wanted dress and shoes, Clarissa put them on swiftly, meanwhile giving instructions to the girl, who, though no longer wailing, now sniveled, instead, at the thought of the terrible change that would befall them, should the Earl die after all.

"Have Pete drive the small enclosed carriage around the corner, and he's to stay with it there. Then, in case I have to leave," Clarissa explained, "that's where we'll join him. And you, Sally, pack as many of my clothes and things as would make two bundles, not too heavy for each of us, you and me, to carry. And then you're to stay with the bundles right here, in this room. Understand?"

"The first thing I'll pack," Sally said, "is all your diamonds, of course."

"Certainly not! Really, Sally, I thought you'd have more *sense.* All the jewels will have to be left behind. Anybody leaving the mansion would, naturally, be intercepted and searched, and if anything so valuable as jewels is found in my possession, I'd be accused of stealing them!"

"But the Earl *gave* them to you," Sally argued heatedly. "And this means that the jewels *belong* to you now. You never *stole* them!"

"All the 'two dry sticks' would have to do is say that I *did,* and with the power that would be theirs on inheriting the Earl's title it'd be enough to send me to prison, and … Tyburn."

Clarissa, as she talked, had been busy putting on some of the diamond jewelry, on her arms and fingers, around her throat, and at her ear lobes, and now, after a quick glance at herself in the mirror, she hurried out of the room, and rustled into the Earl's bedroom.

She made straight for the seated major-domo.

"Stand up, lout! On your feet, I said. Or are you deaf?"

Taken by surprise, the man got up.

"Is … is His Grace better then?" he muttered, incredulous.

"His Grace is not dead *yet,*" Clarissa told him, and to emphasize the fact she slapped the major-domo's big, sly face very hard. "Now go! And don't dare show yourself, unless I ring for you."

"Certainly … madam. Very good, madam."

And holding the side of the face where Clarissa had struck him, the gigantic major-domo beat a hasty retreat, bowing.

"And the rest of you …" Clarissa went on. *"Out!"*

The flunkies ran. The other servants, crowding the doorways, disappeared. And even the physicians at the Earl's bedside were visibly cowed, as they turned round to stare and gape.

"A chair for madam, perhaps?" one of them offered, hurrying over obsequiously.

"Put it there," Clarissa ordered, pointing imperiously at the floor, at a spot some five feet away from the bed's dais.

The chair duly placed at that precise spot, and Clarissa seating herself gracefully, she was at enough distance from the Earl not to excite him by the proximity of her beauty, while being at the same time near enough to watch the physician's activities.

But first—well, the illumination was much too brilliant for the patient's comfort.

"Have those extra lamps and the candelabras taken away," Clarissa said, throwing into her voice again that ring of authority which had so cowed the major-domo and scared the servants. "Pull that bell cord for a flunky! And open the window, it's unbearably stuffy here. And what's that dirty towel doing on the floor? And the overturned water pitcher ...?"

The physician who had brought her the chair, and the one whom she had called "old goat"—both of them strangers to Clarissa—ran about to pull the bell cord, open the window, pick up the dirty towel. The third medical man, who was the Earl's personal physician, and whom Clarissa knew, had remained by the bed. He was the only one among them Clarissa felt she could trust.

A flunky appeared, fully and neatly liveried this time. In a trice, the room was brought into order, the doors decently closed, the air pleasantly refreshed. And the discipline of the household thus swiftly reinstated, and Clarissa's power as the Earl's pampered mistress firmly restored, she could focus her attention on the Earl's own person now.

How small the Earl looked in that great luxurious bed. Smaller than ever! Under that sumptuous canopy of gold velvet which, descending in rich folds from the gilded crown set close to the lofty ceiling, was looped back on either side, how frighteningly inert his small figure lay, prostrate among the rumpled silk sheets and satin covers. The figure of a child, or a doll, with a monkey's grotesque head attached to the little shoulders. But François was putting the small white wig over the Earl's bare-as-a-kneecap skull, and then, with the Earl's personal physician holding the porcelain tray with cosmetics for him, the chief valet deftly applied powder, rouge, lipstick to the little face. The blue and pink satin coat, besprinkled with pearls and diamonds, was then put on the unconscious Earl. And François sprayed him with several perfumes.

Then, the porcelain cosmetics tray hastily hidden out of sight, they all took their places, to await the Earl's return to consciousness. Two physicians stood quietly at the foot of the bed. At its head, the Earl's personal physician stood on one side, with a fat gold watch in his hand, while the fingers of his other hand lay on the patient's wrist, feeling the pulse. François stood on the other side, holding a hand mirror, ready. That's what the Earl, on regaining consciousness, would ask for, first thing. The looking glass.

But Clarissa's attention was suddenly attracted by something that made her feel horribly squirmy. Goose-pimples instantly covered her lovely bare arms. The "something," dark in color, almost black, and obviously *alive,* lay spread on a silver platter, which had been placed on a little table not far from her chair. And then the thing moved, and Clarissa saw that it consisted of a number of tiny creatures, each about an inch long, and somehow disgustingly plump. As if swollen with overfeeding …

"Oh!" she cried. "What is it? What *is* it?"

"What? What?" and they all, including François, looked around in alarm.

"I mean *that!*" and Clarissa pointed.

"Oh, that," one of the physicians said. "That's leeches, madam. The Earl had to be bled. The relief will help him regain consciousness."

"Take them away. Take them away, instantly!"

A flunky was summoned, and as he hurried in, Clarissa motioned at the platter. Taking it up, looking down at the leeches, the flunky said:

"Don't they look good, though! Nice and plump. Yes, they'll make a fine snack."

"A—*what?*"

"We fry them in butter, madam."

"You mean ... you actually *eat* them?"

"We footmen always do. The fellows downstairs can't wait ... A great delicacy, madam. To think that His Grace being so small and shriveled and all, and yet the tiny creatures managed to suck out so much blood from him. Swollen they are with it! Yes, they'll make a fine snack."

And off the flunky went, bearing the platter of crawling leeches with him.

Maybe I'm getting squeamish, Clarissa chided herself. But then she had to jump up, and run to the beautiful big oriental vase which stood in a corner, and be thoroughly sick into it. After which she felt much better. The Earl, besides, regained consciousness just as she resumed her chair. He admired himself in the mirror, which François held over him expertly, nodded, and fell asleep.

The physicians descended from the bed's dais. A collation had been prepared for them in a nearby room, and they were in need of reinforcing their vigor after the recent strain.

"Have no scruples about leaving your patient for so short a while," Clarissa told them, when they seemed to hesitate. "I will be here, and if there's any change I will call you at once. Nobody could be more desirous of His Grace's recovery than I am, since it is I alone who would be utterly ruined should he die. Therefore, it is in my interests to use utmost care in watching over His Grace."

"Quite true, very," they all said.

And hurried out, doubtless thinking of the excellent wine which would be served them from the Earl's famous cellars. François had gone into the dressing room to see about a fresh supply of linen for the Earl's bed, and Clarissa was left alone with the Earl.

She waited for about a minute. Then, very quietly, she rose and tiptoed to the bed. After standing at the foot of the dais, glancing around and listening for someone's possible tread outside the several doors, she swiftly walked up the two steps, approached the bed. She wanted to see for herself just how ill the Earl was. He was indeed sleeping, but his breathing sounded uneven, labored. And because of the paint on the little face, she could not tell just how pale he might be. The hand that lay outside the coverlet, however—and very small the inert hand looked—was completely drained of color. Otherwise he seemed about normal. No sign of heavy sweating. And he was obviously not in pain.

Clarissa moved closer, and the rustle of her rich dress awakened the Earl. He knew her instantly, and nodded.

"Your Grace," she whispered, bending over him.

He stared at her. Then, as if remembering something, his eyes grew anxious. He tried desperately to speak, but no words came. What did he want to tell her? Warn her, perhaps?

But there was the sound of footsteps outside one of the doors. If she was seen so close to the Earl's bedside and anything happened to him now, she'd be accused of killing him. She had barely reseated herself, when the physicians trooped in.

"I have not moved from this chair," Clarissa told them. "But saw His Grace stir slightly, a while back. Maybe he's awake."

They hastened to him, but the Earl evidently had again dozed off. Anyway, there was no perceptible change in his condition, as Clarissa could see by the miens of the physicians, who, after a quick examination, stayed quietly by the bed to watch over their patient.

And then she heard François call to her from behind the dressing room door, which he had opened a few inches, his voice purposely loud for the physicians to hear him:

"If it would please Madam to give me her opinion ... about this linen for His Grace ..."

A mere pretext, of course, to speak to her in private.

"Why, certainly, François," she answered, for the physicians' benefit.

And then she had to force herself not to run, but to walk calmly enough across the floor, and into the dressing room, pulling the door after her. And she gasped.

François was leaving, and in great haste, too. He had exchanged his brilliant livery, with the Earl's crest, for an unobtrusively dark street costume, had hurriedly packed a few belongings into a small bundle, and there he stood, ready to go.

"Yes, and I advise you to do the same," he said quickly, in answer to Clarissa's gasp and stare. "Of course, His Grace *may* recover. But should he die, it would be too late to leave *then*. The great-nephews will certainly take away all the money I've saved," and François placed a hand on the bundle, where he had evidently concealed the gold which the careless Earl was in the habit of leaving about on chairs, tables, dropped on the floor, and which the chief valet would then pick up, and put in his own pocket. "And they'll implicate me in some crime worse than stealing, besides! They'll implicate you too, for sure. Since they hate you so. Therefore, my advice is—leave! Now, at once! While there's still time."

"Suppose I do leave, *now*," Clarissa said quietly. "And then the Earl recovers ..." and she paused significantly.

"Well, of course, he'd never take you back. And another woman will usurp your enviable position. And you'd be kicking yourself for the rest of your life! For being overimpatient, for not waiting ... But if you *are* staying, you must watch very carefully for the slightest change in the Earl's condition," François urged her.

"Yes, yes, I will," Clarissa promised him. "And if there's any worsening, I will immediately leave."

"And the tiny vial with the draught," François reminded her. "Once you decide to leave, throw it away. Get rid of it, somehow. Don't forget, now!"

He was already at the door which led onto the back stairs. Clarissa watched him slip out. Well, it had been easy for François to suddenly make up his mind, decide. He wouldn't be losing much by leaving. He probably had enough of that gold saved to realize his long-nursed ambition of opening a little business of his own, a hairdresser's establishment. And he would doubtless prosper....

She hurried back to resume her chair and keep watch of the Earl. The physicians now were taking turns at staying by his bed. While two of them had gone to sit on the cushioned sofa at the end of the room, and dozed there, the third had seated himself on the dais steps, and his head in its gray-haired wig was also nodding with drowsiness. Which reminded Clarissa that it was still night, and that everybody, including herself, had been roused from sleep.

But I won't fall asleep, she vouched. And she kept her eyes fixed on the luxurious bed. The Earl hadn't stirred once. He was sleeping very peacefully, she thought.

And then one of the two physicians dozing on the sofa sat up, making the sofa creak, and yawned, blinked his eyes, and glanced towards the patient. The casual glance became a stare. And the man, suddenly jumping up, rushed to the bed. Clarissa saw him bending low over the Earl, putting his head against the Earl's chest, grabbing for his pulse. Then, letting fall the lifeless hand, the physician straightened himself. Clarissa didn't have to be told. The Earl was dead.

Very quietly she rose and began to make her way on tiptoe to the door connecting the two bedrooms. There would be commotion, excitement, nobody would be thinking of her, and she would make her getaway unperceived, with Sally and the bundles, and join Pete waiting with the carriage. She was almost at the door. But suddenly it flung open, and the gigantic major-domo stepped out. Clarissa caught a glimpse of Sally's blanched face behind him. Sally's silk cap was all askew, her hair disheveled, and the mouth was wide open in a shriek. The sound of her shrieking was cut off by the slammed door.

"No you *don't!*" the major-domo said, pulling Clarissa away from it by the wrist, which he had grabbed as in a vise.

He grinned all over his big, sly face; how he was going to revenge himself for the slap she had given him!

"Let me go! Lout! Pig!" Screaming, Clarissa tried to wrench her wrist out of the man's painful grip.

She twisted herself about, ducked, pulled, and panting with rage and fear, she suddenly stooped, and bit him in the hand. That's when he began to slap *her* face. First on one cheek, then on the other, repeatedly, making her head loll helplessly, this way and that. And her rich dress torn, her lustrous hair hanging about her tear-stained face in disorder, she was dragged to the center of the room, and jerked to a standing position there.

"Stop your screaming, and stand still," the major-domo ordered, retaining his painful grasp of her wrist. "Or you'll get more of the same with interest!"

She stopped screaming, then, and stood still. The situation was hopeless. And worse was yet to come.

And then the "two dry sticks," the great-nephews, walked in. Alike as two peas, both of them tall, very thin, dressed in somber black, and with long faces, the color of wax, under the small black wigs. They were followed by a short, pudgy man, attired in a dark silk robe and wearing a heavy gold chain around his neck and a large wig of white curls, emblems of his office. A magistrate. The several constables he had brought with him could be seen loitering just outside the door. The magistrate, however, coughing importantly, while at the same time perspiring freely with fear, stationed himself well within the room, to await the powerful heirs' instructions.

The two great-nephews marched straight to the daised bed, and ascending the two steps, halted by the bedside. The bedclothes had been drawn over the dead Earl's face, and now one of the physicians hastened to pull the covering back. The heirs looked down briefly, then they nodded their satisfaction. The covering was replaced. And the "two dry sticks" hastened towards Clarissa.

"Here she is, my lords," the major-domo cried. And he squeezed Clarissa's wrist, making her gasp. "Here's the hussy! The slut! The harlot! She was about to make her getaway, but knowing your desires in this matter, I caught her, and here she is! Please note my participation, my lords, I beg you."

The great-nephews came up close to Clarissa, and stood and stared at her. Preserving a terrifyingly cool exterior, they were burning up inside with the hatred of her. Their breaths, which they purposely let out right into Clarissa's face, were hot with the vengeance they were about to wreak upon her. Like two death's-heads they looked. And how Clarissa wished she could spit in their pale-lidded eyes!

"Now," they said, turning to the magistrate.

"Ahem," that worthy said warningly. "Ahem!" And wiping his perspiring pudgy features on the sleeve of his dignified robe, he lowered his voice to explain, "There are witnesses present, my lords. Better we have no witnesses to *this*. One never knows...."

He meant the physicians, who, uncertain what was desired of them, stood close together, shaking in every limb. But a gesture of dismissal from the great-nephews sent them scurrying to the door, and out. And the "two dry sticks" again turned to the magistrate, with one of the pair saying:

"We want this woman," pointing at Clarissa, "thrown into jail, and, without benefit of a trial, she is to be hanged. Yes, hanged! But not publicly. The jailyard would do. The secret of her identity must be preserved throughout. No one must be allowed to see her, or communicate with her. And she must be strictly guarded to prevent her from making contact with anyone. The wiles of this crafty harlot have doubtless won her a friend or two among people of note, and they may foolishly try to interfere. In short, from the moment the creature is taken out of this house, it's as if she has disappeared. And nobody will ever know *what* happened to her. Understand?"

"Quite. To be hanged. Splendid idea," the magistrate approved ingratiatingly. "There's a gallows in the yard of the jail, for such as must be done away with secretly ... Your instructions, my lords, will be carried out to the letter. But, hmm ... ahem ..." the magistrate coughed, perspired, and at last brought it out, "but what is the *charge* against the slut?"

"Is that necessary?"

"A matter of legal procedure. A mere trifle … Mm! Suppose we make the charge one of common stealing? And the evidence can be fabricated later."

"Evidence?" the two great-nephews exclaimed. "Why, look at her! *Covered* with diamonds! She's been *robbing* His Grace!"

"Quite so," the magistrate hastened to agree. "However, it is common knowledge that … eh, hm … the Earl of Strasford had been showering the woman with jewels, of his own free will, so to speak. Err … hm, a more *plausible* charge shouldn't be hard to invent."

Clarissa, who had been listening to it all as one in a daze, suddenly saw a glimmer of hope, and finding her voice, she screamed:

"I didn't steal them. I didn't! I *didn't!*"

Again she tried to wrench her wrist from the major-domo's viselike grip—the big lout had probably crippled her there—and in the struggle that ensued the tiny vial, which she always carried on her person, concealed inside her bodice, fell out, and rolled on the floor, stopped, and there it lay.

The pudgy magistrate at once ran to pick it up. And holding the tiny vial out to the great-nephews, he declared:

"There's your evidence! And how it simplifies everything. Probably it's just a harmless sleeping draught. But you will tell the Lord Chief Justice that the hussy had been trying to poison the Earl, and his lordship will take your word for it, my lords."

"We will go and arrange it all with the Lord Chief Justice, at once," the great-nephews said together. And one of them took the vial and slipped it into his pocket.

"Err … hm." The magistrate again wiped his perspiring face and, quaking with fear, he hastened to explain, "His lordship is—er—away. Summoned to Ireland, because of the latest rebellion there. Hm, to administer punishment to the rebels."

"Of course, he will have them all shot!"

"Certainly ... the arrogant knaves that they are! And then his lordship will be back in London, in—in about three months."

"Three months! You expect us to wait that long!" and the two great-nephews stepped up to the magistrate threateningly.

The magistrate squealed with terror, and then he pleaded, blabbering:

"My lords ... I will do everything in my power. No trial for the wench. And the hanging to be performed in secret. That alone might cost me my job! But the official document, the order for the execution signed by the Lord Chief Justice himself, must be delivered to the chief jailer, or I'd be jeopardizing my own life for the omission. A three months' wait, what does it matter? So long as she is hanged eventually ..."

The great-nephews were most annoyed, but willy-nilly they had to agree that after having waited so long to wreak their vengeance on the woman they hated, so comparatively brief a delay was really of no consequence. And Clarissa, hearing her doom thus irrevocably sealed, kicked the major-domo in the shins, and screamed at the top of her voice, while the lout, obeying the great-nephews' signal, tore off her jewels, purposely scratching her skin in the process.

"Call the constables! Have her bound, gagged! We can't have her screaming so, it might give rise to talk!"

"Just let me hit her once with *this,* my lords," the gigantic major-domo offered eagerly. And he clasped a hand into a powerful fist. "Not a sound will she be able to make for hours afterwards!"

The last thing Clarissa saw was this fist, swinging out at her. Then, as it hit her, down she went, and total blackness descended upon her.

CHAPTER TWENTY-FOUR

W HEN SHE CAME TO, and opened her eyes, it was to find herself lying in a corner of a dark, dirty cell. So very little light from outside penetrated through the tiny aperture cut high up in one of the slime-covered stone walls, that at first she was aware only of the general grayness and the darker shadows intermingling with it. Then, her sight becoming accustomed to the uncertain light gradually, she saw that the cell was absolutely bare, except for a small wooden bucket which, standing on the unswept floor, was to be used by her, Clarissa instantly gathered, in lieu of a privy. Evidently she would be confined permanently in this hole of a place until led out straight to the gallows, inside an inner courtyard, and therefore completely concealed from outside detection by the jail's looming walls.

The stench of stale straw was in her nostrils. That's what she was lying on, filthy straw. And smelly dampness was all around, collecting in drops and dripping down the stone slabs. She sat up, and the heavy chain rattled. The thick iron ring around her ankle had already bruised the skin there. One end of the chain was attached to this ring, the other to a larger ring set in a nearby wall. The length of the chain would allow her to stand up and even make a few steps. And Clarissa was about to experiment when something cold and sleek ran down her bare arm. A rat. A large one. She saw it disappear. And she heard another rat, in a corner further away, gnawing at something with its sharp vicious teeth. The place was probably full of them. And, meanwhile, she became aware of the lice biting her all over. Hungry for food, the vermin had probably attacked her in droves the instant she had been thrust senseless onto the rotting straw by the jailers. And now she was crawling with lice. She could feel them exploring her scalp, moving there, at the roots of her disheveled hair. But the worst bites seemed to be under the armpits and on the back of her neck. Swiftly, she started scratching herself there, and only then did she realize that her rich dress had been taken away from her, and in its place had been substituted a short shift of coarse sacking. Just an old potato sack, with two holes for the arms, and a third for the neck, and the ragged hem barely covering her knees. Already, in a matter of some few hours, she, the celebrated Clarissa, the radiant beauty of London, had been transformed into a wild-looking creature, unkempt, chained, smelling of rats, vermin, and filthy straw.

And so she just sat there, scraps of anxious thoughts rushing through her mind, still partly dazed by the blow of the major-domo's fist. The blow had broken the skin on her right temple, and a scab was forming there, beside the painful swelling. What happened to Sally ...? To Pete ...? Would they have been arrested, too? Or merely thrown out? After a thorough beating, of course ... And they wouldn't know what happened to *her!* Would have no idea where she was. *Nobody* knew her whereabouts. She had simply disappeared. And there was no way for her to contact someone outside, and let the someone, anyone, know....

Suddenly, Clarissa heard the sound of heavy bolts being removed on the other side of the low iron door. Then the key grated in the lock, and the door swung open, letting in an assistant jailer, wearing his dark green costume trimmed with bits of red cloth at the collar and cuffs, and with the front fringe of his crude circular haircut reaching down to his eyebrows. In one hand he bore a small wooden dish, filled with thin tasteless gruel, doubtless, and in the other a tin cup with water. As he approached, Clarissa saw that the man was elderly, and of a rough, unpleasant appearance.

After placing the dish and the cup down on the floor and within her reach, the assistant jailer was about to turn and leave. But Clarissa was too quick for him. Holding up the heavy chain attached to her ankle to prevent it rattling and so warning the man while he had been busy putting her day's meager portion of food down, she had swiftly crawled on her knees closer, closer ... And now both her hands gripped at his sleeve, and held fast to it, while she whispered quickly:

"You'll be paid ... handsomely. Just let them know, down at the Waterfront Tavern ... Or send someone, to tell them ... that somebody they know is in this jail, in this cell. That's all one has to say, and they'll understand. And they'll pay you, give you money ... gold. You know they will ... the likes of you have dealt with them before."

But the man merely shook her off and, without a word, he leisurely went out, and the door closed. She heard the heavy bolts fall back into place, and then the tomblike silence again surrounded her.

Since she was hungry, she tried to eat the gruel, using the tin spoon stuck in the gluey stuff. But it tasted horrible, almost made her vomit, and she gave up the attempt. The sip of water she next took from the tin cup proved no better. The water was stale, and smelled of rust and mildew. Then something about the wall under which she sat attracted her attention. She moved closer to examine it. The wall was all marked with small scratches. Probably made by the rats' sharp claws, Clarissa decided. But as she studied the markings more carefully, she discovered a sameness about them which seemed to hint at a deliberate purpose, peculiar to the human mind alone.

They were made, of course, by the prisoners who had been confined in this cell prior to Clarissa's own advent. Each scratch, a line of about half an inch, or shorter, in length. And these tiny lines etched on the stone one underneath the other, in short perpendicular rows. Each of the solitary prisoners had made his, or her, own set of these carefully scratched lines. Now what would be the purpose of it? Clarissa wondered. And then she suddenly understood. Each tiny line meant one day. So many lines, so many days ... How else could anybody keep track of the passage of time in this horrible place?

And she would do the same. Was it the tin spoon they had used for an implement? Or, maybe, the tin cup? But first she must find a spot in the wall where she would set down *her* markings. And in order to do that she had to wipe the stone clean of slime and dampness. She quickly tore a piece of the ragged hem of her sack shift, and with this rag she began to wipe the wall until she found a place where the tiny lines had become very faint, or almost obliterated, with time. *Her* scratches, as she made them day after day, would stand out very clearly, because of their newness.

And then she set to work, first with the tin spoon, and then with the tin cup, trying to scratch a mark in the hard stone. She scratched and scratched, sweating with the effort, breaking her fingernails, and—nothing happened. The spoon almost broke in two, the cup was bent out of shape. The metal was too soft, apparently. Then what had the *others* used to make those tiny lines? Nothing else seemed available. With Clarissa's every movement the heavy chain clanked and rattled loudly. And this gave her a sudden idea. The chain was of iron. Yes, that's what *they* must have used. Of course! Selecting one of the links in the chain, she held it against the wall, and moved the link back and forth on the stone to produce a scratch. Her arms ached. Blisters sprang up on the soft palms of her hands, accustomed to creams and lotions. Sometimes she had to stop and rest. But, after a while, there it was! A tiny line, marking her first day here. This way she'd never lose track of time. She would always know exactly how many days had already gone, and how many more there still remained. And that was very important. And she sank onto the filthy straw, and into the sudden sleep of complete exhaustion.

The same assistant jailer brought her gruel the following day. But Clarissa, persevering, again tried to persuade him, with promises of bribes to convey a message for her. The rats during the night had consumed all of the gruel she had left almost untouched the day before, and the man, picking up that emptied dish, and the tin cup, bent out of shape, went out, as glumly silent as before. On the third day, however, it was a younger fellow who came in his stead. The two evidently took turns. The younger assistant jailer walked with a limp, and he seemed kindlier. Clarissa tried to persuade *him*. He remained silent. But when she told him, as she had told the other one, not to mention her name when conveying the message—not that either of them gave any sign of ever *daring* to do such a thing—he glanced around quickly and, lowering his voice, said:

"We don't *know* your name."

She had been most anxious not to have her name so much as breathed, for the simple reason that no matter how cautiously the message might be conveyed there was always the possibility of it being overheard, and the name, Clarissa, catching the eavesdropper's attention, the great-nephews would then surely hear about it in no time. But she had certainly expected the jailers to *know* her name, since a prisoner was always recorded by name in the jail book.

"Not even your sex is designated," the man went on, in answer to her look of amazement.

"But why? *Why?*" Clarissa said.

"You are recorded here by a number," the young jailer told her, mysteriously. "Prisoner Number 17. Which shows how important a prisoner you *are*, the way they're keeping it all so secret. Just talking with you may cost us our heads. So stop trying!"

And with this admonishment, he hastened out.

But Clarissa never ceased trying. Every time one, or the other, of the jailers came in with her starvation portion of gruel and water, she would throw herself upon the man, clutching at his hands, his clothing, his boots, imploring, pleading, promising money, gold. A thousand guineas, two thousand, she'd give him. Once she got out of this place, this horrible cell! She'd *get* the money ... And she would try to use her female charms upon them. Then, realizing that the unkempt state she was in rendered her efforts simply ridiculous, made them laugh, she gave it up. What man would so much as glance at the wild creature she had been transformed into? Her natural beauty concealed, disfigured, by that repulsive shift of coarse sacking. Her hair uncombed, the skin of her face, legs, and arms covered and discolored with grime. And the heavy chain attached to her ankle, the filthy straw pallet, the presence of rats and the smell of lice, the damp half-darkness around, lending her an aspect more animal than human.

The tasteless gruel she now consumed voraciously. And she learned to ration the little water she got in the tin cup. The rats sometimes would overturn it, and then Clarissa knew the torture of thirst. She gave up fighting the lice, catching them with her fingers, squashing them, one after another, swiftly, on her thumbnail. There were too many of them. To be scratching herself continually became a normal procedure. She gave it little thought.

And meanwhile, every single day, she worked hard at making a tiny line on the stone wall with the link of her iron chain. The vertical row of these lines, these pathetic markings, grew speedily. Now and then, she would count them. Always starting with the very first one. One, two, three ... seven ... twenty ... forty-three ... And then suddenly it was eighty. Approximately two and a half months had passed. Only two *weeks* left! And then she'd be hanged. She could feel the rope around her neck. And she screamed. She pounded the wall with her fists. She spat at the jailers, covered them with abuse, cursed them. And while the fit of despair lasted, she would fling the wooden dish, licked clean of gruel with her hungry tongue, at a rat scurrying past. Sometimes she succeeded in hitting the loathsome rodent, and it was a pleasure to hear its squeal of surprise and pain. But then Clarissa sat down on the smelly straw, and thought the situation over. Time was short. Drastic measures were clearly indicated. She racked her brains....

And when the following day the elderly jailer came in, she was very quiet. He had to place the gruel dish and the water cup within her reach, and he now did so, warily, knowing from experience that she might jump at him, in a fury. Slap him, maybe. But she didn't move. Then, as he was about to turn away, Clarissa suddenly said, pronouncing every syllable distinctly:

"Are you a—a Rosicrucian?"

Unhurriedly, as usual, and glumly silent, as always, the elderly jailer went out.

Well, probably the man wasn't a Rosicrucian. Most likely had never even heard of the word. But it was her only remaining hope. After all, according to what *her* Rosicrucian had told her, the most unlikely people were members of their secret society, and in some unaccountable way they all kept in contact with one another.

The next day it was the young jailer who came in. And Clarissa tried the experiment on him.

"Are you a—Rosicrucian?"

His face was blank. Probably he didn't understand what she was talking about. With a shrug, he hurried out.

But Clarissa kept trying. Every time one, or the other, of the jailers came, she asked the man:

"Are you a—Rosicrucian?"

Maybe … maybe, she thought. The question, gradually, became automatic with her.

And then, with only a few days more remaining to her, she was roused in the middle of the night by the glow of a lantern. Blinded almost by the unaccustomed brilliancy of illumination, she blinked her eyes, and suddenly recoiled in horror. Standing beside the young jailer, who held the lantern, was the Spider, the abominable wigmaker, the buyer of human hair from the corpses of the hanged. The young jailer, or maybe the other one, the elderly jailer, or both of them, had apparently noticed the rich abundance of her hair, and they had duly communicated with the Spider and now here he was, to strike the bargain, pay something in advance. The rest of the money they'd get … afterwards.

"Ah, you were right," the untidy, dirty old man said as, coming close with the young jailer, he saw Clarissa's hair in the light of the lantern held obligingly aloft. "A fine head of hair! Even in the condition it is now, one can tell how good the hair is. And of a beautiful color, too. Slightly auburn, eh?"

And the Spider bent down for a closer inspection.

Clarissa shrank away against the wall. Crouched there, with both her arms flung over her head to protect her hair from his sickening touch, she cried out, over and over again:

"No! Not my *hair!* Let them hang me, I don't care … But you can't have my hair! My *beautiful* hair!"

NATALIE ANDERSON SCOTT

"Ah, what a fine head of hair!" the Spider again said. And extending a hand, he picked up a strand to feel the texture with expert fingers. "A masterly job of dyeing has been done on these tresses, a valuable asset nowadays, fashions being what they are. Altogether, exceptionally good hair. And what beautiful wigs I will make with it!"

No wonder everybody in the Thieves' Village hated him as the most dire enemy. All the Spider thought of was their hair, which sooner or later he was certain to get, after they had been hanged. Since his domicile was in the same house where Mr. Davey lived, and Flaxy, and Granny, and the Poet, Clarissa had often had to pass him on the stairs, and always she had shrunk away, in fear, and with a sense of an awful foreboding. But close as he was bending over her now, he naturally failed to recognize her. The way she looked, not even Dumb Clara herself would have known her.

"Very fine hair," the Spider gloated, touching, feeling it, while he chuckled horribly, revoltingly.

"You can't have it!" Clarissa shrieked. "You *won't* have it!"

At last he left her alone, and she collapsed on her pallet of straw, while he haggled with the young jailer over the price. And this agreed on, money passed from the wigmaker's hands into the jailer's, and then the two of them went out, leaving her to rage, and sob, and curse in the darkness. Probably she fell asleep, eventually. And this caused her to lose all sense of time. Because when a light again illuminated the cell, she called out angrily, thinking it was they who had just left returning for some reason:

"Leave me alone. Or this time I'll scratch your eyes out, I promise you!"

"Did you find the document in order, Master Chief Jailer?" a voice said.

412

The voice sounded familiar. Yes, Clarissa *knew* it. Mr. Brummell's. But that was impossible, of course. She was dreaming, hallucinating....

"The document commands me," the chief jailer answered, "to release Prisoner Number 17 into your custody, Mr. Brummell. And it is signed by the Prince Regent. The signature of His Royal Highness is naturally known to me. Yes, the document is in perfect order."

And then another voice spoke, and, like Mr. Brummell's, it also sounded familiar. Clarissa instantly recognized the second voice as belonging to the Rosicrucian.

"Since you are satisfied, Master Chief Jailer," the Rosicrucian was saying, "have your assistant jailer, the elderly one, hasten here immediately with the few articles we shall have need of. He has my instructions."

The chief jailer hurried out, after hanging up the lantern on a hook in the wall. And Mr. Brummell and the Rosicrucian swiftly approached Clarissa, who, sitting up, was staring at them. Strangely enough, it was no hallucination. There stood the quietly elegant Mr. Brummell, holding his glossy beaver, and gloves, in his hand, while he leaned slightly on the slender ebony cane. And the tall figure of the Rosicrucian, beside him, in his long black cloak, and the broad-brimmed black hat, was just as starkly real. Both were visibly shocked by the awful change in her appearance, but they instantly concealed their reaction. Mr. Brummell smiled at her. While the Rosicrucian nodded encouragingly.

"Do not attempt to speak," Mr. Brummell advised her quickly, anxiously. "Try to conserve your strength."

"We must make haste," the Rosicrucian said.

The elderly assistant jailer came in, bringing with him a small bench, on which were ranged, in readiness, a washbowl filled with water, a towel, and a large warm shawl, neatly folded.

Placing the bench on the floor, the man hurried over to the Rosicrucian and, bending a knee respectfully, he raised the hem of the Rosicrucian's cloak to his lips in homage, and said:

"Salaam, Honorable Sir! Salaam!"

"Salaam to you, my Brother," the Rosicrucian answered him graciously.

Then turning to Clarissa he said:

"It was most fortunate that you had thought of asking him whether he was a member. Like the other man, of course, he might not have been. But as it happened, he is. All cases where help is imperative are at once reported to me, and that same night the man sought me out, and the information he gave me left no doubt in my mind that the prisoner in question was yourself. Since the Earl's death, and your sudden disappearance, and knowing that his heirs, the two great-nephews, were bent on doing you harm, I had been trying to find you, but to no avail. Once your whereabouts were known to me, however, I could go to Mr. Brummell and enlist his assistance. And he did the rest."

"I simply told the Prince Regent," Mr. Brummell said, picking up the thread of the explanation from the Rosicrucian at this point, "that an artist friend of mine had gotten himself into some kind of a scrape and that I desired the harmless fellow's release. I then slipped the prepared document for the Prince Regent to sign. And being in a good mood, His Royal Highness attached his signature with a flourish, without even bothering to read the document."

The elderly jailer, meanwhile, producing a big key, freed Clarissa's ankle of the iron ring to which the heavy chain was attached. The ankle was badly bruised and slightly swollen. But the man, taking out of his pocket a little container of ointment and a strip of white cloth, soothed the pain in the marked spot with unguent, and then swiftly bandaged it. The Rosicrucian and

Mr. Brummell then helped her to get up, led her to the bench, seated her there. The jailer threw cold water from the washbowl in her face, and taking up the towel, soaking one end of it, he quickly washed her face for her. And though the grime collected on her skin during the three months' confinement in that horrible cell couldn't be all removed by so simple an operation, it made Clarissa feel wonderfully refreshed.

"And this will give you strength," the Rosicrucian said, giving her to swallow some strange yellow liquid from the little bottle he produced from the deep pocket of his cloak.

The liquid smelled strongly of naphtha, and burned her throat, leaving a bitter taste on her tongue. But it instantly made her weakened blood flow with normal energy through her veins, while the whole of her system was marvelously invigorated. She was then made to sip a small amount of warm broth, which the elderly jailer had hastened to fetch in a cup from his private quarters within the jail.

"For the next few days, partake of nothing but some broth," the Rosicrucian instructed her, "and perhaps a little heated milk. It's the safest diet after enforced starvation."

Mr. Brummell was shaking out the folded warm shawl, and the Rosicrucian then threw it over Clarissa's head and about her shoulders, and she wrapped herself in it. The shawl was large enough to reach down to her insteps, and the ugly shift of sacking was thus completely concealed from sight.

"Will you be able to walk now?" the Rosicrucian asked her.

"Certainly I can walk!" Clarissa assured him.

And she quickly rose. But she had overestimated her strength, for after making a few steps she suddenly staggered, and he had to hold her up. The elderly jailer, however, who had again hurried out, now returned to report that the way was clear, and, with the Rosicrucian and Mr. Brummell supporting Clarissa on either side, they hastened to leave the cell and follow the man. He led the way along several badly lit passages, and to a side door which he swiftly opened and, after letting them through, as soundlessly closed behind them.

A heavy coach, with drawn blinds, stood waiting outside. The fresh air was a shock to Clarissa, and once again she staggered. But this time she was instantly able to control her momentary weakness and, unassisted, stepped into the coach after Mr. Brummell. The Rosicrucian followed her, and taking his place on her other side, pulled the door shut. The coach immediately was in brisk motion. And Clarissa heard both Mr. Brummell and the Rosicrucian heave a sigh of relief.

"I will now explain the situation to you," the latter then said. "To the world in general, the famous Clarissa, the woman who had been the Earl of Strasford's mistress, no longer exists. Having disappeared mysteriously, as everybody knows, on the night of the Earl's demise. And as far as his heirs, the two great-nephews, are concerned," the Rosicrucian went on, "they will *know* that you no longer exist, in something like another four hours, just before the coming sunrise."

"You mean," Clarissa said, "that they will be congratulating themselves *then* on the fact that I have been already hanged."

Her escape had been engineered in the very nick of time. A few hours' delay, and it would have been too late. But the Rosicrucian merely nodded. And he went on:

"They will, of course, make inquiries *after* the supposed event. And the chief jailer then will realize that your release had been obtained by a ruse. But because of the great power which the Earl's evil heirs now wield, since it is they who now pay the Regent's bills and loan him money, the fellow will assure them that he had seen you perish on the gallows with his own eyes, in order to save his own hide from their wrath. He'll take his oath on it. And so will the magistrate who had you thrown into that cell. And the hangman, and the assistant jailers ... In other words, the great-nephews will be satisfied that you no longer exist," the Rosicrucian said. "And to safeguard your life, you must let them think so. You do understand that, Clarissa, don't you?"

"I certainly do," Clarissa said. "Otherwise, they'd be after me again and, being more careful, they'd probably do away with me for sure then!"

"Therefore, you must henceforth assume a different identity," the Rosicrucian instructed her. "A drastic change should be made in your appearance, for one thing ... But perhaps you already have some plan."

"Yes, I have," Clarissa said.

And she did have a plan. And a very definite one. While the Rosicrucian was speaking, Clarissa's mind had been busy casting about for the ways and means of avoiding the pitfalls of her present position, and this plan had gradually evolved itself, and now she was eager to start bringing it into being.

"Where are you taking me?" she asked.

And she tried to peep out through the crack between the drawn blind and the window frame. But the darkness of the night, and the speed of the coach, prevented her from seeing anything.

"Mr. Davey would be glad to put you up, I know," the Rosicrucian said.

Nothing could have suited Clarissa better. The jail being at one end of the city, and the house in which Mr. Davey had his modest abode at the other end, and within a few blocks of the waterfront, they were by now probably halfway to their destination. And then suddenly, through the clatter of their coach wheels over the cobbles, she became aware of the sound of muffled drums.

"Oh, what is *that*?"

And Mr. Brummell, who had been silent till now, said:

"It is the dirge, for Lord Nelson. He was killed in the Battle of Trafalgar, after smashing the French fleet to bits. Napoleon no longer rules the seas, and Nelson fortunately must have realized this before the enemy bullet struck him as, standing on the deck of his flagship, *Victory,* he led his brave men in his last and most glorious attack. Lord Nelson's body has been brought to London and now lies in state. The funeral, which is to be held tomorrow, will be conducted with great pomp and ceremony, of course," Mr. Brummell added quietly.

"Lord Nelson ... killed in battle," Clarissa said. And she thought: and ... and Captain Gray?

But the Rosicrucian, as if guessing her unspoken question, put a hand on her shawl-covered arm, and gave it a quick reassuring pressure. Nothing had happened to "darling Richard." Maybe wounded slightly, a mere scratch.

"And do you know what Lord Nelson's almost last words were?" the Rosicrucian said. " 'Paradise Merton. Happy, happy days ...' That's what he was heard to say, just before the end, as he lay there, on deck, bleeding from that bullet. In his will the cottage had been left to Lady Hamilton, of course."

During Clarissa's last visit to Merton the deed of ownership to the cottage had been legally transferred to Lord Nelson, and now Lady Hamilton would probably have to sell the pretty place, for lack of any other source of income. And Clarissa, naturally, would never see Merton again. To think that so many changes had occurred during her comparatively short imprisonment of three months! While she lay in that horrible cell, completely cut off from the outside world, all these things had been happening, and probably many more, without her knowing anything about it! Clarissa just couldn't get over the stupendous fact. And eagerly she asked for more news.

"Well, for one thing," Mr. Brummell said, "the Princess Caroline was forced to leave the country."

"Oh, no!" Though this was something everybody had expected to happen eventually, Clarissa couldn't help but be sincerely shocked.

"The Prince Regent suddenly remembered that his deposed wife was still in England," Mr. Brummell went on, "and, being in a bad mood, he had the Princess taken under guard to Dover, and put on the boat there, and sent back to Calais, to France, for good. Without allowing her to bid good-by to her child, of course."

The unfortunate Princess Caroline, forever dabbing at her eyes with her wisp of a handkerchief! Never to see her little daughter, the pretty Princess Charlotte, again! Who later, on attaining her fifteenth year, was to marry the heir to the throne of Belgium. Though, naturally, neither Clarissa, nor anyone else, at the moment, could have known anything about such a development.

"And ... other news?" Clarissa prompted eagerly.

"The most important item," Mr. Brummell said, "is that the Duke of Wellington now will be our national hero. Since he's in command of the Allied Armies and it's on land now that Napoleon must be vanquished. Somewhere on the Continent. Meanwhile, there are rumors that Napoleon is planning to march upon Russia. Should he succeed ..."

But the coach had stopped. Clarissa was to be dropped off here swiftly.

"Remember," the Rosicrucian again warned her, "to the world at large, you no longer exist."

"And to further safeguard the secret of your identity," Mr. Brummell said, "should I ever recognize you through your disguise, whatever that might be, I will give no sign of it, Mistress Clarissa." As if he, of all people, ever could, since he had failed so flagrantly once before! The memory of it made Clarissa bubble inwardly with laughter. "Therefore," Mr. Brummell added, "we'll probably never again have the opportunity to speak to one another."

He'd have no one to talk to about Miss Gray, henceforth, he meant. The prospect saddened him acutely.

"Good-by, Mr. Brummell," Clarissa said.

And, turning to the Rosicrucian:

"I'm not going to ask," she told him, "whether I'll ever see *you* again."

"The future, indeed," the Rosicrucian said, "is shrouded in mystery."

Then he pushed the coach door open for her. Clarissa quickly alighted. The coach instantly drove on. And she hurried into the house.

It would be several hours before Flaxy's trained dogs awoke and started barking for their breakfast. The stillness of sleep reigned on and all around the dark narrow stairs. She waited a moment, listening, shivering at the thought of the Spider, who dwelt on the third floor. Then she crept up the stairs to the second-floor landing, and gently knocked on Mr. Davey's door. She didn't have to knock again, for Mr. Davey was a light sleeper, and soon she heard the shuffle of his slippered feet across the floorboards, and the door opened, and she slipped in, and hastily closed the door.

Mr. Davey was small and thin, but because of his black skullcap, his gray hair, and the kindly dignity of his manner, he somehow resembled a little Oriental potentate. Tiny lines radiated at the corners of his gentle mouth, and around his smiling eyes. He didn't recognize Clarissa at once. Then, as she let the shawl slip off her head, he almost dropped the sputtering candle in its tin holder from his wrinkled hand, such was his amazement, disbelief. Evidently he had never expected to see her again.

"I … we … we thought the Earl's heirs," Mr. Davey said, "had had you done away with!"

"And that's exactly what I want 'the two dry sticks,' and everybody else, to *think*," Clarissa hastened to explain.

"Yes, of course. I understand. Or they'd be after you again. But how did you ever manage to make your escape?" Mr. Davey was astounded. "But probably that is a secret and should remain so," he at once added shrewdly. "The important thing is that you are safe. I can just imagine the horrors you've been through, you poor child!" And depositing the candlestick on the table, he put his fatherly arms around Clarissa, and made her welcome. Then, struck by the unkempt condition she was in, he shook his head, clicked his tongue, exclaimed, and said. "You must be deloused, immediately! But do sit down," and Mr. Davey led her to a chair, made her sit down. "You should have a little wine. Some of our sweet holiday wine. I'll bring it."

Clarissa tried to protest. She was anxious for news of Sally, Pete, she told him. What happened to them? Maybe he had heard from them.…

"Yes, yes, of course," Mr. Davey said, staring at her in a curious way. "But first, the wine."

And, with a little chuckle, away he hurried, kitchenward.

The way he got all excited, and consequently rather confused, the dear Mr. Davey! And Clarissa glanced around the familiar room with satisfaction. Half of it served as Mr. Davey's workshop. There, under the window, stood his shoemaker's bench, with the little collection of all the necessary tools. And on the shelves along the walls a great quantity of shoes was ranged, some of them already finished, others in the process of being made. While the material he used was stacked in the corner: small bolts of satin, brocade, of thin and thick leather. And the floor there was strewn with shreds and bits of these materials, since Mr. Davay worked tirelessly, and didn't have the time to be always picking up after himself.

But the other half of the room, where Clarissa sat, was immaculate. And the large table was still covered with a clean white cloth, and on it stood the silver candelabrum which Clarissa had always admired. The preceding day being a Friday, the candles in the candelabrum had been lit and the cloth spread with good things to eat, and Mr. Davey, and his wife and children, all cleanly dressed, and the little boys wearing their black skullcaps, like Mr. Davey's own, they had sat around the table, right after sundown, to commemorate the coming of the Sabbath according to their ancient custom.

But Mr. Davey now was coming back. And he *was* bringing the wine, in a small decanter, and several little glasses. All this he set down on the table. But, right behind him, there appeared ... *No!* It wasn't *possible.* And, yes, it was ... Sally! And, after her, Pete. Sally, on seeing Clarissa, gaped, then she screamed, looked half-demented. While Pete's honest face was almost one idiotic grin. Mr. Davey had purposely not warned them, to give them all a surprise, make them happy. And he stood there, chuckling, watching the commotion that ensued.

Sally, hysterical, had rushed at Clarissa, and her hands clenched into fists, she began to strike at Clarissa with them, while shrieking accusingly:

"We gave you up for dead! We thought the great-nephews had you strangled! You had us scared! How *dared* you scare us so!"

As if it had been all Clarissa's own fault.

"Well, I wasn't sure I'd ever see you again, either," Clarissa told her. "What happened? Did they have the major-domo throw you out?"

And she showered Sally with questions. But Sally answered her with questions of her own. And for a moment there, a regular pandemonium occurred. In the commotion, the shawl had slipped off Clarissa, and Sally screamed:

"Goodness gracious! What's that shift you have on? A potato sack! And you actually *smell!* And your beautiful hair, all matted ... Well, you're certainly a *sight,* I must say!"

And then suddenly, of all things, Yap, yap, yap! And the fluffy little lap dog rushed in. But after one look at Clarissa, failing to recognize her, and with a squeal of fright, back it fled to where it came from. Probably, the kitchen. That's where Sally and Pete would have their makeshift beds, while Mr. Davey was putting them up here.

"To think they let you take that nuisance of an animal with you," Clarissa said. She was astounded.

"And that's about *all* they let me take away with me," Sally cried. "That big lout of a major-domo, I mean. But I better tell you all about it from the beginning." And the general excitement gradually subsiding, Sally went on in a calmer manner:

"Well, first of all, there was Pete, waiting for us with the small carriage around the corner from the Earl's mansion, the way you had ordered him to do. But then, sensing something wrong, he quickly drove the carriage to an inn, and left it there. And that's where it is now," Sally declared proudly, "so at least we saved *that,* thanks to Pete."

"Well, that's something," Clarissa said.

"Of course, you'll have to pay the innkeeper for taking care of the horse, feeding it, and so on," Sally explained. "But he won't charge much.... Well," Sally went on, "after leaving the carriage, Pete hurried back to Grosvenor Square and, concealing himself behind the corner of a nearby house, he watched the mansion, waiting for me to come out. He knew, of course, that *you* were in real danger. But as far as I was concerned, he figured they'd let me go eventually, after a good beating, maybe. And that's exactly what was happening to me, in your bedroom there," Sally said to Clarissa, "after the great-nephews had you taken away. I didn't know just what had happened to you, of course. But I had seen the majordomo grab you by the wrist, before he slammed the door between us, and then, later, when he suddenly comes back to me, and starts slapping me, naturally I understood that something had *already* happened to you. So he slaps me and hits me, and let me tell you," Sally said indignantly, "for days afterwards I was black and blue all over! And then he tells me to get out. And I plead with him to let me take this or that thing with me. But the big pig snatches everything out of my hands, and then just to be rid of me, I guess, he lets me have this homespun skirt and old blouse I used to wear back at Ravisham." To help Mr. Davey's wife with the cooking and the washing she had changed into her old shabby outfit, putting away the gown she was so proud of for a more suitable occasion.

"And then?" Clarissa again prompted her.

"Well, that casket I kept your ribbons in," Sally said, "happened to be right there. So I said to him, 'It's such an *old* thing, of no value, let me take it, *please!*' And after examining it carefully, he shoved the casket at me. But first, he pulled all the ribbons out, just for spite, the lout! And then he *kicks* me out. I picked myself up, and something flies past my face. He had flung the lap dog after me. I thought he'd maimed the poor little angel, but it was all right. And with the casket under one arm, and the lap dog under the other, and clutching the skirt and blouse, I took to my heels, and so out of the house, and then Pete joined me and, right away, we hurried here, and Mr. Davey put us up. I'm glad I got the casket," Sally added, "because you can keep the jewels in it, once you have the jewels back from whoever it was you gave them to for safekeeping."

"But I don't have the jewels, Sally," Clarissa said.

"Well, of course, you haven't got them *with* you," Sally said. "You gave those jewels to someone to keep them for you, to Mr. Davey maybe it was, I don't know. But now you will take them back, and you can sell or pawn a bracelet, and then maybe a ring, and we'll have nothing to worry about! That's what you were saving the jewels for, a rainy day, as they say … You told me so yourself."

"I gave the jewels *away*, Sally."

"I know you did. For *safekeeping*."

"I said, I gave them *away*. Don't you understand?" And Clarissa tried to clarify her meaning. "The person I gave the jewels to isn't supposed to give them back to me. In other words, it is as if I've never had those jewels. And we may as well forget about them."

It was an awful shock to Sally.

"You gave the jewels *away!*" she gasped. She just couldn't get over it. And then she shrieked abuse at Clarissa, "What a *stupid* thing to have done! You must have been *insane!* You, of all people, to give anything *away!* It's fantastic! And I bet I know," Sally tossed her head impudently, "*who* you gave those priceless jewels to. Captain Richard Gray!"

"What difference does it make?" Clarissa said. "And maybe it was foolish of me." But, secretly, she wasn't at all certain that she had been as stupid as it appeared.

"Oh, what are we going to *do!*" Sally wailed. "Because now, you have nothing. *Nothing!* You'll have to start all over!"

"Well, it won't be the first time," Clarissa said. "But now stop your silly noise, Sally. I've had about enough of it!" And to prevent Sally from going into hysterics again, Clarissa hastened to slap the girl's face resoundingly. "There! Or you'd be waking the whole house. And Mr. Davey's wife, and the children."

"Well, naturally, with all this commotion, they did wake up," Mr. Davey interposed soothingly. "But I told them to stay in their room, and try to go back to sleep. Because you, Clarissa, probably have plans to make and business to discuss…. But first, I want you all to have a little of this wine. Let's sit down at the table," and he helped Clarissa draw up her chair. Sally, her face still red from the slap, but feeling much the better for it, though she still gulped a little, took her place next to Pete. "That's right. Like this," Mr. Davey went on, beaming to see them all seated. "Very nice," he kept saying, while busily moving about, filling the little wineglasses he had set in front of his guests.

"Oh, I forgot to tell you," Sally suddenly said, turning to Clarissa. "About your portrait. Just as I was running out of the mansion, I saw a dealer carrying your portrait, with its gilded frame and all, down the steps and to the van. The place was just swarming with dealers, and I heard them discussing your portrait. That it was the first thing the great-nephews sold, and that there was a peculiar condition to the sale. The dealer who bought the portrait could resell it only in the provinces, in some small town or village. So that nobody who could really appreciate a marvelous painting like that would ever see it, or talk about it. And soon it would be even forgotten *whose* portrait it was!"

"My beautiful portrait!" Clarissa said.

"But you mustn't think about it," Mr. Davey told her as, replacing the decanter, he sat down beside her. "Certainly not while we're celebrating your miraculous return. And that's what we're doing, aren't we?" And beaming around at them all, he picked up his wineglass, and raised it to his lips, and sipped.

They all followed suit. The wine had a lovely taste, and it warmed them.

"Is it not a good wine?" Mr. Davey said, proudly. "Our holiday wine."

"Delicious!" Clarissa said.

"And now," Mr. Davey went on, setting down his emptied glass. "If there's anything I can do for you, Clarissa, just say so. While you were at the pinnacle of success and fame as the Earl's mistress, you helped me to prosper by your numerous orders for shoes, and by recommending my work to others. So, now that you have nothing, it's my turn, to be of help to *you*."

"Well, you can start making shoes for me, right away," Clarissa said. "They must be gold shoes. Of gold brocade. A dozen pairs."

"Gold shoes," Mr. Davey repeated, astounded. "Of gold brocade."

And they all stared at her.

There she was, just out of that horrible cell, unkempt, filthy, smelly, her bare feet covered with grime, and the sack shift under the shawl probably crawling with vermin, and—talking about *gold* shoes! It must have sounded ridiculous to them all. If not downright insane.

But undaunted, Clarissa said:

"Gold shoes, yes."

"A dozen pairs?"

"To start with, yes. All the shoes you make for me, from now on, will be gold, of the same gold brocade," Clarissa explained. "Choose the most expensive material you can find."

"Well," Mr. Davey said. "You made good once before, you may make good again. I will start making your gold shoes tomorrow. Anything else?"

"As usual, I'll need the Green Perfume."

Clarissa had debated with herself on the wisdom of using it again, since the scent had been associated with her person while she was the Earl's mistress and, the perfume being unforgettable, it would be instantly recognized, and make people wonder. On the other hand, the famous women on the Continent, among them Napoleon's wife, the Empress Josephine, and the notorious actress Ninon, were known for their use of the Green Perfume, which meant that the scent, priceless though it was, might be bought by more than any one particular person. Besides, Clarissa just couldn't do without the Green Perfume! And so she now decided to take the risk and use it again.

"Very difficult to obtain, as you know," Mr. Davey said. "But I'll get it, of course. Yes, you'll have your Green Perfume in about two weeks."

"That'll suit me fine, because I'll be all ready by then," Clarissa said quite mystifyingly. "But first," she added, "I must find François." The success of her daring plan depended on the assistance of the former chief valet.

"*Find* him?" Sally suddenly cried. And she sputtered with excitement. "Why, we've *already* found him, Pete and I. That's the first thing we did, go looking for François—*he* might know something of what had happened to *you,* we thought. Well, I've heard him telling you, more than once, how he'd like to open a little business of his own, a hairdresser's establishment. So Pete and I, we make the round of all the shops that display a hairdresser's sign, and as we enter one of them, who do we see but François himself! And he's working on a woman customer's coiffure. Was he glad to see us! And when the customer leaves, we have a talk, and, right away, Pete starts working for François, cleaning the place. And Pete could have slept right there, except that Pete," and at this point Sally tittered, "he wanted to be with me, so every night he came here, where I help Mr. Davey's wife with the housework. And that's how we managed not to *starve* while you were away!" Sally declared.

But Clarissa wasn't interested in that. She was already on her feet, hastily pulling the shawl over her head.

"We must go to François at once. While it's still dark. Is his shop very far?"

"It's a very modest place, in a side street," Sally said. "And not far from here."

Jumping up eagerly, Sally ran to the kitchen and returned with the casket and her good silk dress and cap. The latter she could carry herself. The casket she gave to Pete to carry. But they'd have to leave the lap dog here, for the time being, Sally explained to Mr. Davey. Or it might start yapping when outside, and draw attention to them.... Clarissa was already at the door, and there she took leave of Mr. Davey, thanking him for his hospitality. And then Mr. Davey opened the door, and Clarissa, followed by Sally and Pete, crept down the stairs, and stepped out into the street, and the three of them hurried along through the darkness.

On the way they met with no one, and after less than ten minutes' walk the wanted side street was reached, and then François' small shop. But Pete led the way to the back, where there was a little yard, and a light could be seen in a window. The former chief valet, intent on making his recently opened establishment a success, was an early riser. The back door was not locked, and Clarissa walked in, with Sally and Pete hastening after her.

It was strange to see François without his resplendent livery, but dressed, instead, in simple breeches and shirt of dark calico, and wearing over that the hairdresser's short white apron. Nothing, however, had ever seemed strange to François, and though on seeing Clarissa he should have been struck with amazement, he, as usual, evinced no surprise. He simply said:

"I thought Madam had been done away with."

Down and out though she was, and notwithstanding her horribly unkempt appearance, he still called her Madam, respectfully. Which pleased Clarissa no end! She laughed, and then said:

"And that's exactly what everybody must *think*, henceforth. That I no longer exist."

François glanced at her, nodded gravely.

"I understand," he said. "And in that case …"

And he hastened to lock the door, and draw the curtain over the window.

"Madam, doubtless, has some plan," he then said shrewdly.

"Yes," Clarissa told him, "but I must have your assistance, François. For a certain remuneration, naturally. Shall we say, ten percent of my future income?"

"I accept Madam's terms," François said. "But Madam's plan we'll discuss tomorrow. Because," and he took a good look at Clarissa, and then glanced about the room, which though small, and serving as a kitchen, was very, very clean, "Madam must be deloused, immediately!"

And François, at once, became active. Pete was sent to prepare a fire of twigs, out in the yard, and as far as possible from the house. And Sally was to fill the wooden tub with water of as hot a temperature as Clarissa would be able to stand. Since François had to use a lot of hot water in his shop, several large kettles were already bubbling and hissing on the stove. François, meanwhile, briefly disappearing into the shop in the front, returned with some kind of special soap, a large jar of ointment, and several towels. Depositing these articles on the floor beside the tub, which Sally had quickly filled, François approached Clarissa, swiftly removed the shawl, then, taking hold of the ragged hem of her filthy shift, he suddenly pulled the shift up and off over her head. And there Clarissa stood, stark naked, while François, with the utmost composure despite her beautiful nudity, handed the shift and the shawl to Sally, with the order to have Pete burn them instantly.

Sally ran off, and François picked up Clarissa bodily, carried her to the tub, and lowered her into the steaming water.

"Ouch!" The water was so hot Clarissa thought she wouldn't be able to stand it. "I'll be scalded!" she complained. "My skin will come off!"

"Nonsense! Hot water kills lice. See how they're falling off you?"

The water, indeed, was speckled profusely with their microscopic lifeless bodies. Myriads of them!

"And here's where they congregate," François said, starting to soap Clarissa's head and wash her hair.

And another myriad of lice joined the lifeless speckles in the water.

Then François and Sally, who had returned, began to soap Clarissa all over, from her hairline to the tips of her toes. In an instant she was in foams of white lather, while clouds of soapsuds rose over the tub's rim, spilling onto the floor. The soap got in her eyes, in her mouth, and she spat, pleaded for a towel. But François was merciless. She must be soaked thoroughly, he kept repeating. At last, he stood her up in the tub, and she was rinsed with warm water, then rubbed dry with towels. And again François picked her up, nude, but all of her now glowing rosily, and carried her to a cot, which stood in a corner.

"Hot water kills the lice, but it can't exterminate their eggs," he explained, putting Clarissa down, flat on her back. "Only the ointment can do that."

Sally, at his instruction, brought over the ointment jar, and François massaged thick greasy stuff into every inch of Clarissa's skin.

"All this is just preliminaries, of course," he explained, as he worked. "And for the next three days it will be the same. *Then,* the real grooming will begin. Creams, lotions, fragrant oils, milk baths …"

When he finished the ointment treatment, he pulled covers over Clarissa, and said that Sally could sleep on the floor in this room, and he and Pete would make their beds on the floor in the shop. The cot he had given up for Clarissa's use was the only one in the place, but there were enough extra blankets and pillows to make them all comfortable. And then, just before he moved away to start tidying up, François said:

"But now Madam must have her beauty sleep."

How she needed it! Clarissa thought. Yes, *now* she could sleep. Her last waking thought was of Richard Gray. She only hoped she would have her beauty back before he saw her again. And when—oh, when—would that be?

CHAPTER TWENTY-FIVE

T HE FOLLOWING MORNING, right after breakfast, Clarissa, wrapped in the blanket from the cot, and François, already dressed for his work in his shop and wearing his hairdresser's short white apron, sat down at the kitchen table, and Clarissa recounted her plan, and François listened. When she had finished speaking, François thought a moment, and then he said:

"Madam is very clever."

"You think, then, it might come off successfully?"

"With Madam's beauty anything is possible. The plan is ingenious, brilliant, and … daring. If it succeeds it will bring you fame, and wealth. For it has an element of surprise, *and* of suspense, *and*—and this is most important—an element of mystery in it. The public should fall for it. In a big way. Yes, it should be an overwhelming success."

"But why do you say it *should* be, François?" Clarissa asked. "Do you mean it might *not* be … a success?"

"A plan envisaged in the mind," François explained, and tapped his forehead with a finger, "is one thing. Bringing that same plan into execution is quite a different matter. Now," he went on, "the way *I* see it, we shall have two problems. First, to make you look *exactly* as you visualize yourself in this very clever plan. You have a very clear picture of yourself, how you must look, haven't you?"

"Oh, yes, François. I can see myself very clearly," Clarissa said, "and looking quite, quite *different!*"

"So that's our first problem, to change your appearance *drastically,*" François said, "*and* according to your exact specifications. Correct?"

"Absolutely correct."

"Our second problem," François went on, "is to find the right … man. But maybe you already have someone in mind?"

"Well, yes."

"He must be very rich."

"He is."

"And very vain."

"He is that, too."

"As a matter of fact," François said, "I also have a particular man in mind. And *he* answers that description perfectly."

Maybe François was planning to collect his ten percent from both sides; from herself, *and* from the man in question?

"Well," Clarissa said, and she laughed, "since you'll be acting as my procurer, I *might* consider your advice in selecting the man I will need."

"Maybe we're thinking of the same man."

"That's quite possible. Since the choice is limited, for *my* purpose."

"But we'll discuss that later," François said. "Let's consider the first problem *first.*" And he went on, "As I understand it, you will be always clothed in gold."

"Yes, and looking tall and slender. And golden all over. That's how the public must always see me," Clarissa explained.

"Golden all over," François repeated. "Then your hair will have to be dyed—gold. First bleached, of course, and then dyed a beautiful golden color. You want to leave it as long as it is now?"

"The longer the better." And Clarissa turned briefly in her chair, to show François how low down her back her hair rippled.

Without the benefit of occasional trimming during her stay in that jail cell, it had grown quite a lot.

"Golden hair *should* be long," François agreed. "And you will wear it streaming loose like this. Very good. And the gold costume very simple, flowing, highly stylized. And gold shoes."

"I already ordered the gold shoes."

"Very good. What about a piece of gold veiling to be worn thrown over your head and face?" François suggested. "The most transparent veiling *does* conceal the features to a certain degree, you know."

"I was thinking of that," Clarissa said.

"Then have it, by all means. It will add just the right touch of secrecy to the air of mystery in which your person will be enveloped from now on. And what about make-up?" François added. "Since the natural tints of your skin are so vivid, I would advise just a little lip salve, nothing else."

"Oh, François," Clarissa exclaimed, delighted, "you read my thoughts! And is there such a thing," she went on eagerly, "as gold powder?"

"None on the market, but I can make it," François promised. "A light dusting of gold powder over your face, neck, and arms ..."

"Over *all* of my body," Clarissa interposed gravely, "since the audience, towards the end of the performance, will be seeing me stark naked. Except for a narrow loin belt, of gold mesh and dripping with pearls."

"That's right," François said. "As I understand it, from your recount of this remarkable plan of yours, you will appear at one end of the stage, a golden vision of trailing draperies, and, very slowly, you will begin to walk back and forth, in front of the footlights. And then, slowly again, you peel off one long golden glove, and let it drop. And then the other glove. Next, you shed the gold mantle. Then, the gold bodice, the skirt … Then, the exquisite, *intimate,* underclothing. And there you stand, completely in the nude, except for the gold mesh loin belt, dripping with pearls. And, you start to unfasten it. The audience holds its breath. You have unfastened the tantalizing belt, you're about to shed it … When, suddenly and swiftly, the curtain descends, and all the lights in the theater go on. The furore, the excitement, the shouts, the mad applause!" And François was silent a moment, visualizing the scene very vividly. Then, gravely, he declared, "You will be a sensation!"

"I think so," Clarissa agreed, quite calmly.

"Disrobing in public, on the *stage,*" François went on, staring at her in respectful wonder. "Nothing like that has ever been done anywhere in the world! You will be the *first.* Yes, the first to tease the senses of the audience by stripping yourself naked, right before their eyes! It is really extraordinary! Madam is an innovator!"

"Well, right now," Clarissa laughed, "I haven't even a shift to wear. You'll have to advance me some money, François."

"Why, of course." François was very businesslike about it. "I will take your measurements, and order the gold outfit at once. The tradespeople know me; I can get all the credit we need. And I'll get you something to wear around the house. From now on, remember," François pointed out, "you must stay in seclusion. Never venture out."

"Yes, nobody will ever see me, *except* on the stage. So just get me some peignoirs, a dozen or so. And very expensive ones."

"The best," François promised. "But," he instantly added, his mind working very swiftly, "has Madam thought of a name for her new self? Everybody will be asking, Who is she? Who *is* she?! The name should be aptly descriptive, and yet intriguing, and somewhat carnal."

"The Golden Trollop," Clarissa said. She had the name all prepared.

"The Golden Trollop," François repeated slowly, tasting the name on his tongue, weighing it in his shrewd mind. "The Golden Trollop. Couldn't be better," he announced. "Perfect! In no time," he solemnly predicted, "this name, the Golden Trollop, will be famous throughout London, and therefore throughout the nation. It will be on everybody's lips. Popular songs will be made and sung by people in the streets, in the taverns, about the Golden Trollop. But the woman will remain a mystery, a closely guarded secret. And that will only whet the public's appetite...."

It was obvious that the more François mentally studied Clarissa's daring scheme, the less doubts he had about its eventual success.

"And now," he said, "let's consider our second problem. Finding the man who will make it all possible."

"Buy the theater for my performances," Clarissa, starting to enumerate the items she had in mind, used her right hand to bend a finger of her other hand. "And provide for its upkeep, on a grand scale," she bent another finger. "Then, advance publicity, advertisements ... Huge placards on the walls of the buildings. And costumed criers on street corners to announce, with a preliminary flourish of trumpets, the date of the opening." And she bent yet another finger.

"Such lavish publicity alone will cost the man a small fortune," François put in.

"Then," Clarissa went on, and she bent one more finger, "a very handsome allowance for me. And installing me in his unofficial residence," and she bent the last, the little finger of her left hand. Then, realizing that she had used up all the fingers of that hand, she laughed, and then said, "Mr. FitzMaurice is the man

I have selected. But probably it was he you had in mind also, François, wasn't it?"

"Naturally," François said. "Because Mr. FitzMaurice is known to be more vain than any nobleman. He wouldn't be satisfied by merely having a mistress, no matter how beautiful, or popular, the woman might be. He'd want someone who is acclaimed by a wider public, by the man in the street—an actress. That's the kind of glory Mr. FitzMaurice desires to bask in. And you, madam, as the Golden Trollop, will be an answer to his wildest dreams!"

"And is Mr. FitzMaurice as wealthy as he was before my disappearance?" Clarissa wanted to know, just to be absolutely sure. Because of the war, as Captain Gray had often explained to her, fortunes were not only made overnight, but lost, too, and just as suddenly.

"Wealthier than ever, Mr. FitzMaurice is," François instantly reassured her. "His speculations on the Exchange are the talk of London. A financial wizard, they now call him. Has the magic touch, or so everybody says. Mr. FitzMaurice is the very man for you. Indubitably!"

"You can approach him then, immediately," Clarissa said. "He'll want to see and appraise me, of course."

"I will arrange for Mr. FitzMaurice to view you, appropriately in the nude, and from behind a curtain," François explained. "That will make him all excited and he'll forget to bargain about terms. Ten days from now, you'll be perfectly groomed, and as beautiful as ever. So I'll have the appointment made accordingly, when I see him tonight. I know his valet, and the man will arrange it for me, somehow."

And then there was a tinkle of the little bell from the front door of François' shop, and François, getting up, hurried there to take care of the customer. And almost immediately afterwards the back door opened, and Sally and Pete, who had been sent to the market, came in, carrying a basket with the purchased provisions. Clarissa ordered Pete to go and help François, maybe by soothing the waiting customers with cheery talk, since the women always got so irate when forced to wait their turn at a hairdresser's establishment. Sally, meanwhile, hastening to put the provisions away neatly, quickly prepared Clarissa's hot soap bath. And that day, and the next, obeying François' instructions, Clarissa took the required number of these beneficial baths, each of them followed by Sally rubbing into her skin the greasy ointment for the extermination of the lice's stubborn eggs. And François, on shutting up shop, after a day's hard work, absented himself nightly, to pay hurried calls on the tradesmen, the dressmakers, explaining, arguing, bargaining. From tiny samples of materials he brought home with him, Clarissa made her choice, very carefully, of the silks, satins, brocades, cobwebby veiling, and shimmering gauzes, all of the same lovely golden color, and by the fourth day, when François began the process of grooming Clarissa from head to foot, some twenty dressmakers and fifty sewing girls were already busy making the Golden Trollop's outfit, hurrying, working nights instead of sleeping, to have it finished on time.

And how Clarissa's skin, hardened by the grime of that filthy cell, and then made tender by the hot soap baths, welcomed the soothing applications of the creams, lotions, pomades, and oils! Sniffing delightedly at the emollients' delicious fragrances, Clarissa gave herself up completely into François' expert hands, and blissfully relaxed, resting, she would frequently doze off, while François diligently massaged her legs, stomach, her back, arms, and breasts, and the soles of her pretty feet. Milk baths followed. And Clarissa's beauty gradually bloomed anew. Like a rose that had been drenched with dew, her beauty emerged from the tireless treatments, refreshed and glowing, more radiant than it had ever been before.

François also had to attend personally to fitting the golden outfit on Clarissa. He brought it home, with Pete's help, concealed in wrappings of silk sheets, and had Clarissa put it on, so he could mark with pins the few places to be taken in. Then the outfit was immediately returned to the dressmakers and, under François' direction, the infinitesimal tucks were quickly stitched, and he could again bring the golden creation home, this time to be hung up, protected by the silk sheets, in a cubbyhole of an extra room which the former chief valet's modest little place boasted of. The first pair of gold shoes fashioned by Mr. Davey's artistic hands had already been delivered, also, by the boy Flaxy, who had, besides, brought the lap dog, to Sally's hysterically idiotic delight. Clarissa, however, was too preoccupied to argue with the girl about the fluffy animal's bothersome presence. Everything is ready, Clarissa told herself. Everything! *Except* changing the color of her hair. The prospect both excited her, and filled her with misgivings. Would she look good as a blonde? She was very worried. And it made her irritable.

But on the day prior to Mr. FitzMaurice's scheduled visit, François kept his shop closed, in order to spend the daylight hours in transforming her into a blonde. His face grave, but his hands perfectly steady, he set to work. First he bleached Clarissa's hair, very thoroughly. Then, after testing on a wig, the several shades of the dye he had prepared, he began to apply the selected shade, with a little brush, to her hair, strand by strand, starting at the roots, and then drawing the brush firmly down the length of the hair, and over the ends. It took hours! But François was remarkably patient. And he wouldn't let her consult the mirror, not once, no matter how furious Clarissa got. Not until the tedious process was finished, and the hair dried, and a rosy pomade applied to it. Then François held the mirror for her, and Clarissa gasped. She looked lovely as a blonde! Really lovely! And it was a new experience. This vision of golden loveliness, staring back at her from the mirror, was herself! Clarissa just couldn't get over it. She was thrilled.

"Whatever would I do without you, François?" she exclaimed.

And, as a mark of her appreciation, she put out a hand, and with a fingertip stroked the little black mustache on François' upper lip.

"Well," François said, "the ten percent I will be getting from all the moneys Madam will receive will help my hairdresser's shop to prosper, to expand even, perhaps." Very businesslike François was, always.

"Oh," Clarissa said, and she pretended to pout. "What's that heap of dark material in the corner there?" she added, pointing. "I saw you bring it with you last night, but I forgot to ask."

"That dark material will serve as a curtain to divide this room into two parts," François explained. "I'll set it up tomorrow."

And that's exactly what he did the following day, after they had hurried through their evening meal. First, standing up on a bench, he stretched a rope across the room and close to the ceiling, attaching either end of the rope to a large nail he had previously hammered into each of the opposite walls. Then, with Pete helping him, he slipped the piece of dark material, the size of a huge sheet, over the rope. The result was a tolerably decent curtain, stretching from the ceiling down to the floor. But François hadn't finished yet. He always carried with him, in the pockets of his hairdresser's short white apron, the tools of his trade: a collection of combs of various sizes, and several pairs of scissors of different shapes. And now, producing a pair of scissors with flat sharp blades, François suddenly slashed the curtain along the center, from where it touched the floor and as far up towards the ceiling as he could reach.

"This way," he explained to Clarissa, "both Mr. FitzMaurice and I can discreetly part the curtain, and watch you, while sitting comfortably on our chairs."

And to illustrate his point François at once placed two kitchen chairs, close together, on one side of the curtain. Then, fetching from the shop the only cushioned chair there was, he placed it in the center of the other part of the room. Clarissa, who stood all ready, with her newly golden hair rippling down her back and about her shoulders, and her face and arms, and the rest of her body, dusted lightly with gold powder, and wearing a transparent peignoir, immediately sat down, and assumed a reclining pose. François placed a footstool at a certain distance from the chair, and Clarissa, her lovely legs stretched out tantalizingly, rested her feet on the stool. And Sally, who, wearing her good silk cap and gown, and armed with a nail buffer, also stood there, ready, hastened to sit down on the floor, at Clarissa's feet, prepared to polish her toenails. François then handed Clarissa a small gilded comb.

"You'll be combing your golden hair, while your maid polishes your toenails. That will make the scene look perfectly natural," he said. "Open your peignoir, let the hem of it trail along the floor casually. That's right. Excellent! I will now move the table with the lamp a little closer...." And as François swiftly did so, the bright light shone straight on Clarissa, illuminating her golden loveliness.

It was nine-thirty. Mr. FitzMaurice was to arrive at ten. But made excited by François' shrewdly veiled promises of something absolutely extraordinary, marvelous, sensational, and by the air of secrecy with which the former chief valet conducted the negotiations, the portly Mr. FitzMaurice, with his quizzing glass dangling on a black ribbon from his lace-cravated short neck, might become so impatient as to find himself at the door of the hairdresser's shop much earlier.

And sure enough, there was the tinkle of the little bell. François, disappearing behind the curtain, hurried to the front door. While Clarissa instantly began to comb her golden hair, and Sally to polish Clarissa's toenails with the buffer. Neither of them glanced once towards the curtain, and both seemed wholly intent on what they were doing.

Clarissa heard the front door opening, closing, and François' lowered voice greeting the visitor. Then the sound of their tiptoe-ing into the kitchen, and to the chairs on that side of the curtain, and the faint rustle of Mr. FitzMaurice's rich attire, as they cautiously sat down. By straining her ears, Clarissa could listen to the conversation conducted in whispers.

"Nobody knows you are here?" François asked.

"I have kept the whole affair secret," Mr. FitzMaurice assured him, "even from my friend, Lord Cavor."

"The Golden Trollop insists on utter secrecy," François confided. "The creature is capricious. Naturally, she can afford to be, because of her indescribable beauty. Should she be crossed in her slightest whim, she's liable to ... well, just go off somewhere!"

It was good salesmanship, of course. But Clarissa, listening, hoped François wasn't overdoing it, or he might frighten Mr. FitzMaurice away.

"No, *no*," that portly gentleman implored, however. "Everything will be done as the Golden Trollop desires. Everything. Tell her, assure her. *Please* ..." And anxious, excited, impatient, breathing hard, his quizzing glass held in readiness, Mr. FitzMaurice said, "But you promised to show her to me. Just a peep ... This suspense is unbearable!"

"Very well. But I beg you to realize, sir," François then went on, "that the woman you're about to see is of such beauty as men meet with only in their dreams! Therefore, prepare yourself."

"I am prepared! Hurry up …"

"You will be amazed!" And with these words, François parted the curtain a couple of inches.

Clarissa heard Mr. FitzMaurice give a gasp. The famous wizard financier was flabbergasted. Bereft of his voice for a while. Then:

"Extraordinary! Marvelous! Truly, the Golden Trollop. She will be a sensation!"

"Remark the roundness of the breasts," François said in the sugar tones of a procurer displaying his live merchandise.

"Yes, yes."

"The indolent line of the thigh."

"Exquisite! Quite."

"Be kind enough to observe that the stomach is flat and very smooth."

"Yes. I can see that."

"Even her instep is a delight to behold!" François went on, warming to the theme. "I would describe it as *aristocratic*. And since the antecedents of the Golden Trollop are unknown even to me, it is quite possible.…"

But Mr. FitzMaurice was sniffing at the air around. Clarissa had sprinkled the Green Perfume on her own person, and about the kitchen. And Mr. FitzMaurice's shrewd nose had detected the perfume, and he was sniffing at it.

"This scent …" he said. "I seem to recognize it. Yes, of course. The mistress of the late Earl of Strasford, the famous Clarissa, always used it. The Green Perfume."

"It is also used by the Empress Josephine," François was quick to point out, "and the French actress Ninon."

"That's true," Mr. FitzMaurice had to admit.

"The Green Perfume," François went on, "is the perfume of all famous and beautiful women. Therefore, it was only natural that the Golden Trollop, being of their number, should also select it for her use."

"And it becomes her more than any of the others," was Mr. FitzMaurice's sincere comment, as with the help of his quizzing glass he continued to admire Clarissa, while François held the curtain parted slightly.

"But what exactly happened to this woman, Clarissa, you just mentioned?" François asked casually. "Everybody knows, of course, that she was done away with, secretly...."

"She was hanged."

"Is that really so?"

"Fact. I had it from the great-nephews themselves," Mr. FitzMaurice confided, proud of his close acquaintanceship with the powerful pair.

"Well, this Mistress Clarissa, as she was called, was beautiful, of course," François said. "But not to be compared with the Golden Trollop, don't you think?"

"No comparison at all!" Mr. FitzMaurice declared, studying Clarissa through his quizzing glass and panting with excitement. "For one thing," he went on emphatically, "this woman is a gorgeous blonde. Such beautiful golden hair!"

"Yes, the color *is* different," François agreed.

"And she is taller."

"I suppose she is."

"Certainly! And more slender."

"You're very observing, Mr. FitzMaurice, sir." Flattering him.

"Thank you. And then, this woman's skin is so *fair!* So very fair ..."

The gold powder, Clarissa thought listening. It had toned down the naturally vivid tints of her skin quite a bit.

"She is truly golden all over," Mr. FitzMaurice enthused. "The Golden Trollop! She *will* be a sensation."

"She *is* a sensation, already," François pointed out.

"The whole of London talks of nothing else, that's true," Mr. FitzMaurice conceded.

Which was a fact, as Clarissa well knew from François' daily reports to her of the public's reaction to the advance publicity and advertisements he had been able to launch on credit. Thanks to the reputation for trustworthiness established by him among the tradesmen during his years of service with the late Earl. And the huge placards, bearing the name, the Golden Trollop, and pasted on the walls of the buildings throughout the city, and the costumed criers, with their trumpets, announcing on street corners the Golden Trollop's advent, had already made her famous.

"I have secured the theater, by providing a small down payment, my own money," François went on. "In Drury Lane, popular location for a fashionable audience. Every seat sold out for tomorrow night, the opening performance. Thousands had to be turned away." And having thus presented a most tempting picture to the wizard financier's socially ambitious mind, François added, "The accumulated bills, of course, must be paid first thing tomorrow morning."

"A fortune. A fortune!" And Mr. FitzMaurice shrewdly pretended hesitancy, indecision.

"Pay them, and you will enter the theater tomorrow night to be acclaimed, even before the raising of the curtain, as the protector of the Golden Trollop!"

"A fortune!" Mr. FitzMaurice groaned.

But Clarissa, combing her golden hair, feeling his greedy glance on her nakedness, was aware that the portly gentleman was weakening.

"Imagine yourself," François went on, "the center of attention, an object of universal envy."

"Ah, yes!"

"The Prince Regent will ask you to dine with him."

"Aaaah …!"

"You may find yourself sitting *right next* to Mr. Brummell, at that dinner."

"Beau Brummell, *himself!* Ah …"

"The Duke of Cumberland will give one of his famous balls in your honor."

"The luxurious Duke … Oh, dear!"

And Mr. FitzMaurice groaned, panted, produced a silk handkerchief, and mopped his perspiring brow. Then he said, angrily:

"The monthly allowance you're demanding for the Golden Trollop is exorbitant. Exorbitant!"

"The street urchins," François went on, "will be running after your carriage, shrieking, 'Mr. FitzMaurice who owns the Golden Trollop! Mr. FitzMaurice who owns the Golden Trollop!' I'm only telling you the simple facts," François explained innocently. "Even *they* will know you, the street urchins, I mean."

"I suppose you're right," Mr. FitzMaurice said, and he sighed. Then he suddenly asked, "And if I *don't* accept your fantastic terms? And all those bills are *not* paid tomorrow morning? *You'll* be held responsible, since the money for that publicity, and everything else, was advanced to *you,* my good man, yes. The creditors will be here in no time, ready to tear *you* to pieces!" And there was something frightening about the portly wizard of a financier as he said this. His true nature was suddenly bared: malicious, cruel, merciless.

And Clarissa, listening as she steadfastly continued combing her golden hair on the other side of the curtain, shuddered on François' account. Poor François had taken such a terrific gamble on her! And now Mr. FitzMaurice had him in his clutches, as he doubtless had everybody else. Hence his millions ...

"Quite a predicament you'd be in, wouldn't you?" Mr. FitzMaurice went on. "No, you'll have to reduce your terms considerably," he declared. "And even then I'd be doing you a favor, fellow."

"But Mr. FitzMaurice, sir," François protested, speaking quietly and with the utmost respect, "you're not the only person I approached!"

"But you told me ..."

"Because of my admiration for your financial genius," François hastened to explain, "I felt obliged to give you the privilege of a first offer, naturally. But," François lied boldly, "I have several gentlemen lined up, every one of them ready to grab the chance of possessing the Golden Trollop. Gentlemen known to you."

"Who? Who? Name them!"

"Well, Lord Cavor, for one."

Extreme social rivalry marked the friendship of the portly pair, and now Mr. FitzMaurice, shaking with jealousy, almost screamed:

"Lord Cavor! But he can't afford it!"

"He has a title," François reminded him. "Which means that the moneylenders would be glad to give him unlimited credit."

Since this was a fact, Mr. FitzMaurice had to give up haggling over terms, or face the risk of having the Golden Trollop snatched away from under his very nose by his friend Lord Cavor.

"Well," he said, instantly affable, polite, smiling. And adjusting his quizzing glass, he again admired Clarissa through the slightly parted curtain. "Extraordinary! Marvelous! She *will* be a sensation."

Then, getting up, the portly financier followed François out of the room, and into François' shop, to discuss the details of the arrangement.

And Sally, tired of polishing Clarissa's toenails over and over again, immediately whispered;

"Can I stop now?"

"No," Clarissa whispered back. "Continue as before. They may come back."

They both continued as before. But soon Clarissa heard the front door close on the visitor, and then François hurried in.

"Well," Clarissa demanded, sitting up and wrapping the peignoir about her, "did Mr. FitzMaurice agree to all conditions I insisted on?"

"He will be naturally bombarded with questions as to *how* he came to discover the Golden Trollop, *where*, and so forth, but he will preserve an utter silence," François explained. "The deeper the mystery around the Golden Trollop, the greater her fame. And the prestige of her protector will increase accordingly. Mr. FitzMaurice is shrewd enough to understand this. Madam has nothing to worry about. I also advised him," François added, "as to the procedure tomorrow night, and he will have it all arranged."

And so the following night, Clarissa, her golden hair and the gold outfit and gold shoes completely hidden under the long dark cloak with a hood, and followed by Sally, carrying a small box which contained Clarissa's make-up, slipped out the back door of François' modest place, hurried around to the street, and walked swiftly for some half a dozen blocks, without attracting the slightest attention from the passers-by. Then, with Sally, she waited on a corner previously agreed upon. A large coach, with blinds drawn, drove up. Dark hooded cloaks, of the same strange foreign silk of which Clarissa's cloak was fashioned, concealed the attire of the coachman, and of the two big menservants who stood on a step at the back of the coach. Clarissa hastened to enter it, as Mr. FitzMaurice, sitting inside, quickly opened the door for her, and then closed it, after Sally had followed her in.

Having taken her place between them, Clarissa instantly shed her hooded cloak. And there she sat, a vision of shimmering golden loveliness. *Now* she was the Golden Trollop! Mr. FitzMaurice, simultaneously, raised the blinds. And the coachman, and the two menservants at the back, had, at the same time, shed *their* cloaks. The coachman was a Hindu, dressed in scarlet, and wearing a pale green turban on his coal-black hair. The two menservants were big Africans, their skin the color of mahogany. Naked to the waist, with gold hoops in their ears, they wore voluminous trousers of scarlet silk, trailing sashes of a brilliant blue, and both were armed with shining scimitars.

The metamorphosis accomplished in the space of a minute, the coach, drawn by a pair of beautiful black steeds, at once drove on. But now it attracted everybody's attention. Crowds collected on the sidewalks, to stare, gape, and people ran after the coach, and pointed their fingers at it, and at the golden vision of Clarissa visible inside, and cried out, and screamed, and shouted excitedly, "The Golden Trollop!" "The Golden Trollop!" "Here she is, at last!" "Isn't she beautiful!" "No wonder she must be guarded by those big Africans, with the scimitars!" "Yes, or she'd be *mobbed!*"

And they dared not come too close. But they all caught a glimpse of the Golden Trollop, and were struck by the beauty of the woman's face, as seen through the gold veiling, which also partly covered the golden hair, rippling down her back and shoulders. Clarissa's skin, dusted lightly with gold powder, blended exquisitely with the color of her hair and her shimmering gold attire. Golden all over! the people marveled.

The portly Mr. FitzMaurice, seated beside her, acknowledged their acclaim of her by bowing, waving his hand. His vanity gratified beyond his wildest dreams, the financier's thick face was wreathed in cloying smiles. He was really comical, Clarissa thought. She, on the contrary, made no response to the people's voluble admiration. She never smiled. She was aloof, mysterious, bored perhaps. That's how the Golden Trollop should be. And the people loved it. While Clarissa laughed to herself. What clever publicity can do for one! They didn't even know whether she'd be any good on the stage, and yet she was already famous.

The crowd around the theater was so immense that constables had trouble clearing the way for the coach. When Mr. FitzMaurice helped Clarissa out, and then led her up the steps to the side entrance, the crowd gasped, like one man, and then a great shout rose, "The Golden Trollop!" But Clarissa had already disappeared behind the door, which led straight behind stage. And here the theater manager, and the stagehands, met her with the respect due an established celebrity. Her pretty dressing room was right there, conveniently in the wings. Clarissa sat down for a few minutes to rest, then, leaving Sally to arrange the make-up on the little table, she went to look at the audience through a slit in the big curtain.

And what a brilliant audience it was! All the fashionable people were there, come to see the Golden Trollop. Standing in the center aisle, near the fifth row, where he had his special seat, was the Prince Regent. Mr. Brummell was with him. And the Duke of Cumberland. And several other fops. And then Clarissa, through her peephole, saw Mr. FitzMaurice enter the theater, all the heads turning to look at him, the protector of the Golden Trollop. He was being congratulated, and His Royal Highness, as a mark of his sudden favor, gave him two of his fat fingers to shake. And then spoke to him graciously. Probably inviting Mr. FitzMaurice to dine with him. The wizard financier, judging by the idiotic expression on his face, was in seventh heaven!

Not a single court lady present, however. Because the Golden Trollop's performance on the stage had been heralded as something vulgar, even a little obscene, the hypocrites had proudly stayed away. But all the mistresses were there. Most of them Clarissa knew, of course, and she now laughed to herself, as she watched the stupid women already tearing their wisps of handkerchiefs to shreds with envy and rage at the Golden Trollop. Wait till you *see* her! Clarissa told them mentally. You'll hate her even more than you hated Clarissa, the Earl's mistress!

And then it was time for her to walk out onto the stage. Clarissa had rehearsed her act very carefully, many times. She could do it in her sleep. There was nothing to it, really. And so, as the curtain rose, she simply stepped out onto the stage, and began to walk slowly, beautifully, back and forth, in front of the brilliant footlights. Peeling off, nonchalantly, one long golden glove, then the other. Then shedding the gold mantle, as she walked. Then the gold bodice, the skirt, while walking all the time. Disrobing herself, gradually, to the sounds of exciting music that came from the invisible violins in the musicians' pit. And suddenly Clarissa stood there, completely naked except for the narrow loin belt of gold mesh and dripping with pearls. Then she began to unfasten the belt. Such a hush of suspense had settled on the audience that if a pin dropped it would have been heard. She had almost unfastened the belt ... When, suddenly and swiftly, the curtain came down.

The applause that broke out was deafening. The Golden Trollop's success was instantaneous, tremendous. Clarissa could hear the fops jumping up, stamping their feet, shouting, imploring her to show herself, even if for an instant. She could have had hundreds of curtain calls, but adamant despite the excited manager's pleas, she simply picked up her gold garments, and hurried to the dressing room to put them on. The less they see me, the more they'll value me! Clarissa very acutely reasoned.

Altogether, Clarissa was highly satisfied. But the most important thing, of course, was that 'the two dry sticks,' the great-nephews, because of their reputation for extreme respectability, would never come to see such a vulgar performance. It was with this in view that Clarissa had created the character of the Golden Trollop, and her somewhat obscene act on the stage. To keep the two great-nephews away. Since Clarissa was planning to stay in seclusion, except for her trips to the theater and back, they would never see her, and she would never see them. She was safe!

The portly Mr. FitzMaurice, blabbering with appreciation of her success—he'd be like putty in her hands henceforth, Clarissa could see—then joined her, to lead her out triumphantly to the waiting coach. Again the acclaim of the immense crowd outside, as the excited, pushing people caught a glimpse of the Golden Trollop before she stepped into the impressive vehicle, with its turbaned Hindu coachman and the scimitar-armed African attendants. Again people running in its wake in the hope of getting yet another fleeting glimpse of her shimmering golden vision.

She was driven straight to Mr. FitzMaurice's "unofficial residence," a big old house, massive and strangely gloomy. The interior, as the financier, after helping her out of the coach, led Clarissa in proudly, proved even more gloomy. The furnishings, however, though heavy, were luxurious. And the rich oriental silks, huge ornamental vases, and chests of ebony inlaid with mother-of-pearl, or encrusted with precious stones, testified to the owner's extensive travels in distant lands. The elderly dignified menservants, lined up in the entrance hall to greet Clarissa, bowed very low, very respectfully. But she was struck by their utter silence, and Sally, walking on Clarissa's other side, whispered to her quickly:

"Gives me the creeps, this place does, honest!"

But Mr. FitzMaurice hastened to lead Clarissa up the ornate staircase, and into the apartments prepared for her. The rooms were luxurious, and Clarissa's bedroom truly magnificent.

"Since this was madam's opening performance," Mr. FitzMaurice said, "madam is doubtless fatigued. I will therefore leave madam to have her rest."

"I appreciate your consideration, Mr. FitzMaurice, sir," Clarissa said, thinking with painful yearning of Richard Gray. "Yes, I *would* like to rest."

And she curtsied gracefully, while Mr. FitzMaurice bowed. Then he hurried away.

It was a delight to sleep once again between silk sheets, on the down-filled mattresses, under satin quilts, and, in the morning, to have her hot chocolate.

But Sally, who had brought in the tray, was chattering excitedly, hurrying her to come and see something immediately. Sally had been exploring the place, and she had discovered a little staircase which led to the third floor, and from a window there one could see the little house, built at the end of the shady garden.

"The pretty dwelling can't be seen from any of the other windows," Sally explained, "and that proves that Mr. FitzMaurice is trying to hide the existence of this young slave girl. There she was, sitting on a bench outside the little house, and playing on some kind of musical instrument, shaped like a mandolin."

Clarissa set her chocolate cup down and, wrapping her peignoir about her, followed Sally out of the room, and into a side passage, and into what looked like a closet there. But the closet was a sham. For behind some dark hangings inside, there was concealed the beginning of the little staircase. Nobody except Sally, with her insatiable curiosity, would have thought of looking behind those hangings, which as a rule protected a closet from the dampness the stone walls oozed. Clarissa hurried up the stairs after Sally, who then led her to a small window. The garden below was shady with trees and overgrown with shrubbery, and at the end of it Clarissa could see the little house and, sitting on the bench outside, the young slave girl, dark-skinned, wearing a blue sari, white flowers in her coal-black hair, and playing gently on a mandolin-like instrument.

"Isn't she lovely?" Sally whispered. "And so young … Do you think she is being kept here by force, against her will? She looks so sad."

"Just plain homesick, more likely," Clarissa said. She couldn't place the slave girl's nationality. Probably some strange race of the East. "But she looks well cared for, pampered even," Clarissa went on. "Maybe her people were able to render some service to Mr. FitzMaurice, during his travels, and then, if something happened to them, all of them killed maybe, well, he had to take care of her, I suppose."

"Or she might even be his own daughter," Sally said. "I was thinking of that."

"That's quite possible, too," Clarissa agreed.

And as they watched, a black serving-woman came out of the little house, and offered the young slave girl some luscious fruit from a wooden bowl. But the lovely girl merely shook her head. She went on plucking at her musical instrument with her dark-skinned fingers, gently, sadly.…

"Isn't it thrilling, though?" Sally whispered. "We can come here, now and again, and watch her. Don't you think we can?"

"Yes, but we better go now, before one of those silent menservants catches us here."

And Clarissa led the way down the little staircase, and back to her own apartments.

The following night, on bringing her back from the theater after her performance, Mr. FitzMaurice accompanied Clarissa to the threshold of her bedroom, and then, with the words, "I will rejoin madam in a few minutes," he let her go in alone. Thus giving her a chance, in the most polite fashion, to prepare herself properly for his visit.

Swiftly, with Sally's help, Clarissa exchanged her gold outfit for her prettiest peignoir. Hurrying over to the mirror, she drew a comb through her golden hair, applied fresh lip salve, put a dash of Green Perfume behind each of her ears, and between her breasts, and sprinkled the perfume all around. Then, sending Sally out of the room, she jumped into bed and, assuming a very enticing pose, reclined there against the silk cushions.

The portly Mr. FitzMaurice quietly entered. Drawing a chair close to the bed, he sat down and, admiring her through his quizzing glass, he began a pleasant conversation, repeating what the Prince Regent had said of her—"Where has the woman been hiding her so very ravishing charms, pray?" were His Royal Highness' exact words. And what Lord Cavor had said. And all the other fops … A perfect gentleman, Clarissa thought. Paying me compliments before getting into bed. And she smiled at him alluringly. Mr. FitzMaurice, thus encouraged, told her the latest gossip, mentioned some war news, the Duke of Wellington's plans against Napoleon, and his own financial exploits on the stock exchange, which also had a direct influence on the progress of the war. After about fifteen minutes of such polite talk, Mr. FitzMaurice rose, bowed, and, bidding her a respectful good night, he quietly went out, leaving Clarissa to stare after him with her mouth wide open in amazement.

Then, the truth dawning on her, she began to laugh. She threw her head back, and laughed till the tears streamed down her lovely face. She laughed so hard that Sally, alarmed, rushed in from the room adjoining.

"What is it? What happened?" And glancing around, surprised at not finding Mr. FitzMaurice there, "Where *is* he?" Sally cried. "What did he *do* to you?"

"That's just it!" Clarissa said, sitting up among her silk cushions and wiping the tears of laughter away on the sleeve of her alluring peignoir. "He *didn't* do anything! Oh, Sally, don't you understand, you silly goose? Mr. FitzMaurice has me, the Golden Trollop, only for display, for show! While that young slave girl serves him as his mistress ..."

"But you thought she was his own daughter!"

"Well, I thought wrong, then. Some men," Clarissa went on to explain, "can't make love to a woman-unless the color of her skin is different from their own. Brown, or red, or black. And Mr. FitzMaurice, evidently, is one of these men. But because of the terrible social prejudice against such women, he has to keep it a secret. And that's why he hides that young slave girl in the little house he had built for her at the end of his shady garden."

"But even before we found out about *her,* and she's *certainly* dark-skinned," Sally said, "I knew there was something strange going on. Didn't I tell you, the minute we entered this big gloomy mansion, that it gave me the creeps? And I don't like that Mr. FitzMaurice either! To be perfectly frank," Sally confided, "he scares me more than those African menservants of his, with their scimitars! So maybe it's just as well he's not going to bother you with his stupid love-making. Besides," Sally added, with a toss of her saucy head, "this way, Mr. FitzMaurice

will have no reason to make trouble, should Captain Richard
Gray suddenly show up. Whatever could have happened
to *him*, to Captain Gray, I mean? Aren't you going to let him
know *where* you are?"

"Certainly not!" Clarissa told her loftily. "It's ... it's time
Captain Gray took a little trouble to find *me*. It's ... it's time
Captain Gray stopped treating me like a ... a plaything," and
Clarissa's fingers, as she spoke, began to pull at her pretty hand-
kerchief, threatening to tear the fine cambric to shreds. "Yes, like
a ... a plaything!"

But days passed and the brute failed to show up. Except for
her nightly trips to the theater, to give her performance, and
back, in the coach with its fantastic attendants, and accompanied
by Mr. FitzMaurice, Clarissa never went out, but stayed in utter
seclusion. Sally or Pete had to do what shopping she needed for
her. And this they did very cautiously, avoiding those tradesmen
who would have recognized them from having dealt with them
before, when Clarissa had been the Earl's mistress. François, now
and then, came to visit Clarissa, secretly, and very late at night,
to collect his ten percent of the allowance she received from
Mr. FitzMaurice. The former chief valet would stay with her for a
short while and, Clarissa bombarding him with questions about
latest news, current gossip, he would tell her what he had heard
from his garrulous women customers. Thus, through François,
and then through Mr. FitzMaurice, who always, before bidding
her good night, would chat with her politely for ten minutes or
so, Clarissa kept herself informed of what was going on in the
world outside. And almost daily, she and Sally would ascend the
little staircase and, standing at the window on the third floor,
they would watch the young slave girl as she sat outside her little
house playing on her mandolin-like instrument. There *you* are, a
captive, Clarissa would invariably think. And here am *I*, almost

like a captive, too. Through force of circumstance … And it made her feel a little better.

The big gloomy mansion itself and the high stone wall surrounding the garden were scrupulously guarded, of course. But Pete, who slept with the silent menservants in their downstairs room, managed to steal a key to one of the doors opening directly on the street. He had a duplicate made, and hurrying over to François' establishment, he slipped the key into François' hand and told him how to reach Clarissa's apartments. A visit by François, therefore, was always unexpected.

And the night came when it was doubly so. François was there, as Clarissa could see; he had just awakened her by shaking her by the shoulder gently. But he had brought someone with him. And Clarissa, not trusting her senses, rubbed her eyes. It didn't change what she saw, however, not by an iota! For there stood Captain Richard Gray, wearing the same shabby uniform, the tan on his face and hands a little deeper, the forelock falling over his open brow more unruly than ever. And he was grinning broadly. Very proud of himself Captain Richard Gray looked. With no reason for it whatsoever! Clarissa decided. Since he *couldn't* buy himself a new uniform. Just his plain natural conceit! And she was about to tell him so, right there and then.

But François had left, without having said a word. And Sally, after putting her head in, and then giving a disparaging sniff at sight of the unexpected visitor, had shut the door upon them. And Clarissa had jumped out of bed, without realizing that she had done so. The next instant, she was imprisoned in the circle of Captain Gray's strong arms. The usual procedure with "darling Richard."

After he had kissed her expertly on her mouth, throat, and other exposed parts of her body—she had nothing on but her peignoir—he held her away from him, and declared:

"You look lovely as a blonde. So you're the Golden Trollop! François told me," and Captain Gray laughed.

"And may I ask," Clarissa demanded, "*how* you managed to find me, at long last?"

"As soon as I returned to England ..."

"Oh, so you've been away *again?*"

"Naturally. I had business to attend to."

Probably those silly mines. The man was a dreamer, incorrigible!

"So when you came back ..." Clarissa prompted him.

"I went in search of Mr. Davey," Captain Gray said. "You often spoke of him. And he was easy to find. I went into the market place, the one near the Rose and Crown, where I always put up, and the first shopkeeper I asked told me where Mr. Davey the shoemaker had his abode. And I hurried there. But Mr. Davey explained that François was the only person who could take me to you. And he very kindly conducted me to François' place. The former chief valet remembered giving me the loan of his razor that time when you stayed at the Earl's mansion, and he seemed to know all about me. And so ... well, when night came, François hastened to bring me here. And here I am," Captain Gray said, grinning. "You can't say I haven't gone to a great deal of effort to find you!"

"You never wrote."

"I couldn't. But letters wouldn't have reached you anyhow, would they? My poor Clarissa! François told me about what happened. My poor darling." And sitting down in a chair, Captain Gray drew her onto his knees. Clarissa made herself comfortable, and he stroked her hair as he talked. "We haven't seen each other since our last stay at Merton. And so much has happened since! The Duke of Wellington, the Iron Duke we call him, is now the national hero. But nobody can take Lord Nelson's place in the hearts of the people. I was with Nelson, on *Victory*'s deck, when that bullet struck him. He spoke of Merton ..."

"And what about Lady Hamilton?" Clarissa was naturally curious about the lovely woman whom she had so admired.

"Lord Nelson's pension went to his frigid wife, Lady Nelson. All he could will to his beloved Emma was that pretty cottage. But Lady Hamilton, for lack of any other funds, was forced to sell the property. And grief-stricken over Lord Nelson's tragic death, desperate, unable to manage her financial affairs, she began to accumulate debts. And this drove her out of England, and to the Continent, where she is now reported to be destitute, with her mother, Mrs. Cadogan, making a few miserable francs by taking in the wash. Can you imagine Mrs. Cadogan," Captain Gray said, laughing, "deprived of her dish of mushrooms?"

"It serves her right, the horrible glutton," was Clarissa's opinion. "But is it true that Lady Hamilton was cut off without a penny by her husband's, Lord Hamilton's, will?" Among the news which Clarissa had missed knowing while confined in that filthy jail cell, and some of which she later learned from François, was the sudden demise of Lord Hamilton, the one-time ambassador to Naples, the peculiar man obsessed by his strange love of little antique statuettes and busts.

"He left everything to his relatives. After all," Captain Gray argued, "Lady Hamilton made her husband a laughing-stock, because of her affair with Lord Nelson. And maybe Lord Hamilton had been aware of it all along, though he never showed it. But in the end he paid her out!"

"That's all very well," Clarissa said. "But what about yourself, Captain Richard Gray?"

After the Battle of Trafalgar, he had immediately sold his commission. He was now in the reserves. But since the fleet was no longer required in the war operations, Captain Gray could devote all his time to … making his fortune. And that was exactly what he said, shamelessly, and with a grin.

"You're not going to start *that* again, are you?" Clarissa asked him, frowning. More of his silly investments, like those stupid mines.

"I never stopped."

But he made no mention of the mines, though his eyes were laughing at her, at her secret curiosity. Well, she had made him promise not to say a word about it until he was *absolutely* successful. And he was keeping his promise.

"The stock exchange seems very lively, right now," Captain Gray said.

"You'd need a lot of money for that, wouldn't you?" Clarissa observed mildly, humoring him.

First, the mines. And now, the stock exchange. The man was really demented!

"A certain degree of pluck is more important than money in this kind of venture," Captain Gray declared calmly. "Pluck, and … information."

"Oh?" Clarissa said.

"But the needed information, naturally," Captain Gray went on, "is almost impossible to obtain."

"Oh?" Clarissa again said.

"And therefore one has to rely on rumors, or trust one's intuition," Captain Gray explained. "That's what makes it such a risk."

"But," Clarissa said slowly, "if one had a bit of information, now and again, just the *tiniest* bit! It might make a difference, might it not?"

"It *might* make all the difference in the world! But why trouble your pretty head," Captain Gray protested, "about things you can't possibly understand?" And he kissed her.

"No, I'm curious," Clarissa told him. And snuggled against his broad shoulder and strong arm, she said, "I don't suppose you've ever met Mr. FitzMaurice, have you?"

"Not personally. Of course not. But I've watched him from a distance—a cat may look at the king, as the proverb has it!" And the Captain laughed as he said this.

"Mr. FitzMaurice is a perfect gentleman," Clarissa wanted him to know. "And when he brings me back from the theater, after my performance, he's polite enough to chat with me for a few minutes, while he sits in that chair there," and Clarissa pointed at it. "But some of the financial terms, expressions, which Mr. FitzMaurice uses, well, I just don't understand them! And I wouldn't want him to think me *stupid*." And then Clarissa asked:

"What is a stock, for instance?"

"To you, my adorable little idiot," Captain Gray said, "a stock would be just a slip of paper."

"A *little* slip of paper?"

"A small slip of paper. But worth a great deal of money, of course."

"Worth millions, maybe?"

"Well, sometimes. And some of the stocks have strange names, even funny names."

"A little slip of paper, with a funny name," Clarissa said, "and worth millions!"

But then she had to agree with Captain Richard Gray that to worry her pretty head with such things was an awful waste of time, at the moment, anyhow. Because his kisses were growing more and more passionate, and the bed with its silk sheets looked so inviting. And, laughing, she let "darling Richard" carry her to it, and lay her down, and, after so many months, the reunion proved very thrilling indeed.

But the following night, when Mr. FitzMaurice, after accompanying her back from the theater and then conducting her to her apartments, politely sat down in the chair and began his customary chat, she listened with greater care, trying to remember every word he said, while she smiled at him radiantly, and nodded delightedly. She knew that she had never been quite so beautiful as now, in her role of the Golden Trollop, and there she sat, a shimmering golden vision, opposite the portly financier who, while admiring her through his quizzing glass, panted slightly, beamed, and, as usual, bragged about his exploits. And this time she flattered him discreetly, to draw him out, lead him on. And then, at the first opportunity that presented itself, Clarissa exclaimed:

"You're marvelous, Mr. FitzMaurice, sir! Marvelous! Just a little slip of paper, and you'll make millions! And what a funny name this little slip of paper has! You just mentioned it. Begins with a C, doesn't it?"

"Begins with a T. Tasmania, madam. Not *Casmania*."

"Tasmania, of course. That's what you said. What a scatterbrain I am! Naturally, I don't understand anything about it ... But everything you tell me, Mr. FitzMaurice, sir, impresses me so! I'm *so* impressed! So *impressed!* The things you can *do!*" And Clarissa, clasping her hands prettily, gazed at him in amazement. "Do tell me some more."

And Mr. FitzMaurice, flattered by her admiration, told her a little more. But then Clarissa, with the delightful capriciousness of a frivolous female, changed the subject to social gossip. To think that Mr. FitzMaurice had actually dined with the Prince Regent! The financier, naturally, had bragged about that, too, recently. He had actually, Clarissa again exclaimed, sat right next to Mr. Brummell. Next to Beau Brummell, himself. Imagine! And Clarissa again clasped her hands in flattering amazement.

"Mr. Brummell was exquisitely polite," Mr. FitzMaurice told her solemnly. "*Exquisitely* polite! I shall never forget the experience. Never!"

Clarissa let him brag about *that*.

But later the same night, when she was alone with Captain Gray, she said to him, laughing:

"Of course, I don't understand anything about it. But some of the things Mr. FitzMaurice chats about sound so *intriguing!*"

And, word for word, she repeated those boasts of the portly financier which she thought might also rather intrigue Captain Gray.

And almost every time, henceforth, that she saw "darling Richard" she would amusedly tell him something of an equally intriguing nature. François had obligingly had made another duplicate key of the one in his possession, and he had given the second key to Captain Gray, and the Captain thus could secretly visit Clarissa whenever circumstances allowed him. He generally came a couple of hours after midnight, when everybody in the gloomy house had already retired for the night. And then he would as secretly leave, while it was still dark. Sometimes, however, Clarissa didn't see him for days. Well, he was busy, Captain Gray later explained it, grinning. And he would laugh, and take her in his arms, and chase away her jealous poutings with his expert kissing.

But it was from François that Clarissa, about this time, first heard about a Mr. X, who several months hence was to become such a power in the world of finance, and the subsequent revelation of whose identity then so astounded the public.

"The most popular amusement among the fops, at the moment," François said, in the course of this particular visit of his, "is to try to guess the identity of this mysterious Mr. X.

Because of the war, and the possibilities it offers of making a quick fortune, all the wealthy and titled men are trying their luck at the stock exchange, and this Mr. X seems to be outdoing them all. Some say it may be the Duke of Cumberland, which would explain the deliberate concealment of the person's true name, since a royal Duke is not supposed to sully his hands with financial ventures. But the majority are convinced that it is none other than Lord Cavor. And I'm inclined to agree," François declared, "with that opinion."

"I can see," Clarissa said, watching him closely, "that you have a special reason for thinking so."

"Financial success means social success. And there's always been social rivalry between Mr. FitzMaurice and Lord Cavor. And now that Mr. FitzMaurice has jumped way ahead of him socially, thanks to *you* ..."

"Thanks to the Golden Trollop, you mean." Clarissa corrected François, laughing.

"Yes, of course. Anyway," François said, "Lord Cavor is terribly envious of Mr. FitzMaurice, and what better way to pay him out than by competing with him on the stock exchange? So I've placed my bet, fifty guineas—and that's a lot of money to me!—on Lord Cavor, as being this Mr. X."

"You mean they're actually making *bets* on who he might be?"

"The whole of London talks of nothing else. It all happened quite suddenly, just within the last week. The mere idea that someone would dare to challenge Mr. FitzMaurice, the wizard financier, at his own game was enough to cause a sensation. And now the betting on Mr. X's true identity has spread from the houses of the rich to the taverns, to little groups of people gathered on street corners. Even my women customers, while I dress their hair," François said, "are betting their shillings, and half-crowns, and even pennies. But most of them are convinced that Mr. X is no other than the Duke of Cumberland, naturally. Women so admire the luxurious Duke."

"But whether it's the Duke, or Lord Cavor, as *you* think it is," Clarissa said, "there's no actual danger of Mr. FitzMaurice losing … any of his wealth, is there?"

"Of course not!" François instantly reassured her. "Nobody likes Mr. FitzMaurice, everybody would be overjoyed to see him supplanted and that's why this mysterious Mr. X has caught the imagination of the public. The fantastic idea that Mr. X could cause harm to Mr. FitzMaurice is plain wishful thinking, based on pure malice. Mr. FitzMaurice, and very soon probably, will simply wipe Lord Cavor out—assuming, of course, that Lord Cavor *is* Mr. X, which I do. And that's all!"

"*Wipe* Lord Cavor out?" Clarissa said.

"In grand-scale manipulations of this sort, a point is generally reached when only two competitors are left. The combat then centers between the two of them. A cruel combat. Like a duel, to the death. One must wipe the other out. That's a financial expression. Annihilate the other fellow's assets completely. Make him a total pauper. Throw him to the mercy of his creditors. Or into the debtors' prison. And that's what Mr. FitzMaurice will do to Lord Cavor."

"And if Lord Cavor wipes Mr. FitzMaurice out," Clarissa said thoughtfully, "assuming again, as you said, that Mr. X *is* Lord Cavor, then Lord Cavor will be as phenomenally wealthy as Mr. FitzMaurice is now, while Mr. FitzMaurice, well, *he*'ll be a total pauper?"

"Their positions would be reversed, yes. But, since Mr. FitzMaurice has proved his genius so many times, this Mr. X, whether he's Lord Cavor, or somebody else, can't *possibly* win! So you have nothing to worry about."

"I'm not worrying," Clarissa declared.

And she wasn't. Not in the least. Providing the mysterious Mr. X was Lord Cavor—and Clarissa had a great deal of trust in the former valet's worldly judgment—there was no cause for anxiety. She was the Golden Trollop. And Lord Cavor, Clarissa knew, would be delirious with joy to get the Golden Trollop. Something to keep in the back of her mind, anyway, in case anything happened to Mr. FitzMaurice financially. I will simply go to Lord Cavor, Clarissa told herself grandly....

But since she preferred to be prepared for any contingency, she also decided, right there and then, to approach Mr. FitzMaurice himself on the subject of the mysterious Mr. X. So far, the wizard financier had made no mention of his unknown enemy. The mere thought of whom, doubtless, was liable to give him apoplexy. Clarissa therefore, when the following night Mr. FitzMaurice sat down for his customary chat, was especially careful in her choice of words.

"You're marvelous, Mr. FitzMaurice, sir! *Marvelous!*" she exclaimed, as usual, at the first opportunity. Then, with a shrug that set her golden attire to shimmer and rustle alluringly, "The nonsensical rumors one hears nowadays! *Really!* At the theater tonight, as I was going back to my dressing room, there were the stagehands, sitting in a group on the *bare floor,* and ... But probably you won't even believe me! *What* they were doing, I mean. They were taking bets. Can you *imagine?*"

Since the stagehands, most likely, did take bets, if not at the theater then somewhere else, Clarissa felt safe in inventing this little lie.

"Bets?" Mr. FitzMaurice said.

He knew, of course, what the Londoners were currently betting about, and though his voice was calm enough, his well-fed face turned slightly red.

"Bets, yes," Clarissa said. "Isn't it *ridiculous!* And they were arguing among themselves, the stupid stagehands, about somebody absolutely unknown, a nonentity, a nothing, a *nobody!* Can you *imagine?* They called him ... Mr. X. Now, wasn't that silly!"

Mr. FitzMaurice's face turned a deeper red. And he was starting to pant.

"Andtheonlyreasonwhy I mentionthisto *you*, Mr. FitzMaurice, sir," Clarissa hurried on, "is because some of them declared that this Mr. X is none other than ... Lord Cavor. Which, of course, is sheer nonsense!"

The portly financier wheezed through his nose. His pudgy hand, holding the quizzing glass, quivered with indignation. Then, with well-assumed dignity, Mr. FitzMaurice said:

"Nonsense it is, madam. I do assure you."

"Fantastic, I thought it!"

"Certainly! I see Lord Cavor daily, as usual," Mr. FitzMaurice hastened to explain. "We're on friendliest of terms. Naturally, Lord Cavor *is* a trifle jealous of my recent social successes. *He* wasn't invited to dine with the Prince Regent! But not to the extent of trying to harm me ... to compete with me, I mean, in my financial manipulations."

You'd be surprised what a person *might* do when driven by jealousy! Clarissa told him mentally. But then Mr. FitzMaurice, probably, knew that better than anybody else. Aloud, she said:

"And the Duke of Cumberland certainly wouldn't conceal *his* identity under such a plebeian nomenclature as Mr. X! Now, would he?"

"Royalty knows nothing about finance," Mr. FitzMaurice thrust his lower lip out contemptuously. But he frowned worriedly, or maybe angrily.

"And *another* thing those loutish stagehands said ..." Clarissa hurried on. "Well, I just stopped my ears to it!

I *immediately* covered my ears, like this," and she gracefully placed a hand over her either ear, to show how she did it. "But *before* I stopped my ears, I heard them say that this Mr. X will ... wipe you out. And *that's* what made me stop my ears. I didn't want to hear another word, not another word ... I was so *upset!*"

"Wipe *me* out!" Mr. FitzMaurice said hoarsely, when he got his voice back. "Nobody could wipe me out. *Nobody!* Madam shouldn't listen to rumors. Believe me, madam, when I say that madam has no cause for anxiety. I will always be in the position to protect madam financially, I do assure madam. And I have here something, a trifle ..." and he quickly produced it, out of the pocket of his rich silk coat. And Clarissa's hand happening to lie on her lap, palm up, Mr. FitzMaurice placed the trifle there, a sparkling diamond brooch. "As a mark of my esteem," he explained in honeyed tones, ingratiatingly. "In appreciation of madam's beauty."

From the very beginning, the portly financier had made it a habit to slip into Clarissa's hand, now and again, before bidding her good night, some costly jewel. He was never as generous with his gifts as the Earl had been, but a certain pair of earrings he once gave her, of emeralds and diamonds, and a ruby-and-diamond necklace, her favorite, were really priceless. During the last week or so, however, not a night passed without his leaving one jewel or another in her hand, and all of them so fabulous that Clarissa would catch her breath with joy, every time.

And now Mr. FitzMaurice went on obsequiously:

"All these rumors are nothing but calumny. Sheer calumny! I do assure madam."

"Of course they are!"

"Wipe me out, indeed! I'll wipe *him* out, this Mr. X. I ... I'll *smash* him!"

"Of course you will! This Mr. X probably is nothing but a charlatan."

"I'm not interested in Mr. X's identity," Mr. FitzMaurice assured her. "And the higher up he is, by title and wealth, the happier I'll be to wipe him out, *completely!* So long as madam does not worry ..."

"I have never had a greater trust in your financial genius, Mr. FitzMaurice, sir," Clarissa told him, "than at this, so decisive for you, time."

And the portly financier, obviously reassured by her attitude, then left her.

Well, she didn't find out who Mr. X was from *him*. Mr. FitzMaurice seemed not to have the vaguest idea about the mysterious person's true identity. Unless he was deliberately pretending ignorance, for some reason ... But maybe Captain Gray would be able to tell her the latest rumors about Mr. X, and she might deduce some interesting clue from that. Clarissa hadn't seen the Captain for more than a week, and she rather expected him to show up tonight.

And, sure enough, within only half an hour of Mr. FitzMaurice's leave-taking, Captain Gray suddenly walked in. Generally, because of the secrecy of his visits, he would appear much later. But there he stood, grinning, as usual. Clarissa, wearing one of her becoming peignoirs, was sitting at the dressing table, putting fragrant cold cream on her face in front of the huge mirror, while Sally was brushing her golden hair. Sally, on seeing Captain Gray, took one look at his shabby uniform, at his heavy boots, which needed polishing, and she tossed her head, and gave her customary sniff of disparagement, and then went on brushing Clarissa's hair with gusto.

But Clarissa merely said:

"I thought you lost your duplicate key." And she pouted.

"Well, you wouldn't want me to do *that,* would you?" Captain Gray said.

And pulling a chair over, he seated himself close, and again grinned at her.

Feminine reproaches had no effect on Captain Richard Gray, none whatsoever!

Clarissa picked up a soft white cloth, sprinkled something scented from a pretty bottle on it, and, starting carefully to remove the cold cream off her face with the moist cloth, she said:

"I suppose you've heard about this mysterious Mr. X?"

"Mr. X?" Captain Gray said. "Well, one can't help *hearing* about him, certainly."

"The man has as good as made himself famous, actually! London talks of nothing else, François told me. Everybody making bets about his possible identity. Isn't it *something!*"

Captain Gray laughed.

"Some people have all the luck," he said.

But he looked preoccupied.

Clarissa had never seen him look preoccupied before. So she asked him no questions. But, instead, she hastened to send Sally out of the room. And no sooner had Sally shut the door upon them, with a purposeful slam, of course, than Captain Gray took Clarissa in his arms, and she forgot about Mr. X.

But she had occasion to think of him, though briefly, the very next night, while she was at the theater. There was one amusement Clarissa never got tired of. And that was to stand behind the big curtain and watch, through the slit in the heavy scarlet velvet, the arrival of the fashionable audience. And there she stood, in her gold outfit, and with her golden hair rippling down her back and about her shoulders, and one eye close to the slit, she looked the arrivals over. The rich attire of the men vied in brilliancy of colors with the hues of the women's beautiful gowns. Some of the men wore white wigs, and they had gorgeous lace at their throats. But those who followed the prevailing fashion, and had wigs of black or brown curls, sported cravats of fine lawn and of such an extravagant cut that their chins and mouths were completely hidden from view. And this somehow made these fops look especially stylish! And since both men and women wore a lot of jewels, there was no end of glitter and sparkle and glow under the lighted chandeliers. While where Clarissa stood it was absolutely dark.

And all these rich, important, famous people, Clarissa told herself, have come here to see me. *Me!* And the knowledge of it, as always, made her laugh.

But why weren't they taking their seats? What was delaying them? The elegant men and women had come in smiling, gay, ready to be entertained. But some belated arrival had evidently brought with him some kind of news, and the word had spread with lightning-like speed, causing sudden commotion, excitement, alarm. Women could be seen throwing up their hands. And the delicate smelling salts flacons made their instant appearance, and fans and lace handkerchiefs fluttered, in hurried efforts to ward off the faints. The faces of the men wore a gravely frightened expression. And, with the rustle of silks and satins, close little groups were being swiftly formed, to discuss, in whispers, the alarming news.

What in the world could have happened? Clarissa wondered impatiently, while watching it all with intense curiosity. And that was when the thought of Mr. X popped into her head. Some new rumor about *him*, probably … At the moment, it seemed the most plausible explanation of the cause of so much commotion. But then the bell rang, calling everybody to sit down. And since the audience was extremely well bred, it hastened, notwithstanding the distracted state of everyone's feelings, graciously to obey the bell. And Clarissa, suddenly, saw that two seats, in the center of the fifth row, were conspicuously empty. One chair, with the royal emblem, was the Prince Regent's seat. The plain chair, beside it, was Mr. Brummell's. Both His Royal Highness and Mr. Brummell were absent tonight. Well, *that* was certainly unusual....

But another bell now rang, summoning *her* to start her performance. And she hurried out onto the stage, and the heavy curtain rising, and the brilliant footlights flashing full upon her, she went through her daringly vulgar act with her customary aplomb and roguish charm.

She was burning with curiosity, however, and to see Mr. FitzMaurice hurrying across the stage to her, as soon as the curtain came down, was for once a welcome sight. She'd find out from him. Generally, he would come to her dressing room for her.

"I will accompany madam to the house, naturally," the wizard financier at once said agitatedly. "But then I must go and try to learn the details of this tragic event. So come. Let us go...."

His well-fed face was pale, and it quivered. And he kept blinking his little eyes, as if with astonishment.

"But what is it? What happened?" Clarissa cried.

"Later, madam, *please*. Later," Mr. FitzMaurice implored, dropping his voice to a whisper.

And he glanced around swiftly, at the theater manager, and the stagehands, who were within earshot. But the news, whatever it was, must have already reached *them*, Clarissa could see. For they all looked sort of dumfounded.

"I sent your maid to wait for us in the coach," Mr. FitzMaurice went on. "So let's go."

And with customary ceremony, though somewhat hastily, he led Clarissa out to the waiting coach.

"Now!" she prompted him, once they were inside and on their way.

"Oh, it's terrible.... Terrible!"

"But what *is* it?"

"The consequences may be devastating ... on the war, on politics, on *finance!*"

"But what *happened?*"

"The mood of a royal prince can affect the whole nation ..." And then, in a rush, Mr. FitzMaurice told her, "The Prince Regent and Mr. Brummell had an awful quarrel. There was a terrible scene ... behind closed doors, of course. Mr. Brummell immediately left the palace. It is to be hoped that by now he has reached Dover. He had to flee for his life."

"So it all happened today?" Clarissa asked, after a silence.

"Sometime in the afternoon, yes."

"And what was the quarrel about?"

"There were no witnesses to what passed between them. But all sort of rumors are already rampant, naturally."

"For instance?"

"Well, people are saying that the Prince Regent probably was trying on a new coat, and that Mr. Brummell might have made some remark, about His Royal Highness' figure. Which is, after all, eh ... somewhat gross."

"Mr. Brummell, famous for his exquisite politeness," Clarissa protested, "to say anything derogatory, rude? That's just plain silly!"

"They don't mean that he had any such intent! Of course not! But His Royal Highness had, probably, interpreted Mr. Brummell's remark, whatever it might have been, as being ... uncomplimentary."

"So that's what people are saying," Clarissa observed mildly.

And, doubtless, for want of better explanation, that's what the historians would be saying. Something equally silly, anyway!

"But what else *could* have happened?" Mr. FitzMaurice panted excitedly. "*Except* some unfortunate misunderstanding of that sort. The Prince Regent is known for his unreasonableness. His unpredictable fits of rage are proverbial!"

"Well, maybe you're right."

And Clarissa let it go at that, while laughing to herself.

For, of course, she knew what must have caused the historic quarrel. She was the only person who knew the *truth*. And she could imagine, very vividly, how it had all come about. And she was right. For that was exactly what did happen.

"The tailors have arrived, Your Royal Highness," a courtier reported, with a scrape of his silk shoes on the sunlit parquet, as he performed the ceremonial bow. "Does Your Royal Highness desire to try on the new coat now, or wait until Mr. Brummell comes in?"

The Prince Regent, who stood at the window, doing nothing in particular, and with his back turned on the brilliant company which at this forenoon hour always thronged his private apartments in the palace, didn't answer at once. Everybody waited. The tiara of the homely Princess Royal wiggled with the unhappy woman's nervousness, as she sat, like the fabled ass amidst flowers, surrounded by her bevy of young ladies-in-waiting. The luxuriously attired Duke of Cumberland, lounging in a chair indolently, played with the fabulous rings that burdened his white effeminate hands. Or he would yawn with boredom, and then hold a hand in front of his beautiful sensual mouth to cover the yawn. As to the courtiers, they dared not even breathe.

"Well," the Regent said, at last, "I may as well try on the coat now. Since Mr. Brummell won't be getting back till later in the afternoon."

And he strode away from the window to stand before the tall gilded mirror. The fashionable tightness of his white satin breeches accentuated his fat thighs, and since people suspected him of being rather touchy about his figure, everybody stoically gazed, instead, at his face, florid, with haughty eyes, framed in glossy curls of the brown wig, and the double chin propped by the rich white neckcloth.

The tailors and their apprentices had, meanwhile, trooped in. The new coat was passed from one courtier to another, to a third. A fourth courtier, moving around the Prince Regent on tiptoe, carefully relieved him of the coat he was wearing. Then, taking the new coat from the third courtier, he deftly slipped it on His Royal Highness.

"Why not wait for dear Brummell, my dear brother," the Duke of Cumberland drawled, rather belatedly. "Then you'd have his advice. Which, of course, is invaluable!"

"Don't tell me what to do," the Regent told him rudely.

Definitely he was in a very bad mood.

"The dear fellow, doubtless, is enjoying the felicities of solitude," the Duke of Cumberland went on, indolently, "in some pretty rural spot. Admiring scenery, communing with nature, that kind of thing ..."

"As a matter of fact," the Regent said, and he scowled at his brother, "Brummell is still in town. He'll be leaving in about two hours. He had my permission, naturally."

And the Regent began to turn this way and that in front of the mirror.

"Well, what do you think?"

"Beautiful coat, Your Royal Highness!" "Truly elegant!" "Very becoming to Your Royal Highness!" "Marvelous!" "Lovely!" *"Unique!"*

Compliments were showered upon him while, undecided, he examined his reflection in the mirror.

Suddenly he shrieked:

"Wretched flatterers! It doesn't even fit!"

And, enraged, he tore the coat off, ripping the seams. And he flung it into a courtier's face.

"Out! Everybody out!"

The brilliant company hastily left.

"And *you*," the Prince Regent said, pointing a pudgy finger at the courtier who in the general scurry for the door had been pushed to the rear and was now the only one still in the room. "Send those two knaves in."

The courtier disappeared. And the two "knaves," as the Regent called the spies in his pay, hurried in. Two inconspicuous-looking individuals. His Royal Highness seated himself at a table, a magnificent museum piece covered with priceless bric-a-brac, and the two spies came over and stood before him.

"Now," the Prince Regent said. "For the hundredth time, I'm telling you I don't believe a word of your stupid reports, not a single word! Is that clear? Scenery, scenery, Mr. Brummell admires scenery. I'm sick and tired of hearing it! Just a pack of lies! He must be seeing someone there. Meeting with someone. A woman. A slip of a girl with a pretty face and a lot of silly curls!"

Mr. Brummell met with no one, saw no one. He was always alone there, the spies assured the Regent vehemently, as they had assured him so many times before.

"All right. He just stands there, you tell me. *Where?* What kind of a spot is it? Describe it. What *is* there around? Trees, grass, a bench maybe? Come on! *Talk!*"

"We mentioned trees in our report," one spy pointed out sulkily. "Sure, there are trees."

"And grass, too," the other spy said. "We didn't conceal about the *grass*."

"You've been cleverly evasive, that's what!" the Prince Regent accused them.

And since that was exactly what they had been, trying to protect Brummell, the spies quavered with fear.

"But for once, I'm going to get to the bottom of this mighty suspicious business! Yes, I'm *decided!*" and he suddenly banged the table with his fist, making the priceless bric-a-brac rattle. "One more lie," he warned them, "and I'll have you both hanged. I'll have you ... quartered!"

The spies paled visibly, and they licked their dry lips.

"Now, maybe, you'll think of something to tell me *besides* trees and grass!"

"Well," one of the men said, hesitantly, "there are ... headstones."

"Headstones!"

"Very old headstones, most of them are," the other man added, with an innocent air.

"There was nothing about headstones in your reports!"

"We didn't think it important!" the two spies explained, with one voice. And a sly glance passed between them, undetected by the Prince Regent. Maybe it'd blow over, after all ... "We described the spot, a hundred times and more, as being picturesque! But *what* kind of a spot it is—well, what *difference* could it possibly make? Sure, it's a village churchyard. A pretty spot, just like we said it was."

"A churchyard," the Regent said. "Well, of course, those country churchyards are picturesque, that's true enough." And his elbow on the table, and his florid face on his hand, he fell into deep thought. "A churchyard ..." he mused.

But just as the spies were about to exchange a congratulatory glance, the Prince Regent abruptly sat up. He had come to a sudden decision. A pudgy finger pointed, at random, at one of the two men, he said:

"Go to your quarters, and remain there until further orders."

The man immediately hurried out.

"You have your chaise here?" the Regent asked the other spy.

"Yes, Your Royal Highness. We were prepared to follow Mr. Brummell to Halstead, as we always do."

The Regent produced a fat gold watch, studded with diamonds. He snapped the lid open.

"Mr. Brummell will be leaving in exactly forty-five minutes," he said. "But I will leave, at once—for Halstead. You will drive. We'll get there ahead of Mr. Brummell. And I'll see for myself what *attraction* the spot has for him."

And snapping the watch shut, replacing it in his pocket, the Prince Regent led the way, through a secret panel in the wall, down a secret stairway, and along a narrow passage, which brought them out into the street behind the palace. The spy then went to bring his inconspicuous chaise around, while the Regent waited in the shadow of a doorway. When the spy drove up, the Regent at once got in beside him, and they set off at a brisk pace. Thanks to the deep hood which the small chaise was provided with, and to the threadbare carriage rug which the spy hastened to throw over his royal passenger's knees, to conceal the celebrated white satin breeches, the Prince Regent was safe from recognition, and his quick trip through busy London and the outlying countryside attracted no attention.

In less than two hours, they came within sight of the pretty village of Halstead. But to avoid going through the village, the spy drove along back lanes, and into a copse which ad-joined the little churchyard in the back. The chaise was left in the copse, and the spy then led the Prince Regent between the old headstones and to a spot where they could station themselves behind some trees and shrubbery. And thus completely concealed from view, they waited.

They didn't have to wait long. The spy's sharp ear caught the swish of approaching wheels along the country road.

"That will be Mr. Brummell's elegant little carriage, Your Royal Highness," he whispered to the Prince Regent. "Mr. Brummell leaves it in a lane close by, and comes directly here."

In something like five minutes, the Prince Regent, watching through the thick greenery, saw Brummell enter the churchyard from the village side. He saw him walk straight to a simple monument, of gray marble, made in the shape of a stubby needle, and stand before it, the glossy beaver hat and gloves in his hand, as usual, and leaning slightly on the slender ebony cane. The Prince Regent watched. And Brummell just stood there, but he looked contented, almost happy, as he never looked when at the Regent's brilliant court. After staying there so for a little while, Brummell slowly walked away.

No sooner was he out of sight than the Prince Regent rushed from behind the bushes and hurried to the simple monument. He read the name, the two dates.

"Just as I thought! A woman!" he furiously told the spy who had followed him. "A young girl! Gray ... Gray," the Regent repeated with shaking lips, trying to remember if he had ever heard the name before, and jealously wondering where, how, Brummell could have met her. "Probably a local family, since she's buried here. Some impoverished breed!"

"But of gentle birth," the spy said, in an attempt to soothe his royal master. "The young lady went straight from boarding school to be governess at Ravisham."

The Prince Regent recalled his visit there. But, naturally, he didn't remember the governess. Who would so much as look as such a person? A nonentity! A nothing! But that was how Brummell met her, at Ravisham. And the Regent turned his fury upon the spy:

"No mention of *her* in your reports, knave!"

"We made discreet inquiries, and prepared the information, in case Your Royal Highness should ask for it," the man explained defensively. "That was pure routine. But why mention something *harmless,* as we thought it? The young lady being—dead."

"So much greater the insult to me, you fool!"

And swinging away from the monument, the Prince Regent marched out of the churchyard, and to the chaise in the copse, the spy hurrying after him. And all the way back to London he preserved his awful silence. Then, after telling the man that he would deal with him and the other knave later, and for both of them to keep to their quarters meanwhile, he entered the palace by the same door he had quitted it by, and hastening up the secret stairway, regained his private apartments. He immediately pulled at the bell rope.

"Has Mr. Brummell arrived?" he asked the courtier, who hurried in, bowing.

"All of an hour ago, Your Royal Highness."

"He may come in."

The courtier, walking backwards, left the room. And a moment later, Brummell walked in.

The Prince Regent at once confronted him with the words:

"I was at Halstead. I know everything. Do not deny it."

The blow dealt to his immense vanity must have been terrible. He looked awful. His big, usually florid face, was ashen. The haughty eyes gleamed like sharp steel. And the set mouth quivered at the corners.

They had had scenes before, but this was different. And both knew that it was different. And perhaps in the Regent's words, "Do not deny it," there was concealed a plea to Brummell to heal the wound. Perhaps if Brummell had flattered him shrewdly, said something derogatory of Miss Gray, and then made light of the whole thing, everything would have been well.

But Brummell always acted in character. And now he said:

"I loved Miss Gray. She had done me the honor of reciprocating my feelings. The memory of her will be always very dear to me. I wish for nothing else."

"You ingrate!" the Prince Regent suddenly roared.

And grabbing the first object his hand encountered on the table—a marble paperweight—he flung it across half the room at Brummell. Brummell automatically stepped aside, at the same time raising his cane to ward off the threatening impact. The piece of marble hit the cane, breaking it in two, then crashed into the mirror on the wall, splintering it to fragments.

"Don't think you can save your life!" the Regent screamed.

"I saved Your Royal Highness from becoming a murderer," Brummell told him. "And that's more important for England."

The Prince Regent, his high blood pressure affected by his rage, fell into a chair. And Brummell walked swiftly from the room.

"What happened? Why was he shouting so?" the frightened courtiers showered him with questions, as he was about to hurry through the adjoining chamber.

"We heard the crash," the Princess Royal said, her tiara wiggling more than ever. "We thought your life was in danger."

"It will be, unless I leave the country at once."

"Yes, of course. You have your carriage here, haven't you?"

"If I drive fast I'll reach Dover by nightfall."

"But you'll need money then. Take this ring," and slipping it off her finger, the Princess Royal pressed it into Brummell's hand. "It will pay your passage across the Channel."

Brummell thanked her and hurried out. And the Princess Royal and the courtiers hurried to the window. But even as they watched him drive out of the palace courtyard, the Prince Regent, having recovered from his apoplectic-like collapse brought on by his fierce rage, suddenly appeared at the door of his room, shouting, "Guards! Send the guards after him. He musn't get away!"

And very soon the mounts' hoofs were heard thundering over the stone courtyard, as the guards set out in hot pursuit.

But Brummell had had a good start on them, and the guards, besides, since everybody liked Brummell, were probably not particularly anxious to catch up with him. By morning, the whole of London knew that he had reached Dover safely, and then had crossed the Channel to Calais, on French soil, never to return.

CHAPTER TWENTY-SIX

"THERE ARE ROBBERS in the house! We're being robbed!" Sally screamed, shaking Clarissa, trying to wake her. "They've broken the locks on the big oriental chests. The noise of it made me run downstairs to investigate. Starting to ransack the place they are! And those elderly menservants just *stand* there, gaping. Nothing will be left, I tell you, unless you come and *do* something!"

"Nonsense," Clarissa murmured sleepily.

And she was about to snuggle anew against the satin pillows. But then the recollection of quite recent reports about robberies committed in the neighborhood suddenly made her jump out of bed. Throwing a peignoir on, she followed Sally downstairs.

Disorder reigned in the gloomy entrance hall. The big oriental chests had been dragged away from the walls, and the "robbers," all dressed alike in red coats with yellow trim, and with yellow cockades in their black hats, were busy pulling out the contents—rich brocades, velvets, brilliantly embroidered silks—as if looking for something, some hidden treasure. The silent menservants, gathered in a group, just stood there, gaping. And the Hindu coachman, with his blue turban, and the two big Africans, naked to the waist and wearing their voluminous trousers, were also present. But *their* behavior was quite different. They jabbered among themselves in their funny language, gestured wildly, the Africans shaking their sharp scimitars in the air with excitement. Though armed, however, they made no attempt to stop the ransacking, either.

"What is the meaning of this? How dare you!" Clarissa cried, sweeping down the stairs in her peignoir.

One of the "robbers," distinguishable from the others by the fact that he carried a staff topped by some kind of emblem, was moving from window to window, drawing the curtains aside to let the light of day into the gloomy house. And just as Clarissa spoke, he drew yet another curtain aside, and she stood directly in the shaft of sunlight, the gold of her rippling hair vying with dancing sunbeams.

"The Golden Trollop!" the man exclaimed.

And he gave Clarissa a low bow.

The other "robbers" turned to stare. And they also bowed low to Clarissa. To see the Golden Trollop so close awed them.

"Never mind *that!*" Clarissa said. "What is the meaning of this ... this intrusion? How ... how dare you!" she was really angry, indignant. "And you, louts," she turned to the inactive servants, "don't you just stand there! Raise the alarm! Call Mr. FitzMaurice. Have him come here immediately!" And she swung round on the "robber" with the staff. "Mr. FitzMaurice will deal with *you!*"

"But, madam," the man said, quietly, "Mr. FitzMaurice is gone."

"*Gone?* What do you mean, gone?"

"He simply disappeared. Slipped out during the night, evidently. Taking the young slave girl, and her black serving-woman, with him. That's the only information we could get out of the stupid menservants," the man explained, and he motioned at them with his staff, scornfully. "Mr. FitzMaurice abandoned them, dastardly, and yet they refuse to talk! But we know he must have had money put away in gold coins for this kind of an emergency. And that's what we're looking for"—indicating the ransacked chests—"gold. He couldn't have carried it all away with him!"

The man spoke with dignity and authority. And that was what so dumfounded Clarissa.

"But ... but I don't understand!" she gasped.

"We are the bailiffs, madam. Whatever possessions Mr. FitzMaurice left behind him now belong to his creditors. We will be stationed in the house to see that nothing is removed from it."

So that's how the dreaded bailiffs looked! That was the kind of coats and hats they wore! And the one with the staff, topped by the emblem of his office, was the chief bailiff.

And instantly everything became clear to Clarissa.

"Oh," she said, "you mean the Mr. X has wiped Mr. FitzMaurice out!"

"Mr. X certainly did that! The news is all over London by now. It's been a long time since people had anything so exciting to talk about. But," the chief bailiff added, and he coughed politely, "what an inconvenience for madam!"

"Are you inferring," Clarissa demanded haughtily, "that I will be forced to leave?"

"I'm afraid so, madam."

Sally, standing behind Clarissa, at once began to wring her hands.

"We're being thrown out *again!*" she wailed.

Clarissa told her to shut up, rather sharply.

"But I must have time to arrange my affairs," she then said to the bailiff, "and to pack my things ... surely ..."

"I will give madam two hours. It's the best I can do."

"Very well. Come on, Sally."

And, followed by Sally, Clarissa hurried up the stairs to her apartments, and into her bedroom.

"At least, you won't have to start from scratch, *this* time," Sally said. She had evidently thought the situation over, and decided to be brave about it. "There're the beautiful jewels Mr. FitzMaurice had been giving you. And all the allowance money that you've been putting away in that strongbox, under the bed."

Mr. FitzMaurice himself had provided the strongbox. He had also given Clarissa a large velvet case to keep her jewels in.

"Sally," Clarissa said, "I want everything packed and ready, before I get dressed. So be quick about it! Get the strongbox over here," Clarissa pointed at the floor, within a few feet of where she stood. "And I'll pack the jewels."

Sally ran to the bed, half crawled under it, and reappeared, pulling the strongbox with her. She then dragged it along the floor to where Clarissa wanted it placed. Clarissa, meanwhile, taking the velvet jewel case out of a drawer, swiftly picked up a few rings, a pair of earrings, a diamond bracelet, which lay scattered on the dressing table, added them to the larger jewels with which the case was stacked, closed the case, and placed it on top of the strongbox.

"Now get one of those silk sheets," Clarissa further directed.

Sally pulled the sheet off the bed, spread it out on the floor.

"We'll pack my peignoirs, and all my gold shoes, and the cosmetic bottles and jars in the sheet." As she spoke, Clarissa began to gather up the pretty bottles and jars from the dressing table.

Sally, hurrying into the adjoining room, returned with the gossamer heap of peignoirs. Since Clarissa never went out, except to her performance in the theater, she had not bothered to get herself any gowns. But there were many pairs of gold shoes. For her act on the stage, Clarissa never wore the same pair any two nights in succession. And by this simple device, a secret known to all professional actresses, she kept the gold shoes marvelously fresh-looking. Sally had also fetched the old casket with the brass clasps, in which she kept Clarissa's ribbons.

The two of them packed all these things swiftly and knotted the end of the silk sheet together.

"Now you can run down and tell Pete ..." Clarissa started to say, when the chief bailiff, followed by two plain bailiffs, suddenly walked in.

The menservants, strangely loyal to Mr. FitzMaurice, their master, had been stubbornly mum about the whereabouts of whatever valuables, if any, he might have left behind. But owing no such allegiance to the Golden Trollop, they had evidently not been averse to supplying the chief bailiff with the description of *her* cherished possessions. For he walked straight to the strongbox, and picked up the velvet jewel case, while his two subordinates took up the heavy box, lifting it by its thick leather handles.

"No, madam. Not anything of *value!*" the chief bailiff said quietly. "*That* you cannot take with you."

Clarissa, who had never expected such a turn of affairs, stared at him, open-mouthed. Then, getting her voice back:

"But it's all mine!" she cried. "The jewels ... Mr. FitzMaurice gave them to me! *Gifts* ... And the money, the gold, in the strongbox, are my monthly *allowances....*"

And putting both her hands on the jewel case, she tried to pull it away from the chief bailiff. Sally, at the same time, had flung herself bodily across the strongbox, and she was kicking her heels in the air briskly, in the vain attempt to force the two bailiffs, by her sheer weight, to drop it to the floor.

"*Anything* that had been bought with Mr. FitzMaurice's money," the chief bailiff explained to Clarissa, "or any *money* that had been originally Mr. FitzMaurice's, now belongs to his creditors. That is the law, madam."

Well, she certainly couldn't afford to get mixed up with the *law!* She let go of the jewel case. And the chief bailiff marched out of the room with it. His subordinates, having shaken Sally off, despite her shrieks and pleas, followed, with the strongbox.

Clarissa and Sally stared at each other. Then they stared at the bundle, which still stood there. *That,* since it contained nothing of value, was the only thing left.

"Isn't it something!" Sally said, indignant.

But then she broke down and began to weep pathetically.

"Stop your hysterics, Sally," Clarissa told her crisply. "And bring me my gold outfit. I must hurry and dress."

"How can you take it so *calmly!*" Sally whined between sniffles.

She hastened to bring the shimmering garments from the other room, however, and laid them on a chair, and Clarissa immediately began to clothe herself in them.

"But what shall we *do?*" Sally went on despairingly. "Where shall we go?"

"Where do you *think* I intended going, in the first place?" Clarissa said, arranging the gold veil over her golden hair and lovely face, and admiring the result in the mirror. And then she answered her own question herself. "To Lord Cavor, of course."

"Lord Cavor!" Sally stared, but suddenly she brightened up. "Why, *of course!* Since he *is* the mysterious Mr. X. You told me so. And François was certain, all along, that Mr. X is none other than Lord Cavor. And now that he has wiped Mr. FitzMaurice out, he'll be as rich as Mr. FitzMaurice used to be. Maybe even richer!"

"Quite possible."

"And because of the social rivalry that always existed between him and Mr. FitzMaurice," Sally went on excitedly, "Lord Cavor will be *overjoyed* to get the Golden Trollop, become her protector, I mean. In fact, maybe *that* was the reason why he started, as Mr. X, to compete with Mr. FitzMaurice, in all those financial deals—to get the Golden Trollop, to get *you*, away from him!"

"Quite possible," Clarissa again said.

"Then I better run down and tell Pete to bring the carriage around, at once."

Sally meant, of course, the small enclosed carriage which Pete had so cleverly saved from being confiscated by the "two dry sticks," the two great-nephews. After the keeper of the inn where Pete had left the carriage at the time had been paid for the trouble, and for feeding the horse, Pete had put it up at another inn, closer to Mr. FitzMaurice's old gloomy house. And he would drive Sally, when she had to make some purchase for Clarissa, to the other end of London, where the tradesmen didn't know them from their former association with the late Earl's household.

"Yes, have Pete bring it around to the front door," Clarissa said. "And you'll take the bundle down, Sally. And put it in the carriage...."

"And the lap dog," Sally said.

The lap dog had gotten fat from overeating, and it neither rushed around as much as it used to nor yapped as wildly. Right now, it was probably asleep on Sally's bed in the adjoining room.

"Well, the animal also, I suppose," Clarissa said. "And then you just stay in the carriage and wait for me."

Sally hurried out, and Clarissa put on the outer golden garment, the flowing lines of which made her look so slender and regal. She'd have to speak to the African menservants, and to the Hindu, she was thinking, and tell them that they could continue at their jobs, as before, except that it would be Lord Cavor now who'd be paying them. They must know a *few words* in English! Enough to understand, anyway, the good news she'd be conveying to them. Every detail of the setting surrounding the Golden Trollop should remain intact. As to the impressive coach for the drive to the theater and back—she'd tell Lord Cavor to buy one exactly like it, immediately.

And Clarissa hastened downstairs, hoping that the Africans did know a *little* English, and that she wouldn't have to invent some kind of a sign language, which would make it so embarrassing! And there they were, the Africans with their scimitars, and the blue-turbaned Hindu, still jabbering among themselves excitedly. And the elderly menservants stood, as before, in a silent group, wondering, probably, what was to become of them. While the big chests, closed now, had been pushed back to the wall, the bailiffs having carried their search for hidden gold to another part of the house. Only one bailiff remained to guard the front door.

But just as Clarissa reached the foot of the gloomy staircase, an imperative knock was heard. The bailiff, leaving the chain on, opened the door a crack to see who it was. Then he hastened to remove the chain, opened the door wide, and stepped back, with a low bow to the newcomer, who was none other than Lord Cavor.

And I didn't even have to go to him, Clarissa thought with satisfaction. Instead, he instantly comes to *me*....

"May I see madam?" asked Lord Cavor.

His resemblance to the vanquished Mr. FitzMaurice was almost comical. As short of stature, as portly, as richly dressed ... Except that instead of a quizzing glass, dangling on a black ribbon, this one sported a monocle.

"Certainly, my lord," the bailiff hastened to assure him.

And the bailiff again bowed, with all the respect due not so much to Lord Cavor's title as to his overwhelming success as the mysterious Mr. X. Of *that* Clarissa hadn't a doubt!

On one side of the gloomy hall there was a formal grouping of a massive table and two high-backed chairs. And by the time

Lord Cavor, with the help of his monocle, discovered Clarissa's presence, she had rustled over to one of these chairs, and had seated herself in it, in the pose behooving her woeful situation of sudden and shocking bereavement. An elbow leaning on the table, and her lovely face supported by that hand, while her other hand nervously crumpled a handkerchief of gold lace. Even her attire seemed to suggest a widow's weeds, except that instead of being black, it was of shimmering gold.

Lord Cavor hurried over, and stood before her.

"Lord Cavor, madam," he presented himself with a bow and, of course, twirling his monocle. "Mr. FitzMaurice may have spoken of me."

"He did ... mention you," Clarissa sighed. "You find me, my lord," she went on, "in a state of great ... sadness."

And, while crumpling her handkerchief, she managed to pull her bodice down to reveal more fully the roundness and firmness of her exposed breasts.

"Sadness ... naturally," Lord Cavor said, one eye glued to his monocle, and the monocle fixed on Clarissa's bodice. "Most proper, hm ... But I have hurried here, madam, to offer madam my ... protection. Though my means are comparatively modest, I can take care of madam adequately."

His means *modest!* What a hypocrite! The wealthiest man in the kingdom now, more likely.

"I ... I appreciate your offer, my lord," Clarissa said. "And I ... I accept it."

But she mustn't let him suspect how *eager* she was to accept it. The details of the arrangement would be discussed later, and the size of her monthly allowance would increase proportionally to her show of dignity. And Clarissa, therefore, said:

"The feeling of sadness, however, my lord ... lingers on."

"And it does you credit, madam. And please believe me when I say that the awful misfortune which has befallen Mr. FitzMaurice pains me deeply!"

What a hypocrite!

"Mr. FitzMaurice's attitude to you, my lord, was of the friendliest. *He* never suspected you of being the mysterious Mr. X."

"No, of course not!"

"What a shock it must have been when he suddenly discovered that Mr. X was none other than yourself, Lord Cavor."

"But, madam ..."

"Of course, you had your reasons. Still ..."

"But, madam," Lord Cavor again said. And he looked quite agitated. "Madam has somehow misconstrued the rumors!" And Lord Cavor gulped, and then he said, "I'm *not* Mr. X."

"You're not Mr. X?" Clarissa said in a very small voice.

"Certainly not!"

"But that's impossible! The majority were *convinced* you were Mr. X."

"I know. And I can't imagine *how* the idea originated. Naturally, I speculated, like anybody else.... But to dare *compete* with Mr. FitzMaurice!"

"You mean, there never *was* a Mr. X?"

"There certainly was, and *is!* It's really fantastic. Somebody absolutely unknown! A newcomer! Nobody ever saw him before! He was probably there, at the stock exchange, I mean, but merely among the spectators on the balcony. He worked through an agent. And now his name is all over London. Such a plain name, too. Gray! Captain Gray. Captain Richard Gray."

"I beg your pardon, Lord Cavor," Clarissa said quietly. "But I didn't quite hear what you said. That name ... It sounded so *funny!*"

"Captain Gray. Captain Richard Gray. And the latest news is," Lord Cavor went on, "that he's buying Ravisham."

"Ravisham!"

"The Marquis of Trall left no male issue. And the only male heir, a distant cousin, drowned recently while on his yacht. Thus, for the first time in history, Ravisham came to be on sale. The Marquis left very little money, so her ladyship couldn't buy it. The ladies Flo and Sue, in fact, have no dowries. They'll either have to marry pauper parsons, or grow up to be old maids."

And serves them right, too, the horrible brats! flashed through Clarissa's mind, which, otherwise, was in a whirl.

"And now, this Captain Richard Gray," Lord Cavor added, "will be master of Ravisham. Well, he can certainly afford it!"

"Will you please, excuse me, my lord?" Clarissa said very politely.

"Of course!"

"But wait for me, right here. I'll be back directly." And Clarissa rose and began to move towards the door.

"Madam is going somewhere?"

"Something I have to do ... Won't take a minute ... Please wait."

And the bailiff at the door, opening it for her, Clarissa then simply dashed out, not caring what Lord Cavor or the bailiff might think of such behavior. The small enclosed carriage stood right there, waiting. She pulled the door open, and with a cry of, "To the Rose and Crown. Quick!" to Pete on the box, jumped in.

"But I already told him you want to be driven straight to Lord Cavor's unofficial residence!" protested Sally, sitting inside, with the bundle at her feet, and the lap dog on her knees.

Clarissa instantly put her head out the window, and shouted at Pete:

"To the Rose and Crown. And make no mistake about it! And drive *fast!*"

"Goodness gracious!" Sally expostulated. "You must have gone insane! Really …"

She said a great deal more, but Clarissa didn't listen. And Pete drove very fast. In no time, he was pulling up at the busy Rose and Crown.

Clarissa jumped out, dashed in.

"Where is Captain Gray?" she demanded of a menial in a white apron. "He's staying here. Which is his room?"

"Up those stairs, and second door on the right."

Unaware of the stares and gapes her golden raiment and her beauty produced among the tavern guests, Clarissa hurried up the wooden stairs, and to the second door on the right. She put her hand on the doorknob, and it turned. And she walked in.

Captain Richard Gray, still wearing his shabby uniform, and the tall boots in need of polishing, stood in the center of the low-ceilinged room, between the bureau and the bed. Having taken a folded shirt from the pulled-out bureau drawer, he was in the act of throwing it into the old valise, which had been placed, open, on the bed. The folded shirt, Clarissa at once noticed, was brand new. Well, at least he's bought himself a few shirts....

"Oh, it's you," Captain Gray said, glancing at her briefly.

And he tossed the shirt into the valise.

He then took from the drawer a pair of rolled-up socks. Also brand new.

"Are you … packing?" Clarissa asked, very stupidly, of course, and in a very small voice.

"That's right," Captain Gray said. "I *am* packing. As you can see."

Before Clarissa asked her next question, she had to moisten her lips with the tip of her pink tongue. And she spoke very humbly:

"I … heard … you've bought Ravisham."

"That's right," Captain Gray said, tossing another folded shirt into the valise. "Bought it lock, stock, and barrel! And I'm keeping the servant staff, including Mr. Henderson, the butler. The old fellow is supervising the changes I've ordered done to the place. And everything will be ready by the time I come back."

"Oh," Clarissa said. "When you … come *back.*"

"Yes, when I return from Paris."

"You're going to … Paris."

"I'll be leaving, in about an hour or so, for Paris, yes." And Captain Gray, as he tossed two pairs of socks, brand new, into the valise, added, very, very nonchalantly, "To be married there."

Well, she should have expected something like this. A man, once he's made his fortune, would always up and marry somebody. Somebody *else!*

"Ravisham must have a hostess," Captain Gray explained. "People would expect it of me. A very beautiful woman to help me receive the guests, entertain. That sort of thing … And she should be of good family, naturally. Titled, preferably."

"Naturally," Clarissa said. "Of course."

"I'm glad you agree with me," Captain Gray said. "But this matter of a title, *illustriousness,*" he went on, "well, it made it quite a problem."

"Oh?"

"Because, naturally, what Englishwoman of title would consider me, a commoner? All the money notwithstanding, her family would never allow it!"

"Yes, I suppose that's true."

"And it would be the same with any foreign woman of title. A Frenchwoman, for instance. The French aristocracy is just as snobbish as our own English aristocracy. If not *more* so!"

"Probably they are. More so."

"*Horribly* so! So you see, I had quite a problem."

"I can understand *that,* yes."

"But then I solved it," Captain Gray said.

"You did?"

"And very simply, too. Thanks to the co-operation of this woman, who is devoted to me. My fiancée."

"You ... you've known her a long time?"

"Well, I've been seeing her on and off. You know!" and Captain Gray gestured airily.

"Oh."

"Anyway," Captain Gray went on, "to solve the problem, this woman, who is devoted to me, will *pretend* to be a Frenchwoman of title, a Montmorency. She couldn't get away with imperson- ation of an Englishwoman of title, because all the titled people in England know each other. But when it comes to foreigners, well, they couldn't tell a French aristocrat from a French ... *peasant.*"

"Is she an actress then, this woman who is so devoted to you?"

"The role is not difficult. Aside from being beautiful, and dark-haired—the French usually have dark hair—she must be vivacious, very chic, frequently mention the name Montmorency, and then say something like *Tra-la-la, Comme ça, Oui! Oui!* And everybody will be convinced she speaks French, and that she *is* a Montmorency. And that's all that's necessary!"

And Captain Gray, having tossed a few more things into the valise, walked over to it, and closed the lid, and snapped the clasps shut.

"Well," Clarissa said, "I suppose she'll be meeting you here ... this woman. Since you'll be traveling to Paris together, probably. She'll be ... coming here."

"Oh, she's already here!"

"At the Rose and Crown, you mean? In one of the other rooms, I suppose."

"Why *should* she go to some other room? She came straight here, to *my* room, naturally. And that's where she is now. Right here, in this room."

Clarissa glanced around quickly, and then she understood what Captain Gray probably meant. The door of the clothes closet, on which hung a long mirror, stood open a crack. The woman, having arrived ahead of Clarissa, had run to hide herself in the closet, on hearing Clarissa's approach. Even when already affianced, a woman, if she valued her reputation, would have preferred to be found dead in an inn room than to be caught alone with the man in it! And that's where the woman now was. Behind that mirror-hung door. Clarissa stared at it.

"Would you like to see her?" Captain Gray asked. "Go on. Take a look. Move a little closer."

Clarissa was really curious to see the "other woman," and she moved a few steps closer.

"No, you don't have to open the closet door! Just look."

Clarissa looked. But there was only her own reflection to look at. And then she saw Captain Gray grinning into the mirror at her, from behind her shoulder.

"Well, what do you think of her? Do you approve of my taste?"

It took Clarissa fully a minute to realize what "darling Richard" meant.

"I ..." she then said. "You mean ... me? *Me!*"

She had been admired and courted by men of the greatest wealth, and highest rank, in the kingdom. And they had showered jewels upon her; a single ring, a bracelet, worth a fortune! She had known the excitement of being famous, notorious. And the thrill of having her name become a household word had been hers, also. People had run after her carriage to catch a glimpse of her beauty and shout praises to it. Everything an average woman would have given her eyes to have, and enjoy, *that* she had had, and she had enjoyed it all immensely. But—marriage! The highest reward to any woman's achievement, the crowning glory! Marriage!

And for the first time in her life, Clarissa almost fainted. In fact, she would have fallen flat on her face, if Captain Gray hadn't caught her in his strong arms.

"You adorable little fool!"

After a while, still holding her close, he said:

"How long will it take for your hair to grow back to its natural color? A Frenchwoman, a Montmorency, can't be a blonde!"

Not very long, Clarissa told him. Her hair grew so fast. It was so abundant.

"Besides," Captain Gray went on, "I much prefer its natural color. Those auburn gleams are very attractive. You said you used some kind of pomade."

"Yes ... a pomade ..."

She'd have to make secret visits to François, for him to put those "natural" auburn gleams in her hair with his artful dyes.

"And you certainly can't travel in this *unseemly* gold outfit," Captain Gray declared, in a very proprietary tone of voice. "I'll have to go out and buy you a decent gown immediately! Then, later, while we're honeymooning in Paris, you can have all the shopping sprees you want. And ..." he added, kissing her throat, while Clarissa slowly touched his unruly forelock with a fingertip, "we're taking Sally and Pete with us, of course."

PART SEVEN

CHAPTER TWENTY-SEVEN

THE SMALL TOWN of Calais, situated on the blue waters of the Channel, was always famous for its sunny weather. And never had the sun shone so brightly as on the day when the English monarch, George IV, the former Prince Regent, was passing through it on his way back to London, after paying a visit of state to the French capital.

The townspeople, in their quaint multi-colored costumes, lined the cobbled streets to see him go by. Followed by a long line of carriages filled with his brilliant entourage, His Majesty sat in the first landau, with an old courtier beside him, and acknowledged the salutations of the populace by raising a white-gloved hand to the brim of his gaily plumed hat. The red-coated guards, with swords drawn, rode on either side of the carriages, their beautiful mounts prancing and gleaming in the sunlight. From the upper windows of the buildings, a multitude of flags waved in the breeze, the flags of England, and of France, undulating their national colors, proudly and significantly, side by side.

The just-accomplished state visit was the first from an English sovereign since the French usurper, Napoleon Bonaparte, had declared war against the world. Between the two dramatic occurrences, historic events had followed one another in quick succession. Napoleon, his fleet destroyed in the Battle of Trafalgar, began to push his devastating campaign on land. Marching eventually on Russia, he took Moscow, and realized his long-nursed ambition to stand within the ancient walls of the

Kremlin. But the Moscow patriots, inspired by the courageous leadership of their young blond Czar, Alexander I, set fire to the old capital, and Napoleon was forced to retreat across the frozen steppes, with half of his Grand Army perishing in the process. Nothing could stop Bonaparte, however, and his next decisive battle occured in Belgium, when the Duke of Wellington, the Iron Duke, dealt the French forces their death blow near the village of Waterloo. Napoleon fled to Paris, but the Allies followed. And the self-styled Emperor of the French was made to give up his celebrated gold sword as a symbol of his unconditional surrender.

After he was imprisoned on the island of St. Helena for the rest of his natural life, all the European thrones on which he had installed members of his own family as kings and queens were returned to their rightful sovereigns. And a nephew of the guillotined Louis XVI became Louis XVIII of France.

In the summer palace, not far from London, meanwhile, the "mentally deranged" old English King had quietly expired, and the Prince Regent succeeded to his father's throne, as George IV.

As he sat now in the landau, raising his white-gloved hand to the brim of his gaily plumed hat in answer to the populace's salutations, very little change could be remarked in him. Except that the grossness of his figure, perhaps on account of the tight white satin breeches, was a trifle more pronounced. And his large, fleshy face, propped by the exaggerated white neckcloth, looked much more florid. But the haughty eyes were the same.

A red-coated guard, evidently dispatched by a courtier riding in one of the carriages in the rear, galloped up to the landau and spoke to the courtier seated beside His Majesty. The guard seemed to be delivering a message, and the old courtier as he listened became agitated. He cast a hasty glance at his sovereign, grew pale, bit his lip, hesitated. Then he said something to the guard. The latter rode forward a pace to give the order to the footman on the box, who passed it on to the coachman, and the landau stopped.

"Why the delay, pray?"

"Your Royal Highness ..." the old courtier began hesitantly.

"*What* did you say?"

"I beg your pardon, Your Roya ... Your Majesty, I mean."

People had known him as the Prince Regent for so long that they always forgot that he was now King and should be addressed differently. To *them* he was still the Prince Regent. And it was as the Prince Regent that he was to go down in history, thus earning for himself a fame of sorts.

"Your Royal High ... Your Majesty, I mean," the old courtier said, "a citizen of this town has just delivered a piece of information to a member of Your Majesty's entourage, which information, in my ... my humble opinion, should be passed on to Your Roya ... to Your Majesty." And faltering in his speech, not at all certain of the reaction to what he was about to mention, the courtier hurried on, "It is about ... Mr. Brummell, who has resided here since leaving his native shores ... He is now destitute, ill ... alone ..."

For an instant, for a mere fraction of a second, it seemed to the old courtier that something human suddenly gleamed in his sovereign's haughty eyes. Perhaps, in that infinitesimal space of fleeting time, the memory of Brummell and his rare friendship stood, for once, clear, unadulterated, in the mind of the former Prince Regent. But, instantly, that warming memory was blotted out by quite a different recollection. To have preferred to *him,* a royal prince and reigning head of a mighty empire, some insignificant young female, impoverished, forced to earn her bread. A *governess!* The blow dealt to his immense vanity had been shattering. And now the rankling memory of the imaginary insult outweighed his feeling of loneliness, the awful loneliness of kings.... He could neither forget, nor forgive.

The old courtier still waited. But the white-gloved hand merely gestured the command for the landau to move on.

And the brilliant cortege continued on its way; the mounts of the red-coated guards, made nervous by the unscheduled halt, prancing in such a rebellious manner that it took some time to force them back into the normal ceremonial trot.

CHAPTER TWENTY-EIGHT

A ND CLARISSA? She is back at Ravisham. The rows of tall windows in the great stone pile of a house flash and glitter in the sunlight, while peacocks strut on the green terraces that gently slope away from the broad stone steps. And Clarissa can observe it all, with infinite satisfaction, as clad in a trailing peignoir of white lace, she sits in a cushioned chair, which is always placed for her on the lawn, under the luxurious shade of an ancient elm, and sips her morning chocolate. Actually, it's already noon. But Clarissa, never an early riser, sees no reason to get up before noon. And there she sits, sipping her chocolate. And it's very pleasant.

Closer to the house, and romping on the emerald-green grass, are two little girls, wearing beautiful white dresses with rose-colored sashes, and flopping straw hats with rose-colored streamers. Naturally, they're not alone, but have their governess with them. The governess is not *too* old, but she is very homely, positively a *fright.* Clarissa has seen to *that!* Clarissa does not trust governesses.... The younger of the little girls, a mere tot, has a dainty habit of pushing back a curl which, escaping from its fellows, keeps falling over her pretty forehead—just like Captain Richard Gray's forelock does over *his* open brow. While the other little girl has a smile which slightly resembles Clarissa's, but only *very* slightly.

Clarissa can also see, visible from behind the rose garden, which is in full and fragrant bloom, the roof of the cottage that had been built by Captain Gray's order for Sally and Pete, who of course have long since embraced the bonds of matrimony. The housekeeper who used to slap the kitchenmaid Sally on her cheeks so often has been discharged, and it is Sally now who bustles about importantly, with the clank of keys which dangle in a bunch from the chain over her black silk apron. She it is who now slaps the kitchen slavey about briskly. Sometimes she slaps the housemaids' faces for them, also. For Sally, who is starting to look matronly, is very particular about the execution of her duties. She makes her old enemy, the gruff housemaid, Bertha, for instance, do all the weeding in the vegetable garden, behind the house, from early morning till suppertime. And always at Sally's heels, following Sally wherever she goes, there's the fluffy roll of honey-colored fur, the lap dog. Of course, it's not the same lap dog, merely one of its many descendants. But it might be easily mistaken for the original one, the way it sometimes rushes about, yapping.

And Captain Gray, Clarissa knows, is busy right now at the various outbuildings, giving orders, discussing plans with the head gardener, or with Pete, who is in charge of the stables. A great big place like this needs a lot of looking after and "darling Richard," unless he has to go to London to take care of his many investments, is occupied every hour of the day. And when attending to these home chores he always wears his shabby uniform, and the old boots. Which he has had resoled. Or so he assured Clarissa, when she protested. Of course, he did have a new uniform made, and it is beautiful. But he wears it only for his business trips, or puts it on to receive his guests, the nobility from neighboring estates.

And Clarissa, sipping her chocolate, thinks of the resplendent gown she is going to wear tonight. And she's glad that's all she *has* to think about! Not about what food to give the guests.

Or how the table should be decorated. For Captain Gray had his great-aunt from Scotland, a grand old lady with dignified white curls and old-fashioned diamonds in her long earlobes, come to live with them and supervise all such humdrum details. And it is to her that Sally goes to talk about bed sheets, towels, the hiring of extra laundresses, and how big a joint of meat the cook should buy at the Sudbury market.

The great-aunt worships Captain Gray. The two little girls worship him. Clarissa, when he returns home, always greets him with a smile. All the servants, without a single exception, adore him. And even Sally, now that Captain Gray is so rich, has to admit that he is a lovely person. He has won the respect of his proud neighbors. The sight of his great-aunt, with her old-fashioned diamonds, presiding over his magnificent dinner table, convinces them that there is a fine stability in the family, even though the man *is* a *nouveau riche*. Besides, he married a Montmorency! Clarissa charms them all. Her striking, dark-haired beauty is so typical of a French aristocrat, they tell each other. And she is so vivacious. So very chic. And though for the most part she merely smiles, or laughs, or simply listens with flattering attentiveness, when she does say a few words, it's such an attractive-sounding French!

But there is one thing which more than anything else makes the Captain's titled friends lenient to his being a commoner. When they introduce him to strangers, they don't brag about his stupendous wealth, but, instead, explain proudly:

"This is *our* Captain Richard Gray. He was with Nelson, in the Battle of Trafalgar!"

As Clarissa sets her emptied chocolate cup on its saucer, and then places it on the little table beside her chair, Mr. Henderson, the butler, in his black silk costume, with silver buckles on his shoes, and the big white wig on his vulture-like head, comes out of the house and crosses the sunlit lawn towards her. He bears a silver salver, and reposing on the salver is a small package, wrapped in brown paper.

"This came with the morning post, madam. From France. The stamp is French."

"*Tra-la-la. Comme ça! Oui. Oui!*" Clarissa trills vivaciously.

While the old butler deposits the salver on the little table and takes up the package to open it for her.

"Probably from madam's relatives, the illustrious Montmorencys," Mr. Henderson adds respectfully.

Who could it be from? Clarissa wonders. And she is so impatient with curiosity that she almost cries out, Hurry up, and *tear* the wrapping off, you old fool! But, as usual, she controls herself, and waits decorously.

Mr. Henderson unhurriedly removes the brown paper, and a flat long jewel case of blue velvet is revealed. He hands it to her, and then the butler departs, bearing the silver salver with as much ceremony as before, though there is nothing on it now except the piece of wrapping paper, which he had folded very methodically. And Clarissa opens the jewel case.

Inside is a string of gorgeous rubies. A rope of rubies, the glowing blood-red stones are so large. And there's a card, engraved with a crest. The crest is French, but the few lines of writing are in English. Clarissa takes up the card in her hand, and reads:

Madam, doubtless, had her own secret purpose for spreading her little story about the D'Estes having had two identical emerald ropes made. I, therefore, did not contradict Madam, though in point of fact the D'Estes were never partial to emeralds. The family had been always famous for its collection of *rubies*. And I'm sending this string of rubies to Madam, as a mark of my admiration for Madam's radiant beauty, and Madam's cleverness. Perhaps it will somewhat console Madam for the loss of her emerald rope.

And it is signed, FRANCOIS, COUNT D'ESTE.

The erstwhile chief valet, and later the proprietor of a modest hairdresser's establishment, François—like all *émigrés* who had taken refuge in England during the Napoleonic Wars—had hurried back to France on the restoration of the rightful Bourbon king, and his ancestral castle, his exquisite palace in Paris, all his estates and possessions were returned to him, together with his ancient title.

François who used to color her hair so expertly! The *inconvenience* she had had since, in finding another hairdresser ... And Clarissa laughs, as she admires the rubies. She will wear them tonight with her gorgeous new dress. But nothing, of course, could take the place of the emerald rope, which now lies on the bottom of the Thames, under the bridge there, with the low parapet. The gay voices of the two little girls at play ring out through the sun-drenched air, and Clarissa, as the sudden thought of Slippery Jack flashes into her mind, hastens to push it away with a shiver of apprehension. She is superstitious enough to be convinced that if she does not allow herself to think of him *here,* in this beautiful and peaceful place, she will somehow prevent him from making his unexpected appearance in the vicinity. Providing, of course, that Slippery Jack indeed failed to perish in the swift current of the fog-veiled river.

Not that Clarissa adheres indiscriminately to just any superstition she happens to hear about. The bear trainer's instructions, for instance, concerning the casket with brass clasps, in which Clarissa had once kept her little collection of jewels—the "sparklers," as Captain Gray called them, until he had them appraised. Well, Clarissa had never believed the swarthy foreigner's silly gibberish about having to give the casket away, within one week and a day, after she had achieved her good fortune. And she therefore had paid no attention to his warning ... And Sally finding a prettier receptacle for Clarissa's ribbons, the casket was discarded, probably to land up in the attic, eventually, with other unwanted odds and ends. And there it lies, forgotten, gathering dust and cobwebs.

Yes, the rubies will go very nicely with my new gown, Clarissa decides with satisfaction, having banished the thought of Slippery Jack from her mind.

But when Captain Gray goes to London, he stays away overnight, and then Clarissa hurries to the city also, in secret, of course, to pay a visit to the Thieves' Village. As she enters the Waterfront Tavern, she pushes the veil back from her face, and slips her small black mask into the velvet drawstring bag, and opens her plain dark mantle to display her rich dress to the company, which greets her with the usual ribald shouts and observations. Then she sits with old Lafonte, who has grown very frail, and with Dumb Clara, who still plies her rag-picking trade, and gets as quickly tipsy on a sip of gin as she always did, while the others crowd around, grinning. Some of the rough familiar faces are missing. Ugly Frank, for one, has disappeared from the scene, by way of Tyburn. But most of them are still there. And, sometimes, someone happens to mention Slippery Jack.

Once, One-Eyed Tom, drawing Clarissa aside, spoke of a hulk captain who, while drinking there the night before, had talked of meeting in the colonies a man answering Slippery Jack's description. But when Clarissa tried to find the hulk captain all she could learn was that he had been transferred to a regular ship, and that the ship had already left for the Indies. Another time, it was

Black Moll, the procuress, who confided to Clarissa that Honest Gregory had received a letter from the colonies, from Slippery Jack. Black Moll was certain that was who it was from! He did get a letter, the pseudo-parson told Clarissa, when she tried to question him, but it was from somebody else.... And every time that Slippery Jack was mentioned, Honest Gregory would say, "They all come back from the colonies, *eventually*. When the authorities here get tired of trying to find them. And that's how Slippery Jack will return someday, in his own good time...."

But old Lafonte gets nervous from this kind of talk, and to create a diversion he takes out his squeaky fiddle from its shabby case, and begins to play. And then Clarissa, picking up her rustling silk skirts, jumps up on the table, and dances for them, kicking her lovely legs very high, and laughing back at the men's obscene remarks and guffaws. "Higher, Clarissa, higher!" they cry. "What a wench! There's no other like her."

"The only reason you come here," Dumb Clara whimpers tipsily, as Clarissa, her cheeks flushed, eyes shining, throws herself in the chair to regain her breath, "is because this is the only place where you can be yourself. Others may think it's for the pleasure of seeing them, but you can't fool your poor old mother ... hic!"

And Clarissa slaps her on the back so hard that Dumb Clara almost topples off her stool.

Then she throws a handful of gold on the table, for more gin, more rum all around, and leaves the tavern. It is dark, and the fog is dense, and she walks close along the river's edge, and then up the embankment a little way, and at last she stands on the bridge, a hand on the low parapet. Down below, the water glistens blackly. The current there is so swift.... But since, maybe, the current was neither swift nor strong enough, on a certain night, to have drowned a man instantly, it's of something else that Clarissa is thinking. The desolate grave, with the crude marker that still bears her name, in the unconsecrated ground, and so close to Ravisham. The empty grave ... As if waiting for you, Slippery Jack had said, grinning maliciously.

And Clarissa knows exactly how it all could happen. She lured away from the house, with the threat of the harm that would be done to the two little girls. And then ... well, it probably doesn't take long to strangle a woman. And then the earth of the small mound hastily spaded aside, and the hole dug, and the lifeless body shoved in, and the earth spaded over quickly, to form the same mound again, and the crude marker replaced. And nobody would ever know.

But the river fog makes it too damp to be standing there, and Clarissa walks away from the bridge, and hurries across the deserted thoroughfare, and into the narrow side street, where she left the small enclosed carriage to wait for her, as usual. She gets in, and settles herself comfortably beside Sally, and draws the dark mantle closer about her, for she feels slightly chilled, and then she listens to Sally's incessant chatter, while the faithful Pete drives them swiftly back to Ravisham.

www.ingramcontent.com/pod-product-compliance
Lightning Source LLC
Chambersburg PA
CBHW030844030726
47495CB00005B/1367